THE WAY BENEATH THE WOOD

THE WAY BENEATH THE WOOD

I F G O'DONNELL

Chapter 1: *Snip*

Snip. As I sat there at the kitchen table trying to find the cleanest way to remove the pages from Hazel's birthday present I felt a frisson of wrongness: we are taught that books are precious, after all.

She had gone, taking everything that was hers and everything that I would have said was jointly owned too, and her uncharacteristic thoroughness in this said a good deal about the brutal finality of her intentions. The book was the last artefact that had any connection with her in the whole place; a gift I had purchased in secret and hidden away in my sock drawer, not knowing that it was destined never to be given; the tenuous last vestige of her in my life. And here I was, patiently and carefully cutting it up. Snip. Snip.

She would have loved it, too: an aged leather binding, with tiny flowers and animals making a pretty border for the gold-stamped letters on the spine, and the stitch-bound contents an unexpected assemblage of pages of different sizes and textures. Most were articles on cheap, tanned paper from ancient magazines, long defunct, but there were also leaves extracted from other books and occasional handwritten letters and notes. The pages were crammed full of the sort of thing she liked: places visited by the Devil, a cabinet of wonders, mummified remains, hidden faerie gold and so on.

In a trough of self-pity, I had retrieved it from its hiding place and, sitting cross-legged on the floor, had begun to read, hoping, I think, to find some thread, however thin, that might yet connect me with her. It was then that inspiration had struck, and I had gone to fetch the scissors.

This was no mere destructive urge, although there was a morsel of spiteful revenge to enjoy in the act of cutting. No, I had a plan: a plan to slice through her determined silence, to weave a snare that would bind her and bring her back to me.

Snip. Snip. Eventually I discovered that using a razor blade was the best way to obtain a close and neat cut, and after a while I got rather good at it.

Chapter 2: *St. Dunstan's*

I nosed the car up the gravel driveway between two tall, ivy-covered brick pillars, one of which bore the name plate 'St. Dunstan's', and crunched all the way up to the house. The hedges on each side of the drive had been cut back savagely, leaving vast swathes of splintered branches without any foliage. As I drew to a halt the sun broke through the cloud cover, glinting brightly on the chrome parts of my cousin Clifton's yellow Morgan Roadster, which was parked by the porch.

Clifton's new home was a gloomy mixture of architectural styles. The oldest parts were Georgian, constructed in stone with large, airy windows and pleasant proportions. Later additions, which must have been Victorian and were certainly gothic in inspiration, repaired what looked to have been considerable damage, filling in gaps but also broadening the frontage. It made the building resemble a badly scarred and craggy old face. Two single storey wings like hunched shoulders that reached behind to create a courtyard at the rear were even later brick extensions. There was a separate double garage, and behind the house a small stable block and another long, low timber structure like a cowshed. It was all very grand and imposing and very grown up.

It's hard to give up a rivalry you've pursued from childhood, even when your competitor has the benefit of several million quid inherited from parents who both had the generosity to die whilst still relatively young and well insured. The bill for transforming St Dunstan's into a green welly paradise was not something that would trouble Clifton much these days, while I was at least half a dozen inspirational property deals and a not unwished-for

3

bereavement of my own away from parity. I suddenly pictured, with sickening dismay, an entire afternoon spent traipsing around the place listening to his tedious plans to insert large glass panels in its every orifice.

Clifton answered the door looking rather more rotund than I remembered him, his cheeks a touch ruddier, and he was accompanied by a yapping Jack Russell, which was a new accessory. He was wearing a linen shirt under a tweed waistcoat with cavalry twill trousers and tan brogues, every bit the country doctor. "Ah, here you are! Looking not a day older. Portrait in the attic, eh? Come in, old chap. Journey not too bad, I hope?" He pushed the mutt behind him with his foot. "Quiet, Jinx!"

"Two hours."

"Not too bad, then. Well, it's good of you to come. I'm sure your… ah… professional advice will be absolutely invaluable."

We both knew that the only reason I was there was Mother's interference. I would not have offered my property developer's knowledge, and he would not have requested it otherwise, but we shook hands anyway. "Congratulations on your new home," I said, "Looks fantastic. Can't wait to see round it," and I presented him with a bottle of Bollinger, warm from the car, which he wrapped his ham hock hands around greedily.

"Too kind, dear boy."

I followed him down the dark hallway and straight into the very large quarry-tiled kitchen at the back of the house, which was cold and devoid of any cooking smells, where he put the champagne away in the fridge. "Now listen," he said, "Expect you're hungry. Had hoped to cook you some lunch, but it's all gone wrong. Long story, all my fault. So I've booked a table at the pub. Nice grub there, and a decent ale. I thought you and I would take a spin over there in the Morgan and do the tour after. Alright?"

Clifton's casual admission that he hadn't been bothered about making my lunch after my two hour journey was annoying, but being patronised with the offer of a ride in his clown car as if it were a joyous treat capped it all. Did he think I was twelve years old? However, I didn't want him to see he was getting to me, so all I said was: "Sounds great!"

"Come on Jinx! Here boy!" Clifton led the way back outside again, and we clambered, with some lack of dignity on my part, into the Morgan, with Jinx leaping happily in behind us.

A few noisy and hair-raising minutes of rattling blindly down narrow hedge-lined roads brought us to a tiny lane, and then we coasted into the small village of Stoney Hill. Clifton, revving the engine, parked under the pub sign hanging from its white gallows-post. In the centre of the village, around the green, there was a small caucus of ancient and picturesque timber-framed houses with knapped flint and brick walls, including a grocer's shop that was also the Post Office, an antiques shop that looked as if it had been closed for a while, and the pub, of course. The old houses were thatched, individual in design, their gardens defined by low stone walls of flint and ancient trees and hedges: that much had changed little in centuries. Breaking the illusion of time having stood still in the village, surrounding and outnumbering this small group, loitered a red brick, nineteen-fifties council housing estate. These houses were in uniform rows, with tiled roofs, pebbledash-panelled walls and concrete paths and gateposts and patches of poorly kept lawn, and the inevitable sign: *No ball games.* They crowded around the old houses like a gang of pimply teenagers preparing to mug a huddled gaggle of pensioners.

I ducked my head under the low lintel and stepped into the White Horse's low-ceilinged and heavily timbered bar-room. There was a large fireplace at one end, and at the other a sturdy bar. Heavy wooden pillars supported the ceiling at irregular intervals, and arranged around them in haphazard and yet friendly groupings were ancient-looking dark wood tables and a mix of hard and comfortable chairs, some of which were already occupied. The windows, in leaded glass, created a pleasant gloom that made it feel like early evening-time. It was the perfect country pub. By the time I had finished looking around Clifton was already ordering two pints of some undoubtedly ghastly local ale at the bar, with Jinx curled at his feet. It was too late to stop him, so I had to drink it, and of course it tasted like a dog's bathwater that a dozen rotten plague rats had drowned in.

We took a seat at one of the tables. "Mmmm. Er, not bad." I said. "This is a very nice pub. Very cosy."

Clifton began to tell me with surprising candour and volume about the range of ailments of the patients of his new practice. "So I had to conclude that he'd been shagging his girlfriend's grandmother!" he guffawed.

As he continued, I found myself tuning out of his blather and looking idly around the room. There was an old newspaper article framed on the wall, and although my eyesight wasn't quite good enough to read the headline, I had a strong urge to go over and take a closer look. "What's that over there?" I interrupted, pointing.

"No clue," he said. "We should order. What are you having? Steak's good."

"Medium rare," I said, "salad, no chips."

Leaving him to make the trip to the bar to order, I ambled over to the picture. It was a faded and brown cutting from a newspaper called *The Seagull*, dated 27th November 1893. '*The*

Uckford Fairy' was the headline. I skimmed it quickly: some lame hoax concerning a mummified fairy found in a cave, dressed up with pseudo-scientific mumbo jumbo. It reminded me of the Piltdown Man, one of Hazel's obsessions that I was pretty sure she had told me had happened in this part of the world as well. But the main thing about it was that it was the identical twin of one of the pages I had recently cut from Hazel's birthday present. I was idly wondering if that meant Uckford was somewhere in the vicinity when a voice came from behind me: "Anyone would think it was the most interesting thing that ever happened around here, the fuss they make about it."

I looked round. The voice belonged to a man aged about sixty five, perhaps seventy years of age, clean shaven with grey thinning hair brushed straight back, small, piggy eyes, and heavy, ruddy jowls. He was looking at the cutting on the wall, but then turned to face me. About my height, he stood with his back straight and shoulders back in military fashion, which had the effect of accentuating the pounds of extra weight around his waist. He wore a brown tweed jacket over a country check shirt and what might have been a club tie. There were deep furrows across his brow. He nodded curtly.

"Really? I'd never heard of it."

"You're not from round here, then," he said. "I see you're having lunch with Dr Prendergast."

"He's my cousin. I'm helping him with his new property."

"Ah, St Dunstan's."

"Yes."

I must have given him a funny look because he said: "It's a small village. Everyone knows everything about everybody. What is it that you do, then?"

"I'm a property developer," I said. Pride welled in my chest as I said the words. It was true: I had two successful conversions of houses into flats under my belt already, and my next project, an old community centre, was a huge step up from that.

"Ah. I suppose he has big plans for the place."

"We haven't got to that yet."

"I'm just being nosy."

I looked round. Clifton was chatting happily to the barmaid, and it looked as if he was already half way through a second pint. Fine by me.

"What sort of developments are you into? Tower blocks I suppose."

I smiled. "I'm in the process of buying a big old plot in town. I'll make it into eight flats."

"Eight flats. Would you mind telling me what they'll sell for?"

"Around thirty thousand each."

"Really?" He looked impressed. "That's big business."

"Yes. Well, it is quite substantial. I'm trying not to grow the business too fast. It's about finding the right project."

"And how do you know when you've found the right project?"

I tapped the side of my nose. "It's all about what you know and who you know," I said.

The man looked suddenly thoughtful. "I see. You know, I came by some property information the other day that could be of interest to someone like you. I may be able to do you a favour." He squinted at me.

"Really?"

"If it's not too big for you."

I smiled. "Go on."

"No. I'm sorry. We've only just met. I hardly know you. What am I thinking?"

"Please."

"Alright." He looked at his watch and flinched. "Blast! Look, I have to go now, but we could talk later, when you've finished with your cousin. Meet me by the church. Four o'clock alright with you?"

It took me rather by surprise. "Yes," I said, humouring him. "Alright, four o'clock."

We shook hands. "Charlie Price," he said.

"Nick Carpenter."

I followed Charlie's gaze. Clifton was on his way back to the table with more beer. By the time I looked back Charlie was already on his way to the door. "Yes, well, nice to meet you," I said to Charlie's back. "See you later!"

"Here we are," Clifton boomed across the room. "You must be starving old chap. I know I am. It's all ordered, on its way. Got us another pint to wash it down with!"

Chapter 3: *The Dying Shepherd's Tale, by Walter Peachey*

As a physician I have many times been called to the side of the dying, and I have observed that when facing the Hand of Judgement good gentleman and wicked wretch alike are wont to reflect upon their lives, and whilst reason itself may be dimming, the soul requires of its host a most penitent confession of sin before abandoning it to the looming grave. Murder, adultery and thievery long concealed may be laid bare between dying groans in that final anguish of body and soul, and truth long suppressed and sometimes scarcely credible may surface. The time I have served in my profession has inured me to wonder at such *veritas in extremis*, save at one revelation only, received at the bedside of a poor and honest shepherd at the end of his days.

The hovel in which this declining worthy was confined was remote and attended only by an aged sheepdog about to make its own last will and testament, which at my approach had not the strength to do more than rise slowly to its feet and put forth a single bark of warning. Its duties thus discharged it limped forward and sniffed at my trouser, but had no appetite for preventing me and simply followed me in through the door. As I ducked my head to enter the low room I was met by the sorry stink of ripening necrosis originating from where the shepherd lay upon a straw pallet, his lips moving in what I took for silent prayer. There were cold ashes in place of a fire, there being neither firewood nor any family to gather any, care for him or keep him. He greeted me sensibly and attempted to raise himself, but had not the strength so to do, and so I lit a stub of candle I found and by its light carried out my examination at once. His once sure shepherd's feet had failed him and his leg and hip had been broken in a fall upon the hillside, these bones being more brittle in those of such advanced years and poor diet, whereupon infection had set in and by the time of my arrival he was already gone beyond the point of no return. *Acuti morbi in quattuordecim diebus iudicantor,* as our friend Hippocrates says. I did what I could to make him clean and comfortable, but he had no money for medicines and there was little advice I could give that would benefit him. He must have been feeling considerable pain, but he bore it with stoic determination.

At last, with no more to be done, I went to take my leave and wished him God's mercy, knowing that I should never again see him in this life. "Thank ye, Doctor," said he, his cheeks hollow and his eyes swivelling in watery sockets, "For your charity and kindness. Ye have not told me that Death's angel waits for me in the small hours, but I know it to be so and I am not afraid. I have lived a remote and simple life and harmed none, and the Great Shepherd will care for me henceforth more kindly than I have ever known."

"I will stay with you a while longer," I said, ashamed.

"More kindness," said he, "And though I have faithful Bess here to keep me company and so shall not be alone at the end, I am glad for I do confess there is something I should like the opportunity to tell, having spoken of it to no man. Blessed are ye," he recited, "For in all creation only man, favoured child of the Almighty, has no cause to fear death. It is but the gateway to his eternal happiness." He paused to lick his lips. "Those words are not my own, but in the years I have pondered them I have come to understand that in their place they contain a message of prodigious comfort to all mankind, as ye shall hear."

"As a young man," he continued, his eyes shining and the words tumbling out as in a religious fervour, but with them his soul bleeding drop by drop from his feeble frame, "I roamed the hills and valleys hereabouts, finding work when I could and sleeping under the sky when I could not. The trees and the grasses, the flowers and the herbs, the stones and rivers and hills were my dear companions. The sun in the sky served for my pocket watch and the turn of the seasons for my calendar, and no greater happiness had I but to live thus in the gentle bosom of Mother Nature. I would walk under night's canopy for the pure joy of observing the heavens thick with stars. On one such night a blazing comet, swift and joyous, sped across the firmament, the like of which I have never seen before or since. I followed its fleeting course with my gaze across the night sky to the horizon, and it burned its presence into my mind's eye such that I can see it even now; forerunner and warning of things that were to come, perhaps, had I but known.

The following day I set off in the same direction as the comet, on my way to L____. It was a fine morning and I made good time, striding with the carefree vigour of youth across the smooth grass of the downs. It was yet early morning when I came to the dewpond on the south side of C____ at which a flock of ewes with their lambs had been watering, and the ground around the pond was muddied with their tracks. Some disturbance in the churned up earth caught my eye: cloven hoofprints, but not those of any sheep. They were newer than the other prints and carefully skirted the dewpond, preceding me upon my own path, and in appearance were the heavy hoofprints of a large goat, but to my surprise it seemed that this goat had been walking only upon its rear legs! Curious, I set to following the tracks for as long as I could, but I lost the trail upon the grassy hillside despite my best efforts; and further stubborn casting about in all different directions born of overreaching pride in my skill as a tracker came to nought.

Thwarted, I peevishly judged the question of how the tracks had been made to be of no importance; there being a ready solution in that some animals may, when travelling at a certain pace, obscure the imprint made by their fore feet with the imprint of their hind feet; and thus I dismissed the matter summarily from my mind, though I should not have done so, as ye shall hear.

Providence found me work at the next farm I came to, no more than an hour's walk from that place. The farmer was an intemperate brute accustomed to laying about him with a horsewhip when in his cups, after which he would retire to his bed and snore like an old boar; and from this shameful performance no day was spared, be it the Lord's Day or no. He did little enough work about the place, which had suffered much for it, but beyond hiring my services he did not trouble me more at that time, and I resolutely kept out of his way and plied my trade, which is to say minded the flock. Meanwhile, Nature paid supplement to my meagre wages: wild fruit, berries, nuts, mushrooms, and on occasion, wild honey or a rabbit or pigeon caught in a snare, for which bounty I was exceedingly thankful.

That summer seemed to endure forever, as I recall was the way with that season in those glorious days of my youth, and I was kept busy with late lambing and shearing. The farmer's daughter… ahh now, she was pretty, with her fair hair in ringlets and a smile that would charm the pips from an apple. There was a hint of rose in her cheeks when we met, but he guarded her like the mean-tempered old hound he was and there was no talking with her, although we exchanged glances enough behind his back.

For a spell in September it rained more or less every day. In search of a missing ewe and her two lambs, I found myself descended in a valley with steep sides and a flooded gulley at the base, and was making for the shelter of a row of birch trees on the farther side when, across the vale in the beating rain, I spied a shape: thin, dark, moving in leaps and jumps on two legs across the hillside along the line of bushes and trees. It was there but for but a moment and then gone; a man, perhaps a boy, as I thought, moving swiftly and, to my mind, strangely. I tracked cautiously across the steep side of the hill and found the spot, and there I discovered prints again: the trail of a large goat partially obliterated by the rain. Of the man, there was no trace.

This thing I had observed troubled me a great deal. In spite of the rain and the distance, I knew what I had seen; my eyes were sharp enough then, and my youthful certainty in my own powers allowed no latitude for doubt: there was something not right about that figure; something in the gait, the purpose, that jarred with the world that I knew. It did not belong, or rather, it belonged well enough with the hills and the stones and the trees and the rain, but it did not belong in a world in which I was a part.

After that encounter I had no more peace within. Each time I was out I found myself uneasy, watching for signs of something awry. Weeks passed with not a trace of the creature, and yet upon many an occasion I could not help but feel compelled by that hidden, additional sense that tells when the eyes of another are upon us to look around me, but to no avail.

One day the farmer went to market and did not take his daughter because she was taken sick with a fever. As soon as he was gone, however, she came to me and said she had feigned her malady that she might not go with him, and we spent the day together out on the downs in the warmth of glorious September sunshine, my Beatrice and I. I kissed her under an apple tree that was weighed down with ripe fruit, but then we quarrelled and she ran away, and in my pique I let her go. I purposely delayed my return to the farm by hours spent idly wandering, but when I arrived there I found to my further annoyance that she had not herself returned. After that, each minute she was away was a trial, and I called myself every kind of fool as I waited. She did not come back till very late and her father thrashed her, but she did not cry out.

In the morning I sought her out but she would not speak with me, and I felt that all that had passed between us had come to nought. She was a maiden bewitched, her eyes so alive to my intentions only the day before now were evasive, and as the day wore on she took great care to avoid my company in spite of my efforts. That night, after her father had fallen down in a dead faint and begun his customary snoring, she slipped away and ran barefoot out onto the downs, and I followed her. It was a clear, windless night; the stars filled the night sky with drifting skeins of light, and the moon hung heavily like the belly of a lass full with child. I pursued her quietly yet doggedly, keeping far enough away that she might not see me.

Out on the downs she led me, inclining her head slightly as if to catch the strains of a music I could not hear. At last there was a valley into which she descended; a valley I had not known was there and have never found again: like a great bowl it was, with smooth sides and a clump of rowan trees at the centre. I watched from high up on the slope. In a clearing, upon a fallen tree trunk, sat the creature: it was part man, part goat, with a human upper half and the lower part all goat from cloven hoof to shaggy haunches, and the horns of a goat grew at its temples. It was playing on a flute; a wild, eerie sound that, carrying up the hillside to where I was hidden behind a bush, made me afraid. Beatrice danced before the creature no dance of mankind's making: it was a brutal ritual, performed in helpless abandonment under that bloated moon, of primal appetite so intense and fiery that I will swear now I thought her aflame with silvery fire. The music gripped her in its strange rhythm and spun her about first this way, then that, hips turning circles, body swaying, stepping, leaping, reaching. I found myself unable to move, unable to take my eyes from her, and how long this enchantment continued I am unable to measure quite: it may have been minutes, hours, days, years. When at last the music faded away upon a long, quivering note, Beatrice collapsed to the ground as if quite dead. The creature rose, perfectly balanced upon those abominable hind quarters, and stepped towards her. Bowing low it took her hand with infinite tenderness and kissed it, and with this touch she was at once reinvigorated and gracefully took to her feet again. And then...

Nay, I cannot say. Freed of the enchantment of the flute, I rushed from my hiding place and hurled myself down the hillside, leaping with the strength of a lion upon the two, tearing the creature from her and dashing it to the ground. She looked upon me then with no understanding of how she had come to that place, and seeing the creature as for the first time let out a scream of terror. In her abject fear, she reached for me, and I took her in my arms and held her there as she shuddered and sobbed. The creature fled into the darkness without a sound.

How we returned to the farm on that evil night I know not; my mind was full of care for Beatrice and vengeance upon the creature. She slipped back to her bed and I to mine with nary a word between us, and thereafter I knew I could speak of the incident to no man, for it could scarcely be held believable and indeed could only be thought by her father to be a poor device meant to prevent his wrath from falling upon both her and I. Better by far to maintain silence and to perform the duty imposed upon me by the horror I had witnessed: the utter destruction of the evil creature.

The next day I did not see Beatrice and I learned that she lay upon her sickbed, wracked with fever. I was distraught, but the effect of her condition upon me was to reinforce my will and I roamed the downs in search of hidden places and strange signs, and it served only to fan the flames of my fury when I found the creature not. That night when I returned late it was to the news that Beatrice, having been thought by all to be sleeping and too ill to rise, had purposefully slipped from her room and made her way to the barn, where she had hanged herself by means of a rope tied by her own hand to the rafters. My dearest love was dead!

How I stormed and wept that night over her cold, unmoving corpse! How I raged, tearing apart the very hillsides to find my enemy! He had killed her just as certainly as by putting the rope around her neck and choking out her life himself, and I had no thought but to serve God in delivering the justice the devilish creature deserved. I strode across the dark downs with the might of giants in my bones and sinews, and all things hid from me and were afraid, but when the first rays of the sun broke over the horizon I had not discovered the creature's lair and my strength left me and I fell insensible upon the turf.

Thereafter I could not work or eat until I had found and dispatched my enemy. I did not attend the bitter interment of my dearest Beatrice in unconsecrated ground: time enough for that reconciliation when she had been avenged. Days lost patrolling the hills passed into weeks and there was no trace of the creature anywhere. I became ill and wild-eyed, and the farmer and his men shunned me; but still I would not relent until I was so weak from the ague and hunger that I could not move from my cot. There I was at last visited by one of the labourers' wives with some thin broth. She bore the usual signs of a hard life: deep lines upon her brow and around her mouth, a bruised cheek and eyes that were sad and watery; but there was something in her that put me in mind of my poor Beatrice when I first had seen her, and I began to weep. Too weak to send her away with curses as I wished, I received her charity and in that moment was touched by the care of one being for another that she barely even knew. The rage that had sustained me almost to my destruction left me, although implacable hatred of the creature remained, and the will to recover my health, become strong again and pursue the creature to its destruction took the ascendancy.

Reason told me that I had never seen the creature far from the flock, and this chimed with the feeling I had of being watched all the time, and so I began an improved campaign of greater cunning and patience. As my strength grew, I proceeded with my duties as usual, knowing that my quarry must be carefully observing me whenever I was near the flock to ensure it should avoid detection. Only when it was certain I and my kind were far distant would it show itself, and thus I must take it unawares by seeming to be elsewhere and make use of such devices that might aid my cause. Therefore I procured from the farmer musket and powder, on the pretence that wild dogs were threatening his flock and must be dispatched on sight; but thereafter I hid the weapon so that my enemy might not see me with it and be warned.

My plan was simple: I would leave the flock day after day at the same time until one day when I should double back and, taking the musket from its hiding place, seek to surprise my quarry who may be lulled into taking no precaution, thinking me gone. Unfortunately, this excellent strategy did not reach fruition because after only a few days the farmer must have back his spare musket as he is going shooting and wishes to lend it to his good friend, and so I must hurry to return it to him that very morning. I recovered it from its hiding place in the hollow of an old tree out on the downs near where the flock was grazing. It was wrapped in oilcloth and already loaded that I might waste no time when the beast was sighted. No sooner had I unwrapped it to check the damp and rain had not got to it but I felt a presence and turned to find, to my surprise and immediate delight, the creature not twenty yards away with its back to me, slowly creeping across the hillside. It had not seen me. I cocked the musket, and the sound caused the creature to turn and face me. Contrary to my expectation it did not try to run, but holding its ground fixed me with a baleful stare. I took a step nearer, and then it spoke with a voice like a high wind rushing through the trees: "Kill me if you must. It is in thy nature."

"I shall!" I replied boldly. "Fear not any other fate, demon." Its eyes were yellow, with a rectangular pupil like a goat's, and its skin pitted and aged.

"There!" it cried in bitter triumph. "No more can you deny your nature than I mine. We are as we are created."

"Indeed, we are not alike," I said hurriedly. "You may, like the beasts and the birds, be unable to deny your nature, but the Lord has placed my fate in my own hands. I shall kill you because it is what you deserve, and not because it is in my nature to kill."

"Do the beasts and the birds deserve to die for being beasts and birds?"

"Wicked creature! Do you excuse your evil thus?"

There was silence between us and around us for a long moment. Then the creature said: "Wretched am I, and ancient. I danced in the youth of the world with the first men. I saw the pyramids rise from dust, and I witnessed great cities hatch from humble huts of dung. I have seen grand estates and empires of men rise and crumble. I have seen the dominion of man spread to every quarter of the globe, and I have seen my kindred hunted down and mercilessly murdered by thy brethren. Now I am alone. I may be the last of my kind, I do not know. It seems there is not room enough for mankind and such as I in this world. I would leave. I would leave, but I cannot find the way. It is hidden to me. Kill me, then, and have done. It will be a mercy."

The creature bowed its head and closed its eyes in preparation for my bullet. I raised the musket to my shoulder. "Mercy? Think ye that the Lord our Father will show you His mercy? The fires of Hell await thee!"

"Not I!" The creature shook its head. "There is no afterlife for such as I! Time I fear not; I age not as ye do; but my death shall be an ending of me, a conclusion, a ceasing to be. Blessed are ye, for in all creation only man, favoured child of the Almighty, has no cause to fear death. It is but the gateway to his eternal happiness." It began to laugh, a terrible low grating like two heavy boughs chafing together in a storm.

"You laugh in the face of your destruction?"

The creature raised its face and its bulging, slotted eyes met mine. "Kill me and that is an end to my sorrows. But in committing this act, O son of Adam, ye shall be banished from God's side for your sin of murder, and condemned to wail in the shadows for all eternity."

The creature was in my sights: only slight pressure of my finger would bring me vengeance for my Beatrice. Its eyes continued to meet mine and seemed to grow like waxing lamps. I breathed in, held the air in my lungs, and I could feel the blood pulsing through my body, even in the crook of my finger around the trigger. Time itself stretched.

Then the world tilted and the moment passed. I could not kill it, I did not wish any further dealings with the creature, and indeed I could not bear even to look upon it. I lowered the barrel of my gun and, turning upon the heel of my boot, I strode away without a backward glance. There was no sound other than my own footsteps upon the turf; not a bird, not an insect stirred. I went thence immediately to the graveside of my darling girl, and there I humbly begged forgiveness and made my peace with her spirit.

You may think that is the end of my tale. It is not. Grateful for perhaps the first time in my life to have human company, I resolved to settle at the farm for the winter at least. November came and went in a blaze of thin sunshine and golden leaves interspersed with dark storms. December brought the first truly cold weather: heavy frosts, driving sleet carried on swirling winds, and snow. The men and women on the farm gathered around roaring fires under snow-laden roofs. Heavy snowfall is hard work for a shepherd: sheep will find shelter where they may, but caught unawares may be trapped in a snowdrift and must be rescued if they are not to be frozen to death. When there had been a heavy fall the farmer would let me out on his old nag Bluebell to patrol the hills in search of such trouble. On one such morning, which was very bright and crisp, I took to the saddle and travelled northward for a mile across the hills towards where I knew the flock would be. They had settled in the lee of a cliff where the snow was thin, but for a few that were missing. I had an idea where the stragglers might be, and thought to bring them back to the flock if I could find a way; but the drifts pushed me further eastward than I would have wished, and I was on the point of turning back and trying to find another way when I saw tracks in the snow. I knew at once that it was the trail of the creature. The tracks were fresh and erratic: the beast was injured or ill. They led towards a spinney of snow-topped elms; I followed on horseback and then crept carefully into the trees on foot. Not far inside I found the creature huddled and shivering in a rude bower made of branches and leaves. It saw me leaning in, but its gaze showed little interest in my presence and turned away. Its cheeks were hollow, its eyes sunken into their sockets, its body emaciated: the creature was dying.

In my saddle pack I had with me a blanket, a day's food and water, and a small flask of strong spirits. These items I retrieved and brought back to the bower. The creature did not stir even when I climbed inside and lifted its head to pour a few drops of spirit into its mouth. The liquor had its effect, though, and the creature was soon coughing and somewhat revived. I wrapped the blanket around it and helped it to take some water, and then some small pieces of bread, which it chewed thankfully enough.

"You cannot remain here," I said, "Or you will die."

"Where would you take me where I should be safe?" the creature croaked. "Better to leave me here and forget you ever saw this place."

There was indeed wisdom in these words: the creature could not come anywhere near my fellow man or its days would be numbered short indeed. There were no places of natural shelter that I knew of nearby that would be any better than this spinney.

"Very well. Here you shall stay, and here shall I come every day until you are recovered."

"I deserve not your kindness," the creature said weakly.

"We are each one alone in this world," I replied, "But for the kindness of strangers."

When I returned the next day through the snow with supplies, I found the blanket and flask abandoned in the remains of the bower. The creature was long gone. What became of it I know not: I never saw it or its like again."

The shepherd's breathing was laboured, and his voice had fallen away to a husky whisper: the effort of relaying his tale and thus reliving it had greatly hastened his journey to the *portas caeli*. He tried to lift his hand and reach towards me, but there was not strength enough left in his arm. "I have never forgotten the words of the creature: the comfort of knowing with certainty that life eternal awaits at the side of the Lord our Father has changed me and the way I have lived my life since. Good doctor, every word is true. Rejoice… rejoice…"

And with that the old shepherd closed his eyes and fell silent, and inside the hour his soul was gone to God. His face was set in a beatific smile, and with his hands clasped across his chest he looked the very image of a saint of old. His loyal sheepdog was also at peace, lying at his feet with her head turned toward her master as if she had been faithfully attending his last words.

Greatly moved, I drew the rude covers over him and made ready to depart, resolving in my own mind that the shepherd, whether there was truth in his strange tale or no, deserved more than a pauper's grave and that I would give the farmer enough of my own money to see him properly buried in the churchyard and erect a stone ad perpetuam rei memoriam; and so I did, and indeed, no money have I

23

bestowed since that gave me greater return. I closed the shutters and, stepping outside, fastened the door to the hovel firmly shut, proof against beasts at least until someone should come for the body. It was late afternoon, an hour or so before dark, and the wind had dropped away to nothing. I noticed that my horse, tethered at the gate, was standing stock still, its ears turning this way and that as it strained to pick up a distant sound, and so I listened myself. Far away, at the very limit of my hearing, I thought, for a moment, that I could hear a flute playing; its unearthly theme unlike any I had heard before and yet so aptly mournful and bucolic that it might have been composed by an angel solely for the passing of that good shepherd.

Chapter 4: *Charlie's Van*

"Come in," Charlie said. "It's not much, but it's home." Some call them 'mobile homes', some 'static caravans'; Charlie called it his van, and patted the doorframe affectionately as he took the two steps up. The outside area included a rusty rotary washing line, old clay pots stacked up, some rotting garden furniture, and in a corner a soggy-looking compost heap. Inside, the carpet was worn, but not dirty, and there was a smell of sweat, old clothes and damp. Everything was faded, but mostly clean and subject to some sort of order, although to say it was tidy would have been definite overstatement. The area just inside the door was designed as a compact lounge: a banquette of green sofa cushions stretched in a horseshoe around a coffee table. Beyond that was a kitchen, which consisted of a linoleum floor in a terracotta tile pattern, a block of small kitchen cabinets with aluminium trim, and a stainless steel sink. The cooker was of the type powered by a gas cylinder.

"Tea?" Charlie asked, filling an old-fashioned whistling kettle from the tap. I sat down on the banquette where I could still see Charlie in the kitchen area. Squeezed in across the aisle from where he was standing was a diner-style booth with yellow and green flower print cushions and a wood-pattern Formica table top. Farther in there were more doors, leading presumably to bathroom, toilet and bedroom. The walls were finished with textured plastic in cream, which had started to yellow in places, and every spare inch of wall space that could be was covered with shelves groaning with books. There were rows of old Pelican and Penguin paperbacks with tanned pages and cracked spines, books on history, archaeology, languages, and even a long run of ancient Reader's Digest magazines. Other shelves held spiral bound notebooks of varying sizes. As if there were not enough of a fire risk already, papers and newspapers had been sorted into piles on some of the seats and on the floor.

"Great," I said. "I could murder a cuppa."

"I keep meaning to have a clear out," Charlie said, lighting the gas ring with a match, "But somehow I can't seem to get round to it." He pottered around the kitchen setting out two mugs and producing a carton of long life milk from the fridge.

"Have you lived here long?"

"It doesn't feel like it's been a long time." He looked around the interior of the mobile home. "I suppose it has been a fair while now."

There was a long pause while the water heated and Charlie fussed about. To fill the space I picked up an old book that was lying on top of the pile of newspapers next to me: Shakespeare's 'A Midsummer Night's Dream', printed in 1930. Inside the cover the owner's name had been inscribed in childish handwriting: Charles Anton Price.

"Charlie, what is it you do for a living?"

"Oh, I'm strictly a pensioner these days. How do you take it?"

"Er… milk, no sugar thanks." There was another long pause. "So what did you do when you were working?" I asked. The kettle began to whistle. The sound grew to a shrill crescendo, where it remained until Charlie eventually removed it from the heat. He filled the waiting teapot with boiling water.

"How many flats can you get out of St Dunstan's?"

I laughed. "I do wonder what he's going to do with all that space. It could be amazing, but Clifton's very traditional. He's more interested in restoring than transforming."

"Quite right. Everything was better in the past."

When we were both seated with mugs of murky-looking tea in front of us, Charlie cleared his throat rather formally and said: "Now, about this property. If I may speak in strictest confidence..."

"Of course."

"You didn't mention it to your cousin, did you?"

"No. None of his business."

"Good." He frowned, deepening the ploughman's furrows on his brow. "I can't tell you how I found out. Let's just say a little bird told me."

"Okay."

He paused for effect. "Wychwood Hall is going up for sale. The owner's bankrupt."

"Wychwood Hall. Sorry, I don't know it."

Charlie looked surprised. "Stately home? Just down the road?"

I shook my head.

"House, outbuildings, and about two hundred and forty acres."

"Really?" I leaned back, disappointed. "It's kind of you to mention it to me, Charlie, but that's not my kind of thing, to be honest. A property like that'll be Grade One listed I should think. It's not like you could do much with it. It's probably a complete money-pit."

Charlie nodded. "Yes," he said. "Without a doubt it is. Best thing to do with the house is put a match to it, trust me. Dry rot, the lot. No, it's the land, you see."

I shook my head. "It's agricultural or ancient woodland or something like that. You can't build on it."

Charlie acknowledged my point with a jab of his finger. "You can't build on it. If you could, the owner wouldn't be skint. He wouldn't have to sell. He could develop it himself, or just sell off some of it to a developer. But he can't."

"Okay." I tried a sip of my tea. It was too hot and had an odd taste; old man's tea. I could already tell this was going to be a waste of time.

"The estate has drained him of all of his money and more besides, and now he's having to put it up for sale to clear his debts, but no-one will want to buy. He'll have to sell it for next to nothing."

I couldn't help smiling at Charlie's naivety. "And you thought I might want to take advantage of the knock down price. Well, that's a nice idea, Charlie, but unless I could develop it there's nothing in it for me. I'd just be lumbered with a useless asset."

"Indeed." He paused. "But this is where it gets interesting."

I waited for him to say more, but he just sat there and said nothing.

"How," I asked, "Does it get interesting?"

Charlie tapped the side of his nose. "It's who you know. If you wanted, I could introduce you to someone."

I gave it a few moments' consideration, and then shook my head. "Thanks Charlie. I appreciate it, but I'm really busy right now and it's a long way off my home turf."

"Please yourself."

I scratched my ear, feeling the touch of a thread of spider's gossamer snagged on it. "Just as a matter of interest," I said, "Who is this someone?"

Charlie shook his head. "If it's not your kind of thing…"

We fell into an uncomfortable silence. Charlie took a long swig from his mug. The tea was hot enough to burn, but he swallowed it down with no sign of discomfort. He adopted a vacant look.

"I suppose it wouldn't hurt to meet them," I said.

Charlie's eyes came back into focus. "I wouldn't want to mess him about."

"Who is he?" I had a good idea of the sort of person it must be now, but I wanted more from Charlie.

"If I do this for you, your complete discretion will be required. Complete discretion, you understand?"

I laughed. "You're making it sound very dodgy. Come on, Charlie. Don't play games with me. You brought this up, not me."

"Alright. My acquaintance is, shall we say, someone in a position of authority. And he thinks something can be done. Possibly. Definitely, for the right person with the right ideas."

"I see. And that could be me. Charlie, that sounds suspiciously like an invitation to bribe a public official."

"Absolutely not."

"No?"

"No. That would be criminal."

"Yes it would."

"Yes it would."

"Yes."

Charlie went silent again, but this time his eyes held mine, trying to read my thoughts.

The prospect of doing a massive development just down the road from Clifton's new country pad was just too delicious to resist. "I'll meet him," I said. "I'm intrigued."

"Alright then, I'll speak to him. And if he's willing, I shall arrange the meeting."

"You'd better take my phone number," I said.

"I don't have a telephone," Charlie said, as if the telephone was some new-fangled invention he hadn't quite got around to adopting yet. "But there's a phone box in the village."

I didn't drink my tea. When Charlie had finished his, I said I had better be going, and he said he would walk me back up to the church.

The sun was out and it felt pleasantly warm. There were bees working the hedgerow and crickets chirruping in the long grass. An airplane from Gatwick was inching by far overhead, leaving a double white jetstream across the blue expanse. We walked slowly for a few moments without talking, and then Charlie said: "The church dates back to Saxon times. Well, some of it anyway. That's the trouble: people are always adding and embellishing. They can't leave things alone. That tower was added much later, you see." I could see the church tower over the line of trees that followed the churchyard wall. Suddenly a magpie shook the branches of an elm tree to our right and rak-rak-rakked aggressively. Charlie fell silent, following his own line of thought. After a dozen paces he stopped. "And those *fucking* church bells," he spat, "They're enough to drive you mad!"

The bells were silent enough for now. I tried to imagine how loud they must be from Charlie's van, but it wasn't as if he was so close that it would be uncomfortable, more a nuisance if you didn't like it. "I expect they are," I said, but Charlie had started walking again and was grumbling under his breath. I kept pace. We had passed the lich gate and were nearly at the road when he stopped suddenly again and I heard him hiss.

"What's the matter?" I asked.

"Fuck it!" he said.

I looked up and saw a man was approaching purposefully. "Who's that?" I asked, but it was too late for Charlie to answer because the man was upon us.

"Still alive?" he demanded of Charlie. "Really Charlie, I was hoping you'd be pushing up the daisies by now; then I

30

could get my hands on that nice little plot of yours." He took up a boxing stance and jokily punched Charlie in the arm, a little too hard for it to be a purely friendly greeting. Charlie did not take it well. The man was short, broad shouldered, and bald, except for a line of hair joining his ears around the back of his head. His face reminded me strongly of Mr Punch: a hooked nose over a thin mouth and pointed chin, and deep-set, fierce brown eyes. He was wearing a tailored dark green tweed suit with a cream shirt and brown knitted silk tie, and tan brogues.

"Charmed, I'm sure," Charlie replied, still wincing. "Nick, this is Duncan Brockbank. He's an obnoxious little bastard."

Brockbank looked at me like a blackbird eyeing a worm. "How do you do?" he said, offering his hand to shake.

"Nick Carpenter," I said, shaking it.

Brockbank disentangled himself from my grip prematurely and looked at his watch. "Well, I'd love to stay and chat but I'm late for rehearsal. The christening's tomorrow so we're having a run through and I'm the godfather." He caught my arm at the bicep. "He's not really a grumpy old git," he said, giving a nod in Charlie's direction. "He's much worse than that! Cheerio gents." And with that, he hurried off towards the church.

"Who the Hell was that?" I asked Charlie.

"Local tosser." Charlie shook his head. "And people wonder why I'm anti-social.

Chapter 5: *The Uckford Fairy*

from The Seagull
London, Monday.

Tonight the learned, the studious, the sceptical, the enthusiastic and the curious gathered in the theatre at the Natural History Society, Hanover Street, invitations having been issued by the president and committee, to witness the examination of mummified remains believed to be the best evidence yet discovered of the existence of beings commonly known as fairies. The discoverer of the remains told his story to a crowded room of scientists, including Sir Arthur Conan Doyle, the celebrated author and doctor. The first announcement of the find was made exclusively in the "Seagull" on the 2nd October.

Professor Titus Ogg said that "the specimen may be regarded as presenting a hitherto unknown species, for which a new name is proposed."

The lecture was eagerly awaited and is expected to produce the keenest controversy and discussion. The discoverer, Mr. Walter Peachey, a Sussex naturalist and writer, who exhibited the remains, told the story of his find, and Dr. David Rackham, of the Natural History Society, read a paper on the result of his examination of the relic and his conclusions. The paper was entitled "On the discovery of winged human-like remains in a Neolithic mine near the river Uck at Uckford (Sussex)." Dr. William Chester-Hayward, the president of the Society, occupied the chair, and the members were much interested in the specimen that was exhibited.

Mr. Walter Peachey said that the subterranean complex in which he made the discovery occurs in a chalk escarpment some 800ft above the level of the river, and forms part of an extensive network of Neolithic mine-works in the area. It was reached by excavating a filled-in shaft to the depth of 15ft, and consisted of a tunnel with a series of three chambers. The tunnel was about four feet wide and five feet high. The remains were discovered upon crawling through a deep horizontal crevice in the tunnel wall some thirty feet south east along the tunnel from the excavation to a small chamber.

Professor Charles Clark said the South Downs are topographically formed of chalk, a soft, very fine-grained limestone that may be dissolved by rainwater and contains such features as caves, sink holes and karstic cavities, which occur along faults, flint seams and marls. The chamber in which the discovery was made was likely a karstic cave connected to the tunnel due to water action sometime after the Neolithic period.

Dr. Rackham then described the specimen. The lecture was fully illustrated by lantern slides and diagrams. He said that the skeletal remains were complete although with some damage, adult human in proportions but very small. Of course, the frame had much shrunk with age, but the length of the limb bones argued a creature measuring no more than 280mm in length from top to toe. The bones of the skull had remarkable thinness, and the face was damaged, although large orbits could easily be discerned from the fragments. It was an intelligent head of civilised contour, with an upright forehead and weak mandible.

The long bones of the human-like limbs, the tibia, the fibula, the femur, the humerus, radius, and ulna, were intact, but of light construction like the long bones of flying birds. The small bones of the hands and feet were present but dispersed, possibly disturbed by insect action; reconstruction suggested long, delicate fingers and proportionally small, narrow feet.

A capacious rib cage with a slightly keeled sternum strongly suggested the ability to fly, and the desiccated remains of wing structures comprised of a forewing and hindwing like a butterfly's were visible beneath the remains, but the means by which the musculature that would enable flight might have operated could not be determined without further study.

The entire skeleton bore curious markings of size and depth proportional to the bone upon which they appeared that resembled marvellously engraved runes or pictograms, although with no connection to any known language or code. Dr. Rackham said that the markings may be an effect of decomposition and Dr. Talbot Alexander offered that they were unlikely to be typical but could be caused, for example, by bone growth disorder.

It was not possible to say how long the specimen had been preserved in the cave, but the state of decomposition suggested many decades at least.

A debate followed, in the course of which several points of disagreement emerged, the chief of which being the taxonomy of the specimen. Professor Titus Ogg proposed the name "Anthropus Volans Peacheyii" for the type. The principal speakers in the discussion were Lord Eysham, Professor Jacob Stenger, and Dr. Talbot Alexander. Lord Eysham argued that classification as a hominid could not be considered to have been satisfactorily established, and challenged whether there was evidence enough even to consider the creature mammalian given the insect-like venation and chitinous appearance of the wing structures. Professor Stenger emphasised the extreme significance of the discovery, claiming that the find supported the view that ancient legends and tales of interaction between human and fairy had foundation in fact, and that further study by the Natural History Society of the literature would reveal clues that would evidence the conjectures so far drawn based upon anatomy alone concerning the creature's activities and social behaviour.

Dr. Talbot Alexander, on the other hand, saw no reason to doubt a close kinship to humans but felt the presence of the structures interpreted as wings was likely coincidental and lacked the significance that had been assigned to it.

A long discussion followed from which no final conclusions were drawn, other than that a subscription should be made towards the splendid work being done. At the close Dr. Rackham and Mr. Peachey were thanked and Dr. William Chester-Hayward added a few words as to the Natural History Society.

The specimen is to be presented to the Natural History Museum at South Kensington.

Chapter 6: *Unleashed*

"Hello Hazel."

"Oh." She paused, collecting herself. "Hello."

"How have you been?"

"How have I been? Free, actually. Liberated. Out from under the jackboot. Unbound. Unburdened. Untethered. Unfettered. Unleashed."

"That's quite a list. Therapy going well, then?"

"Oh, Jesus! Don't start. I was in a good mood."

"Er… it wasn't me who started."

She was silent for a moment. "Alright," she said at last, and I heard her take a breath. "Let's begin again. I didn't mean it. Well, not the jackboot, anyway. Not entirely. So, hello. How have you been?"

"I've missed you."

"Och, you big jessie."

"Did you get my letter?"

"What do you want, Nick?"

"Did you like it? The story?"

"We agreed you wouldn't contact me."

"Come on, Haze."

"Oh, you're such a bloody psycho! Can't you just leave me alone?"

"But did you?"

"Do you think I don't know what you're doing? It's a trap, a juicy bit of Hazel-bait to suck me into your orbit again. I'm not falling for it."

I waited.

"So… goodbye, Nick."

"Don't you miss me at all?"

"No."

"I wish I could talk to you."

"You mean you wish you could control and manipulate and mind-fuck me the way you used to."

"No, really. There isn't anyone I can talk to the way I can with you."

"Christ, this is pathetic. That's it, Nick. I've had enough. I can't bear it. You can just leave me alone. Just stop it. Don't ring me again. Not… for a while." There was a moment before the connection clicked out in which I thought I heard a muffled sob, but I couldn't be sure.

Chapter 7: *The Journal of Davey Bone*

Wednesday 16th June 1779

It were a day afore yesterday when the strange happenings did begin, and they may be over with now and they may not be over with yet, but for fear I shall forget some important nugget I must set pen to paper and in doing so I shall hope I may also arrange these matters in order of sorts in my own troubled mind. That day was in many respects much alike to the day before it, and that one to its own forerunner, and so on, save that when I sat upon the kitchen step of the White Horse Inn in the sun and closed my eyes for a moment there came into my thoughts a memory of my father, also called Davey, who was a good man and is much missed by his children for his wise head and warm heart, putting out a dish of bread and milk upon that very step after it were dark and calling me and my brothers to come and hush and wait to see a hedgepig or prickleback as some calls them. That memory came to me so clear I were nine years old again, hiding in the kitchen and brim full of excitement. We did wait and after a while, and it were a good long while mind and not easy to keep hushed when there is six young boys with nothing to do but keep quiet and Harry whispering and wanting a sharp stick to stick it with when it comes, there was something a-moving in the bushes and then it did come waddling: a fat hedgepig with black beads for eyes and a twitcher of a nose and a thick coat of brown needles. It stopped to sniff and look around three times afore it came up to the step. We was quiet then all right, and not even Harry wanted it hurt and he joined the army for want of fighting and was shot dead in the American colonies eight years gone, and we was all willing it to come upon the step so as we could get a closer look and I thought I wonder if I shall see its fleas jumping about, but I could not. It put its claws up on the step and reared up and heaved and wriggled and then it reached the dish and I don't remember its way of eating but for it lapping like a cat sometime and its black eyes did glisten in the light from the kitchen. So now I thought I should try putting out a dish of bread and milk so as my own children might have the wonder of seeing such a thing afore they was too old to care much for it. My own young Davey being twelve years of age and like another man about the place might not marvel to see such a thing the more, but the others, well I should like to see their faces and hear them when they see one for the first time, especially my little Lilly Grace, who is just four and whose smile does light up a dark room better than two dozen church candles. That very night I did begin it, although it was fair busy in the inn and I had no time to watch, but I thought I would try it out afore telling the children so as I could be sure a hedgepig would come for them; and so out the dish went on the back step just where my father hisself put it all them years ago and no-one but me knew it. When I looked later in the evening it was still there and untouched except for a fly was swimming in it, and when I looked later still it was yet untouched, and when I came down early in the morning to start work before any others of the family had waked, as is the way of this life of mine, it was untouched also. And I thought try again and this time I shall warm the milk so the hedgepig shall sniff it and come forth, and so I did later that day leave it on the step where I had before, and when I locked up after ten o'clock it was still there untouched and I made to bring it in and try one more time on the morrow, but on a thought I left it there for the night and see what would be.

That was last night, and last night was I visited with a dream, which to a man that sleeps ever soundly in his bed and without dreams was in itself cause enough to feel unsettled, never mind the strange tenor of the vision itself. I dreamed I fell in beside a man as we travelled through an ancient wood of tall oaks and elms that made a great canopy over our heads, through which bright sunlight did flash and flitter, and pressing upon each side of the road was a tangle of dense brambles, briar-rose and ferns from which Spring flowers did peep like shy maidens from between curtains. He was young, of countenance fair, in stature tall and lean, and dressed all in green finery save for a white cloak across his shoulders, and his face and hands were white as alabaster like they had never seen the sun. As it seemed his wish to keep pace with me I bade him good day in all politeness and did enquire of him whither he was bound.

"I am off to Wychwood Hall!" he replied in a friendly enough way.

"Wychwood Hall? Why, I know it! Indeed, it is not far from where I live."

"Is that so?" says the man. "Then you are a singular fellow! I believe you may be able to do me a service."

"I hope I shall."

We did walk on a little farther together and then he said: "Are you a hunting man?"

"I have never seen the attraction of it."

"A singular fellow indeed! I have taken a liking to you already, quite a liking. I vouch we shall be the best of friends."

The wood was ringing like a belfry with birdsong and there was a breeze that set leaves and stalks a-quiver as the two of us passed by on our way. "What is your business at Wychwood Hall?" I asked.

He smiled then, with long, white teeth, and in his nimble grasp did appear, as by magic, a gold coin, which he handed me with a genteel flourish. As we walked I turned it over in my fingers: it was heavy, and so bright in the sunlight that it might have been struck in the King's mint only moments before, save that there was no picture of the King upon it but rather a bull's head on one side and a cross upon the other. I was much taken with it, but when I turned to give it back, as I thought he had intended, I found my companion gone and the only signs of the means of his departure were a faint rustling of leaves and a fleeting shadow glimpsed through twisted undergrowth.

I awoke this morning much out of sorts and afterwards went about my duties begrudgingly, but when at last I thought to look outside on the kitchen step to see what was, the dish was clean of bread and milk, and that was something; but then, much more to my surprise, left in the middle of the dish neat as neat was a coin and that like none I had seen before except in my dream. I was sorely taken aback and snatched it up to look more closely, and I thought at once it must be gold, by the weight, and of great age, for the pattern upon it was rough and much faded and I could make out little but what might be the head of a bull upon one side. I was caught up then in feverishly wondering how it came from my dream to the dish, but soon after did come to my senses and with that the welcome certainty that this must be no more than coincidence and no less than someone making a jest with me, and I laughed aloud, as much from relief as any other cause. An immediate attempt to guess the name of the culprit was confounded, for I could think of no-one as would chance such a thing as that coin upon a mere jape, and I have waited all day and mentioned nothing to anyone to see who would speak to me upon it in the end, but none has. So now I am thinking as I shall put out a dish of bread and milk again and perhaps in doing so I shall mock the author of this jest and make them quiet, or perhaps I shall earn another gold piece and then it shall be an expensive trick for whoever-it-is and to my advantage, and we shall see who is laughing in their sleeve and who has gold in their purse!

Chapter 8: *I Told You I Wasn't Nice*

Highgate, overwhelmed long ago by the inexorable bloating of the London corpus, has nonetheless retained something of the character of a true village. The building that houses my flat shares its hilltop perch above the ugly aggression of the surrounding sprawl with a characterful crowd of what the estate agents would call 'period' dwellings, all jostling for the view. The village remains an enclave of privilege, boasting its own traditions, its own characters, its own life; and whilst it is possible, as in any city, to live there anonymously and in ignorance of one's neighbours, there is a readily accessible community which, whilst not always entirely friendly or benevolent, will at least take an interest in your business should you choose to allow it. The shops are thriving on local clientele, and the pubs and restaurants are rarely empty.

It was just over two weeks since my visit to Clifton. Normally I make a determined effort to arise early every morning and make a strong start in spite of the relatively few demands placed upon me by my work, but on this particular morning I had slept late and I woke to light creeping in around the edges of the blind and, most unexpectedly, the sound of loud and tuneless singing coming from outside.

I slipped out of bed and went, in my dressing gown, to the large, balconied bay window in the open plan kitchen and living area at the front of the flat. The sun was coming in through the shutter blinds there too, revealing a very thin sprinkling of dust that had settled on the dining table and kitchen counter. From force of habit I checked the mantelpiece: Hazel had been a devil for moving things out of position. Of course, it was all still in perfect order: a framed photo of Mother and Father with yours truly in their arms on a long-ago holiday to Tuscany, possibly the last time we were all happy in each other's company; a small frog by Eduardo Paolozzi, much loved by me and detested by Hazel; black ceramic candlesticks from Heal's; and a Schatz German mantel clock from the 1950's in a glass case, which still kept time with relentless Teutonic accuracy.

I opened a two inch crack in the shutters. Gathered on the pavement below were half a dozen people carrying placards that said 'Save Footsteps Community Centre' and 'Hands off our Centre' and the like, chanting something I couldn't quite make out. Of course, I knew what it was about, but I hadn't seen it coming at all and so it was a nasty shock, not to mention something of an embarrassment that I would have to live down with the neighbours, who I was surprised hadn't been round to complain already.

I wondered if I should just call the police. Surely these people couldn't just organise a protest outside my house like this and harass me! Then I realised that the police would just say they were very busy and they might have someone available in about six hours, so I decided not to bother; and in any case, if this was going to be a problem for my flagship development project then the best thing I could do was to confront it and sort it out myself. I threw some water on my face and quickly got dressed, trying to weigh up whether there was any risk of violence. They looked a bit grubby: just what you'd expect from rent-a-mob Socialist Workers. More of them meant more witnesses, a wider range of views, which suggested aggro was less likely; but on the other hand there was a risk that numbers would just make them bolder, like a pack of hyena. I certainly didn't want to face them all at once. Perhaps I should invite just one of them in for a civilised chat; the leader. Yes, that was better, and perhaps that would even offer an opportunity to negotiate a... ah... financial solution.

When I opened the front door downstairs, they didn't notice at first. A tall man with an American accent was leading a chant to the tune of La Donna è Mobile: "We want our centre back, we want our centre back…". Leaving the door open behind me, I strode up to him purposefully, on the principle that when in doubt it's best to at least look as if you know what you're doing.

"Hi," I said, "I believe you may have something you want to say to me."

"Hello Mister Carpenter," he said, recognising me straight away, which was rather unnerving. He was in his forties, clean shaven with a square jaw, and sporting old-fashioned browline glasses and a Western-style bootlace necktie. There was the air of a clergyman about him. A Goth woman next to him had stopped singing and was grinning at me, twisting her thick black hair round her finger and grinning at me in a coquettish way that could only be ironic.

"Look," I said, "If I agree to talk to you right now then can you make the others go away? You're spoiling people's breakfasts."

The flat seemed a little stuffy when I came back in, so I opened the blinds and the doors to the balcony to let in some air and at the same time make sure the other protesters had dispersed, which they had. It had proven impossible to detach the little Goth woman from the American ringleader, and so I had allowed them both to enter. Now they were sitting on my sofa and I heard myself ask in a polite voice if they wanted a cup of tea. They both refused, but I made one for myself anyway, taking the time to calm my nerves and thinking that the delay might soften my visitors up a bit. While they waited for me the man sat as upright as he could, his knees and feet together, looking uncomfortable. "Nice place you have here, Mister Carpenter." he said. His gaze darted around the room.

"I like your frog," the woman said, jabbing her heavily be-ringed index finger at it. She was much older than I had first thought. Her long, very thick hair was dyed jet black with a white streak on each side. Heavy eyeliner with thick mascara and pale foundation gave her round face a mask-like appearance, but there were faint laughter lines at the corner of her eyes that softened her expression. Dark lipstick accentuated a wide mouth under a small, pierced nose. She curled her legs under her, boots and all, on my sofa. I decided to live with the risk of dirtied and torn cushions and said nothing about it.

I sat down in my armchair with my mug of tea. "Without wishing to seem rude, can we please get to the point? You want to talk to me?"

The woman grinned. "Got your attention, have we?"

The man produced a notebook and pencil from his pockets. "Mister Carpenter," he began, "My name is Conrad Goldblum. I'm the co-ordinator for the Save the Footsteps Community Centre campaign." He gave me a fake smile, which consisted of his teeth, which didn't look like they were properly attached to his mouth, being given a brief outing like an attacking shark's. "And my colleague is…"

"My name is Mary Flowers. They call me Shitty Mary. You don't need to know why, you just need to know I deserve it." Shitty Mary drew her fishnetted legs out from under her and crossed them, putting the heels of her boots heavily on my coffee table. I winced, but neither of them seemed to notice.

Goldblum continued. "We understand you are the developer in the process of buying the centre from the council. That is correct, is it not?"

"They are selling it to me. Yes."

"And your plan is to turn it into flats, I believe?"

"The planning application is lodged for all to see."

"Yes. The thing is, we don't think it's in the best interests of the community to close the centre, you see. We want to keep it open. It performs a very important function, hosts lots of services that people need, that people depend upon. Drug and alcohol abuse. Mental health."

Shitty Mary put her feet down and leaned forward. "A lot of crazy people depend on that centre," she said.

"Ahem! Yes, so… ah… we'd like you pull out of the sale." Goldblum continued.

"Really?"

"Yes. We think the council will change its mind if you do. You'll be doing everyone a favour."

"I see."

"And if you don't, then we're going to fuck it up for you." Shitty Mary said. "We're going to fuck it up for you big time. So big that you will regret the fuck out of it for the rest of your unhappy fucking life."

Goldblum held his hand up, trying to calm things down. "What my colleague means is, we will continue to campaign until we achieve our objective. Some important people are backing us, Mister Carpenter. People with influence."

"Who? I mean, what are their names? Perhaps I should talk to them?"

"I'm not at liberty to discuss that. Suffice to say that they are capable of intervening, if necessary. Your planning application has no chance of success."

An orange butterfly flew in through the balcony doors and made a jerky circuit of the room. The conversation halted. "Oh, fuck off!" Shitty Mary snarled at it, waving her arm as it came close to the sofa. We all watched as the butterfly came to rest on the rug just where the sun's rays reached farthest into the room, on the balcony side of the coffee table, nearest to Shitty Mary, and stretched its wings wide. Each was adorned with a huge eye pattern. The eyes stared at us, slight movements of the wings making them come alive.

"Well," I said. "I've never seen…"

Shitty Mary jumped to her feet. "Fuck off!" she spat vehemently, addressing the butterfly. Surprisingly, it didn't move. "Fuck off, I said! Get out of it!" She waved her arms. In response the defiant insect angled its wings to follow her, flicked them wider so that the eyes joggled, and, extraordinarily, suddenly hissed at her. She glared at it. The eyes jiggled again and it hissed more loudly. "You see that?" she said, turning in our direction and rolling her own eyes upwards in disgust. "That's taking the piss, that is." And then, without warning, she lunged forward with frightening speed and stomped heavily on the creature with her Dr Martens boot. Twice.

There was a bronze smudge on the rug where the butterfly had been. I was too shocked to say anything at first. Shitty Mary sat down again and proceeded un-self-consciously to wipe the remains of the butterfly from the sole of her boot onto another spot on my rug.

"Would you mind," I said when I had regained control of my jaw, "That's my rug!"

She looked at me without a care. "I told you I wasn't nice," she said, and I realised that the unexpected and uncontrolled violence she had perpetrated was meant as a message. She had no boundaries, and I was not safe. I leaned forward and looked each of them in the eye in turn, weighing my options.

"Please, I'm a reasonable person," I said, sounding reasonable. "In my experience there's always a way for everyone to get what they want. What would it take to make this go away?"

"I don't understand." Goldblum replied.

"Well, I can't afford much, but a financial contribution from me towards a campaign to find a *new* home for the community centre, perhaps?"

"No. No, Mister Carpenter, that does not interest us at all."

"Alright, then. No doubt you've both found all this campaigning a bit of a strain on your personal finances. If I could help you out in some way..."

"He's offering us money," Shitty Mary said to Goldblum, keeping her eyes on me. "We thought he would."

"We're not interested in money," Goldblum said.

She turned to him. "Is it time to go now?" she said. They stood up. So did I.

"Okay. I've heard you out," I said. "I will give what you have said due consideration. In return, you will please leave me alone and stop annoying my neighbours."

"No. I'm afraid we can't do that, Mister Carpenter. We're trying to help you. You'll just be wasting your money if you go ahead. We don't want that any more than you do."

Shitty Mary folded her arms. "We're not going to stop. We're not going to go away. Not ever. We're going to annoy the shit out of you until you give up."

"Thanks for your hospitality," Goldblum said, turning towards the door. "We'll see ourselves out."

They walked to the front door and opened it for themselves. I followed them out into the hallway. "Pull out of the deal," Goldblum said. "Find another community to destroy."

"Money isn't everything!" Shitty Mary said over her shoulder, strutting out. The latch clicked shut behind them.

Chapter 9: *You Have Been Warned*

Dear Nick,

I'm sorry I was so horrible on the phone. You shouldn't have called. I did ask you not to. Quite what I'm supposed to make of you – of all people - sending me an old fairy story I do not know. I liked this one very much; it has a faun and it's sad but quite beautiful. But please don't write to me or call me any more! If I get more letters I shall simply bin them without opening them. You have been warned!

H

Chapter 10: *The Brodie Cabinet*

"The ideal collection should be nothing less than a theatre of the universe... keys to the whole of knowledge." Samuel Quiccheberg (1529-1567)

On visiting the town of Lewes, one of the sights that the inquisitive traveller should not miss on any account is the Brodie Cabinet, which is now accommodated outside the Mayor's parlour in the Town Hall. The combination of a mania for completeness and order and an academic, enquiring mind of the kind that has been sharpened in one of our great universities led John Brodie to acquire an extraordinary collection of curios on his extensive travels around the world, and subsequently to display them in a purpose-built cabinet. The cabinet, as with others of its peculiar ilk, juxtaposes natural phenomena side by side with artificial wonders in an heroic attempt to encapsulate wisdom and shed light upon the world. Nowadays the futility of attempting to capture the essence of all of nature and artifice thus in one small collection has led to the practice being eschewed in favour of the larger and more accessible museum; however, at the time the assembly of such a collection was considered a laudable, valuable and indeed fashionable pursuit. Several such cabinets survive and still provoke gasps of amazement from the viewer at their horrors and delights.

John Brodie was born in Antioch Street, Lewes, Sussex on January 18th 1721 into a family grown wealthy in the wool trade. His older brother, James, inherited the family business on the death of their father, and John Brodie, having completed his schooling at Brasenose College, Oxford, went travelling in Europe on the route followed by those taking the "Grand Tour". His interest in collecting curios was no doubt rooted in visits paid to the Schloss Ambras, where the extraordinary collection of Ferdinand of Tyrol is housed, and to Italy, where he encountered the magnificent collections of the Medici family in Florence and the cabinet of Manfredo Settala in Milan. Brought up in the Church of England, Brodie was strongly influenced as he made his acquisitive way through Europe by the dominance of the Catholic Church. In Rome Brodie converted to Catholicism, and soon after went to Liège where he studied at the Jesuit College. He was brought back to England by the death of his brother in 1752, and on selling the family business came into a sizeable fortune.

He purchased Wychwood Hall, a country house previously destroyed by fire, and with it an estate of some 5,000 acres. In 1762 work was completed on the renovation, into which he moved immediately. Brodie had no remaining family, and never married. Pursuing scholarly ambitions, he amassed an extensive library and a small circle of friends. Pursuing also a surprising passion for hunting for a man of such an academic bent, Brodie became master of the local hunt; a position he held with a grip of iron for twenty-one years, housing a large pack of hounds and a stable of horses on his estate at his own expense. He died in September 1783 of a stroke following a hunting accident in which he was unseated by his horse and dragged into a tree with his foot caught in the stirrup. The instructions in his will donated his library and collection to Stonyhurst College, the Jesuit school in Lancashire. Unfortunately, another fire at Wychwood destroyed the bulk of the library before it could be claimed, and in the ensuing confusion it appears that the cabinet was rescued by the constables and put on public display in Lewes, where it has remained ever since.

The cabinet itself is twelve feet in width by seven feet in height and perhaps eighteen inches in depth. It is made of mahogany in an asymmetric design in which no alcove or shelf is the same size. It was custom built to precise specification around the collection, and it is plainly intended that each object should take on meaning from its positioning within the cabinet and the nature of the neighbouring exhibits. In this way, the relationship between art and nature is utilised to provoke and to reveal. The damage caused by the fire is evident along the left hand side and whilst the structure has survived, albeit with severe blackening, several exhibits upon that side have been destroyed or lost. The catalogue of items was also lost in the fire, and thus we are left to speculate upon the nature and provenance of the items on display for ourselves: each is a cipher.

There is a thematic order to the objects, imposing a familiar structure upon the world: earth, water, fire and air arranged in hierarchy from floor to ceiling. Meanwhile, items set side by side explore the dialectic between life and death. Objects have distinct virtues and properties, by which they are grouped, and each has also some symbolic quality. Together, they represent a body of learning, accumulated and frozen in time, for which the key has now been lost.

Occupying the lower shelves in the cabinet are the objects of the earth. On the left, jars and vials of unidentifiable powders and liquids crowd together beside a set of metal implements like a surgeon's kit. There is a collection of crude pottery items, cracked and broken, in odd designs with no obvious use, and beside it a set of tiny pans and pots in copper, no doubt from an apothecary's kitchen. These items are manufactured, chiefly mineral in content. They symbolise, perhaps, primitive history and progress through science in medicine and technology.

Farther to the right, the remains of an unidentifiable burrowing creature preserved in a jar, head down, stands beside the jawbone of a troglodyte bear, canine teeth carved with ancient designs. There is a specimen of an abnormal human foetus also preserved in a jar, and beside that a deformed human skull showing the nubs of bony horns. This section is animal in content, mostly in natural state, and symbolises subterranean origin, birth, death, and in its brutal ugliness comments upon the primeval harshness of existence.

Moving to the right again, the exhibits remain of animal origin but are now embellished or worked upon: a bezoar set in sumptuous silver and gold, a collection of horse whips with horn handles, and a large hunting horn, inlaid with silver and painted with hunting scenes. A very realistic mask, carved from wood and polished until almost glowing, sits beside a display of coins stamped with strange runes. There is a large fragment of a classical statue of the god Pan in anthracite. And also at this level, a crude iron cross and beside it a smooth stone with a hole through it.

Water, the bringer of life, is next: amongst other exhibits there is an automaton of a mounted knight with a spear, stabbing at a fleeing water nymph; an ill-favoured doll made of sealskin; the horn of a narwhale carved fantastically; other items of scrimshaw depicting fantastic beasts; a Jenny made of a dried fish; a shell made into a goblet with a stem of red coral.

Fire, creator and destroyer, is represented at the next level. Here we find amongst other things an egg crusted with semi-precious jewels, a black candle in a holder made of carved bone, a crude clay oil lamp, a small lizard in a jar with the appearance of wings – an embryonic dragon perhaps! – and an ancient hammer. This part of the cabinet is – ironically enough - the most damaged by the fire and there may be as many as three exhibits missing, presumably destroyed at the same time the house burned down.

Air artefacts include a display case of bright tropical insect wings pinned out, a fly whisk made from a horse's tail with a bone handle, a curling musical instrument of the wind family, but of design unlike any other, a pot containing bronze arrowheads, a machine with complex and delicate parts that appears to measure something, and a portrait of what may be the Madonna made entirely of feathers.

The visitor may also witness how the exhibits are classified in other ways: one may trace a vertical path in objects that are scientific or medicinal, in objects that are natural in origin, and objects wrought for aesthetic purposes from that which was formerly living. Note also the juxtaposition of life and death: the skull beside the baby, the egg beside the bone carvings, the medicines beside the weapons. Art and nature vie side by side. This is an attempt at a system of classification that engages, provokes, challenges, and in so doing attempts nobly to unify and explain.

John Brodie may now be forgotten, but his extraordinary cabinet has survived him and grants him some small measure of immortality for as long as men remain curious about the condition of their species. As a result of the fire that damaged it, the cabinet will remain an incomplete and undecipherable mystery: we shall never know if Brodie had indeed succeeded in expressing a unifying theory of all things. Nevertheless, the cabinet remains one of the wonders of our age.

Chapter 11: *Exfoliation*

I arrived at the beauty salon in Knightsbridge a few minutes late. There was a clinical serenity to the place that was not unpleasant, but it was without doubt a haven intended for women only and even though the receptionist was perfectly civil I couldn't help feeling a little unwelcome. When I asked for Mother she nodded, suddenly a lot more deferential, and shepherded me carefully to the door of a treatment room at the back, where she knocked and checked it would be alright to let me in. Mother's commanding voice from inside quickly cut her off, talking over her and instructing me to hurry up, and, battered, she slipped hurriedly away, leaving me to make my own way into the room and shut the door.

There I found Mother lying on a treatment bed, her head swaddled with white towels, her eyes covered with cotton pads, and being attended to by a therapist in a white uniform who was rubbing something onto her forehead with cotton wool.

"You're late," Mother said.

"Hello Mother."

"Hazel with you?" Mother asked hopefully.

"No. It's just me."

I leaned back against the wall, taking in Mother's appearance before the inevitable onslaught of questions began. She was more stick-thin than ever, her legs long and elegant and her toes manicured. Her skin had transformed from the orange peel it had been the last time I had seen her to the tan and texture of ostrich leather.

"You look well," I said.

"You sound thin. You're not eating properly."

"I'm eating all the right things. That's the secret." Mother barely ate anything ever, so she was hardly an expert. "Perhaps you should have taken me for lunch."

"I'm on an impossible schedule. You know I'm flying back tomorrow. How's Hazel? Why isn't she with you?"

I was ready for Mother on that one. "I did tell you. We're on a break."

"I don't know what that means."

"It means she's moved out for a bit."

"She's left you!"

"No, we're just having some time apart."

Mother took a moment to digest this.

"Can I get you something to drink?" the therapist offered, without looking up. "We have mineral water or green tea."

"Has she met someone else? Have you?"

"No, thank you," I said to the therapist, and then to Mother: "No, it's just as I said, time apart."

Mother harrumphed.

"There we are, I've finished cleansing," the therapist announced soothingly. "Now I'm going to exfoliate."

"Yes, just get on with it." Mother snapped. "Do sit down, Nicholas. Don't skulk by the door."

How did she do that? I lifted a chair out of the corner and set it down. "So you've seen Clifton's place. Quite a project he's taken on, isn't it? It's going to cost a fortune." She had found more time for Clifton on this trip than she had for me. Not that that was something I would complain about.

Mother sighed impatiently. "He's got a fabulous home for next to nothing. And he's being very shrewd about the renovations. I didn't think he knew anything about property. I'm very impressed."

I knew better than to argue.

"He has a new girlfriend, too. She's rather lovely, actually."

"Has he? Shame they never last."

"Hmm. I have a feeling about this one. I think she might be the one."

"Well if he's found someone who can put up with him at long last, good luck to him."

"I wish you could find someone who'd put up with you, Nicholas. I live in hope."

I could tell she was building up to a full broadside, and it was coming any moment.

"Now look, about this development, the community centre. You haven't exchanged contracts yet. What's the hold up?"

"We're getting very close."

"Is there a problem?"

"God, no. It's all going fine."

"You would tell me, wouldn't you?"

"Mother, I assure you it's all fine. You know what councils are like to deal with."

The therapist started in on Mother's face again. "You'll feel the grittiness of this," she said. "It's not too harsh. Just lifting all the dead skin."

"Well, I'm concerned. After all the money we've sunk into this already, I don't want to lose it."

"You think I do? Walk away from… a hundred thousand quid profit after tax, maybe more?"

"Alright, Nicholas. It's your company, I don't dispute that. I don't wish to interfere, but it's my money, and as your funder I do have a say in these things."

"Of course. Sorry. Look, I'll make sure you're kept better informed, okay?"

"I'd appreciate it."

The truth was that I was on the verge of pulling out of the community centre deal. The threats from the protesters had coloured my thinking about it, naturally: it was entirely possible that they would be able to block the planning permission; but the main reason was that if Charlie's contact turned up trumps, and I had a hunch it would, I would need the money for that, and there was no way I could fund two big projects at the same time. Charlie's project would be a life-changer if it came off, and that was what I needed to get back on track. Also, I didn't want to miss a chance to get one over on Clifton. I didn't want Mother interfering until it was a done deal. Quite what supernatural sense had given her a whiff of there being an issue I had no idea, but her acuity was as scary as ever.

"Can you feel the roughness?" the therapist asked.

"It's fine," Mother replied dismissively.

I seized the opportunity to change the subject. "How's the extension coming along?"

"It's exhausting. Honestly, I don't know how I find the patience. Those Spanish builders just turn up when they feel like it."

I reflected that they probably lived in mortal terror of Mother and stayed away whenever they could, but I said: "Perhaps they'll get it finished while you're away. That would be a lovely surprise."

"Yes, it would." Mother fell silent as the therapist worked the exfoliant around her lips and cheeks. I sat watching her face growing redder by the second. When the therapist had moved on, Mother said: "Nicholas, it's lovely to see you but you don't have to stay and chat. I'm going to be here another hour at least and I would like to spend some of that time relaxing."

And that was it: she had delivered her message and now I was dismissed, without her even taking the trouble to remove the eyepads and actually look at me. Well, I had got off lightly, with time off for good behaviour. "Actually I *was* thinking of getting a spot of lunch. Build myself up a bit." I said. I stood up. "I'll be off then. Lovely to see you too, and, er, safe trip tomorrow."

Mother waved her hand vaguely by way of a goodbye, and I headed for the door. It was a strange thing with Mother: I always fell into the trap of looking forward to seeing her, but when I did see her I always came away feeling like I'd been mugged.

Chapter 12: *The Journal of Davey Bone*

Thursday 17th June 1779

Last night I walked again in that ancient wood in my dream, and as I passed by the great trees they did catch aflame and blacken and twist, and as they burned they cried out with the voices of men and women and did wave their branches as arms in their suffering and the fire did hiss and roar like a great beast all around. I discovered beside me once again my companion, the man all in green, and he smiled and greeted me with warm looks and a calm manner.

"Be not afraid," he said, "For as they are consumed, like the phoenix are they reborn. Fire does cleanse and return all things to their beginning."

"I am not afraid."

"Singular fellow that you are! Why, I wish I had known you sooner, indeed I do sir. You shall do, indeed you shall."

"Shall I? How may I assist you?"

"All in good time," was his reply. "All in good time, I beg you."

We walked on and soon the flames were done but there was much smoke and cinder in the air, and when it settled I found on all sides a snowy covering of fine silver ash, broken only by the charred tree-stumps that were the remains of those forest giants. There came rain then, and sun, and we had not progressed very much farther along the road before there were green shoots pushing through the blackened turf.

"How long must it take for the wood to grow back to its former glory?" I asked. "It must be a hundred years."

"It is but the blink of an eye." The man pointed at the ground by the side of the road. "Take this nut tree," he said, and where he pointed there was a new sapling pushing

62

through the sod. "It is yet so small that it can bear but a single nut." He reached down and plucked the nut from the tree. "But soon it shall bear fruit enough to feed a village." He handed me the nut, and it fell into two halves in the palm of my hand. As I looked, each half became a bright gold coin.

I woke in a sweat to find the hour no different to my usual hour of waking and yet I felt I had barely rested. I feared then and I fear still that I must be sickening with some ailment that lays in wait and has yet to show its true form but is foreshadowed in dreams and broken sleep. But fears do not feed families and life must continue, and so up from the comfort of my bed and downstairs to my duties, and I made the first of these to look outside the kitchen door to see what had happened to the bread and milk; indeed, I was anxious to see that the events of the day before had not repeated themselves and that normal life had been restored. The dish was clean once again, and that might have pleased me were it not that there were two gold pieces in the dish, one neatly lying atop the other, which instead did cause my gut to twist like rope and my heart to pound louder than a blacksmith's hammer: how it could be that the dream should foreshadow the event I did not know, and no sense could I make of it. I stood as one dazed for some moments, and then I became suddenly possessed of great anxiety that, whatever the cause, there may be danger for my family in it, for none but a madman would give away such things and yet there they were stacked nicely in the dish, and so I took up my stout walking stick and beat upon the bushes all about to discover anyone hiding there to laugh or for a reason more sinister, but with no result other than looking foolish to myself. Next I picked up the coins, which were both much alike to the first in condition but of design different in as much as I could tell, and although I looked at them long and very hard they made me none the wiser.

Once again the day long not a soul breathed a word of it to me. Later, when there was a quiet moment, I took the opportunity to speak to my dear wife Anne on the subject as she can be trusted not to repeat our talks to others and is wise in ways I am not, although I did not mention my dreams to her for fear that she may entertain the same worries as I concerning my health. She laughed at my grave face and said it must be no more than a rascally trick being played upon us by one of our many friends, and was not afraid as she had not heard of any strangers hereabouts and felt sure that another day would see all revealed. She was so cheery and unconcerned that I felt foolish and after much consideration I thought to myself: well, this may indeed be a jape at my expense but I am, in all, three gold pieces the better for it and that is a handsome return indeed upon bread and milk, and so I say long may it continue! Therefore shall I put out the dish again tonight, and tomorrow morning we shall see what has occurred and if it is more of the same then soon I shall be rich!

Chapter 13: *Footprints of the Devil in Our Own County*

One night under a full moon long ago the Devil, it is said, angered by the conversion of the local folk of the Weald to Christianity and by the number of churches they were building, resolved that he would drown them all by digging a channel through the South Downs to let in the sea. He began his excavations at Poynings: his elbows and knees flew and his titanic efforts sent great clumps of earth flying, creating what we now call Chanctonbury Ring, Rackham Hill, Cissbury Ring and Mount Caburn. A wise old woman saw the Devil at his work and quick as she could pushed her rooster off its perch and held up a candle behind a sieve. The Devil heard the loud protestations of the rooster and saw the soft, round light and, fearing that the dawn was breaking, broke off his efforts and the great ditch he had begun is now known as the Devil's Dyke. In some accounts he fled from the dawn by leaping across the Channel and a clod of earth fell from his hoof and created the Isle of Wight, and in others he perished and where he fell is known as the Devil's Grave, and it is said that if you run seven times widdershins around the Devil's Grave holding your breath the Devil will appear. In another version of events he jumped into Surrey, and the impact of his landing created the Devil's Punch Bowl.

The Devil was indeed frequently to be seen in England in those far off days: the results of his often ridiculous antics are to be found in many more topographical features that are named for him, and in no place more than our own County of Sussex, one of the longest inhabited and last proselytised areas of the country. At West Lavant there is a six mile long earthwork called the Devil's Ditch; the Devil's Bog is to be found in Ashdown Forest; the Devil's Race is a field on

Cradle Hill near Alfriston; Devil's Rest Bottom is at Norton; Stoney Down is known as the Devil's Burrow; Moulsecoomb Pit is known as the Devil's Footprint; the Devil's Humps are at Bow Hill; and at Treyford Hill is a series of barrows called the Devil's Jumps, so named because the Devil was once amusing himself by jumping between the barrows and irritated Thor who was sleeping there. Thor threw a great stone at him and caught him squarely in mid-jump, and the Devil ran away.

The arrival of the early Christians into what had been a pagan stronghold worked the Devil into an infernal rage. Saint Wilfrid, Bishop of Northumbria, spent five years in the Kingdom of Sussex converting the pagan Saxons following his exile by the King of Northumbria, Ecgfrith, in 680AD. New churches sprang up, often upon the sites previously used for pagan worship. Saint Dunstan (909AD-988AD) had several direct skirmishes with the Devil as the fiend tried to prevent Christianity from extending its influence in the area. A famed metalworker and already the Archbishop of Canterbury, Saint Dunstan was at work in his smithy at Mayfield when the Devil approached him in the guise of a beautiful girl seeking spiritual help, but then began an attempt at seduction. Saint Dunstan was not easily fooled and spied the Devil's cloven hoof peeping out from under the girl's skirt. He picked up his red hot blacksmith's tongs from the fire and grasped hold of the Devil's nose, who, writhing and screeching, fought and changed into a series of fearsome monsters, but could not win free. At last the Devil changed into his true form, and only then did Saint Dunstan release him, whereupon the fiend fled to Tunbridge Wells and cooled his nose in the waters there, which is why they are red in colour to this day. The saint's smithing tools are still on display in Mayfield. The deed is remembered in this ancient verse:

> *Saynt Dunstan (as the story goes),*
> *Caught old Sathanas by ye nose.*
> *He tugged soe hard and made hym roar,*
> *That he was heard three miles and more.*

Also in Mayfield, Saint Dunstan was approached by a man with a request to shoe his horse. Saint Dunstan recognised him as the Devil and instead of shoeing the horse, seized him and nailed a horseshoe to his hoof. The Devil hopped about in pain, but Saint Dunstan would not release him until he had sworn that he would never enter any house with a horseshoe over the door. This was the origin of the custom of nailing a lucky horseshoe over the front door of one's house. Another version of this tale has it that the Devil, enraged by the building of a nearby convent, threatened to knock down all the houses in the village. Saint Dunstan bargained with him and tricked the Devil into conceding that he would leave alone any house with a horseshoe nailed outside. Armed with his hammer and nails and a supply of horseshoes, Saint Dunstan hurried around the village and before the Devil had begun his work there was not a single house left without a horseshoe over the door, and so the village was saved. Saint Dunstan has become the patron saint of goldsmiths and silversmiths, and the tongs are his symbol.

The directional alignment of the new church founded by Saint Dunstan provided another opportunity for the Devil to continue his harassment of the people of Mayfield: churches are generally aligned to face the East, and this church was no different until the Devil intervened and moved it from its proper alignment overnight. Saint Dunstan corrected it repeatedly only to find that the Devil had moved it again. Another attack on a new church came at Hollington, where the Devil, having failed to prevent its construction, moved the building to another location in the middle of a wood. In another version of this tale, the wood sprang up to defend the church from the Devil after he had moved it. The Devil's assault upon the church of Saint Nicholas of Myra in Brighton took a different form: the Devil disguised himself as a devout woman and gave out vases of oil to pilgrims with which, they were told, they should anoint the church. The oil turned out to be a liquid that would burn the church walls! The plan was thwarted when the bishop met the pilgrims and the plot was exposed.

The people of Sussex make use of a variety of sobriquets for the Devil: Old Nick, Old Scratch, Mister Scratch, Old Man, Old Harry, the Naughty Man, the Poor Man, and Old Grim being the principal names, although the Devil is also confused sometimes with Pan and with Puck. It is thought that these nicknames have evolved in order to avoid having to name the Devil and thereby run the risk of summoning him or being the recipient of a dose of bad luck. However, it has also been argued that some of these may be a corruption of old Saxon fairy names; thus Old Nick may be a corruption of Nicor, a Saxon water sprite, and Skrat, a wood spirit of Norse origin, has become Old Scratch.

The phenomenon of the replacement of ancient pagan culture with new Christian extends beyond the names of spirits and the use of pagan worship sites for building churches. As the newly converted were diverted away from old pagan places, legends of such spots being haunted by the Devil gained currency. Walking around Chanctonbury Ring at the right hour was said to lead to an encounter in which the Devil would steal your soul. A similar outcome could be achieved by circling the Devil's Humps seven times. More recently some locations such as old tombs and deserted buildings have earned a reputation for being haunted by being the hideouts of smugglers; the stories of terrible consequences such as being chased by the Devil for those foolhardy enough to risk a visit having been propagated by the criminals to keep people away.

The association of the county of Sussex with the supernatural is of very long standing. Early beliefs in spirits inhabiting stones, plants and animals have over the years given way to more complex theologies imported from elsewhere: Saxons, Celts, Norsemen, Romans and Normans each brought with them a different framework for understanding the spiritual dimension of men's hearts. It could be that the sightings of spirits and strange creatures that haunt the Weald and that continue to this day are no more than the feverish imaginings of the impressionable; but if challenged with the prospect of a lonely midnight stroll around an ancient pagan site under a full moon, perhaps on Walpurgis Night, we may yet be surprised by how many of even our most robust local yeomen would sheepishly plead a prior commitment to another, unbreakable, engagement whilst privately shivering in their stout farmer's boots.

Chapter 14: *The Bewick Horse*

When he answered the door of his van, Charlie was dressed in light tweeds and walking boots. He grabbed his stick and stepped out, pulling the door shut behind him before I had a chance to say a word. "Come on," he said, "We're going for a walk."

"I thought I was meeting your friend."

"He likes a walk."

"I wish I'd known," I said. "I'd have dressed for the occasion. Brought, I don't know, some water and Kendal Mint Cake and stuff."

Charlie set off at a surprisingly brisk pace. "We're not going on a transcontinental expedition," he said over his shoulder. "Come on." He strode away down the lane away from the village, barely using his stick, and after a moment's hesitation I chased off after him.

We had not travelled far from the village when the ground began to rise and the open fields and grazing meadows on each side gave way to mature woodland. The ancient lane dipped beneath the level of the tree roots, and branches reached across high over our heads to make a tunnel. I caught Charlie up. "So where are we going?"

"We're meeting him at the Bewick Horse."

"Bewick? I don't know it. How far is that?"

"Half an hour or so. Not that far as the crow flies, but a bit up and down."

"Okay. Nice day for it." A half-hour's ramble across the downs in the sunshine to some obscure pub sounded quite pleasant.

"How's your community centre development coming along? Knocked it down yet?"

"No. Actually, Charlie, I'm holding off on exchanging contracts until I've met your man."

"Thank you. I'm relieved to know you're taking this seriously. My friend wouldn't like being pissed about. But then, I wouldn't have offered to introduce you if I'd had any doubts about you. I knew you were smart from the moment I met you."

I didn't say anything to Charlie about it, but I had done some homework on Wychwood Hall and its owner, and from what I could find out Charlie's analysis was spot on. The cost of maintaining a stately home with huge grounds and ornamental gardens requires the kind of large income an asset like that just can't generate. Wychwood Hall had become badly dilapidated and the situation was getting worse by the day. The owner, Lord Wychwood, had mortgaged it up to the eaves and beyond and was in massive arrears with payments. His planning applications had all been rejected. Short of a miracle, it was inevitable that the bank was going to force a sale imminently.

"So, who is this guy?"

Charlie's face gave nothing away. "An old friend of mine. I've known him a very long time, since before the war. He's one of a kind, a singular fellow. I trust him absolutely. And he just happens to be the chair of the council planning committee."

The lane sank further into a steep-sided valley, and at the bottom we came to a wooden gate on our left. Beyond was a path leading downwards into a deeper dell of oaks and sycamores. We descended cautiously, in single file, and the heavy shade kept the air cool, almost chilly despite the sunshine. At the bottom of the slope was a plank bridge over a tiny stream in which the water, which was running slowly but steadily, was a translucent black due to the deep shade.

We crossed over and started up the slope on the other side. Charlie slowed considerably, maintaining a constant pace and planting his feet carefully. As I followed him I found it difficult to travel at the sluggish pace he was setting and kept getting too close behind him and having to mark time to let him get ahead, but we made progress nonetheless and before long we stepped out of the shade of the trees and onto a grassy slope, where he paused for a rest.

"This part of Sussex is known as the Rape of Bewick," Charlie said when he had got his breath back, apropos of nothing. "A rape is an old name for a division of land."

"Really? I've never heard of that."

"Bewick's always been a deathly quiet corner of the world. Too far from the river Adur, you see. No trade. Nothing here of interest. Even the Romans couldn't be bothered with it."

"It does seem incredibly unspoiled."

Charlie snorted. "But we'll soon fix that, eh?"

"Last leg." Charlie jabbed the air with his stick to make up in emphasis for the breathy weakness of his voice. We had followed a drover's path over one of the downs, crawled around the base of the hill and joined a well-maintained and broad path that came from the South; a welcome development that suggested civilisation could not be far away. I started to think about the pub. The path wound its way confidently upwards at a comfortable gradient, and was wide enough for Charlie and I to travel side by side. We walked in silence, Charlie with his head down in grim determination to keep going, using his stick heavily. A wooden rail appeared on the downward slope side of the path as we got higher.

About two thirds of the way up, the path and rail suddenly came to an end in a flat patch of worn ground. We halted.

"Okay Charlie, where to now?" I said, but Charlie shook his head and pointed with his stick. I followed the direction it was pointing in and saw a tall and stooped figure descending the slope towards us. It was a man, about Charlie's age I thought, although he moved with long, even strides that suggested he was much sprightlier.

"Is that him?"

Charlie nodded.

"Where's the pub?"

"Pub?"

The Bewick Horse, I was about to say, but I realised at that moment that I was an idiot and it wasn't a pub. Of course it wasn't a pub! As I tuned in I began to see the long patches of chalk on the grassy hillside beside us for what they were. "Oh!" I said. "I see."

Charlie let me know he thought I was an idiot too with a look. I took a few steps sideways, trying to get a better view of the giant white figure on the slope while still keeping an eye on Charlie's friend.

"Lovely day!" the man called, lifting an arm to greet us. His voice rang with authority: here was someone who was used to being shown respect, deference even. When he reached us he seized Charlie's hand, giving it a firm shake. "Charlie," he said. "Charlie, Charlie, Charlie. You look well! All this walking, eh? Keep it up." He turned his head to look at me. "Now, won't you introduce me to our friend here?"

Charlie released his grip, dropped his hand to his side. "This is Nick Carpenter," he said, in a strained voice that suggested he was only just staving off a major heart attack.

"Nick, this is Howland Greenwood. *Councillor* Howland Greenwood."

Greenwood came over. "Very pleased to meet *you*," he said. His hand was large and bony, and it felt like shaking hands with a giant skeleton. I tried to look him in the eye as we shook, but he turned his head slightly and looked at something over my left shoulder.

"Pleased to meet you too, Councillor."

Greenwood had swept-back white hair and wore small, round-rimmed glasses. His mouth was thin lipped and contained a tangle of snaggly rat-teeth that made him look hungry, and his thick jaw muscles made him look like he could bite, too. He was wearing a lightweight anorak over an open-necked grey shirt and tan corduroys, with high top mountain boots.

"I want to thank you," he said, "For coming all the way up here to see me. I really appreciate it." He surveyed the view. "Marvellous, eh? Just look at that." He put his hand on my shoulder and left it resting there. "There's Wychwood Hall, you see? It's over there." He pointed. I tried to make out what he was pointing at, but the countryside all looked the same to me, so I shrugged, taking the opportunity to step away from his hand. "It's there, man! There!" Greenwood insisted, pointing again, and I renewed my efforts to find the house, but it was hopeless. I shook my head. "Well of course you can't actually see the house because of the trees," he continued. "It's that small wood there, looks like the trees are crowding around something. You see it now? Ah, well, I suppose you have to know what you're looking for."

"So tell me what this is all about, Councillor? What have you got in mind?"

"I like a man who comes straight to the point. No tiptoeing about, no bullshit. Alright, look, I've known

Wychwood for a very long time. A very long time." He shook his head. "He's a very stubborn man. Stubborn to the point of being pig-headed. The trouble is, so am I." He grinned. "May I call you Nicholas?"

"You can call me Nick."

"Nick. That's a solid, dependable name. Very good. Well, Nick, that stubborn streak of Wychwood's is the trouble. We want to build houses. Good, sound council homes for people who need them. We want to build communities, you see. Gatwick Airport's just down the road. Plenty of jobs. Wychwood has all that land, just look at it, and not all of it is impossible to build on. But he won't hear of it. He's resisted for years. He's stubborn and he's selfish. The estate's going to ruin because he can't afford to maintain it. Oh, he puts in planning applications alright, but only for a luxury home here or there in a far corner where he won't even notice. He wants money, but he doesn't want the great unwashed on his doorstep. We can't agree to that. We won't! We want council houses. We *need* council houses."

"I understand completely," I said.

"He won't give in, and I won't give in. I'm the chair of the district planning committee, have been for twenty two years. I'll tell you this, Nick: that man will never get planning permission to build anything. Not a fucking sausage. Not while there's breath in my body."

"Is it true he's bankrupt?"

"Yes. Well, not technically as yet, but he is hugely in debt. He's sinking fast; it's only a matter of time. There's nothing he can do. We have him blockaded. He won't sell to us, and no-one else will buy because they think we won't give them planning permission."

"Then he'll have to give in and do a deal with you."

"He won't. And we won't do a deal with him."

75

"Okay. So let's see if I understand you properly: if someone else came along and offered to buy the estate for something in the region of the current valuation, with no plans to develop it, you think he'd sell to them."

"He'd absolutely have to. He's out of options. The bank would force his hand. And for that someone, we would then be very happy to hurry through a major planning application. So long as we got our council homes, we'd approve pretty much anything else you fancied."

I thought about this for a moment. "You're sure you can deliver it?"

"The committee's had many years of frustration at Wychwood's stubborn attitude. It won't be an issue, I can assure you."

"What if he only sells me part of the land? Why not let him keep the house if he wants it so much. It must be listed. That's a giant pain in the neck."

Greenwood went red in the face. "No. Absolutely not. It's all or nothing. I want him out and I want Wychwood Hall demolished. It all has to go, you understand. That's the deal. Every brick, every timber." He started pacing up and down. "That place has become a symbol of everything that's wrong with this country: entitled aristocrats living in privilege in huge ancestral homes on land that their grandfathers stole by force of arms, waited on by servants, and idling away their time fox-hunting and shooting things. It's a disgraceful anachronism, and it's time it made way for progress. It has to go."

"What about English Heritage?"

"You leave them to me. I'll sort it."

"How?"

He smiled cryptically.

"I understand," I said. "And the council will buy the new homes?

"As many as you can fit on the land."

"Alright," I said. "Suppose I was interested. Exactly how does this work? What can I do for you personally?"

He gave me a cunning look. "The satisfaction of getting my own way after all these years will be more than enough for me; seeing Wychwood Hall and all it stands for razed to the ground..." He paused. "Gah! He's such a snob. I'm sorry, you can tell this has become very personal. I'd be happy to see those council houses built, too, after all this time."

"I was wondering if you needed to… oil the wheels, so as to speak. That's what I meant." I waited with a smile fixed on my face for the inevitable request.

"Oil the wheels? Oh, I see! No, not at all. That would be illegal, wouldn't it?

"I wouldn't want to suggest anything illegal."

"Quite so."

"Good." This was a surprise. I cleared my throat. "You'll appreciate you're asking me to accept an awful lot on trust. What if you can't sort out the planning? What if English Heritage won't play ball? I mean, it's a listed building. I could be left holding the baby."

"That's simple enough to fix. How's this: the council will give you a guarantee to buy the estate for what you paid for it plus a five percent premium, at any time. There. You can't lose."

"Fifteen. Plus my costs and any overage."

"You drive a hard bargain. But just so."

"At any time of my choosing and not yours."

"As you wish." He looked me in the eye. "So what do you think? Any other questions?"

"What do I think? Well… based on what you've said, I think it sounds almost too good to be true. I want you to know that I understand how you feel about this. I understand why it's important, and I sympathise with what you are saying. This is for the greater good. You want someone you can trust." I paused. "I'm very honoured that you would consider me."

"Just a few questions from me then, if you don't mind. You have the funds available?"

"Yes."

"Loan funding?"

"Cash and yes, loan funding from a private source."

"Private source?"

"Family."

"Ah. You won't mind evidencing that for me?"

"No problem at all."

"What other projects have you got on at the moment?"

"I have a community centre development in London that I will put on hold so that I can concentrate on this."

"How committed are you?"

"I haven't exchanged contracts on it yet. I might just pull out of it completely."

"That would be my preference."

"Alright."

Charlie came over from where he had been loitering. "Do we have white smoke?"

Greenwood slapped me on the shoulder approvingly. "We do!" he declared. "Nick's our man. Absolutely!"

Charlie grimaced. "Well I'm very happy for you both. Fuck old Brockbank, that's what I say."

"Brockbank?" I said. "What's he got to do with it?"

"You didn't tell him about Brockbank?" Charlie demanded.

"I thought you said *you'd* briefed him!"

"No. It's not my business," Charlie said. "But I can't stand by if you're not going to tell him."

"I have every intention of telling him!" Greenwood said firmly.

"What about Brockbank?" I asked.

"Brockbank is a local developer."

"I've met him! Charlie and I bumped into him."

"Ah, have you? Well… he's been on at me for ages about the Wychwood estate, trying to get me to pull some strings for him. He knows Wychwood can't last out much longer, and he's been circling like a vulture."

"I can imagine," I said, thinking of the little man's greedy face with its hooked beak. "Why not do a deal with him, then?"

"Frankly, I can't trust him. I've had too many dealings with him in the past. I know what he's like. And he's too close to Wychwood. I'll admit I was getting to the point of thinking I'd have to do a deal with him because there was no-one else. But then you came along, thanks to Charlie here."

"Brockbank is an arse and I wouldn't trust him to build a cheese sandwich." Charlie said. "Nick's your boy."

"I'll be straight with you, Nick," Greenwood said. "I like you, but I don't know you. Charlie here is vouching for you, and that counts for a lot in my book, but right now I only have your word you have the funds available and I can't be certain you'll commit. I do know Brockbank and there's no doubt he's got the money and wants to do a deal. I don't want to mess about. You understand? Why don't you have a chat this week with the estate agent who's going to be handling the sale. It's Wagg's in Lewis. They'll tell you when it's going on the market."

"I will," I said. "And I'll provide proof of funding as you ask."

"Good man."

"We're going to do this," I said. And with that, we shook hands.

A light breeze had come up, and while we continued talking I looked out, taking in the nearby groves of lithe birches, knots of ancient oaks and tall limes, leaves a-flutter, and beyond them the rippling hills and rolling meadowlands of the Weald. A skylark was making circles above us, its melody carrying a joy that corresponded with the feeling rising in my chest. This was it! This was the deal that would make my fortune, give me my independence, and put me on a par with, or even ahead of, Clifton. I could run rings around these country bumpkins, already had. Brockbank was after it, and he was local, so it must be the real thing. And the sweetest of sweet things about it, the wonderful irony of it was, it had all come about solely because of Clifton. He it was that had chosen the area to move to. It had been his thoughtless laziness that had taken us to that pub for lunch. Without him, I would never have befriended Charlie. And the development was all right in Clifton's back yard, too! He would hate that. It was almost enough to make me want to pop round and thumb my nose right in front of his big, pudgy face.

Greenwood suddenly bent over and plucked something from the ground. "Well I never!" he said, "This must be an omen." He held up a dirty old coin to us between his forefinger and his thumb, and then scrutinised it closely. "Pre-Roman if I'm not mistaken. Here, Nick – you have it. A precursor of riches to come, eh?" He pressed the coin into my hand. It was cold and heavy, and I guessed immediately that it must be made of solid gold.

Chapter 15: *Amusingly Literal*

Nick,

I opened it in spite of myself. Not even a note from you? I suppose that is you being amusingly literal and complying with my request not to write to me.

'The Uckford Fairy' is one of those obscure hoaxes that pops up from time to time. I've seen it before. I think most people have. I suppose it would be more popular if there were any photographs, but all you ever get are disappointing artist's impressions. Anyway, if you thought you were going to surprise and delight me with it, you've failed.

By the way, I don't know where you got the cutting from, but it looks original to me. I really hope you aren't stealing from the library – however, I fear you must be. Where else would you find these things? And what of these mysteriously similar scissor marks on both pieces? I wouldn't put it past you, really I wouldn't, and shame on you if it's true. Does your evil know no bounds?

Should I make something of your choices? Fauns and fairies? That much is obvious: something to draw me in. Sussex? And Walter Peachey, who I didn't even know was a writer until now?

The truth is, I don't care. This is all going in the bin. Go and bother someone else with your fabrications and leave me alone now.

H

Chapter 16: *The Devil's Footsteps, by Walter Peachey*

An excellent shoulder of roast mutton having been dined upon to the satisfaction of all, Professor Jacob Stenger invited his two companions, as was his custom, to settle into armchairs by the fire in the parlour and enjoy a cigar of his favourite Punch variety with him. Seward, his manservant, uncorked a bottle of brandy and poured each a generous measure before retiring, leaving the bottle conveniently positioned at his master's right hand. Stenger lit a splint from the fire and drew upon his Havana, and once it was going well blew a luxurious plume of smoke up to the ceiling.

"Ah, nothing like a good cigar, eh Stenger?" The man who had spoken was Clayton, a former major in the British Army with a broad chest, a proud bearing and a magnificent waxed moustache. Stenger regarded his companions with a troubled expression: it appeared that he was weighing up whether to tell them something.

"What is it, old man?" Clayton said. "You haven't been yourself all evening."

"Yes, you look as if you have something on your mind," added Purcell, the third man; a writer of some renown whose fictional works chiefly dealt with the sensational subject of ghosts and the supernatural. "Spit it out, man! A problem shared…"

"I confess there is something. I hesitate because you will no doubt think me foolish when I tell you. However, it has reached the point at which I feel if I don't tell someone then I shall go mad. You see, in the last two days some very strange things have been happening, very strange indeed: in short, I have come to believe that I am being haunted."

"Haunted?! Good heavens!" Clayton leant forward, frowning concernedly.

"I strongly suspect that you are not," said Purcell, lounging back in his seat with an indulgent smile and conveying with a raised eyebrow his anticipation that he would be able to solve the mystery without taxing his considerable intellect more than a little; but even he had to admit surprise at what came next.

"You see," Stenger continued, "I am being followed. I hear footsteps behind me, always the same footsteps; but when I turn around there is never anyone there. It began the very next day after they published my last piece in S_____ magazine; the one on places in Sussex named after the Devil. I was walking down Regent Street at about nine o'clock in the evening when I realised that the same distinctive footsteps had been following behind me all the way from Oxford Circus, keeping pace with me, never faster and never slower. I was curious to see who it might be, so I looked over my shoulder, but the footway was busy with people and I couldn't tell. A little farther on I stopped on the pretence of looking in a shop window, and the footsteps also stopped immediately. That made me feel uncomfortable, I can tell you! It should not have been hard to see their owner, but I could discern no likely pursuer among the shoppers and homeward-bound workers. I tried an experiment and turned right into Vigo Street, then right again into Savile Row, and right again into New Burlington Street, which as you will appreciate brought me back out onto Regent Street. I had completed a circuitous detour: never once did the footsteps fail behind me; never once did I catch a glimpse of my pursuer. I decided then and there to take refuge in my club, which was only five minutes away: I made it there in four. I was so unnerved by the whole episode that after a brace of stiffeners in the bar I took a cab all the way home."

"Most disconcerting!"

"Indeed. But the most perturbing thing is that since then those footsteps have dogged my every journey, and not once have I been able to identify the culprit."

"That is really most peculiar," Purcell said, frowning.

"That is not all! Someone, or something, is moving the books about in my library. I leave them out on my desk, and when I come back they are neatly stacked to one side and a new set of books is arrayed there as if someone has been studying. But that is impossible because, as you know, there is only myself and Seward, and I have trained him never to touch them."

"You must go to the police," Clayton said.

"I have considered it. But what would I say? I fear they would not take me seriously."

"You are quite right," said Purcell. "They would not." His cigar was going out, since he had neglected it during Stenger's tale, so he paused to puff furiously upon it to revive it, indicating that he had more to say by raising a hand. "On the subject of the books," he continued at last, expelling a satisfactory quantity of smoke, "They would immediately assume that either it is Seward and you have misjudged his character, or it is you and you are an absent-minded old fool. Either way, they would have no interest in the matter. On the question of being followed, they would ask if there is a particular reason someone might pursue you: a large inheritance, a difficult business transaction, a debt, an amorous dalliance…"

"And I should say no, of course. There is nothing of that kind, I assure you."

"…Or if there is anything that may be making you more than usually anxious."

"I say, you're not suggesting the whole thing is nothing more than an attack of nerves, are you?"

"I'm simply running through the questions the police would ask."

"Well, there is nothing." Stenger folded his arms.

"Next they would wish to know if you have any enemies: anyone that may intend you harm."

"And again, the answer would be no!"

"In which case they would tell you to go about your business and come back if the situation did not resolve itself in a few days."

"Which is a polite way of telling me to pull myself together and stop wasting their time, I suppose!"

"Has anyone else heard these footsteps?" asked Clayton.

"Now you're both at it! I tell you, I am not imagining it!"

"Now, now, Stenger… of course you're not. We're your friends. We don't doubt you for a minute, do we Purcell?"

"Without wishing to appear rude, I must say I consider you one of the most unimaginative men I know," said Purcell. "Any evidence you offer must be taken as indisputable truth, and I believe we should be alarmed accordingly." He lifted his brandy snifter and swirled the golden liquid inside around. "The question is, old chap, what is to be done about it?"

The next morning Clayton and Purcell arrived together at Stenger's house and were shown by Seward to the library, where they found Stenger pacing up and down in front of the fireplace. "I'm damned if I'm going to let this ridiculous nonsense stop me from going about my business!" Stenger said as soon as they entered.

Clayton clapped him on the shoulder. "That's the spirit!"

"On the contrary," Purcell said, "You must desist from your normal activities at once, until we have resolved the matter."

"But why should I?"

"I have an idea that this ridiculous nonsense, as you call it, may in fact be very serious indeed and not a little dangerous. If we are to put a stop it, we must understand cause and effect. And for that, my dear fellow, I am afraid we shall need your full and undivided attention for a day at the very least, and perhaps two."

"I see." Stenger stopped his pacing. "Very well, Purcell; on reflection, I believe you are right. I cannot go on like this, and so I place myself in your hands. For now, at least." He rubbed at his temples with this fingers. "I am sorry. I hope you do not think me ungrateful. This is difficult. There are pressing publication deadlines, very pressing indeed."

"I understand." Purcell was watching Stenger closely. "Later, we shall observe you taking a walk as you follow your route of two nights ago back to where you started. Perhaps en route we shall identify and apprehend the owner of the footsteps following you. But for now, I should like to see the books that were moved."

"Very well." Stenger led Purcell and Clayton to his bureau. "Here," he said. "Of course, I have now restored the books I am currently using to their former places on my desk. The others are back on the shelves where they belong. However, when it happened, I found that…" He looked down. "Great Heavens!" He staggered and had to put out an arm to steady himself against the desk.

"What is it?"

"The books… they've been moved again!"

"This is not how you left them?"

"No it is not. This is impossible!"

Purcell rang the bell for Seward, and then turned back to Stenger. "What is the subject you are researching?" he asked.

"Rituals of the ancient Danes."

Purcell inspected the books open upon the desk. "And these books are..?"

"The ones I was using before, to write that piece about places named after the Devil. I swear I had put them back on the shelves."

Seward arrived. "Ah, Seward," Purcell said. "Have you moved these books?"

"No sir. The professor does not like anyone to touch his books."

"And has anyone else been in this room since Professor Stenger was last in here working?"

"No sir. No-one else has been in the house."

"Thank you Seward. That will be all."

"Yes sir."

When Seward had gone, Purcell said: "He seems truthful to me."

Stenger nodded. "He has been with me for a long time. I trust him completely."

"Always thought him a sound fellow," Clayton concurred.

Purcell looked around the room thoughtfully. "Are you able to lock this room, Stenger?"

"Yes, and there is only one key."

"Excellent! Well, it is almost time we went for that walk; but first, with your permission, I should like to spend a few moments examining the room more closely. While I do so, could you possibly put these books back where they belong on the shelves once again, and set out the books you need for your current project on ancient Danes on the desk, just as you had them?"

"Of course! You are proposing an experiment, to discover whether the books will be moved again by some ethereal force even after we have locked the door." Stenger shook his head. "Why didn't I think of that?!"

They began their journey outside Stenger's club in Pall Mall. Stenger and Purcell walked together down the street with Clayton shadowing them twenty yards behind. It was a busy time of day, with carriages and carts moving nose-to-tail, and a good variety of pedestrians in both directions.

"No-one would risk following me with you and Clayton parading alongside like bodyguards," Stenger said after a while.

"Unless they were a ghost!" Purcell said. "By the way, what were you doing in Regent Street?"

"Regent Street?"

"When you first realised you were being followed."

"I was on my way home."

"Yes, but where had you been?"

"Oh, I don't know," Stenger said with a dismissive wave of his hand. "It can't have been important, or else I should remember."

"I believe it is important. Are you sure you can't remember?"

They walked on for a while in silence, and then Stenger said in a strange voice: "No. No, I can't remember anything between when I left work and when I found myself walking down Regent Street with those footsteps behind me. Confound it! I don't know what's the matter with me."

"What time did you leave work?"

"Well... it was my usual time. Half past five exactly. I always leave at the same time as Carter, and you can set your watch by him."

"I see. If that is correct, then there is more than three hours of time unaccounted for, would you agree?"

Stenger did not reply but continued walking, looking uncomfortable and staring straight ahead. After a few more paces, he turned to his companion and his face was ashen. "Purcell," he said in a shaky voice. "The footsteps... they're back!"

Purcell gave no external sign of being troubled by this news and indeed continued his perambulation along the busy pavement as if he had not a care in the world. A close observer may have noticed a glint in his eye. "Remember the plan," he said in a conversational tone. "Don't look round. I'll give Clayton the signal." A few moments later he took out his large white pocket handkerchief and made considerable play of dabbing his face with it and then blowing his nose as he walked. "That should do it," he said, putting it away. "Can you still hear them?"

"Can't you?" Stenger hissed.

"Not sure, old chap. There's a lot of noise. We'll turn up towards Regent Street in a moment. Perhaps I shall be able to pick them out with more ease."

"But they're so loud! He must be right behind us."

"You must trust that Clayton will ensure we are safe. They would be very foolish indeed to take Clayton on, whoever they are." Realising that Stenger was preparing to turn and face his pursuer anyway, Purcell put a restraining hand on his shoulder. "Steady, old chap. Just a bit farther."

They turned the corner, and after another twenty paces Purcell gave Stenger a firm nod. They turned as one to find Clayton approaching quickly, and, caught between, a man in a hounds-tooth coat and a broad brimmed top hat who had been walking with his hands in his pockets. Realising his predicament, the man tried to take evasive action, but it was too late, for Clayton had seized him in a bear hug, pinioning his arms to his sides. The man struggled, but there was no escaping the massive soldier's iron grip. He spluttered into his beard and seemed about to cry out when Purcell sprang forward.

"Why are you following this man?" he demanded, indicating Stenger.

The captive shook his head furiously. "I'm not following anyone," he pleaded, looking thoroughly frightened. "What do you want from me? Please... let me go!" He looked around him wildly for help.

"Where are you going?"

"Back to work. I work at the Criterion, just up here."

"The Criterion. I see! Then you will be able to tell me the name of the manager of the Criterion."

"Mister Charles Wyndham is the manager. Please, what is this all about?"

Purcell turned to Stenger. "Have you seen this man before? Is he the one who has been following you?"

"I don't believe I've ever seen him before." Stenger hesitated, and then said: "Ah, Purcell... I don't think this is the person we are seeking."

Purcell followed Stenger's gaze down to the man's feet. Beneath his coat the man was wearing a theatrical costume: the ends of striped pantaloons finished at his ankles, and in place of normal shoes or boots he wore soft-soled Turkish slippers.

Purcell broke into a broad grin and muttered something that sounded like "Better than I had hoped", and then addressed the detainee: "My good sir, I offer you a most sincere apology: it appears that this is a grievous case of mistaken identity. Please, continue your journey. My companions and I offer our deepest regrets for inconveniencing you and wish you a very good day." He gave a short bow and signalled to Clayton, who released the man as a naughty child might a stolen rag doll. The man brushed himself down, straightened his hat, gave each of the three companions a long look in turn, and then marched off harrumphing and checking his pockets.

They hurried on to Stenger's office in Bloomsbury after that, and no more footsteps were heard on the way unless they had an owner and that owner was minding their own business and intent upon going their own way. The building in Tavistock Square belonged to the University and was home to several academic departments, including the Department of Anthropology, in which Stenger was employed. Once inside the terraced house Stenger took his two companions to his office, a spacious, high-ceilinged room with a view of the garden square, where he shortly arranged with Lizzie, the maid, for tea to be served.

"I don't do much of my real work here," Stenger confided as they settled into well-worn armchairs. "I use this mainly for teaching. My library at home is much more comfortable, as you will appreciate, and there I can work uninterrupted…" He paused reflectively. "I *could* work uninterrupted…" He tailed off into a reverie of sorts, and as he plunged into the depths of thought his eyes glazed and his head dropped.

"I should very much like to meet your friend Carter," Purcell said quickly. "I don't suppose he would be free to talk to us now?"

"Oh, I expect so," said Stenger, livening up. "He only delivers three lectures a week." Stenger rang the bell to summon Lizzie, who was duly despatched with a message to his colleague. Carter, a thin man with a black goatee beard who carried himself with a good degree of nervous energy, arrived shortly afterwards, and introductions were made. He perched on the edge of a chair and, unbidden, poured himself a cup of tea with long, thin fingers.

"Would you say you and Stenger keep the same hours at work?" Purcell asked him.

"I am an early riser, so I tend to be here before most of the other academic staff. But, ah…" Carter looked at Stenger.

"There is no requirement for an alibi of any sort, if that is on your mind. Professor Stenger is in no trouble on his own account, I assure you, although he may be the victim of a serious crime. The truth will do nicely, and may I thank you on his behalf for your loyalty, which I am certain is very much appreciated."

The normally erudite Stenger was only able to muster a faint nod of agreement.

"Professor Stenger and I regularly leave together, at exactly half past five," Carter finished.

"I should like you to cast your mind back to earlier this week, if you would: to Monday, to be precise. Did you leave together then?" Purcell asked.

Carter nodded his head twitchily several times. "Oh yes," he said. "Yes, we did." He paused, twiddling his fingers. "No," he corrected himself. "No, I remember now. We went to leave at the same time but Stenger had visitors. I left him talking to them in the porch."

"Visitors?" Purcell exchanged looks with Stenger and Clayton.

"Yes." Carter's gaze moved between all three, a puzzled expression on his face.

"May I ask you to describe them?"

"Yes. Well, I didn't get a very good look. I didn't wait to be introduced. It was a man and a woman, anyway. The man was in clerical garb, tall, American I think; and the woman… Carter tailed off. He was looking at Stenger, whose eyes had rolled upwards and whose mouth was opening and closing in a strange way.

Purcell and Clayton reacted quickly, and had soon loosened Stenger's clothing and arranged him with his feet up on the couch. Carter was despatched to find some brandy. "He's had a fit of some sort," Clayton said. "We should send for a doctor."

"No, no," Stenger protested weakly. "I shall be fine in a moment. I don't need a doctor. I just felt very light-headed all of a sudden, but the feeling is gone now."

Clayton looked to Purcell for support, but Purcell seemed less concerned than perhaps he might have been in the circumstances. "You'll be alright, won't you old chap." Purcell asserted cheerfully. "Come on, Clayton – let's sit him up." As they lifted him, however, Purcell whispered in Clayton's ear: "Keep a close eye on him for a bit, will you old chap?"

While Stenger was recovering, perched on the couch with a glass of brandy in one hand and a sweet biscuit to nibble upon in the other, with Clayton hovering protectively over him, Purcell went to Carter's office to finish his questioning. Carter had very little else to tell: he could not remember any more about Stenger's visitors, and said he had gone straight home that evening. He expressed his concern for Stenger and offered his help in whatever capacity Purcell thought apposite. Then Purcell summoned Lizzie, and asked her if she knew anything about Professor Stenger's Monday visitors.

"I'm a plain speaking woman, sir; that's the way God made me, so I 'ope you'll pardon me if I speak out of turn. I didn't take to them at all, God forgive me, but they 'ad no respect; no manners, and this a place of hedgycation. I only opened the door, and they barged in past me without so much as a by-your-leave. And him a man of God, although she weren't no better than she ought to be if you ask me, wiv her tattoos and all. They must've seen Professor Stenger in the lobby, I suppose. I was put out by it, I was, but I didn't like to say nuffink as they seemed to know him at first. Anyway, they was standing in the lobby together for a long while talking, and then they left together, laughing and joking they was, and all got into a cab outside."

"They knew him?"

"Knew who he was, yes sir, but I don't think he knew them. They was all smiles and compliments, and he was quite taken with them, what with them saying they wanted to give him twenty-five Pounds and all."

"Twenty-five Pounds!"

"Yes sir. I'm not mistaken. Pardon me for eavesdropping but I couldn't help myself, being as they was so rude and I was worried for the Professor. He's a lovely gentleman, sir, but he wouldn't know a villain if they picked 'is pocket and 'anded his wallet back to him hempty on a gold cushion."

"In your estimation they were villains, then?"

"In my hestimation, sir, yes, they was up to something alright."

"Did you hear where they were taking him?"

"No sir, I did not."

"But you saw them getting into a cab outside."

"Yes sir."

"Did you hear them say anything to the cabbie?"

"No sir."

"Nothing at all?"

"No sir."

"Think carefully, Lizzie: did you see or hear anything at the time, anything at all, that could provide us with a clue about where they took the Professor?"

"No sir."

"Very well." Purcell's shoulders slumped in dejection. "Thank you, Lizzie, you may go now. You have been a good girl. I shall be sure to mention it to the Professor."

"Thank you sir. Begging your pardon, sir, I took the trouble to ask the cabbie when he got back where he had taken them. The cabbie works in the square regular, you see. It was number __, _____ Road, Hampstead." Lizzie bobbed a curtsy and sauntered archly from the room.

Several hours later a cab pulled up in _____ Road, Hampstead, and the trio of Purcell, Stenger and Clayton emerged from it. Purcell took Stenger by the arm casually as they waited while Clayton conversed with the driver about waiting and payment arrangements. "Right-oh," said Purcell when Clayton was done, "Let's pay a visit to your friends, shall we?"

Stenger made no attempt to move. "This is very strange, Purcell. I would swear I have never been here in my life. That cabbie must have made a mistake."

"Let's see this through, old chap. Courage to the sticking place, and all that. This address is the only clue we have. If I am right, the answer to the riddle of the footsteps and the moving books lies behind that door."

The three walked through the gate and up the garden path and Purcell gave several loud raps with the doorknocker. After a short interval there was a scuffling noise and then the door opened a crack.

"Yes? Who is it?"

"Professor Stenger is here to see your master," Purcell announced loudly.

"What do you want?" A pale and very hairy face hovered in the dark gap between door and door-post.

"He will wish to see us. Please go and tell him at once."

"Wait there." The door slammed shut again.

"That is a very impertinent footman!" Stenger commented.

"At least we know now that the master is at home," Purcell said.

The three waited for just over a minute and then the door opened to reveal the same man, who looked as if he had thrown on a tailcoat over his scruffy nightclothes. He ushered them inside without ceremony.

"The master is in the upstairs drawing room," he said bluntly, gesturing at the wide staircase that swept grandly up in front of them. The entrance lobby was impressively large but had an air of neglect about it, and the light from the gas lamps gently sputtering on the walls failed to lift the gloom. It was decorated in the oriental style with large Chinese urns and dark lacquered cabinets, and was overlooked by ancient, fading portraits in rows like crows waiting for a death.

Stenger appeared to be badly affected by the atmosphere in the house, and leaned heavily upon Purcell's arm. "He's fading fast," Clayton whispered. "Perhaps we should – "

"We must carry on," Purcell interrupted firmly. "Give me a hand, there's a fellow."

Clayton took up a position at the professor's other shoulder, and then the two friends climbed the stairs with Stenger, who appeared to be sinking further into a walking catalepsy with every step, supported between them. The footman, following behind, offered no assistance but occasionally muttered and chuckled to himself.

The upstairs drawing room was large and high-ceilinged. There was an ornate mantelpiece on the interior wall, with a fire burning steadily in the grate, and above it a large and dingy landscape of hills and distant sea in a gilded frame. The walls were painted a solid green with the woodwork finished in white, the windows, which otherwise would have looked out onto the street, were shuttered, and wall-mounted gas lamps provided light and shadow. At the far end there was a stained and worn boardroom table, at which two men were sitting. The first of these leaped down from his chair immediately, revealing himself to be a dwarf of no more than three and a half feet in height with a huge head and ape-like arms and chest. He had bright, almond-shaped eyes in a swarthy, wrinkled complexion, possessed a very full shock of hair, and was dressed in a morning coat with a cherry red waistcoat. He darted towards the newcomers, waving his arms and chattering in an unintelligible language that was punctuated with clicks and whistles and moments in which he simply bared his teeth. He stopped short just out of reach, where he continued to grimace and gesticulate, hopping from foot to foot excitedly. The other man stood also, revealing himself in contrast to be over six feet tall, with long, powerful limbs. He had a full, dark beard, which was greying in places, and a thick mane of long, dark hair with grey flecks at the temples. His apparel was well tailored and made of expensive cloth.

"Perfessor Stinger and friends," the footman announced, and then slipped away.

"Professor Stenger?" The tall man addressed his remarks to Purcell, whom he had evidently picked out as the leader of the three as he approached them. His accent was foreign, perhaps Russian. "I have heard that name... and you have brought some friends with you! You must forgive my prodigious companion: he is excited by your presence, as we do not often receive unexpected guests. I am afraid you have me at a disadvantage: I do not know the purpose of your visit."

"My name is Purcell. *This* is Professor Stenger, as I believe you already know despite this unconvincing charade, and this is Major Clayton of the King's Royal Rifles." Purcell did not step forward or offer his hand to either man in greeting.

"Charade? I do not know what you mean by this. There must be some misunderstanding."

"There is no misunderstanding." Purcell drew himself up to his full height. "We have come to seek redress for evil inflicted upon the person of Professor Stenger."

"You have made a mistake. I cannot help you."

"On the contrary, you will do as we ask willingly when you have heard us out."

The dwarf scampered back to the master of the house and plucked at his trouser leg, pulling him towards the door.

"Remain where you are, please!" Purcell commanded in a compelling tone his friends had never heard before, his eyes locked upon his target. "You do not know who you are dealing with. I am an officer of the Court of King James and a Knight of the Order of St Dunstan. You will hear me out."

The man inclined his head slightly in acquiescence. "I shall hear what you have to say," he said, but the dwarf gave a hiss and slipped out of sight under the boardroom table. Purcell took a few paces towards the fire without lowering his gaze, leaving Clayton to support Stenger, whose eyes were glassy and whose jaw was slack.

"A man followed by the sound of footsteps," Purcell began, "When there is no-one there that could possibly be making them; who is also the owner of a library where the books move themselves when he is out of the room! What is one to make of such a mystery? Is this a manifestation of the supernatural? Is my friend Professor Stenger haunted by a spirit from beyond the veil?" He paused. "The supernatural does indeed play a part in this case, but it most definitely is no haunting."

He leaned upon the mantelpiece with an elbow. "I put you on notice that I am well aware of whose house we are currently visiting and the nature of the organisation whose headquarters is situated here. You are surprised, Viktor Oleksandrovitch Lysenko?" The man's eyes flashed as Purcell spoke his name. "We have retraced the steps our friend took on Monday last; the day upon which these strange goings-on commenced. It appears that he was induced to come here by your associates – to that we have witnesses – with offers of a generous commission. Curiously, he remembers nothing of it; but I believe I am able to fill in the gaps in his memory, and so I shall do this very moment, although I am certain that you would rather I did not. You entertained him here, and asked him to continue the line of research he had started concerning places in England named after the Devil, having read the piece he published in the S_____. However, when you put the specific nature of your request to him, he refused. Why so? After all, your offer of twenty-five Pounds was an exceptionally generous one."

"Here we come to the nature of your interest: you, sir, are the head of a secret organisation that believes there is a physical gateway to Hell here on Earth and is dedicated to locating it! That malignant organisation is known as The Devil's Footsteps. That I am aware of this and of your identity is due to my own profession and interest in the occult; however, my dear friend Stenger would have known

99

nothing of it and would have had to rely only upon what you told him. It appears that notwithstanding this he found your proposal either absurd or abominable: in any case, he refused."

"You, however, were not satisfied with that honest refusal, and when you were unable to persuade him you proceeded with an ingenious and utterly despicable plan to ensure that he would carry out your wishes even against his will. You drugged his drink and while he was under the influence of the drug you used the technique of Mesmerism to install in his subconscious mind the imperative to carry out the research on your behalf."

"This is preposterous!" Lysenko interjected.

Purcell continued. "He would not remember the encounter with you or your colleagues, his visit to this house, or be aware of having been so tasked. However, when working alone he would succumb to the influence of the subconscious instruction, carry out the research, and ultimately would be compelled to report his findings to you. This is the explanation of how the books in his library apparently moved by themselves: he moved them himself whilst in the Mesmeric state, and afterwards, with no memory of having done so, concluded that someone else had done it! This is further confirmed by a completed set of research notes on the task you had set him, freshly written in his own hand, that I found hidden in a drawer when I searched his library this morning." Here, he reached into his coat and produced a small wad of papers, which he waved about.

"The human mind works in peculiar ways. Following his encounter with you, Stenger was almost immediately haunted by footsteps dogging his movements. We ruled out the possibility that there was a real pursuer by carrying out an experiment. When Stenger said he could hear the footsteps behind him – we were in Regent Street at the time – we apprehended and questioned the only person walking close enough behind to be the culprit. By happy coincidence the man was wearing soft slippers and could not possibly have been making the sounds Stenger had been hearing, and this led very quickly to the confirmation of my hypothesis that only Stenger could hear the footsteps. They were a somewhat literal message to his conscious mind from his subconscious: the Devil's Footsteps pursuing him everywhere he went."

"Your hypnotic instructions sought to ensure secrecy by causing Stenger to feel ill any time the plot came close to being exposed. Pondering the unexplained - where he had been that evening, what had caused the books to move - made him uncomfortable; our discovery of his having been approached at work by your people led to him having a nasty turn. Indeed, I became concerned that he may have been driven to harm himself had the facts emerged in the wrong circumstances."

"And so we find ourselves here, having followed the trail back to its source. We have brought Professor Stenger here this evening so that you may remove the subconscious compulsions you have implanted and restore him to his old self. In return, you shall receive his research notes – he has quite finished his study upon the subject – and an undertaking that we will not take the matter up with the police, unless, of course, we are troubled in any way by you or your associates in future. Should you refuse, then these notes will go on the fire, and we shall put the matter in the hands of the authorities immediately."

Lysenko momentarily lifted his arms in surrender. "Mister Purcell, that is an extraordinary feat of reasoning. I congratulate you. I admit, of course, to nothing." He paused, seeming to weigh things in his mind. His eyes kept wandering to the sheaf of papers in Purcell's hand. At last, he appeared to come to a decision. "You leave me with no choice. I agree to your terms."

"You will complete the task here in front of us."

"Very well." Lysenko drew out a chair from the table and set it theatrically in the middle of the room. "Please…" he said, patting the cushion absurdly like an Italian barber beckoning his next client to be seated.

Clayton helped Stenger to the chair and settled him in it, where he remained slumped as if already in a trance. "Stand back!" Lysenko insisted, waving Clayton away. The big man backed off slowly and took up a position near the door.

Lysenko began speaking into his subject's ear: "Listen to me, Professor Stenger, listen to me, listen to my voice…" He continued, his tone droning and insistent, and Stenger followed his instructions compliantly until at last he was sitting completely still with his hands clasped loosely in his lap. Lysenko lifted an arm and then dropped it, and it fell back loosely into place.

"Professor Stenger, tell me please, what is the exact location of the Gates of Hell?"

"Hey, what are you doing?" Purcell shouted, waving the papers. "Stenger, don't tell him anything!"

"He cannot hear or see you, Mister Purcell."

Lysenko clapped his hands and suddenly two dark figures armed with shotguns stepped through the door into the room. The first, a tall, rangy man, was in clerical garb that belied his evident professional skill with the weapon he was carrying; and the second was a woman in mourning clothes, equally comfortable in wielding the firearm, who announced herself with an incongruous "Hello ducks!" They cocked the shotguns and aimed them at Purcell and Clayton.

"Professor Stenger's research notes may be complete, but if they truly identified the location of the Gateway to Hell I very much doubt that you would bring them here," Lysenko continued. "In any case, I have no need of the notes when the Professor can tell me himself! Stay where you are!" This last was directed at Clayton, who had taken a step towards him. "Stay where you are and I may allow you to escape with your lives." He directed his next instruction to his newly arrived henchmen: "Shoot them if they try to interfere." He turned his attention back to Stenger. "Professor, you have something to tell me, do you not? It will be such a relief to tell me. You cannot wait to tell me. Your research is completed. You have found the location of the Gateway to Hell. Where is it to be found? Tell me!"

"The footsteps!" Purcell shouted. "Stenger, listen to the footsteps!"

"Quiet, you fool!"

"The footsteps! Behind you!"

Stenger began twitching and muttering.

"The footsteps, Stenger! Look behind you!"

Stenger cast a worried look back over his shoulder. "Footsteps…" he muttered to himself, "Footsteps…"

"The footsteps! What do they want?!"

Lysenko was overwhelmed with rage. "Silence him!" he bellowed. The gun-bearing cleric left his post by the door and stepped towards Purcell with his gun raised threateningly. He had taken no more than three paces when Clayton, who had his back to the door, span suddenly round and connected with the gunman's jaw with a magnificent right cross. The blow sent the gunman cannoning into the woman. Clayton was upon them in a moment, and as the bogus clergyman slid to the floor, already unconscious, Clayton wrenched the gun from the woman's hands and with impassionate efficiency used the butt to knock her out. He turned quickly, the shotgun ready for use at his shoulder.

In the confusion of the moment, no-one had noticed the dwarf emerge from under the table and creep along by the wall towards the fireplace. With a sudden burst of speed, he launched himself at Purcell and snatched the papers from his hand. "Hey!" Purcell yelled. With a cackle of glee, the dwarf dodged past Clayton and scampered out of the door, clutching the notes in his fist. Clayton turned in pursuit.

"Never mind him!" Purcell shouted. "Lysenko's the one we need."

Clayton turned back with the gun at the ready. "Where has he gone?"

Purcell's jaw dropped. "He was here!" He looked frantically around the room. "He must be here!"

Purcell made a hurried circuit, looking behind curtains and under the table while Clayton quickly retrieved the other gun and provided cover. Every possible hiding place was uncovered and explored, but there was no trace of Lysenko to be found. "Damn and blast! Where the Devil is he?" Purcell cursed.

Satisfied after his search that for the moment at least there was no threat, he turned his attention to Stenger, who was still sitting motionless in the chair. "Stenger? Can you hear me?"

"Yes I can. There's no need to shout."

"Thank God! How are you feeling, old chap? Can you walk?"

"Walk? Of course I can walk! To tell the truth, I feel better than I have done in a while."

"That's good, old chap. That's very good. Because it's time we left. Up you get, now. Take my arm. That's it. You come with me. We're going home."

The next day, the three friends reunited at Stenger's house for dinner. In accordance with habit, they refrained from any serious discussion until they had retired to the parlour.

"So how are you feeling?" Purcell asked Stenger at last as Stenger's cigar box was being passed around.

"I feel much better, thank you. It's as if a huge weight has been lifted from my shoulders."

"You're not feeling under any compulsion? No more inexplicable urges? The books have stopped moving around by themselves?"

"I am back to my normal self. Last night's extraordinary visit to *that* house," and here Stenger shuddered, "Seems to have done the trick."

"I am so glad. I feared that we had failed you when Lysenko got away. But I have been thinking: when you were under his spell last night he told you that your research had been completed. When he did so, I believe that freed you from the Mesmeric compulsion."

"Why would he have said that?"

"He was trying to coax you to tell him your findings. My bringing your notes along and waving them under his nose must have convinced him that you really had finished the task."

Stenger leaned forwards. "My dear Purcell, my dear Clayton; I must thank you from the bottom of my heart for all you have done for me. I couldn't ask for two better friends. Now, I must know: what happened when you went back with the police?"

"The house was deserted," Purcell said. "Lysenko and his friends had obviously abandoned it. It turns out they had the place on a short lease. We found nothing at all of any interest. Now that the police are involved, I don't think you'll be hearing from the Devil's Footsteps again."

"What about my papers?"

Purcell shook his head. "They got away with them."

"Oh dear! Well, I do not know what I wrote, but I sincerely hope it is of no help to them."

"I shouldn't worry, old chap. They will find the notes they stole of no use at all, unless they have developed a sudden interest in the rituals of the ancient Danes." Purcell drew on his cigar and sent a large cloud of curling smoke up towards the ceiling. "As for the research notes you produced whilst under the Mesmeric influence, I destroyed them without reading them, and I sincerely hope you will agree that that was for the best."

Chapter 17: *Beast of a Horse*

My first impression of Annabel was that she bore more than a striking resemblance to a Knightsbridge shop window dummy. Perfectly coiffed, manicured and dressed, her expensive clothes were precisely chosen to flatter her slim waist and long legs, and despite her toils in the kitchen preparing lunch, she was in elegant heels.

"Congratulations!" I said. "Fantastic news!"

We kissed cheeks. "I'm so glad you could come," she said, sounding unexpectedly genuine. Somehow she had managed not to smell of roast lunch, and instead I received a delicate waft of a rather delicious perfume. I produced a large bunch of lilies from one of my bags and presented them to her. She seemed pleased with them, although it might just have been her being polite; she had an easy confidence that made it hard to tell.

The excuse for issuing the invitation to Sunday lunch was presumably so that the charming couple could receive my congratulations and, I dare say, engagement present, but the main purpose was undoubtedly so that Clifton could rub my nose in it even further. That being so, I was determined to rise above it. From another bag I produced my now standard bottle of Bollinger and passed it to Clifton.

"Cheers, old chap," he said, unimpressed.

"There's more," I said, bending down and bobbing back up with another gift: a Georgian cut-glass and silver claret jug, for which I had overpaid hurriedly in an antiques shop in Camden Passage the day before, out of time and ideas. "Here's your engagement present."

Clifton unwrapped it and took it out of the box, making appreciative grunts as he turned it in the light. Annabel said:

"It's beautiful! Really beautiful! Nick, you really shouldn't have."

"Nonsense!" I dove down again, wondering with slight annoyance this time if I had perhaps overdone it with the gifts, and came up with a nice bottle of Pauillac. "This goes with it."

Clifton looked at the label and smacked his lips. "Thank you so very much. Too generous by far, really old chap. Lovely."

The dining room had a long, mahogany table that could easily seat twelve, but we sat together at the end nearest the door, eating with ancient silver cutlery from willow-patterned china laid out on a linen tablecloth. There was a large fireplace facing the window, above which was a large and rather old-looking oil painting of a country landscape. A grandfather clock ticked loudly in a corner.

"This lamb is absolutely delicious!" I said to Annabel. It truly was.

"Yah," Clifton said, his mouth full. "I get it from the local butcher. It's local meat. So much better than the supermarket stuff."

"The potatoes are fabulous as well."

"Home grown. I roast them in goose fat with rosemary from the herb garden." Annabel smiled sweetly, showing her perfect teeth. "The mint sauce is home-made too."

"No wonder Clifton's marrying you."

"Too right!" said Clifton, helping himself to more lamb from the carving dish with his thick fingers. "Tell you what, I'll show you the garden later. Bags of home grown. We have asparagus beds. And a greenhouse. And an apple orchard."

"Must be nice to have such a big garden, after living in London."

Clifton grunted. "Lot of work involved. Backbreaking."

"Not that Clifton knows anything about that," said Annabel. "That's what we're getting a gardener for. Too busy doctoring, aren't you, lovely."

"How's business, Nicko?" Clifton asked dryly, changing the subject.

"Great."

"Clifton said you're a property developer?" Annabel said, compliantly picking up the thread.

"That's right. I'm currently developing twenty four flats on a disused community centre site…"

"I thought you said eight before," Clifton butted in. "I'm sure you said eight."

"That's right, but things move on and now it's twenty four." Damn Clifton, I could have sworn he never listens to a word I say. How did he remember that? "Anyway, there's even better news than that: I'm on the verge of closing a really big deal. I can't say anything about it, it's all top secret, but it's really exciting."

"Well done Nick!" Annabel said.

"Tell us something. Just a little clue." Clifton demanded."

"Really, I can't. Soon." If Wagg's of Lewis were to be believed, Wychwood Hall would be on the market in the next three months. "Really soon."

"I can't wait to hear all about it." Annabel's genuine enthusiasm made me warm to her considerably.

"How's my favourite aunt?" Clifton asked.

"Your only aunt. She's well. Disgustingly well, actually. Still living in Spain. On a macrobiotic diet now, apparently, although I don't believe she actually eats anything."

"Good for her! How long is it now since…?"

"Since the accident? Just over five years."

"Is it really? Good God! Doesn't time fly?" Clifton wouldn't meet my gaze. "I was very fond of Nicko's Dad," he said to a spot on the ceiling. "Terrible business. Still, your Mater's just the same as ever. She doesn't get any older, does she? That must be where you get it from. Good of her to fly over for the wedding, anyhow."

The absence of any scrap of communication from Mother to me about this unwelcome manoeuvre added to my annoyance. "Oh, you must be delighted!" I said.

Annabel chipped in with mischief in her eyes. "She asked me if I could find you a nice girl to marry. I told her I know lots of girls who would jump at the chance."

I rolled my eyes. "She never ceases to find new ways of embarrassing me. Anyway, I'm sure you don't."

She smiled wickedly. "I do, actually. If you haven't got anyone to come to the wedding with…"

"Pointless. I shall be sulking all day, wishing it was me and not Clifton. No-one else will get a look-in."

"I don't think you should be flirting with me quite so openly with my betrothed actually in the room," Annabel said, looking pleased.

"So how are the plans for the house coming along?"

"Haven't done anything yet," Clifton confessed. "Been too busy. Had to do some stuff in the paddock, though. We have a stable now."

"Really?"

"For my gorgeous Merryman," Annabel said.

"Her beast of a horse," Clifton clarified.

"He's not a beast. He's a poppet."

"He bites."

I intervened. "A dear old Shetland from pony club days?"

Annabel fixed me with a withering stare. "He's a gorgeous hunter," she said. "Seventeen hands."

"Crikey!" I said. "That *is* a monster!" Annabel stuck her tongue out.

"Soon to be two monsters, old chum. It seems I must take to the saddle myself and ride with the local hunt. It's expected." Clifton looked at Annabel. "And I shan't ride anything smaller than Belle's beast. I'd look ridiculous, a fine figure of a man like me." He patted his belly with both hands.

I was thinking that Clifton would look ridiculous no matter what size horse he was on, but I said: "I didn't know you could ride."

"It's like riding a bike." Clifton waved a hand dismissively. "Must embrace the country way of life and all that, eh?"

"Two horses. Crikey."

"I'm used to it. I grew up with horses. It's not work really." Annabel smiled. "I've been mucking out stables since I was six."

"Perhaps we could go and say hello to Merryman after lunch?"

Annabel's smile was white, her teeth perfectly spaced. "Of course!"

Clifton unexpectedly insisted upon doing the clearing up in the kitchen, leaving Annabel to take me on the promised tour of the garden and encounter with the beast. "How have you managed that?" I asked Annabel. "I've never seen him lift a finger."

She smiled craftily. "He's a sweetie," she said. "Really he is."

The garden must have been rather grand in its time. The crumbling remains of nineteenth century landscaping could still be discerned: several lawns, one of which might once have been a tennis court; a tumbledown gazebo; and there was a large greenhouse, its panes now green with moss and algae, white-painted wood split and stained, and alongside it a row of cucumber frames in a similar state of repair. Farther away from the house, towards Stoney Down, there was an overgrown orchard of ancient and gnarled fruit trees: apples, pears, plums and medlars; and beyond the orchard was the large paddock in which the seventeen-hand biting monster lurked. The original design had been twisted out of shape by time and the wild, and if it had any feelings of its own then they were undoubtedly dejection and abandonment. Annabel and I strolled through this faded glory while she explained to me what her plans were for the gardener, who would have his work cut out by the sound of it.

"How did you and Clifton meet?"

She stopped and looked at me for a moment, squinting slightly in the sunshine, and then said: "It's awfully dull. It was at a dinner party held by one of Daddy's business friends."

"And your eyes met over the pommes dauphines?"

"Something like that."

"And..?"

"Are you *sure* you want to know?"

I gave her a look.

"Alright. Actually I didn't think Clifton even noticed me at first. And to be honest, I went home thinking he was... well... a bit boring. It's okay, I've told him. He knows. But then Andrew, that's Daddy's friend, told me Clifton really liked me; said he kept going on about seeing me again, and I got talked into going to a drinks party to meet him again. And we got on much better. He's awfully shy, you know. Underneath all that bluster he's really quite thoughtful and generous. He just can't express himself."

It didn't sound like the Clifton I knew: to my certain knowledge all of his ex-girlfriends had left him citing thoughtlessness and selfishness. Annabel's attractions must have hooked him pretty seriously if he was willing to change his entire personality for her. "And then what?"

"He asked me out. To the pub. And that was it, really. I told you it was dull."

It was horribly dull, confirming my suspicions that Clifton had not a romantic bone in his body. Even Annabel seemed unexcited by it.

"Well he didn't waste any time in popping the question."

"When you know it's right…" she said, formulaically. "And let's face it, at our time of life there's no reason to hang around." It all sounded very transactional and dispassionate. The conversation needed rescuing.

"So how are the wedding preparations going?"

Annabel's face brightened. "It's all under control, just about. I'm having the dress made in London, so I've been backwards and forwards. Lots of lists. Clifton has been lovely. He's letting me manage the whole thing, and hasn't complained once. The only thing he's organised is his stag do."

A night out drinking with Clifton's rugby friends was not my idea of fun, so I was secretly grateful that I hadn't been invited to it. I said nothing. We were approaching the paddock through the orchard, and I could see the new stable building between the trees. It was bigger than I'd imagined; a two storey timber affair.

"And where are you having the reception? A marquee in the garden? You've got the room, haven't you?"

"We could have, absolutely, but luckily Daddy's letting us have Wychwood, which is perfect."

"Wychwood," I said, and my tongue suddenly felt thick in my mouth. "Wychwood Hall?"

"Yes."

I stood still, silently processing the information for a long moment.

"Are you… Are you Lord Wychwood's daughter?"

"Yes. Are you alright, Nick? You don't look well."

We had reached the paddock gate, and I grabbed hold of it gratefully, transferring the weight from my legs, which were feeling unsteady.

"Actually I'm suddenly not feeling all that great," I said.

Annabel peered into my face concernedly. "You've gone white. Do you want to sit down?"

I was going to be sick. I pushed off from the fence. "Will you excuse me? I'm going to pay a quick visit."

I set off without waiting for the answer, heading at a half walk, half canter for the house and the sanctuary of the downstairs toilet. Fortunately, when I came in through the back door Clifton wasn't to be seen in the kitchen and I was able to slip through to the hall and into the toilet, where I shut myself in and sat down. There was a taste of bile at the back of my throat, and beads of sweat were running down my forehead.

So Clifton was marrying Lord Wychwood's daughter. Of course he was! Of course! It made complete sense. When anything good came along for me, he always found a way to trump and degrade it. It happened without conscious effort on his part, it happened with monotonous inevitability, and it was the main reason I hated him. And now he had done it again: the deal with Greenwood, the deal that was going to put me on the map, was in tatters.

There would be no question now of Lord Wychwood having to sell the estate, because Clifton's money would stave off the creditors indefinitely. It all came into focus suddenly: Clifton and Annabel were introduced by 'one of Daddy's friends', were they? Were they, indeed! It was an arranged marriage, nothing more, nothing less. Wychwood had traded his only daughter to Clifton in return for money that would keep the estate in the family. She didn't even like Clifton that much – it was obvious – but she was the old-fashioned sort of girl who would dutifully do what Daddy told her for the good of the family. It explained a lot about the way he was treating her. And Clifton would in due course inherit the stately home and lord it over me and everyone else for the rest of our lives.

I spent a long time in that toilet, getting to know the contours of the walls and floor with unhappy intimacy as I mulled over the consequences of my discovery. When at last I was ready, I flushed the loo for convention's sake and washed my hands and face at the sink. I didn't want to face Annabel or Clifton, but I made my way back to the kitchen anyway.

"How are you feeling? Annabel asked, looking genuinely worried.

"I'm so sorry. I'm feeling terrible. I'm just going to go home."

"Poor you. What do you think it is?"

"You do look a bit pale. Hope we haven't poisoned you, old chap," Clifton chipped in. "Will you be alright to drive?"

"I'll be fine. Please don't worry. And I was having such a nice time too."

"Me too! " Annabel said. "Nick, I'm so sorry. It's been really lovely to meet you. You must come for a weekend. Wouldn't that be nice, Clifton?"

"Thank you," I said, noting Clifton's not unexpected silence.

They showed me out and waved from the front porch as I drove away. On the long drive back to Highgate I replayed the conversation with Annabel over and over in my head. It's like a curse, I thought. How does he do it? How does he do it?

Chapter 18: *List of Suspected Victims*

Dear Nick,

This is vandalism of the worst kind, not that my saying so will stop you, of course. You know I don't have the strength to actually put these pages physically in the bin because I know they belong somewhere, wherever it is you stole them from, and there's a chance, a very faint chance I know, that one day they could be restored to their rightful place. But please stop. I can't bear it.

That piece about the footprints of the Devil puts into words something I've thought for a long time. The footprints of the Devil aren't his footprints at all (hoofprints?) but the footprints of a pagan past subverted and overwritten. When you think about the vicious and systematic way Christianity rooted out the old beliefs and hijacked the ancient myths and legends, you realise what a bloody pogrom it was. It's hard to know what's true and what's been corrupted. History is written by the victors, and most of it is just lies. That's how I feel about us, too. Your version of events, anyway.

The Brodie Cabinet is completely new to me and it sounds brilliant. I have tried to find out where it is now so that I can go and see it, but no luck so far. It's not in Lewes Town Hall anyway. The piece didn't mention that the elements – earth, air, fire, water - are used in classifying elemental beings like fairies, and in astrology too. The thought of how much that last sentence is going to annoy you is making me smile.

Anyway, you're sticking to Sussex, I see. On this basis I have narrowed down my list of suspected victims to the regional libraries of the South East. If you've anything else you've already cut out, then I suppose you may as well send it to me. Otherwise, stop it! Stop it at once!

H

Chapter 19: *The Journal of Davey Bone*

Friday 18th June 1779

Great curiosity concerning my unknown benefactor remained with me throughout the day, but as for my strange dreams, they had faded to nought in my thoughts following my jolly talk with Anne, who is my joy and comfort in all ways and without whom I should flap gasping like a trout tickled from the stream. It was another late night with more than usual takings and as much talk of crops and raillery about the weather as ever and toward the end much cheery tomfoolery, and I did not have a spare moment to keep an eye upon the dish I had set out. It was after midnight when finally I came to it, and finding that it had not been disturbed as I had feared, I sat quietly in the kitchen in darkness with the intention of discovering the culprit, leaving the door part way open so as I could see the dish upon the step, and so I remained until I could no longer keep my eyes open. When I went a-bed it was nigh on two o'clock and clear skies and the bread and milk had been cooling there for hours. I fell into a dream at once in which the great wood had grown back taller and thicker than ever and we were surrounded by it as we walked onward upon the road, my companion all in green and I. Sunbeams fought like knights to find their way through the thick canopy above, and but a few emerged triumphant, and yet the light was pleasant enough, like swimming deep in a summer mere. My companion stepped but daintily, seeming almost to float just above the ground, and travelled at a pace that was more than a match for my own long strides, and so we arrived just before sunset at our destination: a great clearing in which loomed a monstrous castle with a black moat, high towers and unscaleable walls of smooth stone.

"But this is not Wychwood Hall," I said as we stood surveying this menacing view from the very edge of the wood.

"I assure you it is," the man replied, his eyes bright in the gathering twilight.

"It is not the one that I know."

"Perhaps not."

"This is a gloomy and desperate place."

He clapped me on the back. "You are a singular fellow! How discerning you are! How judicious! There is no-one more perceptive!"

"Look: there is a light at the window. Shall we go in?"

My companion took fright at this suggestion. "Indeed no!" he cried, taking a little leap backwards. "I mean," he continued, collecting himself, "I cannot go in there. They are my enemies. They would not let me in. No indeed! But you could go in. You must go in!"

"And what then?"

"Why, then you shall show your mettle. You shall have riches beyond your dreams."

"Riches..? Truly?"

"Follow my instruction with care and do not falter, and indeed yes, you shall!"

"And what are your instructions?"

"Take this." He presented me with a small and marvellously carved wooden box. "You shall have need of it."

"What is it?" I asked. There was no reply, and so I slid back the lid. Inside there were three more bright gold coins. When I turned to seek more explanation, my companion had gone.

Once again I awoke to find that the whole night had passed. First thing I did go to the back door and sure enough the bread and milk is gone from the dish and in its place three ancient and worn gold pieces in a stack. I took the dish inside then and took up the coins, and much like they were to the others, and now I had six and several worries more besides. After that when Anne asked had there been any more gifts from the fairies I said there was nothing and Almighty God forgive me my lie to her but I was greatly troubled and feared that if I told her I should not be able to stop myself and would tell all, and I did not wish to frighten her.

Chapter 20: *Pick Up a Booklet on the Way Out*

I found Charlie at the village hall, which was next door to the church. There was a constant drizzle from a relentlessly grey sky; the kind of rain that clings to your clothes and eventually wriggles its way through to your shirt collar and cuffs. I had tried the pub and then his van, so by the time I passed the church on my way back to the road I was damp and ready to give up, but on hearing the strains coming from the hall of 'Teddy Bear's Picnic' being belted out on the piano, I knew it could only be him. A quick dash up the path to the porch and I was out of the wet.

Inside the lights were off except for a solitary lamp illuminating the keyboard of the of the piano, by which I could see that it was indeed Charlie, completely absorbed in his playing. Certain bass notes caught the natural frequency of the prefabricated walls of the building, making them thrum in rhythm. I walked over, but either he didn't see me or he chose to keep playing; either way I ended up standing at his shoulder until he had finished. As the final chord faded away, he turned his head abruptly. "Sorry, I don't do requests," he said.

"Hello Charlie, I need a word."

"About?"

I had forgotten about his habitual rudeness. "About Wychwood Hall," I said.

There was a pause, and then Charlie played a long, crashing discord. As it faded dramatically he swung his legs round slowly. "Shall we sit over there?" he said, indicating the nearest row of seats.

By the time we were installed the hall was utterly quiet, but for the patter of the rain on the flat, tar-paper roof.

"You know, church bells have been made of an alloy of copper and tin for hundreds of years now," Charlie said. "It makes for a much sweeter sound than the old iron ones, but the sodding bells in our church are still made of iron. What do you make of that?"

I didn't bite. "It's a bit dark in here for me," I said. "Aren't there any lights?"

"Nervous? Don't worry, you're perfectly safe with me."

"Oh, for God's sake." I shook my head. Charlie could be rather annoying when he put his mind to it. "Charlie, if I may get right to the point: Annabel is Lord Wychwood's daughter."

"Sorry, I don't follow. Annabel?"

"Let me put it another way: you know your friend Howland Greenwood? Well, his grand plan, the thing we shook hands on, is completely fucked. My cousin Clifton's fiancée is Wychwood's daughter."

"Your cousin is marrying Wychwood's daughter?"

"Exactly!" I paused, allowing it to sink in and waiting for Charlie's response, but he didn't say anything; he just sat there twiddling his thumbs absently. "And Clifton is absolutely loaded," I added. "You see what I'm saying."

I had expected Charlie to be horrified by this revelation, or at least show some surprise, but all he said was: "Alright, but your cousin's not stupid, is he? Why would he sink his fortune into that money pit?"

"No. He may be an arrogant fat lump but you're right: he's not stupid. However, his entire fortune *is* going to be poured right down the ancestral plughole anyway, because he wants to be the sodding lord of the sodding manor and that's the price. That poor girl. I couldn't understand what she saw in him. I just put it down to Cupid's random arrow, you know, at first. But the truth is, she doesn't feel anything

122

for him. She tried to fool me with a lot of talk about warming to him and he's better when you get to know him." I shook my head slowly. "Funny, isn't it? The only time she sounded passionate was when she started talking about the wedding arrangements. She's sacrificing herself for the benefit of her father. And to Clifton of all people!" It was very quiet in the hall. The sound of raindrops on the roof had suddenly stopped. "I bet he wasn't even first choice. I bet he was near the bottom of the list. Scraping the bottom of the barrel."

"How much is he worth?"

"Well he's not rock-star rich, but I'm afraid he has enough cash to stave off Wychwood's ruin for a few more decades. So that's it, Charlie. It's all off."

"Annabel," Charlie said, pointing a slightly shaking arthritic finger at me. "Why are you going on about Annabel so much?"

"She's Wychwood's daughter, Charlie. Don't you get it?"

"No, that's not it. I know what's going on here."

"What are you saying?"

"Well, it's obvious, isn't it?"

"What is?"

"You're absolutely smitten."

"Smitten?"

"Yes! Infatuated. Head over heels."

"You've lost me."

"With this Annabel woman!"

"No I'm not!"

"You can't stop talking about her. You're jealous of this Clifton fellow, your cousin. What did you just call him? Arrogant fat lump? Come on, man!"

"Oh my God! Charlie, please listen to me."

"Fat lump, you said. See? I'm right."

"Oh my God!"

"You're mooning over her."

"No I'm not!"

"You're a good liar, sir, but it won't do you any good with me."

"Charlie, please. You're starting to really piss me off."

"Alright." Charlie was chuckling to himself. "But please allow me to express my admiration."

He had lost me completely.

"It's brilliant! She'll fall for you. Hoo hoo! Probably has already! You steal her from the arrogant fat lump, right under Wychwood's nose." He laughed uproariously. "I'd like to see that! You could be the next master of Wychwood Hall!"

"You're out of order, Charlie."

"Rumour in the village is she has the hots for you too."

"Charlie!"

He stopped laughing after a while. "I suppose you want me to tell Howland?"

"Why don't you just give me his phone number? I'll do it. I expect he already knows, anyway. Everyone knows everyone else's business around here."

"I thought you agreed no direct contact. Too risky."

"Yes, but that was when there was a deal. Nothing is going to happen now."

"I see what you mean. Let me talk to him first, make sure he's comfortable with the idea of speaking to you."

"Oh, for God's sake, Charlie. You tell him, alright?" I got up and began an undignified shuffle along the row of seats so that I wouldn't have to squeeze past Charlie, and then I was heading for the door.

"You should find out about the church bells." His voice receded as I neared the exit. "You can pick up a booklet on the way out. They're 50p. Just put the money in the box. If you're feeling honest, that is."

I ignored him and stomped out into the rain.

Chapter 21: *The Haunted Hunt: Tales of Hunting and Ghostly Happenings*

Fox hunting as we recognise it today may be considered a relatively recent development, its customs and etiquette being attributable, according to popular belief, to the discipline of the Quorn Hunt of Leicestershire, which was founded as lately as 1696; however, it has, despite this relative youth, a well-established tradition of its own in ghost stories and tales of strange happenings.

Its ancient sibling, equestrian deer-hunting, was the recreational passion of kings for centuries before the idea of hunting foxes was ever hatched, and indeed, entire forests have been saved from the woodsman's axe over the years by monarchs concerned only to guarantee the abundance of good sport. This earlier form of hunting has a widespread and somewhat grander tradition of gods and hellhounds rather than common-or-garden ghosts. The legend of the Wild Hunt is common to many European countries, with many variants: in medieval romances the participants are identified as fairies; in other stories relating the origin of the Wild Hunt the Devil plays a part in tricking the hunters into their eternal pursuit. It is said that the Wild Hunt has strengthened its numbers over the years with the very best of huntsmen, who mysteriously disappear from their lives and are never seen again: characters of renown such as King Arthur, Hereward the Wake and even Sir Francis Drake have all been identified as participants, but whether willing or unwilling is not told.

In England the hunt is led by Herne the Hunter, who appears as a huge antlered figure riding his horse, sometimes seen in Windsor Great Park beneath the great oak tree from which he was hanged, accompanied by the hounds of Hell.

There are eye-witness accounts of the terrifying appearance of the hunt: jet-black or milk-white hounds possessing great saucer eyes and blood-red ears, and the riders, titanic and sinister figures mounted upon great black horses, making blood-curdling cries and winding their horns, all careering in the vanguard of a great storm.

The object of the Wild Hunt varies according to locality: in some traditions it is a mythical creature such as a great boar, a white stag, an ominous dream-beast; in other places the hunters' quarry is a nymph or dryad, or a maiden to be captured, bound, and borne away. In some accounts the hunted were sinners, or the unbaptized.

However, with mounted stag-hunting now only an historic footnote, for which we must give thanks to the proponents of the enclosure laws that were introduced at the end of the last century, only fox-hunting continues to develop a new mythology of ghosts and demons. It is a pastime that certainly lends itself well to the purpose, concerning encounters with a foe of legendary cunning in the mysterious depths of the English countryside, together with a good deal of risk of physical harm to the participants.

The huntsman, whose skill in working the hounds is so finely tuned that it may itself appear supernatural, is often the source of such tales. Neither a history of volatility nor an obsessive mindset is unlikely in such a profession, and thus one has the solid foundations of the classic ghost story immediately to hand. Henry Crighton, it is related, was the professional huntsman of the Ashdown Bewick hunt. Famed throughout the county for his doggedness and cruel blood-lust, Crighton was not one for allowing his prey to escape with its life once the hounds had scented it. He died whilst in the thick of the chase and running well ahead of the Field, the victim of a hitherto unsuspected weak heart, and his stallion was eventually discovered wandering many fields away with his corpse still slumped in the saddle. Strangely, there were many that day that swore they had seen him at the kill, urging the hounds on with his usual shrill cries, even though he would have been dead for several hours by that time.

Twenty years later another huntsman, Joseph Kenworthy, was said to have become obsessed by a particular fox that could not be caught: it would throw the hounds off the scent by various devious means, or in the end simply outrun them, and then stand proudly on the skyline before slipping away to fight another day. Kenworthy complained that the fox was mocking him, and swore on the horns of the Devil himself that he would take it, mask, brush and pads. He died before he could do so, but his ghostly, transparent figure, ripened as a corpse, was glimpsed in the vanguard of the chase on many occasions thereafter by the horrified members of that hunt, and it was commonly held that he would never be able to rest in his grave until he had fulfilled his contract.

The hounds are also a rich source of ghostly tales. The pack that disappeared into a dark dell in Yorkshire and never emerged, every hound having vanished inexplicably, is still, we are told, on some occasions to be heard giving voice at night as if from some great cave or hole in the ground. At Castle Dreygh the pack disappeared under the ice following a ghostly grey fox across a frozen lake, and some ten years later the tragedy was repeated again at precisely the same spot. Another tale concerns Patrick Hanrahan, who was the Master of Hounds at Brindley Edge, and his two favourites: Perseus and Rogue. These two hounds would run together, leading the pack, and between them could pick up and track a scent infallibly over any terrain. They were both large, powerful dogs: Perseus was belligerent and gave voice frequently and loudly, whilst Rogue was silent and efficient, often a few paces ahead of Perseus. Hanrahan loved them both and kept them out of kennels, allowing them to sleep in the house and feed in his kitchen, and they were inseparable. When he died of influenza, both hounds instantly went berserk, attacking each other viciously. Rogue killed Perseus, but was terribly injured in the process. He was attended to, and subsequently put in kennels with the other hounds in line with the wishes of Hanrahan's daughter Charlotte, but they turned on him immediately and tore him to pieces.

In 1799 a rider in the Field of a well-established hunt was unseated at a jump, and rose uninjured only to find his horse Hildie acting very strangely: she was turning and stamping as if being remounted but he could plainly see that there was no-one there. He attempted to grasp the reins, but she turned sharply and galloped off after the hunt. Hildie caught up with and passed the Field, and continued in pursuit of the hounds, passing the Master, whippers-in and huntsman all. The Master swore afterwards that he saw the reins being manipulated but no-one in the saddle. When the hounds lost the scent, Hildie continued on and disappeared from view. She was later found to have gone over a cliff and died from the fall. The huntsman said Hildie had followed the scent trail faithfully ahead of the hounds, and must have been ridden off the cliff because "…no horse would jump from that giddy height of its own accord."

The fox itself is oft-times credited with uncanny intelligence or ability, deliberately luring the hunt on into danger, or somehow laying a curse upon huntsman or hounds. Sometimes the fox is even depicted as enjoying the sport itself. After the death of its Master, one hunt that had experienced the worst season of its entire history up to that moment, with every meet having been confounded by weather, injury, scents lost and never found again, or worst of all, no fox to be found anywhere, suddenly found itself giving chase to the gamest quarry it had ever known. A strong dog fox with a black patch upon its shoulders like a waistcoat was picked up in a covert that had been empty for years. It tore away from the hounds and across the countryside with a spring in its step, just as the sun came out from behind autumn rain clouds. Away it ran, with the hounds streaming behind in full cry, and the huntsman hunted the hounds and the new Master led the Field, hunting the huntsman. A full twelve miles that fox took them, never fast enough to lose the pack, never slow enough to allow them to gain, and all the while in glorious sunshine. They crossed fields and none of the jumps was too easy or too high for the riders, forded streams and never for more than a moment did the hounds lose the scent, and the route took them by all of the most magnificent sights of the county. Towards the end of the day the hunt, tired but elated, found itself coming back towards its starting point. The fox made a beeline for the dead Master's house, where the meet had begun, went right through the main gate, across the gardens, and was found in the end taking refuge in the Master's favourite bath chair that had been left out to air on the lawn. Was this the spirit of the former Master in fox form, determined to give his beloved hunt one last idyllic outing?

In a similar tale, one vixen led the pack a merry dance, over hill and down dale, doubling back through coombes and copses, running down streams and ditches, through the village, and up the way to Old Nan's Cave. The hounds were singing that they had cornered her in the ravine, and when the huntsman and the Field had arrived, the pack was sent in. When the riders followed up, expecting to see a kill, all they found was a little old lady with red hair and a red coat who was sitting upon a tussock, knitting a black woollen stocking and glaring at the hounds whilst puffing furiously on a cob pipe. Addressing the huntsman she thanked him kindly for a fine run out on such a lovely day and regretted that she could not stay for more due to a prior engagement. Then she packed away her knitting, tapped out her pipe on a stone, and in the blink of an eye she had turned into a fox and raced away. But the hounds were on her in a flash and first they took her hind legs, and then they took her front legs, and then they found her neck and it was all over bar the devouring, and not a man there could look away or lift a hand to stop them.

It can be deduced from this small selection of tales that there is no shortage of ghostly imaginings among hunting folk. Whether they are more susceptible to such things than other people, more exposed to them because of their proximity to nature, or simply following in a grand hunting tradition we cannot say for certain. We may, however, as we turn out the light and settle down to sleep, be grateful to them for supplying such a wide-ranging canon from which to draw our desired nightly quota of shudders, chills and enervations. Tally ho!

Chapter 22: *Stuck With Pins*

"Hello darling," I said, kissing Annabel on both cheeks.

"I'm so glad you called me," she said, sitting down at the table. "Sorry I'm late. It took them forever to unpin me." I dismissed the inconvenience with a tiny shrug and was rewarded with that brilliant smile of hers. A waiter helped her with her chair and opened her napkin.

I sat down again myself. "How's it coming along?"

"That's top secret, I'm afraid. Nothing will be revealed until the big day. Ask me about anything else you like and I promise I'll be the soul of indiscretion, but not that." I raised an eyebrow. "I will," she insisted, her eyes laughing.

We were in my favourite fish restaurant in Mayfair, which I had booked hurriedly after a speculative phone call from me a few days before, when I had known Clifton would be at work, had elicited the expected news that Annabel was due in town for a fitting of the dress. It was still early for lunch, but the dining room was filling up steadily and there was already a background buzz of conversation. I really wanted her to like the place, to the point of being a little nervous about it. The anticipation of the event had even eclipsed, albeit only temporarily, the painful disappointment of the Wychwood Hall situation.

"What shall we drink?" I asked.

"I'd love a glass of champagne."

"Let's get a bottle!"

"Good God, no! I have to go back later. I'll need to be able to stand up."

I ordered two glasses from the hovering sommelier. Annabel looked around her. "This is lovely," she said. "I came here once before, with my aunt. It must've been about ten years ago."

"Yes, it's actually been here forever. It's good for celeb-spotting. I once had Prince Andrew sitting at the next table."

"Well, it's an absolute treat. Thank you, Nick. We sort of got out of the habit of coming to London as a family, and Clifton isn't one for going out much, unless it's the pub."

"It's absolutely my pleasure *and* my treat."

"Oh, no. I didn't mean that. I thought we would split it. Is that alright?"

"No," I said firmly. "I chose it, so it's on me. I insist."

"If you're sure." She beamed. "You're so lovely."

The champagne arrived after some inconsequential chatting, and I raised my glass. "Cheers!" I said. "Here's to indiscreet revelations." We clinked, drank.

"How's the property business?"

"My community centre project? I've pulled out," I said.

"Oh no!"

"It's fine. It was a good project, would have made me a lot of dosh, actually, but in the end the community needed that centre. I don't know why the council even contemplated selling it. As soon as I realised how much damage had been done… well, I talked the council into reopening it."

"Nick! That's such a kind and generous thing to do."

"Don't sound so surprised."

"I'm not surprised. It's just that there aren't many people who'd sacrifice their own interests that way for… for the greater good."

"You're just embarrassing me now. Something better will come along, don't worry."

"Of course it will. That's karma! I like your shirt, by the way."

"Thank you."

"What are those buttons? Are they silver?"

"They're supposed to be different flowers I think."

She leaned forward for a better look. "I love them. Clifton would never wear anything like that. He's so conservative."

"We should order," I said. We looked at the menu and I waved the waiter over. It turned out that Annabel was on a crash diet for the wedding, so she ordered a salad starter as a main and nothing else. I decided on the scallops and then Dover sole Meunière.

While we were ordering, four people arrived at the next table and made a big fuss of settling into their seats. One of them, a woman in her fifties wearing a bright green two-piece and pearls, was very loud and started giving our waiter instructions before we had finished ordering. He managed the situation magnificently, but Annabel was seething silently, rolling her eyes.

"Why is it that when you come here you get Prince Andrew and when I come here I get *that*?" she demanded, whispering.

"It's like having my mother at the next table. We can move if you want." I whispered back.

She shook her head. "It's okay. But if she does it again I'm going to stab her in the eye with the butter knife."

"It's not okay. Let's move." I went to lift my arm to beckon the waiter back over, but Annabel pushed it back down again.

"Nick," she said. "We're fine." She left her hand on my forearm.

"Okay," I said, but then went to raise my arm again, and we had a jokey little wrestle, which brought the mood back up.

"So what's happening with your ex-girlfriend. You said you were on a break.

"Hazel? Actually things are pretty difficult."

"Oh. I'm sorry. You don't have to tell me if it's too personal."

"It's okay."

"So have you broken up now then? I mean, is that it? Is it over?"

"It's over. It's definitely over. But it's complicated."

"Go on."

"Well… it's a real rollercoaster at the moment. She's needy and clingy half the time, and unreasonable the rest of it."

"I thought she'd moved out."

"She has." I leaned forward. "But she rings me at all hours, usually in a state. And she keep sending me things in the post. She has some serious issues, to be honest. We can't go on like this, I know, but I can't just walk away from her when she's in such a mess. It wouldn't be a kind thing to do. She needs help."

My scallops arrived, seared and in the shell with chilli butter. They looked wonderful. "It sounds a bit feeble, I know. I should be cruel to be kind."

"No." She looked at me thoughtfully, her eyes shining. "You *are* being kind."

I dabbed at a gobbet of butter at the corner of my mouth with my napkin. "Enough about me. Tell me about you," I commanded.

"What do you want to know?"

"Oh, I don't know. So many secrets to unlock. Okay, what's the most wicked and evil thing you've ever done?"

"I've led a very wholesome life, I'll have you know. Practically angelic." She hesitated for a moment and then said: "I did run away from school once when I was fifteen."

"Did you really?"

"Yes. I went to boarding school. I actually quite liked it there, but my best friend, Caroline Appleton, hated it and was always talking about running away, and one day we actually did it. We got the bus to the main road and then we hitched as far as we could. We ended up in the middle of nowhere, and had to sleep the night in a hay barn. She tried to snog me, but that didn't work out at all, and in the morning we were so cold and hungry we gave ourselves up to the farmer, and he rang the police. It's funny: we thought we'd be punished, but they never did anything."

"Crikey! That's a proper adventure. Runaways, police, haystacks. It's got everything! What happened to Caroline?"

"I actually don't know. We sort of lost touch after we left school."

"You're the first person I've ever met who said they liked it at boarding school."

"I'm an only child who grew up on a country estate with no friends my own age. It was very lonely. So when I went to boarding school and there were all these other children there, I thought it was rather wonderful."

"Oh dear, what a terrible childhood you had," I said insincerely. She had started to give me the big, sad eyes, but when she realised it wasn't working she reached over and pinched me hard on the back of the hand.

"Ow!" I said.

"Don't be beastly," she said, laughing.

"But I am beastly."

She gave me an appraising look and then nodded slowly. "I suppose I'm one of the privileged few. Most people would see it that way. But looking back on it, it was lonely. And it wasn't as if I had the run of the estate; lots of it was out of bounds, and there were rules and I had chores to do all the time. At least I had the horses."

I laughed, and so did she. "So one day it will all be yours," I said. "And Clifton's."

She looked suddenly haunted. "Sometimes it feels like a great millstone tied round my neck, dragging me down, and I wish I was free of it. Sometimes I hate it."

"Why not sell it then?"

"It's been our family home for seven generations. It's part of me. And I feel responsible. You know that corny thing about 'we're only custodians for the next generation'? I truly feel that. Is that silly? Besides, it would break Daddy's heart if Wychwood were ever sold."

"What about your heart?"

Annabel thought seriously about it. "It's bigger than me. What I want doesn't really matter."

"Now who's sacrificing their interests for the greater good? You've got some pretty good Karma coming too, I'd say."

The waiter took my plate away. "That was fabulous," I told him. He gave a nod of acknowledgement and smiled.

"How is it," Annabel demanded, "That this is only the second time I've met you and it feels like we've been friends for years?"

"I know what you mean. It must be something to do with you, because it never happens to me."

"I'm serious. Meeting someone who's on the same wavelength. It doesn't happen very often."

"No, it doesn't." I gave her a steady look across the table.

She looked away, flustered, but regrouped with admirable speed: "Your mother came round again last week."

"Christ! I thought she was in Spain!"

"I think she feels responsible for Clifton. With his parents not being around, you know. She keeps offering to help with the wedding."

"I should keep her as far away from it as possible if I were you."

"She's only being nice."

"Mother doesn't do nice."

"Well I like her."

"You'll learn."

"You look like her."

"Everybody says that."

"It's a compliment."

"Ah," I said, "Now you're talking. Compliments. Tell me more."

The sole was excellent, and I would have had a chocolate fondant for dessert had Annabel not announced that she was overdue back at the dressmaker's.

"What? You promised me indiscretions, and I've had nothing. I'm feeling rather let down."

"Well I can only apologise. I did tell you about Caroline Appleton."

"Well tell me something else before we go."

She smiled broadly. "I'll have to owe you."

"That's all very well, but the next time I see you probably won't be until after you're Mrs Prendergast."

"Come for a weekend. The first hunt meet of the season is coming up. I'll call you with the details."

"I don't ride."

"I shan't expect you to."

"Alright." I gave her a big hug. "Go and get stuck with pins, if you must."

She kissed me on the cheek, and left. I sat down again and wondered if I should have the chocolate fondant after all. Also, that kiss had been a fraction warmer and longer than it should have been, hadn't it? I was sure it had.

Chapter 23: *The Arms of Another Man*

Dear Nick,

Thank you for 'The Devil's Footsteps'. If your Machiavellian idea is that this stuff will tempt me to allow you back into my affections, then I'm sorry but you have miscalculated by a mile. You have only succeeded in driving me into the arms of another man: Walter Peachey, my new favourite author. His books are out of print so I am having to track them down, but that's the kind of problem I love most, as you know.

A Knight of St Dunstan, eh? Makes you wonder what they get up to when they're not snuffing out plots to open a forgotten gateway to Hell hidden somewhere in the Home Counties (such a delicious idea it's bound to be true!). Dunstan was such a scourge of the old ways. Persecuting dear little dwarves, gnomes and pixies I shouldn't wonder, given half a chance.

Where is all this going, Nick? Don't expect me to believe you've somehow assembled it all yourself. You haven't, have you? Where are you getting it from? Please tell me.

H

Chapter 24: *The Journal of Davey Bone*

Saturday 19th June 1779

I am considered a strong man by all accounts, and I never ran away nor was bested in a fair fight my whole life long, and that is the truth, and what is more I have many friends and few enemies, and a little learning to my credit, and all this has served me well; but today I have felt helpless as a new-born kitten drowning in a sack in a river. As the day wore on I became strongly resolved to remain that night hid well in the dark of the kitchen and watch a new dish of bread and milk upon the step and try to bring this to an end one way or another. Old Hodge's tale about the Devil's hoard under Stoney Down tickled me about the ears like a fly in the heat of summertime, though I was not listening, having heard it a hundred times and more, and yet it made me think of gold and more gold, and all day I had bad nerves and kept my eyes open for trouble, but there was naught amiss in the end, although I almost wished there had been so that I should not have the trial of further waiting. So at last I finished my work and the place was quiet, and late it was, but I was installed quickly and neatly then in the dark and my vigil was begun. It was quiet, but for a little owl hooting, and I fell to thinking about my wise old Dad and what he might say of these events. He had little in the way of schooling and could read nor write, and there was nothing much to set him apart from a long line of Bones living here in Stoney Hill in the same way. He believed in things as they did too, and I could hear him saying in my ear: "Take care, Davey, as the coins is the gifts and the work of the pharisees living on Stoney Down, fond as they are of bread and milk, and t'would be bad luck to pass them coins on to any man for fear of the pharisee's curse. Keep your wits about you, for they are sure to try to trick you!" With these and other late musings I must have fallen asleep in spite of my intentions, nerves or no.

The dream that night was unlike the ones that came before it: I was no longer in a humble wood but transported to a magnificent royal chamber with a high dais at one end upon which there was a glittering throne made of spun silver and gold. Rich tapestries hung all around; the vaulted ceiling was supported by pillars like silver trees, with branches reaching up and disappearing into it between which fireflies did perform courtly dances in the lofty air; the floor, strewn with grasses and the petals of flowers, did spread a delicately sweet perfume through the chamber; and the space within was lit in places with bright moonlight, although from whence it came I could not see. Creatures fabulous and grotesque lined the route between where I stood and the throne: dryads and nymphs, fauns and centaurs, goblins and dwarves; I could not recognise or name them all, and indeed should not wonder if many of them did not have a name. They were chattering and gibbering and pointing at me in a way I did not at all like, and yet despite the strangeness of my situation I felt no fear.

"Come forward," came a clear voice over the hubbub, and the throng fell silent. I looked up to see that the throne was occupied by a shining figure: it was the man in green that had accompanied me in the wood, his face still white as chalk, but now about his brow he had a silver crown and he had grown to the stature of a giant. Across his shoulders the white cloak, made, I could see now, from swan's feathers, caught the light brightly. I walked slowly towards him. A hideous old crone in fine brocade curtsied as I went by. "Hail to thee, opener of the way. Fair shall be thy children beyond the measure of man."

A bloated creature in a powdered wig and with a face like a toad croaked: "Hail to thee, bringer of destruction to our foes. Hale in health and long-lived shall ye be."

"Come forward," said my companion. "Wealth shall be thine, beyond thy dreams."

I halted before the dais. "Have you the box?" my companion asked.

I found that I had.

"Open it."

I did so, and inside there was flint, steel and tinder.

"Ye know what ye must do."

"Indeed I do. Your purpose is plain enough. You wish me to enter Wychwood Hall and burn it to the ground."

There was a roar of approval and delight from the assembly. Their leader rose from his seat. "A singular fellow! Did I not tell you how clever he is?"

"It is an old Saxon hoard you are offering me in return, is it not? And where shall I find it?"

"Clever did I say? Why, he is as cunning as Reynard and as sly as Tybault! Ye shall find it upon your own doorstep, indeed you shall, just as soon as the deed is done. Burn Wychwood Hall to the ground and all inside, before the longest day of the year is done, and it shall be yours."

"Burn it! Burn it to the ground!" the throng cried in strange voices. "All inside must perish!"

"Tell me, why do you wish this?"

"They are my enemies. They wish me harm. They hide a great secret that must be revealed."

"Burn them! Char their bones! Pound them to dust!"

"And if I agree to this thing, how shall I know that ye may be trusted to fulfil your part of the bargain?"

"Such as we are bound fast by the bargains that we make. It is in our nature: I should have no more choice in effecting it than in breathing."

I thought of how little money I had hidden away in my strongbox for my dotage after all these years and the great comfort the gold hoard would bring, and I knew that I should never have such an opportunity again to improve the fortune of my beloved family to such a degree.

"I will do it." I said, receiving immediate cheers and hearty commendations from the creatures around me.

"Then witness all: our bargain is struck! Beware, for it may not be unmade, not even should both of us wish it so, for such are the ways of our folk. Breaking it carries a heavy price." My companion bowed deeply and long. "Farewell. We must both hope that we shall never have cause to renew our acquaintance."

I remember no more until waking in my chair with a bad head and feeling the ache of my bones as I tried to get up. Upon the doorstep the dish was once again clean and in it a wooden tinder box, heavily carved with a dense forest on the sides of a high hill. I have it on the desk now beside me: upon the lid, which slides back, is carved in marvellous detail a knight fighting with a demon or such that has smoke and flames coming from its nostrils; the inside is as one might expect, with flint and steel and charred cloth under a damper. It is as fine a piece of carving as I have seen and in condition barely used and no doubt stolen, as is the way with fairies.

Chapter 25: *The Hunt*

On the Saturday morning at Clifton and Annabel's house I had to get up for breakfast at an unholy hour because of the hunt, which, since I hadn't been sleeping at all well, was the last thing I needed and it took a superhuman effort to drag myself out of bed.

My hosts were both already at the table in the kitchen when I came downstairs: Clifton was dressed *de rigeur* in fawn breeches and a pre-season tweed, or 'ratcatcher' as Annabel called it, jacket. Despite what must have been extensive tailoring, he looked scruffy and uncomfortable in the way only ex-public schoolboys can. Annabel was, as usual, impeccably turned out, but not in her hunting apparel.

"I'm not riding today." She got up slowly from her chair and straightened up, grimacing. She looked very annoyed. "I've done something to my back, lifting boxes upstairs, and the pain is making me utterly wretched."

"Only a muscle strain, not a prolapsed disk." Clifton chipped in with professional cheer over the top of his newspaper.

Annabel made her way slowly over to the kitchen counter. "I had hoped I'd be better this morning, but it woke me up early. Clifton has given me some super-strong painkillers, so I'm as high as a kite and getting higher by the minute. Soon I shan't be able to feel my toes at all. I shall be alright to drive us over in the Land Rover and watch, but poor dear Merryman won't get a run out today, and I know he was so-o looking forward to it."

"You poor thing! I thought you were moving around a bit stiffly yesterday." I went to help her with the breakfast things.

"Oh, do sit down. I shall be fine. Now, there's porridge and bacon and eggs. And toast. And tea or coffee."

"Why don't you let me do it?" I said.

"Nonsense!" Clifton said. "It's all under control."

I looked at Annabel, who did not react, but avoided my gaze.

I sat down. "I'd love a cup of tea," I said, reaching for the teapot. Annabel walked stiffly over and lifted it away from my hand. "I'll make some fresh," she said, and then added mumsily: "You had better eat something. It's a long day and there's no lunch. Although I have made some sandwiches for you."

"Unfair! Where are my sandwiches?" Clifton looked hurt.

"You'll be far too busy to worry about sandwiches, dearest love," Annabel said. "You'll see."

"It's such a shame you don't ride," Annabel said as we rattled along empty country lanes in pre-dawn half-light.

"I've never ridden a horse in my life. I'm a complete townie."

"You couldn't be worse than Clifton." She rolled her eyes. "He tries so hard, and I know he's just doing it to please me, but..."

"I'm sure he'll get the hang of it."

"He always looks so... uncomfortable. You, on the other hand, would be a natural. Don't shake your head: I'm absolutely sure of it. You can tell, you know. Perhaps you might try one day. I could teach you."

"Really?" I found myself saying, "Well that's an offer I can't refuse. That's very sweet of you."

We slowed behind a horsebox and followed it at twenty miles an hour. I pulled a face. "Oh, for heaven's sake!" I said.

Annabel smiled at me, a paragon of patience. "Slow down, Sterling Moss. They're going as fast as they can! Think of the poor horses!"

The horsebox eventually turned off into a field in which other vehicles were already parked, but we carried on a little farther and arrived at the gates of Wychwood Hall. We passed through large flint and brick pillars onto a long gravel drive overhung with dark trees, and then instead of following the last section of the drive up to the house we turned off to the right and followed a straight, tree-lined avenue. All I could see of the house itself was a silhouette of tall chimneys, which was tantalising, but then the stables, a Georgian brick-built structure with a large paddock beside it, came into view.

"Jesus! How many horses has your Dad got?"

"Six. The stables were built for twenty, though. Those were the days! Can you imagine?" Annabel parked outside and switched off the engine.

No wonder he was in debt, I thought. "What are we doing?"

"I borrowed a lawnmower from Daddy and he wants it back. You'll have to lift it for me, I'm afraid." She eased herself out of the door and opened the back of the Land Rover.

Pushing the mower angled up on its rear wheels, I followed Annabel round the back of the stable block to the outhouse where the gardeners kept the machinery. Inside there was a brick floor and there were workbenches along the walls, with various ancient and modern gardening tools bracketed above, but most of the space was taken up with lawnmowers. Petrol vapour, the sour smell of old oil, and the musty richness of old grass cuttings filled the nostrils. There were old cylinder mowers, powered by two stroke engines and just the job to finish off a cricket pitch. There were rotary mowers, for the rougher jobs, and in pride of place there was a miniature tractor with a rotary mower underneath and a trailer that picked up the cut grass. Fuel and oil, in a variety of tin cans of different sizes, were stored under one of the workbenches. I pushed the mower into a vacant space, and turned to exit, only to find Annabel standing in the doorway. I very nearly knocked her over, but managed to stop just in time and caught hold of her arms just above the elbow to steady us. She looked up into my eyes and we stood awkwardly, chest to chest, for a moment.

"Sorry. Nearly killed you!" I said.

"You saved me," she said, and, reaching up, gently stroked my temple and the back of my neck as if I were a horse. "Thank you, darling boy." Then she turned and marched off at an impressive pace for someone with a bad back. "Come and meet Daddy," she commanded over her shoulder.

We stepped into the dusty atmosphere of the stable block, with its triple notes of straw, slightly sweeter hay, and horse-dung, which blared pungently above the other two like a trombone over cello and viola. It was busy inside: two horses, manes plaited and coats gleaming, were already tacked up and being led out of their stalls. Annabel led me over to a man in riding gear who was yanking on the girth of a third in a bad-tempered way. It was a huge stallion, and a stable hand wearing an apron was holding tightly onto the bridle while the skittish brute nodded and pulled.

"Good morning Daddy," she said. "This is Nick Carpenter."

"Pleased to meet you," I said.

"I don't give a shit!" Lord Wychwood said forcefully, not looking up. Much to my relief, there was an immediate, muffled reply from someone in the next stall and I realised that we had walked in on a conversation. Wychwood fastened the girth and tucked the strap away, and then held up his hand to us, rather rudely I thought, to stop us from saying anything further until he had finished. "In any case, the drag has already come back, for God's sake!" he barked. "We pass Compton's whether you like it or not."

He turned to us, barely noticing me. "Good morning," he said. It seemed strangely formal. The stallion stamped impatiently.

"Nick is Clifton's cousin. He's been very kindly helping me with the Hayter."

"I see. Well, that is very kind. Please don't leave it out. Just put it in the shed."

"Nick's already done it."

He acknowledged my foresight with a brief nod, and then took the bridle from the stable hand and began to lead his mount out of the stall. "How are you feeling?" he asked Annabel brusquely.

"I'm just sorry for poor Merryman. He'll miss the run out so badly."

"Piers will be whipper-in instead of you."

"I'm sure he'll do famously."

He grunted doubtfully, and looked at me for the first time. He had a strong nose and an angular jawline, with eyes set slightly too close together like a predatory bird.

"Nick's going to follow today. I'm going to look after him."

"It's very kind of you to let me tag along," I said.

He gave a curt nod. "Enjoy your day," he said, and led the stallion out into the yard.

"Friendly sort of chap, your dad."

148

Annabel shook her head. "Sorry. He's not always like this."

She took the Land Rover rattling back along the drive. I complained that I still hadn't even seen the stately pile, so instead of turning towards the gates she continued straight on, following a huge beech hedge until we suddenly emerged into open space. My first view of the house in the improving light caused me a sudden intake of breath: I hadn't realised just how grand and overbearing the hulking edifice that was Lord Henry Wychwood's home would be. Annabel stopped the car. There was a large fountain comprised of a centrepiece of four stone horses rearing and spewing water from their mouths into a great round basin, around which the driveway circled. Wide steps up from the driveway led to a tall, six-pillared portico that sheltered the front entrance. The central part of the house, onto which the portico had been added, was built of stone and the wings were of brick, rather like Clifton's house; however, there the resemblance ended. I counted eight tall, small-paned windows on the ground floor, four each side of the entrance, each guarded by an ornate iron grille, and nine on the floor above. The roof was hidden by a parapet wall, but clumps of very tall chimneys were visible even at such close quarters. The driveway was bordered by neatly kept lawns that had been landscaped in banked terraces that rose to meet the dense surrounding woods. There, thick tree roots laced and twisted the green sward like gnarled old hands gripping velvet cloth. Sculptures of various mythical creatures presented in well-trimmed topiary arbours punctuated the dew-laden open space, placed seemingly at random. The overall effect was impressive, yes, and intimidating, but also somewhat unreal, as if the house and grounds belonged to a different world.

"Miniscule," I said. "The word 'shoebox' comes to mind. Very disappointed." Annabel gunned the engine and took the Land Rover around the fountain and back down the drive towards the road.

The field where everyone was parking had filled up, and although the sky was overcast the proceedings were now illuminated by the full light of morning. Horseboxes had been emptied and everyone was heading on foot towards an open gate into another field. We parked and followed the crowd. At the gate, I was stopped by an elderly man wielding a biscuit tin with intent.

"Good morning," he said.

"Good morning."

"I don't know you, do I?"

"I'm with Annabel," I said, looking at Annabel and then back at the man.

He screwed his face up for a moment and then shoved the tin at me. "It's 50p," he said.

In the field the riders had mounted up and were cantering towards the gate on the far side. The ground was soft and muddy, and I was grateful for Clifton's wellingtons, which I had borrowed and were not a bad fit. I could see lots of people and horses gathered beyond the next hedge.

"An important tip for complete townies," Annabel said as we approached. "Don't stand behind the horses, especially if they have a ribbon in their tail." I was about to ask for an explanation when a woman in a tweed suit and wearing a head scarf, who was walking a few yards in front of me, lost her footing. I found myself instinctively leaping forward to help her, and caught her arm before she went down, skidding a little myself in the process but carrying it off in the end.

"Thank you," she said. She must have been in her early forties, but her outfit suggested she was of an older vintage. She paused, collecting her thoughts and looking me up and down. "Would you mind hanging on, just until we get to the gate?"

"Of course not, it will be a pleasure. It's a bit treacherous, isn't it?"

"Oh, I'm quite used to it really. I just like having a handsome young man on my arm." She smiled. "Cecilia," she said, holding out her free hand. I thought for a moment she was expecting me to kiss it.

"Aunt Cissy," Annabel said, catching up and neatly taking the outstretched arm in her own. "This is Nick Carpenter, one of Clifton's rellies, and it's no use at all you flirting with him because he's with me today."

Cecilia and Annabel both had the same big eyes, and they both had the same sharp jawline as Henry. "You can't be Annabel's aunt!" I said quickly.

Cecilia laughed, not at all taken in by my flattery. "I'm Henry's much younger and much better looking little sister," she said. "So I am, I'm afraid." The smile her laughter had left on her lips lingered. "So you're the eligible bachelor who's staying at St Dunstan's. Oh yes, we know all about you. Belle has been talking you up with all the local girls. She's become quite the matchmaker now she's brought down her own quarry."

"Nick knows about all that, don't you Nick? He's coming to the Hunt Ball."

"They may just eat you alive. Fresh meat, you see."

"You're not riding today?" I asked Cecilia.

"Evasive subject change, deftly done, and not without charm. Bravo." She observed me with her head on one side for a moment, and then shook her head quickly. "No, I don't ride any more. Used to once upon a time, but I broke my back, I'm afraid, in a fall."

"I'm so sorry to hear that."

"It broke my heart too. Horses were my first true love. It was a jump I'd taken a hundred times before. I can only think that it was the evil fairy's curse."

When we went through the gate into the next field I was surprised to see as many as forty riders there, ranging from the hunt officials to the mounted followers, who included Clifton and a wide variety of other tweedy folk and pony club members. They were slowly milling around on horseback, chatting and taking drinks and snacks that were being offered by staff from the Hall. The hounds were being kept away from the horses for now in a far corner. The hunt supporters, of whom there may have been as many as a hundred, were mostly gathered in knots at the periphery of the mounted group, watching the proceedings and enjoying their own drinks and snacks from Thermos and Tupperware, except for a privileged few who it appeared were permitted to mingle between the horses.

Annabel and Cecilia led me straight into the equestrian melee. When Annabel let go of her arm to stop and speak to someone, Cecilia seized the opportunity to drag me away. I craned back, trying to catch Annabel's eye, but to no avail. "Let me introduce you to a few people," Cecilia was saying. "The etiquette is to say good morning. Had you got that? After that you can say what you like. There's usually plenty of gossip, which I freely admit is my principal pleasure at these events these days..." She spotted Henry and made a beeline for him, pulling me with her before I could say anything.

"Good morning, Master," she said formally and took the bridle of his huge stallion, patting it firmly on the shoulder. Henry turned and looked down his nose at her, whereupon she introduced me. He treated me with a blank look, as if we had not met earlier, and with the same perfunctory courtesy. Then he briefly turned his attention back to his sister. "Another young friend, Cissy?" There was no time for her to reply: with a short surge, his horse bore him away from us.

Cecilia turned to me. "I'm so sorry," she said.

"Not at all. I was flattered."

She spent a moment weighing me up unguardedly, and then smiled. "Possesses more charm than is good for him. Good liar. Calm in a crisis. Possibly quite dangerous."

While my attention had been on Henry, Annabel had somehow conjured up a staff member with a bottle of port and some silver stirrup cups on a tray. At that time of day, and after a bad night's sleep, the thought of drinking anything alcoholic was less than appealing; indeed, I wasn't keen on drinking port at any time of day; but I couldn't help worrying that I might be committing a terrible faux pas by refusing: everyone seemed to be taking hunt etiquette very seriously. Following her lead I picked up one of the stirrup cups, each of which had the ugly head of a different fantastic creature on the base, and righted it, holding it while it was filled.

"Death to the evil fairy!" Annabel and Cecilia said together.

"Happy hunting!" I replied, and swallowed down the contents in one, placing the cup back on the tray upside down. There was time after that only for Annabel to introduce me to Lucinda and Henrietta, two identical-looking women with big front teeth who had drawn up their mounts side by side and were apparently childhood friends of hers, before Henry made a speech. Everyone stopped and listened intently except for Cecilia, who whispered comments in my ear throughout, some of which were helpful embellishments and some rather less helpful but more amusing observations about her brother and the people he mentioned. In speaking, Henry was nothing like the haughty grandee I had encountered earlier. He was authoritative, yes, but he seemed kindly and approachable. He made a few jokes, introduced the hunt officials, and then, with brisk efficiency, gave a clear and comprehensive outline of the plans for the day that would have done credit to a three-star general. Finally, and with convincing sincerity, he thanked the various people who had contributed. By the time he had finished I felt that I knew everything, even though the names of the places he had mentioned were meaningless to me and the identities of the hunt officials had slipped out of my head almost as soon as they had arrived there.

The crowd began to move away, making room for the riders to turn their mounts and make their way to the gate. I lost Annabel and Cecilia for a moment in the melee, had to take several quick paces backwards to avoid being knocked over by an anxious horse, and then caught sight of Annabel again a small distance away talking urgently to her father. She was very much in her element: I could see how happy and relaxed she was despite her bad back; much more relaxed, in fact, than I had ever seen her. She had a way with horses: her father's enormous steed was oblivious to the excitement around him due to her absent-minded caresses.

She came over. "Come on then: let's go over by the gate and see the hounds out."

We somehow managed to find a place right by the gatepost. The hounds shouldered by us and padded out through the gate looking lean and hungry, accompanied by some riders, who Annabel said were the huntsman and the two whips. I guessed at thirty-seven hounds, but Annabel insisted that there were forty. "We say twenty pairs," she said. The huntsman led them off at a trot in the direction of a small copse at the bottom of a steep slope. Henry followed through the gate with the remaining riders behind him.

"Right," Annabel said, "A quick jog up the hill and then we'll have a perfect view."

I was out of breath by the time we got to the top, but Annabel had somewhat surprisingly taken the climb in her stride. The vantage point gave me a three-hundred-and-sixty-degree view of the surroundings. Down in the valley the hounds were swarming around the trees and bushes, egged on by the huntsman who was calling instructions in a strange language: "Leu-in try. Leu-in"; and sounding short, encouraging notes on his hunting horn. The whips had stationed themselves so that they could see both sides of the copse. The other riders were watching, chatting quietly, and offering each other drinks from their hip flasks.

"They'll all be pissed," I said.

"It has been known." Annabel produced a flask of her own, which she unstopped and offered to me.

"Annabel!"

"Don't you think it's time you called me Belle?"

"Belle. Okay. What is it?"

"Port with a touch of brandy. Strictly for medicinal purposes, of course. Dulls the pain. Go on, Nick. Don't be a stuffed shirt."

Still feeling the shock of my encounter with my pursuers I didn't need any more encouragement to take a good, long

155

pull. After a while there was some excitement among the hounds: several of them emerged from the copse sniffing the ground and one of them howled. This leading group loped off, giving out high-pitched squeals and whines of excitement, and the other members of the pack streamed after them. The huntsman was calling something new, which sounded like "Huick tew-im," and then "Harrk foorrard." He rode off with the hounds, with the whips alongside. There were cries of "Hulloa!" and "Gone away!" from the other riders, and at the signal of the huntsman's horn they were also on their way, with Henry in the lead.

"They've got it. Come on." Belle led me off on a hike down the hill.

"Where to now?"

"It's a five-minute walk, but we need to be quick."

"What about your back?"

"I'm practically floating. It's fine."

We followed the hedge along the side of a field and then negotiated a wobbly old stile and started to climb again under some overhanging chestnut trees, whose branches reached down over our heads like great spreading fingers. We came out into the open on a steep hillside that led up to a hawthorn hedge.

"Come on, look lively!" Belle said, taking the slope in long strides as if it wasn't there. At the top we followed the hawthorns to the left, crossed another stile, and found ourselves rewarded with a magnificent vista of countryside bursting with vivid oranges, reds and greens. Belle pointed out the manor house and the field where we had parked. They were a surprisingly long way away. So, too, was the hunt. She read my mind. "Don't worry," she said. "They'll come this way in a minute or two. Trust me."

I followed her down a steep slope until we reached another hedge, and climbed over a gate. "This is the spot," Belle said firmly, stopping.

I caught my breath, hands on my knees. "How do you know they're coming this way?"

"Shhh!"

The slope continued before us for a while and then levelled into a narrow valley that was prime grazing land. At the heart of the valley was a dense clump of bushes and trees growing around a chalky knoll and surrounded by a thick fringe of dry bracken. "Look there. That's Compton's. One of the most famous coverts in the county. That's when we used to hunt properly, of course."

From our vantage point we could see the hounds emerge over the crest of the hill and stream down into the valley. Next came the riders: the huntsman and the whippers-in, and then Belle's father, and then, some way behind, the other riders in small clusters. The leading hounds were running with powerful assurance, only periodically dropping their heads to check the scent trail. They hurried along the length of the valley towards us, passing Compton's Knoll on the western side and running by without even acknowledging our presence. Just behind the leaders came a group of three. One of these turned its head suddenly, having caught wind of something as they came past the knoll, and changed direction sharply. The other two peeled off after it, yelping and whining, and in a moment all three were burrowing deep into the undergrowth the covert. The remaining members of the pack, arriving, followed suit. The leading hounds turned and hurried back to join the others.

"What's going on?"

Belle's eyes were shining with excitement. "They've found something in there."

"Oh my God! A fox? That's not supposed to happen."

She made no reply. The huntsman galloped up to the knoll, blowing long, even notes on his horn that had no apparent effect on the hounds. Reining to a halt, he began to shout and crack his whip, but still the hounds did not emerge. The two whippers-in joined in, raising quite a din. Then Belle's father arrived and, halting alongside the huntsman, leaned in for a conversation that resulted in even more shouting and whip-cracking, but all in vain: the pack was out of control.

Suddenly there was baying and yammering from the bushes, followed by a high-pitched squealing.

"They've got it!" Belle said, grabbing my arm.

More of the riders caught up and came to a stop, forming up in a wide arc behind the Master, mounts facing the disturbance in the covert. The squealing mounted in volume and pitch and the bushes began to shake. Tails and hindquarters emerged, followed by muscling, tugging shoulders and heads yanking and pulling this way and that.

"Oh no, they've got something alright." I said, but Belle was too caught up in the moment to even know I was there. Her fingernails were digging into my arm through my coat. There was more tugging and jostling of black, white and tan as the pack emerged, tails in the air, many jaws locked firmly onto the limbs and flesh of something thin and grey and hairless that twisted and kicked and shrieked.

"Oh Jesus! What is that?" I moaned. The hounds on the fringe of the frantic melee were trying desperately to push in to reach the centre, whining with excitement while their prey gibbered and screamed. The huntsman dismounted and edged carefully towards the rioting pack, leaning in to get a better view. When he did get a good look, he stared for a long moment and then took a few quick steps backwards.

At that moment there was a long, thin scream that cut off suddenly. After that, the urgency of the hounds quickly abated. The huntsman stepped forward again to look, and then turned and gestured, and the Master dismounted and walked over to join him.

They did not interrupt the hounds, which carried on in a more leisurely, almost casual way with their pulling, ripping, and tearing. Some lost interest and wandered off, and then came back again for more. It was a long process. I spent a good deal of that time looking at Belle, whose rapt attention was fixed upon the gruesome events unfolding in the covert. Cheeks flushed, tiny nose wrinkled, teeth bared, she was like a savage at a cannibal feast.

At last, the frenzy over, the huntsman stepped in between the few remaining hounds and, picking up several indistinct objects, placed them somewhat gingerly into a bag. Mounting up, he sounded his horn and as easily as that the hunt was on the move again, the hounds resuming their mindless pursuit along the scent trail that had been laid that morning, the huntsman and whippers-in on their tails, and the Field spreading out behind.

Belle had not released my arm throughout the entire episode. We stood together and watched them pass from our vantage point. No-one looked at us; not even Clifton who was huffing and puffing at the tail end on an under-powered mare. I felt drained and nauseous.

"Belle, what was that? The thing they killed."

"That was a fox, Nick. An old one, I think. And mangy." She produced the flask. "Feeling a bit woozy? Here."

I took it and swallowed a couple of long gulps. She was right: it made me feel less nauseous, but it didn't change what I saw: that thing the hounds had torn bloodily apart was not a fox. Not. A fox.

Belle grabbed my hand. "Come on, Nick!" she said, "Follow me!" She pulled me along and I followed her back up the hill at a breathless pace. "Come on!" she shouted when I flagged, and I was somehow dragged into the moment and her mood. We ran pell-mell down into the next valley, laughing. At the bottom there was a path leading into a grove of ancient beech trees, which she took.

The foliage high above our heads was in the process of turning from lustrous green into vivid orange. The ground was covered with last season's dead leaves, with only a few early arrivals from above flecking the rotting brown with vivid red. It was strangely silent beneath the technicolour canopy: no birdsong, no scuffling of squirrels, no buzzing insects.

The leaves were a tad slippery underfoot. Belle halted, a little out of breath, and produced the flask from her pocket, taking a hefty swig. "Refreshment break," she announced, offering it to me.

"So how far is the next stop?" I asked, taking a mouthful and handing it back. There wasn't much left.

She ignored the question, apparently lost for a moment in thought.

I said, a little jokily: "Well, here we are, Belle. Just you and me. All alone. All alone, lost in the deep, dark wood."

She looked up at me, her chin tilted. "Yes," she said. The air between us suddenly felt thick with meaning. As if cued by an unseen director, a songthrush started warbling prettily.

"Not really," I said. "I bet the woods are swarming with people. The hunt…"

"They won't be coming through here."

I walked slowly over until she was very close. She was putting the flask back in her pocket when I reached out and pulled her to me. I kissed her, and she responded readily, greedily. She tasted of boarding school secrets, gymkhana, bloodlust. I couldn't stop. At last, grasping the lapels of my jacket suddenly, she pulled back and caught my eyes in a direct and unwavering gaze. We had crossed a line together and we both knew that nothing now could stop it. "I am feeling so fucking horny, Nick," she said, grinning like a devil, and the delicious vulgarity of it shocked me. "I want you to fuck me. Right here. Right now."

"You planned this, didn't you? There's nothing wrong with your back…"

"Shhh!" She let go of my jacket with her right hand and slid it slowly down my chest. "You and me…" Her hand continued until it found the buckle of my belt, delved farther. "All alone…"

"Lost…" I breathed.

She leaned forward to kiss me, but when I responded she bit my bottom lip almost hard enough to draw blood. "Lost," she continued, "In the deep, dark… the deep, dark wood…"

Chapter 26: *A Letter From Mrs Gladys Rudkin*

Dear Mr Peachey,

I write in response to your advertisement in Far Horizons magazine seeking true accounts of sightings of fairies. I cannot say that I have seen one, but thirty years ago I did have a strange experience in which you may be interested. I was on my way home from lunch at my aunt's house in Snedley on a quiet Sunday afternoon in July with my sister, aged seven. I was thirteen at the time. It was a pleasant walk across the downs that we had undertaken many times before, the sun was shining, and we were following a well-worn path and talking away happily. We were very close, and prone to becoming engrossed in our own little world when playing games, and we were little more than half way through our journey when I realised that the path had taken us away from our normal route and that we had entered a wood of oak, alder and hazel trees that did not look at all familiar. As I was trying to get my bearings my sister remarked that she felt suddenly cold, and I realised that the temperature had indeed dropped uncomfortably by several degrees.

I knew that we could not be far from our way and, since I could not tell what direction the path was taking us in, I resolved that we should retrace our steps until we were in the open and I could find the right track again. We were both amazed to find that when we looked behind us the path, which we had thought to be clear and well-used, petered out after only a few yards. Casting about did not pick up any further trace of the route we had followed. At that point I did not yet feel lost, but I did have a vague sense of unease that I took care to try not to transmit to my sister. We attempted to pick our way back in the direction we had come anyway, but we quickly discovered such a proliferation of brambles and low thorn bushes that it was quite impossible to progress that way. Indeed, it was soon apparent that the only direction in which it was possible to progress was the direction in which the path wanted to take us.

We followed it with growing reluctance as it took us deeper into that wood, which was becoming darker and more dense with every step. There was no birdsong and even our footsteps failed to carry any sound. We tried to continue our jolly conversation from before, but we were distracted and our words fell flat. When at last we came to where another footway crossed the path, we were both relieved and took the left turn in the hope that this new direction, which felt right, would lead us out into the sunlight. However, the new path came to an abrupt halt after about thirty yards, ending in a small loop, and when we investigated we found that the same was true of its sister turning on the right.

Forced back onto the main path, I was now feeling seriously rattled, and my sister had fallen silent, which was most unlike her, and had taken tight hold of my hand for comfort. After several twists and turns that made me feel even more lost and confused than before we arrived before a five bar gate, behind which the shadowy shape of a cottage could be made out in the gloom. I recall the landscape had changed to towering fir trees around us, and the building itself having an air of long neglect, although I did not think it was abandoned. I was on the point of going in and asking for help when my sister began to cry and to keep her spirits up I said: "Don't worry darling Sis, it is only the fairies playing a game with us."

As if a veil had been lifted, the sun came through the branches overhead, and the five bar gate was revealed to be nothing more than the branches of a fallen tree. There was no cottage beyond it, and when I looked down at the path I was able to follow it with my eyes quite clearly in both directions. A songthrush burst into joyful song at that moment, and after that we soon found our way home.

I have walked that route many times since and I have never again been able to find where we left the way that day, or the location of that oppressive wood. I am not a great believer in the supernatural, but I can tell you that my sister and I both feel we were under an enchantment of some kind that was broken only by chance when, in attempting to comfort her and make the situation lighter, I happened to mention the fairies. I do not know what might have happened had I not had the fortune to do so.

Yours sincerely,

Mrs Gladys Rudkin, June 18 1896

Chapter 27: *The Worst Kind of Rival*

"Hazel is not at home. Please leave your name and number and she'll get back to you, unless your name is Nicholas Carpenter, in which case…"

"Hello Hazel."

"This really is Hazel's voicemail. She's not picking up her messages right now… What do you want?"

"Did you get 'The Haunted Hunt'?"

"I did. Tell me right now: where on Earth are you getting it all from?"

"Here and there."

"No you're not. Please tell me."

I kept quiet.

"I'll hang up on you."

I said nothing, knowing it was an empty threat.

"It's a breadcrumb trail. I'm like a little sparrow hopping along, pecking up the morsels. But what's at the end of it?"

"Hansel and Gretel find their way out of the woods?"

"They didn't. They nearly got eaten. No, it's for luring a poor little bird hungry for breadcrumbs further in, isn't it?"

"At least they were together."

"They were brother and sister, Nick. What's your point?"

"I'm very hurt that you prefer Walter Peachey to me. Perhaps I won't send you any more."

"Oho! Are you jealous? He's only been dead for seventy five years."

"That's the worst kind of rival."

"True enough! There's no contest, I'm afraid. It's Walter Peachey for me."

"Alright. If he's so great, how come I'd never heard of him?"

There was a tinkle of laughter.

"Hey!" I said.

"Okay. In fairness, I've only just discovered him myself. Well, he was clever, for one thing. A real polymath. Writer, scientist, historian. The thing he's best known for is the Stoney Down fairies."

"Stoney Down?"

"Yes. Well, one day he just up and announced to the world that he'd encountered a troupe of faerie-folk on Stoney Down. There was a lot of hysteria about fairies and the supernatural at the time, and some prominent people were wrapped up in it, and, anyway, he had a lot of people convinced. He claimed the fairies took him through a secret door in the hill into their… timeless halls, I think he called them. The descriptions he gave were all very elaborate: marble pillars, fountains, tapestries, a library of books in strange languages, a great stone table upon which food appeared by magic. Pure pastiche, the critics said. There was an attempt on the part of the… er… fairy enthusiasts to find the evidence to support his story. They crawled all over Stoney Down, but no-one could find a fairy doorway into the hill or anything else, and so it all fizzled out."

"Well that is sexy. Phew! I can see why you prefer him to me."

"You wouldn't understand."

"Thanks. Well, I can't hang about on the phone all day listening to you drooling over other men. I've got…"

"No, you can't go until you tell me where you're getting it all from. I have to know."

"I miss you."

"Nick!"

I hung up.

It was *working*.

Chapter 28: *No Sign of a Scar*

We stepped inside my flat and I closed the door. Belle and I found ourselves standing face to face in the hallway. She adopted an amused smile. "You're looking at me as if you don't know what happens next," she said.

"Sorry. Come in. Come in and I'll open a bottle of something. What would you like?"

"No, that's not it."

"It isn't? Okay, how about a cup of tea?"

"Oh Nick! Come here!" She took a step forward so that we were nearly touching, and then we were lost in each other so completely that there was no room for anything besides Belle and I in the entire universe.

Later we lay in bed with the covers kicked back, side by side, slick with sweat, not touching, too exhausted after our exertions to move. We lay there for a long time without speaking. It was true: I was falling for her. I wanted to tell her how I felt, but before I could find the right words she gave a comedy groan and croaked: "Nick... need water... dying of... thirst..."

"Coming up!" I found myself saying with too much alacrity, and then I was up and moving. I came back with two glasses of bottled water from the fridge and touched one to her back to make her jump. She shrieked and twisted round. "You...!" she said. Her breasts were small and pointed, her nipples a gorgeous pink. She took the glass and drank greedily, and then I nestled in beside her. "So you're taking me to the Hunt Ball," I said into the nape of her neck.

She craned round to give me a smile loaded with mischief. "I told you: I'm going to find you the woman of your dreams."

"What if I've already found her?"

"You mean me, of course. Well yes, that does set the bar rather high."

"What makes you think I mean you?"

She gave me a haughty look and looked away, slowly.

"I do mean you," I conceded.

"You're very pretty, Nick. You'll make some lucky girl a gorgeous husband."

"Are you really going to marry Clifton?"

"Of course I am. Don't be ridiculous!"

"Don't marry him."

"Stop it."

"We could run away together…" I suggested.

"No we couldn't."

"Why not?"

"Poor Nick," she said. "Cuddle up to me."

I did, and there were long minutes of drifting in and out of drowsy sleep.

"Your mother told me lots of interesting secrets."

"Really?"

I could hear the smirk in her voice. "Like the time you caught your willy in the zipper in your jeans and they had to take you to hospital."

"Oh my God! I hate her!"

"Did you really set fire to her favourite china doll in the garden when you were five?"

"Yes I did. That doll was evil. It had to go."

"Mm. She said you're still Mummy's little boy, and if you don't get your own way you have a huge tantrum and throw things around."

"Also true. I'm still only two years old. Didn't you know?"

"Nick. I have inspected your anatomy all over very closely, and I can testify that you are definitely not." She

168

giggled. "Also, you'll be pleased to hear there is no sign of a scar."

"Ha bloody ha. I'm still a bad loser though. Are you sure you won't run away with me?"

"Perfectly sure, thank you." There was silence again, and then she said: "It's such a shame you don't ride. You could join the hunt."

"It may have escaped your attention, but I don't think your father took to me particularly."

"I'm sure I can talk him round."

I didn't reply. After a long moment she sighed. "You have such beautiful eyes," she said. "You look as innocent as a china doll."

"It's all a front. I'm actually an evil genius plotting the end of the world."

"Really? Go on, what's your evil plan?"

"Kill everyone with giant robots leaving you and me sunning ourselves together in a tropical paradise somewhere."

"Now you've spoiled it. And you were doing so well." She kissed me on the forehead and turned away again. There was another long silence, this time not entirely comfortable.

"You know when we were watching the hunt," I said. "What was that thing the dogs got hold of in the bushes?"

"Hounds."

"What?"

"They're not dogs. They're hounds."

"Hounds then."

"I told you."

"You told me it was a fox."

"Yes. Duh! That's because it was a fox."

"It wasn't. I saw it."

She was silent.

169

"It was a weird looking thing, like a monkey or something. It was grey and had long legs and arms. And it was screaming. Words."

She squirmed round to face me again. "Don't be silly, Nick." There was an amused smile on her lips, but her eyes were dead like a poker player's.

"I saw it," I insisted.

More silence. Then she sat up suddenly. "I really have to go now," she said, "Or I'll be late."

"Don't go," I said, but she had already swung her legs over the side of the bed and was on her way to the bathroom. While she was gone I lay on the bed looking at the ceiling. I knew then I wanted her more than I had ever wanted anything in my life. I listened to her pee and flush the toilet, and then run the taps. After a while she came back in wearing my bathrobe, which had never looked as good on me, and bustled around picking up her expensive underwear from where it had been abandoned on the floor. Then she tossed my bathrobe aside and dressed in front of me, apparently at ease with my silence. When she had finished dressing, she deftly applied makeup, peering into the mirror on top of my chest of drawers.

"Mirror, mirror on the wall…" I said.

Belle's reflection narrowed its eyes at me. "Evil stepmother is definitely not me, Nick." She primped her hair. "I'm a princess."

Then, suddenly, she was ready to leave. I reclaimed my bathrobe from where she had discarded it and put it on. "Was it the robots or the tropical island?" I asked, walking with her to the door. Belle didn't reply.

Before she left we held each other and I kissed her gently under her ear. "When will I see you?" I said, trying not to sound plaintive.

She gave me a big smile. "At the ball, Prince Charming."

Chapter 29: *The Journal of Davey Bone*

Sunday 20th June 1779

To church this morning, though I could think of little else but my dream of the night before and the fortune in ancient gold that had been promised to me. As I muttered my prayers I was at the same moment contriving how I might complete my own part of the bargain by gaining access to the house to set the fire and somehow securing the doors and windows to prevent any from escaping. It would be simple enough, I thought cheerily to myself, to choose an hour of the day when all must be trapped within. As the service wore on, however, the zeal with which these bloodthirsty notions continued to present themselves in my mind made me at first uncomfortable and then, in that consecrated place, so distressed that I could barely follow the service and I remained standing when all sat down for the sermon until my wife tugged upon my coat and brought me to my senses. After that I sat quietly and listened, and I am glad to say that the more I did so the calmer my thoughts became and the more I came to feel like myself.

Since then, as the day has progressed, I have become stronger and more able to know my own mind, although having none I may talk with upon the vexed subject has been a sore hindrance, for without the spur of company my thoughts generally follow one another as slowly as a train of mules. The words have warmed themselves upon the tip of my tongue ready to depart upon the short journey into the ear of a ready listener only to be stopped cold more than once, for who would hear the tale and not think me mad? Only my dear wife, in whom the Cardinal Virtues have an enduring home and who I should not wish to weigh down or discomfit further with such troubles; not for the wealth of kings.

Indeed I am mad, if madness is engaging wilfully with those things we are taught to fear because they defy God's laws and the teachings of the Church; mad, if madness is to commit oneself to felony punishable by death for no better reason than a dream of riches never seen and likely never to be delivered, ending priceless lives out of petty and selfish greed. In my dream it seemed but a small thing: among those timeless creatures the destruction of an entire forest was as nought, and so how little meaning there was in the passing of a mere house and its occupants, the span of whose lives counted as little as those of insects and might be as easily crushed out and as soon forgotten.

In truth, it wears ill indeed with me that I am become, albeit through my own foolishness, the servant of unseen masters whose purpose is obscure and whose methods savage. I have been possessed by the sin of greed and carried to the brink of damnation, for what is this pact if not a pact with the Devil that shall earn me eternal flames in the pits of Hell in the hereafter?

And so I am resolved: I shall not do the deed and I shall face the consequences as a man and try henceforth to be worthy of a place in Heaven.

Chapter 30: *That Night I Dreamt*

That night I dreamt of Belle. In the dream I was in my childhood bedroom, or somewhere that felt like my bedroom, anyway, and suddenly she was standing there in an elegant, flowing black dress. There was an aura around her, as if she had been backlit with a spotlight, and her arms were outstretched in front of her in offering, hands cupped together. She lifted them towards me, inviting me to look, and slowly opened them. Pale slivers of light escaped the cracks between her fingers, joining and expanding until there was a shivering ball of soft radiance resting upon her open palms; at the heart of which was a tiny figure like an illustration from a Victorian children's book of fairy tales: a beautiful woman with wings like a butterfly's, her translucent form revealing the source of the light to be her tiny, beating heart.

It was like looking directly into a candle's flame, and I fought the instinctive urge to look away so that I could take in as much as I could of the minute details. Dressed in a simple white dress, belted at the waist, bare footed, the fairy was slowly looking about it, its face a picture of innocent curiosity. It wore finely twisted bands of gold about its neck and wrists, and its hair fell loose to its shoulders and seemed to shine of its own accord.

I looked up into Belle's face, and she looked searchingly into my eyes. "It's beautiful!" I said. She smiled, and her eyes travelled back down to her hands. I followed her gaze to find her fingers closing over the glowing fairy. "Wait!" I said. "I want to see!" Her smile broadened and her eyes opened a little wider, and she tightened her grip, squeezing and then brutally crushing. "Stop!" I shouted. The light between her fingers was flickering, fading away. "Stop! You're killing it!"

Belle began to work and rub her hands together, and a light dust escaped from between her fingers, spilling in tiny, luminous clouds onto the ground.

Chapter 31: *Business Expenses*

"No thank you, Nicholas. No tea. No coffee. Nothing." Mother held up her hand. "I just want to know what the Hell is going on." She was sitting in the living room of my flat, having arrived without warning and so early in the morning that I had been obliged to answer the door in my dressing gown.

"Well I'm putting the kettle on," I said. "I need caffeine. Can I get you a mug of hot water, perhaps? I'll just throw some clothes on, won't be a…"

"I don't have time for all that," Mother snapped. "Come and sit down. Now, please tell me: what exactly is happening with the community centre development."

"We haven't exchanged yet."

"You've pulled out. I found out from Annabel."

"Yes. It was the right decision."

"And when were you going to tell me? Really, Nicholas, you might have consulted me about it first."

"I've only just instructed Wyn." Wyn was our family solicitor. "What chance does that give me to discuss it with you?"

"You had time to discuss it with Annabel. Anyway, You're missing the point. I expect you to discuss these sorts of decisions with me before anything happens."

"Well it's not as if it was debatable. There was a massive protest, the council was wobbling about it, and we were never going to get the planning permission through. We had to get out before we exchanged contracts and Wyn is going to try to get some compensation out of the council, which is about the best we can hope for."

"Why was I kept in the dark about this?"

"You weren't kept in the dark! There was no time. It's not my fault. I had to act quickly. We were going to exchange."

"I've spoken to Wyn, so I know exactly what happened." Wyn, the treacherous bastard who didn't call to warn me.

"Then he must also have told you he's confident we're going get our costs reimbursed. You really don't need to worry. I'm sorting it out."

"I hope so, Nicholas, I really do, but that is not the main issue." Mother leaned forward threateningly. "The fact is, I'm very disappointed in the way you have behaved. You have demonstrated that I can't trust you to do as I ask, and as a consequence I will have to take action."

"What are you going to do?"

"I haven't finished yet. Why is there so much cash being drawn?"

"Expenses. You know, architects, structural engineers, planning fees."

Mother looked at me incredulously. "They prefer to be paid in cash nowadays, do they? Nicholas, you draw a generous salary from the company. You have to live within your means."

"Business expenses." I said firmly.

"It's not good enough. Another reason why you've lost my trust. In the circumstances, you've left me no option. I am afraid I'm going to cancel your line of credit and call in my loan to your company."

I found myself on my feet again. "What?"

She smirked, her eyes gleaming.

"But how do you expect me to run a property development company with no funds?"

"You've left me with no choice. I won't have you taking silly risks with family money. I asked you to consult me, you decided you knew better. That is unacceptable."

"Don't you think this is a tiny bit of an overreaction?"

"Do sit down, Nicholas," she barked, and I sat down. "No, I do not. My mind is made up. I've been very foolish, supporting you when you need to stand on your own two feet." She took an envelope out of her handbag. "Seven days. That's how much notice the agreement requires. Seven days in writing." She put the envelope on the coffee table. "There. That's done."

"Please. I'll do whatever you want. I'm sorry, okay. I should have listened."

"It's a bit late for that now."

"Please?"

Mother stood up.

I stared at the envelope. "This is a business arrangement. I'm not a child. I won't accept it."

"Of course you will. In any case, I've lodged a copy with Wyn."

"You appreciate that if you do this you're putting an end to my career. What am I going to do?"

"There's no 'if' about it. And as for what you're going to do, well, I rather think that's up to you, Nicholas. You had better start with liquidating some assets so that you can pay me back."

"Fine. You know what? That's fine. I'll do that. Because then you won't be able to stick your nose in any more."

Mother thought about this for a moment, and discarded it. "You might think about getting a job," she said.

"Oh, for God's sake! Why do you have to be such a… such a…"

"Yes?" She held my gaze, goading me.

I couldn't muster any words. Mother smiled tolerantly. "I'm doing this for your own good." She moved towards the door gracefully, holding her handbag with two hands on the top edge.

I stepped in her way. She locked eyes with me and waited. There was a long moment of silent mental struggle, and then I stood aside and Mother continued down the hallway. Before leaving, she turned back and said: "I shall see you at the wedding. Please be on your best behaviour."

Chapter 32: *White Tie, Scarlet If Convenient*

The traffic in South London was bad, and by the time I arrived at St Dunstan's it was already late afternoon and Belle and Clifton had to go ahead to help with the preparations for the ball, leaving me to get ready on my own. I took much longer than I would care to admit: plucked eyebrows, ear and nose hairs, shaved, flossed and brushed my teeth, showered and washed hair, applied hair gel, applied aftershave, and polished my shoes. The invitation said: White Tie, Scarlet if convenient. I had no tails, but Belle had assured me that only the hunt officials bothered with it and that black tie would be perfectly acceptable. The final effect, appreciated by me in the bathroom mirror, was, I thought, as close to perfection as I would ever get. I hoped Belle would appreciate it.

I arrived at Wychwood Hall in a taxi cab, feeling slightly nervous. I was late, but although most people would have already arrived, there were still cars queueing in the driveway. The fountain was floodlit and on overdrive, virulently spouting into the air water enough to drown out the sound of crunching gravel, slamming car doors, and excited voices as others, who I didn't know, were dropped off around me in groups and couples. Reassuringly, the men were in black tie too.

Then I was at the grand front entrance, going in under the floodlit portico. Inside, beneath an impressively grand crystal chandelier, there was a line-up of hunt officials to meet and greet the guests, led by Belle's father, the Master of Foxhounds, in a scarlet swallowtail coat. Belle was there too, and once I saw her I lost interest in everything else. Wearing her hair up, she had on a long, black, sleeveless gown, and, curiously, seemed much taller and thinner than I had expected. She hadn't noticed me yet, and was busy laughing and chatting, glittering as she turned from one arrival to the next. Hardly conscious of my surroundings, I shuffled forward; and then, suddenly, Belle's father came into focus right in front of me. He was saying something, which I missed. I shook his proffered hand. "Thank you," I mumbled.

"I said," he replied firmly, leaning forward and not releasing my hand, "Be kind to Cissy. You understand."

The enormity of the misunderstanding hit me like a hammer, but it was no time for lengthy explanations. "Thank you," I said again. "Thank you." He let go. I moved forward, head spinning, and shook more hands without even taking in who I was meeting. Then I was waiting for the couple in front of me to finish their conversation with Belle, which seemed to take forever, and at last I had her to myself for a moment.

"Hello Nick," she said, and the peck on the cheek she gave me was only fractionally less warm than I had expected, but it set alarm bells ringing.

"You look utterly gorgeous."

"Thank you." She jokily struck a coquettish pose. Diamonds in her necklace and earrings flashed. "Clifton's already inside. He's keeping an eye out for you. I expect he'll be by the bar."

I took this to mean that she would be joining us when she had finished the line-up. "I'll see you later, then."

She flicked a glance up the line to see who else was coming. Then she met my gaze and her eyes were soft and warm. "Handsome boy," she whispered, and suddenly all was well again.

I took a glass of bubbly from a tray that was proffered at the end of the line-up and followed the other new arrivals down a long wood-panelled hallway to the right that was lined with dark family portraits until we suddenly emerged into an enormous marquee filled with raucous voices. To my left, under a ceiling of midnight blue that was illuminated with hundreds of fairy lights, the great tent stretched away containing what must have been thirty tables with bright white cloths, all set for a formal dinner, and each with a different elaborate centrepiece. There was a large chart set on an easel alphabetically listing the guests and their table number. Immediately in front of me was a dance floor with its own lighting rig suspended above it, and to my right was a long bar with seven or eight bartenders. Behind the dance floor was a small raised stage with an upright piano on it. Both the dance floor and the space in front of the bar contained a tight press of people dressed to the nines, all busy chatting and laughing, and more than anything, drinking.

I checked the chart: I was on table 27, which was at the far end. Belle and Clifton were both on the high table. I had been hoping, perhaps unrealistically, that Belle had engineered things so that I would be sitting next to her, and the disappointment hit me hard. In immediate need of a proper drink, I went in search of Clifton. Worming my way through the throng was not easy, and I didn't see a single face that I knew until I got all the way to the bar and found him perched precariously on a bar stool. He welcomed me with a bonhomie no doubt born of several preparatory gin and tonics. "Nicko! There you are! Welcome to the Hunt Bonk!"

"Hi Clifton." We shook hands. He hooked out a bar stool he had been hiding for me with his foot. "Thanks," I said, and then I noticed he had his big fist around the neck of a bottle. "What have you got there?"

"Brandy, old chap. Works a treat to perk up this filthy champers. Allow me." He took my glass from my hand and placed it on the bar. Then, stooping closely over it like a chemist, he poured brandy into it, sprinkled some sugar from a sachet, and then topped it up with champagne.

I took the glass from him. "Does it have a name?"

"Ah! Well, it's a stripped down champagne cocktail, I suppose, so how about... a Shamcock?"

I laughed. "You're a genius. Shamcock it is. Cheers!" We clinked glasses.

It drew the attention of two women who were standing next to us in the crush. One was tall and willowy, with short-cropped blonde hair and a square jaw. She rested her hand on Clifton's forearm, which had the effect of preventing him from raising his glass. "That looks interesting. What is it?"

Clifton shook his head. "I can't tell you that," he said. "It's only just been invented and... er... the patent is pending, you see. Top secret."

She pressed up against him. Her friend, who was shorter and more rounded, had sidled round to stand next to me. "Go on," the taller one said. "You can tell us, can't he, Helen?"

"Oh yes," Helen agreed in a squawky voice. "We're very trustworthy."

"Are you really?" Clifton leaned forward, eyeing them both beadily. "Alright then. It's called..." and here he paused, drawing them in, "...A sham-cock!"

They pulled back, laughing. Clifton roared too. "That's right, isn't it, Nick?" He turned his attention back to the tall woman. "What's your name?"

"Vicky," she said. "What's yours?"

"Tim," he said, giving me a sly wink. "Well, Vicky, would you... would you like a mouthful of my shamcock?"

She giggled. "Go on then. What's in it?"

"I can't say. Here you are."

She took the glass and sipped from it. "Oh, no. I don't like that." She gave Clifton his glass back, pulling a face. "Ooh no."

"Can I try yours?" Helen asked. Her plump hand was on my shoulder.

"Any time," I said, in the spirit of the moment.

She took the glass and sniffed the contents. "Uh-huh," she said, and then took a decent swig. "It's alright," she pronounced. "I'd drink it."

"What will you give me if I make you one?" Clifton demanded.

"How about a massage?"

Clifton's eyes bulged. "Now you're talking," he said. "Give me your glasses." We all complied, and he turned round to face the bar and began pouring furiously from the bottles behind him.

Vicky nudged my arm. "You're not from round here, are you?"

"No, I'm Tim's cousin. From London."

"It's alright," Helen whispered in my ear, "We know he's not really Tim."

"You do?"

"Oh yes. He's Doctor Prendergast. Everyone knows who he is."

Clifton turned around with two glasses in his hands. "One large shamcock for you," he said, handing Helen one of them, "And straight bubbles for you." Vicky took the second glass. Then he reached back, handed me a full glass, and raised his own. "Death to the evil fairy!" he said loudly, and the two women repeated it. "What's the matter, Nick?"

"That toast. What does it mean?"

"That's what we say. It's the hunt toast."

"That's right. Whenever anything goes wrong on the hunt, we blame the evil fairy." Vicky said.

"Now then," Clifton interrupted. "Someone owes me a massage. Shall we just slip away now..?"

"No need for that. We'll do it right here."

"Here?!" Clifton exclaimed with wide eyes.

"Yes. Now, give me your hand." Helen put her glass down, took Clifton's large, red hand with both of hers and steered it until it was resting palm upward on his knee. She began to knead it with firm fingers.

"Hey! What's this?" Clifton demanded.

"A hand massage," Helen replied, digging both thumbs into his palm.

"Ow! But that's not fair!"

While they wrestled, I realised just how much I had come to dislike Clifton.

"Now now." I said loudly. "No fighting, really! A gentleman never raises his hand to a lady."

"Do you want one?" Helen demanded obligingly, turning to me.

"Aha!" I announced, looking across to the entrance to the marquee from the house. "Here's your fiancée, Tim." Everyone looked, and there was Belle, arm in arm with one of the whipper-ins, who was in a red tailcoat like Belle's father. She was laughing at something he had said.

"Oh no," Vicky said, winking. "That can't be Tim's fiancée. That's Lord Wychwood's daughter Annabel. She's engaged to Doctor Prendergast."

"She's a lucky girl in that case," Clifton said quickly. "I heard he's got an enormous… er…"

"That's not what I heard," Helen said. "I heard it was tiny. Like a thimble."

"Yes, that's what I heard too." Vicky held up her little finger and wiggled it. "Teeny weeny."

The man Belle was with whispered something in her ear, and she smiled. I felt a pang of jealousy. Then she gave his arm a squeeze, and he went off in a different direction, leaving her to find her own way through the throng to the bar. I lost sight of her for a few moments. The women in the crowd were for the most part in dark-coloured low-cut sleeveless ball gowns with skimpy straps, but with the occasional brilliant crimson or sequinned number livening things up, and they fell into one of two categories: the more mature, wearing their hair up and sporting real diamonds; and excited young women with very high heels and enormous costume jewellery. The men, by contrast, were in black and white and distinguishable only by hairstyle, shape, and size, except for a very few in Highland dress or in scarlet. When Belle hove into view again she had made barely any progress and was conversing intently, apparently heedless of my impatience.

"To be honest, it's an easy mistake to make. He's a very handsome fellow as well," Clifton was saying. Belle must have felt my eyes upon her, because at that moment she turned her head and gave me a beautiful smile that was all for me. I held her gaze and sent her a telepathic message that went into graphic detail about what I wanted to do to her next time we were in bed. The message failed somewhere en route, and she turned away long before it could all have reached her, but I told myself not to worry: I would find another opportunity later.

It took another fifteen minutes for her to reach us at the bar, by which time Helen and Vicky had drifted away and Clifton was in the process of placing an empty plastic beer glass on the top of his head, which was the final stage of something we had become embroiled in with some Young Farmers.

"It suits you," she said, unfazed. "Hello boys. We're about to sit down for dinner. You can finish Colonel Puff later." Cowed, the Young Farmers mumbled together, then gathered up the pints of beer they had lined up on the bar and went off towards their table.

"Spoilsport," Clifton harrumphed. "Had 'em on the ropes, didn't we, Nicko?"

"You did," I said. "I was rubbish."

"You were a bit rubbish," he agreed. "It's a good job they were off their faces already or else we would have been in a spot of bother."

I turned to Belle. "You took your time getting here." I knew as soon as I had said it that it was too familiar, betraying a degree of intimacy that should not be there.

"I know you both missed me terribly." She had the unerring skill of always knowing the right thing to say to smooth things over. She didn't look at me.

"We did not!" Clifton said emphatically, having thankfully missed it. "Well, that is… I did. Nick was chatting up some girls."

"Were you indeed?"

"They were just being friendly. They went off with some chap called Tim to give him a massage," I said, watching Clifton squirm.

"Nice chap, Tim," he said under his breath. "Enormous… er… talent."

187

Chapter 33: *Not In Love*

We joined the people drifting towards the dining area, and, having received assurances from Belle that she had put me on a table with some lovely friends, we parted company and I struck out for the far corner. The large table decorations were on a hunting theme and consisted of flower arrangements among which cardboard riders in red jackets pursued their quarry. Some had butterflies floating on stalks above the riders. One had a flock of black birds made of tissue paper, and another large cardboard sun and moon cutouts. I didn't see a fox.

My own table was dominated by a display of twigs, grasses and flowers around which cardboard foxhounds, rendered by a variety of childish hands, were racing. The display was so large that I wouldn't be able to see the people on the other side of the table when I sat down.

I found myself standing next to Jenny-from-Oxford. She was tall and skinny with very long legs, big-boned, with very full lips, which I found it hard not to watch a little too closely when she was speaking. "No, I don't ride at all," she was saying. The tip of her pink tongue popped out nervously. "This is all…" She waved her hand around and giggled. "Don't tell anyone, but I don't even approve of hunting. I used to go out with this guy who was an anti-hunting activist. I mean a serious one. I can't even tell you what he used to get up to."

"If they find you out they'll probably chop you up and feed you to the hounds," I said, "But don't worry: your secret is safe with me."

"Well, thank you. My life in your hands and I've only known you two minutes."

"So what are you doing here?"

She shrugged. "Sounded like a laugh," she said. "I suppose I was curious to see if they all had horns."

"Do they?"

"Possibly. The jury's still out." She reached up and rubbed my head, checking. "You don't, anyway."

"Thanks." I combed my hair back into place with my fingertips.

"What about you?"

"Oh, I'm a complete townie. I don't even like horses. The countryside gives me the creeps. And I'm starting to think all these people do have horns, just like everything else around here. I like concrete and tarmac and glass and shops that are open when you want them."

A girl arrived at the table on my other side and tapped me on the shoulder. "Hello Nick," she said. She had big front teeth, dark hair and freckles, and was looking at me as if I ought to recognise her. I didn't.

"Hello."

"It's Henrietta. Belle's friend. We met at the last hunt meet."

"Oh yes," I said, pretending that I remembered. "At the hunt. Henrietta, this is Jenny-from-Oxford."

"Oh, we know each other already," Henrietta said with a short, insincere smile. "Jenny is one of Belle's *university* friends."

Fortunately, at that moment there was the tapping of a glass and then a voice that I recognised as Henry's boomed out from the PA system.

"Good evening, good evening. Please take your seats, if you would. Yes, that includes you, Tommo, if you please. Members of the hunt, official hunt followers, esteemed guests, my name is Henry, Lord Wychwood, and I am the Master of the Ashdown Bewick hunt. On behalf of the committee, I should like to offer you a very warm welcome to the annual Ashdown Bewick Hunt ball."

There was much applause and cheering in response. As Henry continued, Jenny whispered in my ear: "You don't look anything like Clifton."

"Well thank goodness for that!"

"Oh, no. He's much more handsome."

I shot her a look and she started laughing. "Just kidding," she said. "Your face was a picture, though. Don't worry, you've won the best-looking man contest hands down."

"Have I?"

She waved her hand around. "Not much competition around here. Anyway, you're cousins, aren't you?"

"Right. How do you…? Oh, Belle told you."

I had tuned out of what Henry was saying, but suddenly there was raucous laughter, and an enthusiastic round of applause. "Have you noticed how pissed everyone is already?" Jenny said, leaning over in order to be heard.

I nodded. "I'm a bit pissed myself," I said, and her hair brushed my cheek as I leaned in.

"…So the more you drink, the more support you are giving! I hope you have a wonderful evening." Henry sat down to more applause, and then conversation broke out like the waters of a dam bursting through a breach.

The serving staff brought out the food. The starter was duck and green peppercorn pate, served with French bread. Next there was roast beef, brought to each table as a joint and carved by one of the guests themselves, who had to don an apron and a hat of random variety: there were toppers and bowlers, chef's hats and riding hats, flat caps and even a motorcycle helmet.

Belle was sitting next to the man in the scarlet jacket I had seen her talking to earlier. They were laughing together in a way I really didn't like. She seemed to hang on every word he said, looking up at him like a spaniel. When I looked back a few minutes later they were still wrapped up in each other, now talking earnestly, heads close together. Clifton, sitting several places away, was talking away animatedly to others at the table and paying her no mind.

Jenny interrupted my surveillance. "This would be a perfect location for a haunted house movie, don't you think?"

"I've not really seen the inside." I said.

"Only there's no stuffed animals. I thought there'd be gruesome trophies everywhere, but there's nothing. Got to have animal heads mounted on the wall in a haunted house." The tent was getting hotter and hotter, the talk louder and louder. Despite my evident success with Jenny, I thought perhaps I would go outside and get some fresh air. Then I felt a hand on my shoulder and turned.

"Our charming eligible bachelor. I thought you might have come and said hello by now."

"Cissy! I've been looking for you everywhere!" I stood up.

"Silver tongue and brass neck," she replied. "But shame on me for wanting to believe you." She pecked me on the cheek. "How are you enjoying our little soiree?"

My tongue was not shaping my words with its usual effortless accuracy. "I've drunk too much and we haven't even finished dinner yet," I said. "I've met some new people. And your brother has already had a very stern word with me." I gave a half laugh to show that I didn't think it completely ridiculous. "He thinks we're an item."

She removed her hand. "I don't see what's so funny about that."

"Sorry, I didn't mean…"

"Got you back for being insincere." She smiled wryly and then frowned as her thoughts turned to Henry. "Has he, indeed? You leave that to me."

I bowed. "Of course."

"You're not in love with Belle, are you?"

The question jolted me sober. "Whatever makes you say that?"

"We've been seeing an awful lot of you. It made me wonder what the reason was."

"Belle's already spoken for."

"That dunce?" Then her scathing tone changed. "You're not denying it, then?"

"I do deny it."

"Good. I shall dance with you later. There's no escape."

"I shall look forward to it."

"There you go again."

Pudding was a choice of pavlova or cheesecake. After a spoonful or so of fruit and meringue I found I wasn't hungry any more. Jenny was engrossed with the man next to her, and Henrietta had gone wandering. Around me the conversation in the marquee was being conducted at maximum volume. Then, unexpectedly, everyone fell silent and stood up, so I did too. Jenny was alone in remaining in her seat. As I looked around I realised that all the guests were looking expectantly at the mayor. He raised his glass with a practiced hand. "The Queen," he said loudly. We followed suit, and then everyone swigged and took their seats again.

"I'm a republican," Jenny whispered as soon as I was back in my chair.

"Don't worry. I have a feeling there will be plenty more where that one came from," I said, and I was right. We toasted the farmers, and the hunt supporters, and the huntsman, and the whippers in, and the Pony Club, and the Young Farmers, until I lost track of who or what we were drinking to. At last Henry rose again. "It's time for our final toast," he said, "So if you will please stand." Many had anticipated the request and were already on their feet. "Death to the evil fairy!"

"Death to the evil fairy!" the guests intoned, and then they drank, and sat down. Immediately, the lights were dimmed, hushing everyone and causing a ripple of oohs and ahhs. There was a pool of light drenching the raised stage where the piano had been set up. Then a man dressed in a green and red Enid Blyton elf costume ran in, to immediate catcalls and a smattering of applause, and climbed up onto the stage, installing himself behind the piano in the spotlight. His eyes were smudged with heavy mascara, his mouth comically outlined with misapplied red lipstick. On his head was a green pointy cap with a bell at the end. He adjusted the microphone and smiled. "Good evening!" he said, and played an arpeggio. "I hope you are enjoying yourselves! Here's a little ditty that came to me when I was riding Mrs Carson out on the Downs." There was a silence, and then a few of people tittered. "Mrs Carson is a mare," he continued. There was more laughter, and then he added: "That's what her husband says, anyway." He played a few bars of introduction, and then broke into song, accompanying himself on the piano in a fair imitation of Noel Coward.

> *"Oh, how I wish that I could be a fairy.*
> *How I'd love to be a brownie queen.*
> *How gay to be a ghoulie, I long to be one, truly;*
> *Trick or treating folk at Halloween.*
> *You don't know how I ache to be a goblin,*
> *Down among the pansies in the grass.*

To ride astride a talking badger with a stripe upon his tadger
Would be a fable in a different class.
Once I took a jolly cruise by starlight,
Not knowing what adventures it might bring.
From behind a bracken frond a pixie waved his magic wand,
And invited me into his fairy ring."

He held the last note of 'ring' for an absurdly long time, jumping up an octave and then then down two.

"Oh, it must be nice to be a raving fairy.
It must be wiz to be a brownie queen.
If you're lacking in conviction or consider them a fiction,
You can always join the merchant marine."

He finished on two short chords. "Thank you very much." There was laughter and applause, and there were calls for more, but the man jumped up, bowed to the assembled company, and then ran out of the room. Next upon the stage was a comedy sketch performed with enormous enthusiasm by some of the Young Farmers. It contained a lot of in-jokes, which had some of the audience members and most of the cast bursting their sides with laughter, but which went over my head completely. When they had finished and enjoyed rapturous applause, the lights went up again. I looked over at Belle, to find her talking to her neighbour on the other side, the mayor; a small relief. The man in the elf outfit reappeared on the stage and settled behind the piano.

"Now it's time for Puck and the Huntsman. Most of you will know all the words by now, but if you don't then they're on the back of the menu cards on your tables. I want you to all join in, and let's see if we can sing the roof off this tent."

There were cheers. As he played the introduction, Jenny leaned in and said: "Do you know this?"

"Never heard of it. The tune sounds familiar, though." Out of the corner of my eye I saw Belle get up and edge out from behind the top table.

Chapter 34: *Puck and the Huntsman*

The Stoney Down huntsman was Trumpeter Jack;
As rosy dawn broke he unkennelled the pack;
Drawn from the covert the vixen did run -
Puck saw the chase and the chance of some fun.

Tantivy! Tantivy! The call of the horn!
They sailed over hedges and ditches that morn;
Hard on the scent until Puck waved his hand
And the horses and hounds set to dance l'Allemande.

Faster and faster in circles they stepped;
To see such cavorting a stone would have wept.
To whip and spur none of them paid any care,
Then the hounds and the horses flew up in the air!

Up through the clouds they continued their rounds;
If it wasn't for Jack they'd have left the world's bounds!
On his sweet-sounding horn our man winded a tune,
And the hounds and the Field made a turn round the moon.

Led by Jack's horn they swooped down to the ground;
And danced a light jig as they circled around.
Jack cast the hounds: though Reynard was long gone,
They sniffed out old Puck and the chase it was on!

Hark forward! Hark forward! Hark forward, away!
O'er hills, dales and valleys, if it takes all the day,
With a spring in our step and with fire in our eyes,
We'll bring down that Puck and assure his demise.

The zeal of the hounds it was quite unconfined;
  Soon the heat of their breath he felt on his behind!
He gave a great leap and a sky-rending wail,
  And all they were left with was Puck's pointy tail.

The Stoney Down huntsman is Trumpeter Jack,
  And thanks to his pluck, Puck will never come back.
So here's to his health with a flagon of ale!
  Now he carries a whip made of Puck's pointy tail.
  Now he carries a whip made of Puck's pointy tail.

Chapter 35: *The Journal of Davey Bone*

Monday 21st June 1779

How should a fool undo a bargain made with the Devil himself? Last night after all had gone to bed I thought to put the six gold pieces and the tinder box into a dish outside the kitchen door before retiring myself, in the unlikely hope that this may communicate my intention and indeed provoke some sign of acceptance; namely that in the morning these accursed objects should be gone and I should be free of my curse. That I expected little from this plan and was resigned to receive the vengeance of the faerie for my betrayal, in whatever shape that may take, you may be assured. It was a warm night and I could barely sleep, what with the stirring and snoring of Bone family members and the yelping of foxes and the like. I lay imagining writhing creatures of strange and terrifying aspect creeping around outside the walls of the inn and looking to find their way in, and every unfamiliar sound became testament to their sinister presence. What little sleep I did have was without dreams. I was up with the farmer before dawn and fearfully looking out upon the step to see whether my offer had been received. I was half expecting to find scratched signs of attempted entry upon the door and the marks of twisted limbs and claws upon the ground, but there were none: all was as I had left it, and, to come to the point, much to my disappointment the gold pieces and the tinder box remained undisturbed in any wise.

There being no other manner I could think of in which I might contact the donor of the coins and the box, fairies or no, I decided to continue to press my point in the same way, and so the dish and its contents remained upon the step all day, causing much inconvenience to the Bone family who were all forbidden the use of the kitchen door and the yard outside. By way of explanation I told them all I had put down poison for rats, and for this I received a mild rebuke from my dear wife who said, with excellent justification, that she had not been troubled by a rat around the place in years and that in any case there were better places to place a bait than upon the kitchen doorstep! In spite of the very little hope I had that the strategy would yield any result, I nonetheless checked at frequent intervals during the day. At around three o'clock in the afternoon I put my head out of the kitchen door only to find my little Lilly Grace sitting upon the doorstep and playing happily with the objects I had left there. She had laid all the coins out in a row and having discovered the sliding lid of the tinder box had removed it completely and was occupied in placing the coins one by one into the box and saying some such nonsense as: "One for Robin Goodfellow, two the fairy queen, three the sisters of the wood, four the prince in green…"

I confess that I shouted at her and reminded her had I not said there was poison laid there, and asked what did she think she was doing?! She was in tears immediately, and all I could get from her was that she had forgot. I was so angry that I lifted her bodily over the wall of the yard and sent her on her way and she ran off sobbing with her face in her hands with me shouting imprecations at her until she ducked under the bushes and was gone. I hastily rearranged the items on the step, although quite why I did so and what difference it made I know not.

Lilly Grace at supper seemed happy enough and conversed cheerily with her mother and siblings, although she made her protest by not speaking to me and I felt sufficiently ashamed of myself for the injustice of my actions earlier to allow her the satisfaction without rebuke. When it was late and shadows had chased the sun from the downs I thought to put out some warm milk in a dish beside the other to see if that would have any effect. It succeeded only in attracting a small hedgepig that I did not dare to frighten away, which simply ate with admirable industry and then went merrily upon its way, after which I continued to watch and wait fearfully, in terror of what must happen.

It is now after four o'clock as I write this. Midnight came and went without event, and I have spent the small hours wrestling with my understanding of what has happened. Could I have been mistaken? Were the dreams really encounters with the faerie folk, or were they, as I have already suspected and feared, my own imaginings, causes by a mind beset with a disease not yet manifest? Were the objects I found upon the step left there by a sprite, or was it more likely that they were placed there by someone as a jest, or, as seems ever more likely to me now that I have seen Lilly Grace making games with them, are they the found objects of a child, played with upon the step and then forgetfully abandoned? If so, then I am ashamed and affrighted by the wickedness of which my own mind is capable; the mission to burn down Wychwood Hall and murder all inside being plainly a twisted design of my own invention. I thank merciful God that I did not succumb to my own snare, and I pray with every fibre of my being that I have reached the end of this sad matter.

Chapter 36: *A Dreadful Stew*

I followed Belle out of the marquee and down the dim hallway. She heard my footsteps behind her and turned. I caught up with her and I pushed her into the dark recess of a doorway.

"Nick! Don't."

She didn't sound too displeased with what I was doing. "You've been avoiding me all evening," I said. "I need a kiss."

"Yes, but not now. Not here. This is really not the place. Nick, let me go."

"Just a kiss," I insisted, leaning in.

She pushed me away suddenly, glaring at me. "Nick!"

"What's all this?"

I turned my head to find Belle's father in the hallway behind me.

"Nick's not feeling well," Belle said in an even voice.

"Really? Look here, young man. I thought we had an understanding. Now I find you're making a regrettable nuisance of yourself. It won't do. Either go back to your table and behave yourself, or go home. Which is it to be?"

He was staring at me expectantly like an angry parent with a wayward teenager, and I had to resist the strong temptation to fall into my prescribed role and say something that I would undoubtedly later regret. "Thank you for your kindness and hospitality," I replied at last. "I'm sorry we've got off on the wrong foot. I hope we can put it behind us." I put out my hand to shake his, but he just looked down at it disdainfully and then marched off down the hallway into the house.

"What was that about an understanding?" Belle asked.

"For some reason he thinks I'm Cissy's latest boyfriend."

"Please tell me he's mistaken!"

"Of course he's mistaken!"

"Well why would he think that?"

I put my head in my hands. "It's just an awful mix-up," I said, and then looked up and grinned. "Are you jealous?"

She smiled coyly. "I may have been, for a tiny moment."

"I want you, very badly."

Her smile grew. "You're giving me naughty ideas," she said. "Look, I have some jobs to do right now. Why don't you go and sit with Clifton. I expect he'll be at the bar by now. I'll come and find you and then, well, maybe I'll give you a personal tour of the house. If you're not too busy with Aunt Cissy, that is."

I followed Belle's directions and found Clifton, not at the bar but still at his table, alone and watching vacantly as the staff swiftly removed some of the other tables to expand the dance floor. I settled into the chair next to him and started looking for a bottle that had something left in it. Clifton reached under the table and produced a bottle of red, which was still three quarters full, and without a word poured me a glass.

"You okay?" I asked.

He nodded. "Just drifted off for a bit. Thinking about the wedding and… other things. Funny how things turn out, eh?"

"You're a lucky man. Belle is so… perfect."

He huffed dismissively. "Yes. Yes, she is."

"I've been meaning to ask you. Will you inherit the title?"

He shook his head. "Doesn't work like that. Has to pass to a male heir, and if there isn't one, as in this case, it dies out. No Lord Clifton, not that it matters." Looking up at the ceiling for a few moments, he sighed deeply. "Estate's all in hock. It's going to cost a pretty penny to put it right." He sat glumly for a while, and then said: "At least I get the girl." He raised his glass. "Cheers big ears!"

The band, a group of five gentlemen with silvering hair and beer bellies, struck up a nineteen-fifties rock and roll number, playing tightly and loudly. The dance floor filled up immediately with cavorting, drunken bodies.

"I'm going for a boogie. You coming?"

I shook my head. I watched him walking towards the dance floor, pumping his arms and waddling like a great ape in time to the music.

All the wine bottles were empty, so I tipped the contents of several partially consumed and abandoned glasses of red into mine and drank a silent toast to the health of the evil fairy. In the depths of dark ruminations, I felt the touch of a hand on my shoulder and a soft voice in my ear. "You look so thoughtful. I would love to take off the top of your head and see what's simmering in there."

For a wonderful moment I thought it was Belle, but even as I was turning my head I realised in a crash of disappointment that it was Cissy. Their voices were almost indistinguishable, but Cissy's perfume gave her away: it was darker, muskier, more complex. Suddenly our mouths were in uncomfortably close proximity. I pulled back; enough to give breathing space but not enough to give offence. "Nothing exciting, I'm afraid. A dreadful stew," I improvised lamely, trying to make it sound unappetising. "Boiled beef and carrots. Maybe a few dumplings."

She patted my shoulder and slipped into the chair Clifton had vacated. "Sounds delicious, darling boy."

I needed to get rid of her before Belle came back, and I was preparing to deliver a fairly direct cold shoulder when it came into my mind that Cissy did not deserve such treatment from me. She had been nothing other than kind and charming towards me, and therefore deserved at the very least that I should try to find a way to extricate myself without giving offence. To buy time, I steered the conversation onto safer ground. "This is such a fascinating old house," I said. "Did you grow up here?"

She looked surprised to be asked about herself. "When I was very young we had a nanny. Then I was sent away to boarding school. Wychwood wasn't a very child-friendly place."

"What do you mean?"

"Oh, father and mother weren't all that interested in children." Her eyes evaded mine momentarily.

"But it must have been wonderful to have all this space to run around in, and the grounds."

"No, it wasn't the slightest bit like that. It was more like living in a museum. You can't go there. Don't touch. Do as you're told. Do as you're told. Do as you're told."

"Did you?"

She smiled and arched an eyebrow. "I was always getting into trouble."

"You surprise me." There was something of the same magnetism that drew me to Belle about her. She had snapped me effortlessly out of my misery and now she actually had me enjoying flirting with her.

"Now about that dance," she said. "That's what I came for. I warned you: I shan't take no for an answer."

On the dance floor a general combination of excessive enthusiasm and helpless inebriation was causing mayhem. People riding piggy back raced back and forth, whipping their mounts with napkins. Clifton, red faced and sweating profusely, was himself galloping around the dance floor like a charging bull in pursuit of several young women who deftly avoided him like seasoned matadors. I tried hard to dance with Cissy, but it was like an obstacle course: we kept being bashed into; we couldn't hear each other at all; and it wasn't as if I could really throw myself into it, as I was still keeping an eye out for Belle; so I wasn't very surprised when, after a few chaotic numbers, she announced in mime that she had had enough.

I followed her off the dance floor, overheated but slightly less drunk. Cissy stopped and firmly took my arm, trying to steer me in the direction of the house. "Come and see seen my apartment in the east wing," she shouted in my ear. I removed her hand gently. "I'm in enough trouble with your brother already," I said.

"Fuck him!" she said vehemently. The disco lighting highlighted tiny drops of spittle flying from her lips.

"You flatter me," I said, not moving.

There was a moment in which our wills battled. "Fuck you too!" she said at last, and lifting her chin she turned and stalked away a little unsteadily towards the doorway into the house.

As she reached it, Belle emerged from the doorway looking utterly radiant. Belle's gaze sought me out, and we exchanged a look that left me exhilarated: it was the moment I had daydreamed about. Cissy stopped her and whispered something in her ear that made her frown, but she shook her head and patted her aunt gently on the shoulder as she replied, and Cissy continued on her way and disappeared into the house.

I went to Belle, and we met half way. "Time for the grand tour," she announced as we approached each other. "Come on, quickly!" She turned and headed back to the doorway. "We can't be seen," she said over her shoulder seriously as I followed her. "Not by anyone." Then she grinned at me like a nine-year-old with a sled in a snowstorm, and, turning suddenly, flitted into the house and along the hallway with a rapidity I hadn't anticipated. I scurried after her.

Chapter 38: *The Grand Tour*

"The Wychwood library!" Belle announced, clicking on the lights as we entered a very long and high-ceilinged room that was lined with well-ordered bookshelves from floor to ceiling, with still more tall bookcases dividing the room crosswise into thirds. Some books were behind glass doors, others open to the dry stillness of the room; they ranged in size from enormous folio editions on deep lower shelves to tiny travel editions; all were bound in black or tan leather with decorated spines and gold lettering. There was a tall ladder on a rail that ran around the walls of the room above the height of the windows.

Even a confirmed biblioclast like myself could hardly fail to be impressed by the age and scale of the collection. The library somehow rose above the thumping music and the hyena clamour of party voices coming from the marquee, insisting upon its own dignity and peace.

My gaze was drawn to a large display case on the wall to my right and, curious, I walked slowly over. It had an irregular structure, as if it had been built around its contents, and displayed an extraordinarily diverse array of strange objects. One side of it had been damaged by fire. The collection was not easy on the eye: many of the exhibits were grotesque and unnatural, and my vision, already a tad blurry from all the alcohol I had consumed, thankfully slid over them without registering much. A breath of air from a nearby window open window brushed my face and I shivered involuntarily.

"We can't stay here." Belle took my arm and I was reminded that her excitement at our adventure was tinged with real fear about being caught. "There's something I want to show you. Come on."

She practically dragged me along the length of the room to the far wall, where there was a large polished-wood door, which she opened with an old-fashioned mortice-type key. Inside there was a wooden staircase leading steeply down into darkness. The first flight turned to the right and disappeared, but I had the impression that the shaft continued a long way further.

I whistled in appreciation. "Wow! Where does it go?"

"This is the grand tour. I'm going to show you!" Belle flicked some switches: the stairs were suddenly illuminated all the way down by a series of low wattage bulbs, and the library lights behind us went out.

"Come on," she said. Then we descended with the exaggerated care of the very inebriated on worn oak treads in eight flights that turned at right angles, winding down to a deep subterranean level. The walls of the shaft were whitewashed plaster, with, at intervals, dark oil paintings in warped frames hung upon them; their subjects hard to identify in the gloom as we passed: oddly proportioned people in hunting attire, I thought, standing in groups or mounted on horses with straight, spindly legs and arched necks. About half way down the walls changed from whitewashed plaster to stone blocks and after that the pictures changed too: now almost nothing was discernible to the passing gaze, but I could tell through some sixth sense that the theme had moved on from hunting to religion. Saints subduing demons, perhaps: a smudgy Saint Anthony menaced by a hint of lion, and then a blotch amid blotches that made me think of Saint Teresa of Avila.

"Just wait," Belle said, anticipating impatience that I wasn't feeling. Another flight, and then the staircase ended and we were in a vestibule with a flagstone floor and walls of stone blocks. It smelled and looked like the entrance to a church. On one side loomed a high gothic arch of stone in which an ancient wooden door was set. The door had a heavy iron ring by way of a handle and was thickly studded with nails. At the far end there was a deep alcove, containing a clothes rail bearing a large number of what I guessed were ecclesiastical robes.

We stood facing the door, submerged in a liquid silence. I could not help swaying slightly, but Belle seemed not to notice. She flicked some light switches on the wall by the door with the flat of her palm. "The chapel," she said, and turning the great metal ring with both hands, lifted the latch and dramatically pushed the heavy door open.

It was a huge crypt. Two rows of pillars supported a vaulted ceiling of surprising height, from which twin wooden chandeliers hung, providing atmospherically dim electric light. There were no windows – we must have been deep underground - but small side chapels with their own light sources created the illusion that there was an outlook. There were two parallel rows of heavily carved wooden pews, stained with age, leaving an aisle down the centre that led to a raised quire, in the centre of which there was an undecorated altar. Dominating the space behind it, and indeed the entire chamber, there loomed a huge, menacing reredos of ornately carved wood. Almost as high as the ceiling, it exuded an extraordinary energy that seemed to set the rest of the space thrumming.

Belle took my hand and led me down the central aisle. "Don't say anything," she said. "I want to tell you something. Something serious." We passed banners on each side hanging in dead air from poles above the entrances to the side rooms. On the walls between were carved representations of what I took to be the *via crucis*; but the deep shadows on the carvings moved as we walked, and I could not be sure whether the story depicted was Christ's final journey and death or some other tale of torture populated by devils and monsters. Our feet clattered on the stone flags, and the echoes of it roosted like bats high in the ceiling above us.

"We don't allow strangers into the chapel, Nick. You have to swear to keep this a secret."

We halted at the end of the aisle, before the altar, and it suddenly felt as if we were enacting some kind of arcane ceremony. Belle stepped up into the quire, taking me with her as she still had hold of my hand. Behind the altar the reredos throbbed with dark energy. The central scene it depicted, which I could see properly now, was the Razing of Hell: a triumphant Christ leading the patriarchs out through Hell's gate, his foot upon the neck of a hideous depiction of the Devil. The level of detail was extraordinary. Kneeling in rows upon one side were men and animals, and upon the other an array of hideous mythical creatures of every shape and description. I couldn't take my eyes from it.

"You can never tell anyone you've been here with me." Belle's voice shook. "You can never tell anyone about us."

I knew I was drunk, but there was something else now scrambling my thoughts and preventing me from thinking straight. Belle took my other hand and turned me away from the altar so that our bodies were facing each other, and then she reached up and gently turned my head away from that disturbing carving with a soft hand on my cheek. Then we were eye to eye, and so close that we were touching; legs, chest, loin. An irresistible wave of arousal washed through me, driving out any vestige of other thoughts. "Swear it," she whispered. Swear to me, Nick, that you'll keep our secret. Swear that you would rather die than betray it. And... And death to the evil fairy."

210

I leaned forward just as she artfully lifted her chin, and suddenly we were kissing wildly and both of us were utterly beyond any self-control. I frantically hitched up her dress and ran my hand up between her legs, slipping in her ready wetness; she was unbuttoning my trousers, tugging with frustration at her slow progress and then reaching inside, grasping. "Swear it!" she demanded.

I lifted her to sit on the altar. She pulled the long skirt of her dress up around her waist, I tugged at her knickers, she wriggled, and then she was urging me to get inside her and a moment later I was on the altar too. There was thick fog in my head and sensations crowded in on me: my heart pounding at my ribcage, lungs gasping for air, the bursting hardness of my manhood, her hips grinding under me, her fingernails clawing my back, our tongues thrusting and intertwining. "Swear it," she moaned, "On God's holy altar."

Befuddled with desire, I could do nothing else. "I swear," I whispered, and she wrapped her legs around me, and as I pushed she swallowed the length of me with what felt like a greedy gulp. She gasped with the pleasure of it, and breathed: "Oh, Clifton!"

Time froze.

In the silence the stone walls whispered her words cruelly around the chamber. I was whisked out of the moment into a detached, empty place floating some feet above the altar from which vantage point, looking down, I witnessed myself frozen in the act while Belle, unaware at first that anything was wrong, only gradually ceased her movements as realisation slowly forced its way through the fug of drunken lust. She clutched at me, trying to sustain the moment, but then stopped and lay still.

Restored suddenly to myself, I withdrew roughly, disentangled myself from Belle's limbs, and climbed carefully down from the altar. She sat up and looked silently down at me from her perch as I buttoned up my trousers over my wilted manhood, while behind her the reredos glowered over us like the face of a frowning god. Then she slid down, graceful as ever, smoothed down her dress, and bent down to pick her knickers from the floor.

"Nick, I didn't mean…" she said, reaching over to touch my arm. I stepped away, not looking at her. She bowed her head. "I don't know what happened. I don't know what to say."

I finished dressing and said nothing. After a long moment she made a decision and walked off with as much dignity as she could muster towards the door, but the air was tense with my humiliation, and each step reverberated in the vaulted ceiling in a gradually quickening slow handclap.

Chapter 39: *In The Nest*

I walked from Wychwood Hall back Clifton and Belle's house. It took me longer than it should have done, since the roads were incredibly uneven, twisty, and much narrower than I remembered. Also it was very dark, and it took me a while to get my bearings. By the time I got there, Clifton and Belle had long gone to bed. I crunched down the drive and found the house dark and deathly quiet. The back door was locked.

I went wandering. In the stillness of the night the garden's wistful daytime vista was transformed into something eerie and threatening. The moonlight made the greenhouse appear larger and more sinister: a moon-palace nurturing who knew what kinds of noisome fruit. Inside the ruined gazebo lurked a heart of impenetrable, rotten darkness. Trees reached down, clutching with long, bony fingers.

I had been thinking vaguely of Belle's story about sleeping in a hayloft and of the new stable they had built by the paddock, but long before I came anywhere near it the simple fact that I had drunk a great deal too much and now badly needed to lie down took the ascendancy. The prospect of surrendering to the cold, damp, hard ground seemed quite wonderful to me, evil moonscape notwithstanding, but I was determined that I should not, at least, be seen from the house by Clifton and Belle, and so I stumbled on in search of a spot that would screen me from that embarrassment.

Flower beds tangled with thistles, couch grass, deadnettle and brambles, choked with long-dead growth and delineated by rusting wrought-iron decorative borders, became lethal man-traps in the gloom, to be carefully avoided. The paths, uncleared for dozens of years, were so overhung by branches and haunted by deep, clustering shadows that they were unusable. Flaking brick walls, round-shouldered with age, their faces spotted with lichen and rusty nails, loomed and receded. Clumps of trees that might once have been delightful groves but were now impenetrable thickets lurked like huge, brooding monsters. I gave a wide berth to the ornamental pond, which in the dark was reduced to a melancholy bog haunted by the ghosts of frogs and mosquitos.

The orchard radiated aged but faithful benevolence in a way that the rest of the garden did not, and offered plenty of cover. It was a huge relief to reach its welcoming turf. The grass was much longer than it should have been, and had collected into dry, pale clumps beneath the twisted, unpruned branches of the fruit trees, but despite its uncared-for appearance there was no menace to the place as there was elsewhere in the garden. I came to a halt by an ancient, warped medlar tree that occupied a clearing at the centre. It stood like a proud old man jutting his chin at the moon, his arms thrown upwards in pique, or perhaps supplication. There was a small clearing beneath its spread that looked like a nest. It felt like the destination I had been seeking. I pitched forward into it, and within seconds I was asleep.

I awoke with the last vestiges of a dream draining from my memory too quickly for me to retain. It was morning; the sun a moving dapple overhead that I could sense through my closed eyelids and upon my cheeks and nose. As I became conscious, the multi-layered sounds around me asserted themselves: the soft shushing of branches; the electric buzzing of unseen flying insects; birds calling from their secret vantage-points: wood pigeon, blackbird, thrush. I was only disoriented for a moment, and then memory returned and with it the dark edges of a fierce hangover. I lay still with my eyes closed, not daring the discomfort of movement: I was not cold, at least, but the ground had been hard and surprisingly lumpy, moulding my back to its own shape and ensuring that I would suffer the consequences the moment my muscles shifted.

After several minutes, in which I drifted between consciousness and sleep, half-listening to Nature's susurrus, I became aware of a new sound. It was very faint, but I was certain that I could hear the hesitant, ultra-cautious footsteps of someone, or something, very nearby that was trying not to wake me up. A foot being gently placed on dry grass causes a certain kind of sound as the blades fold under the pressure of the sole, crowd together and are crushed. As the foot moves away again, when the broken stems pursue the memory of their former shape, a short rustling resettlement follows. It was too faint to be human, and it wasn't Jinx, who would have crashed through like a rhino and licked my face, and so I reasoned that it might be a cat, or perhaps a squirrel. The curious thing was that the sounds seemed to be slowly going away from me, as if the thing, whatever it was, had been poised over me as I had slept. There. Three careful, irregular steps.......... four...... five... I lifted my head and opened my eyes. Light poured in, blinding me to all but a sudden flurry of movement, which was accompanied by frantic rustling and the swish of branches displaced. My vision came into focus then, upon the low-hanging boughs of an overgrown beech hedge swaying in the wake of something moving with speed and stealth. My temples were pounding. I strained to see into the shadows beyond, but the creature, whatever it was, was long gone.

With my attention fully now upon a stocktake of my suffering anatomy, I realised that for some unknown reason I was holding my right fist upon my chest, fingers clenched tightly. I relaxed, allowing my hand to slowly open, and as I did so it became apparent that I was holding something. A faint squeeze gave me a sense of what it was, and I sat up abruptly, provoking a landslide of pain inside my head, and opened my hand. Resting upon my palm were two ancient, dirt-ingrained gold coins.

Chapter 40: *A letter from Mr. Walter Peachey to Professor Titus Ogg*

29th July 1901

Dear Titus,

There are few people that I would trust with my life: you are foremost among them. I must beg your forgiveness for what I am about to impart, since it will place you in the impossible position of having to betray either our friendship or your reason, but I have an urgent duty to our mutual friend and colleague Doctor Horace Rackham to report what has become of him. I am afraid you alone must be the recipient of this knowledge from me since you are the only person I trust to judge this matter correctly. I know you will behave honourably; for my part I shall of course abide by your advice, and if that should be to turn myself over to the police or the asylum you may be assured that I shall abide by it none the less.

It is no secret that following the embarrassment with the Natural History Society, Horace became determined to prove them wrong and deliver incontrovertible evidence of the existence of the Fae, and to this end devoted all of his spare time to crawling inch by inch over the South Downs and pursuing with relentless vigour every rumour, tale or legend he encountered. To this activity he roped me in regularly – not against my will, I should add, for as you know this has long been an interest of my own – and I have documented our expeditions at his request for posterity. His letters to the Society were not answered and I believe he may, regrettably, have become something of a figure of fun with some, although I know you have always remained a true and loyal friend.

That we found little or nothing of substance only drove his determination until it became nothing short of obsession. He adopted a more academic line of attack, seeking out rare old texts in the libraries of academia and of the Church, and kept a notebook in which he would copy down passages or drawings that caught his attention. When he showed it to me, the contents had at first glance the butterfly haphazardness of a lost intellect, but on more detailed inspection there was a design to his research that circled ever-nearer to his favourite theme of encounter with the Fae. He tracked down many instances of the same first-hand tales being told by people who could not possibly have met, drew timelines and plotted locations upon maps.

Two weeks ago exactly we met for lunch at Bentley's in High Holborn. When dining out, which he did seldom with friends and never alone, Horace had adopted the habit of frequenting only those establishments that could offer the security of a private booth. He could not, he said, enjoy his mutton when he could not speak freely and must endure the prospect of being recognised and subjected to whispered ridicule.

"I am sorry," I told him, "That it has come to this."

"Many scientists have suffered the same indignity. They scoffed at Pythagoras for believing the world is round. Galileo was tried by the Inquisition for arguing that the Earth revolves around the sun. It was many years after their deaths that the truth of their findings was at last generally recognised. I am afraid we must accept, dear Walter, that were we to put Titania herself on exhibit in Trafalgar Square, as large as life, we should still be pilloried as charlatans."

Then he told me that he was ready to go back into the field again, and had devised a method to predict the appearance of a fairy, based upon historic and topographical calculations. "Time and place," he declared, "Do not mean the same to the Fae as they do to us. It is remarkable that they are seen in the same place at the same task by different people at different times, often decades apart. There has been no pattern or regularity detected in these appearances, until now."

"Then you have a place and time in mind," I hazarded.

"I do indeed. Sussex is, and has been for many hundreds of years, the very epicentre of fairy activity in this country, and possibly in the world. But to be more specific, the location is, conveniently, a place that you know well: the Devil's Burrow, by your own village of Stoney Hill; and the time is midnight a week from today."

"The twenty first of July."

"Indeed so. Will you come?"

I agreed that I would, of course, and soon it was time to call for the bill. As usual, Horace found something to occupy him when it arrived and I settled it for both of us. I believe he always intended to repay me, you know, but as he could never afford a practice of his own, nor could he hold down a position for long in someone else's as he was always distracted by his researches, he never had any money. That this was an embarrassment to him I have no doubt, although he never spoke of it. For my part, I never begrudged him a farthing of it.

On the evening in question I accompanied Horace out onto Stoney Down. It was a balmy night, warm and clear. The stars seemed closer overhead than usual – some kind of atmospheric illusion – and the bright moonlight rendered our lanterns unnecessary. In the lee of a solitary pear tree we halted and Horace explained his plan, reading at times from his notebook, which he always carried with him.

"It was by this very tree that, in 1773, a local man named Hodge claimed he met a fairy struggling to push an empty wheelbarrow up the hill. The fairy, a short and stooped creature with long arms, dark, wrinkled skin, and a broad, grinning mouth asked for his help, offering gold as a reward; but when Hodge agreed and tried to lift the handles of the barrow he could not. He pulled and strained harder until his arms nearly came out of their sockets, but with no result. It felt to him that there must be a great weight inside, but all he could see was a few seeds rolling about. When he admitted to the fairy that he could not lift the barrow, let alone push it up the hill, the fairy took it from him and, raising the handles with only slight difficulty, set off on its way again without a further word."

"Earlier, in 1699, it is recorded that a farm labourer encountered a creature answering to the same description going up the hill with a wheelbarrow. He also was offered gold to provide assistance. Being an exceptionally strong man, he succeeded in lifting slightly one of the handles, which tipped the barrow and one of the seeds rolled out and fell onto the ground. At this, the fairy cursed loudly and, pushing the labourer out of his way, snatched up the handles of the barrow and hurried away up the hill, muttering to himself. The next day the labourer found a mature pear tree growing in the spot where none had been growing before."

"I believe this tree, beside which we are standing, is the very same tree that features in *both* stories. It is a normal pear tree, you may rest assured, although very aged: I have carried out every test. So we are in the right place."

"There are other folk tales of this fairy and his wheelbarrow, going back many hundreds of years. They have the same elements in common. No-one has ever succeeded in earning the gold, by the way. But the importance of this example is that the incidents are better recorded than most, and my analysis shows that the frequency of the appearances has a pattern. It is not an easy pattern to detect: I have delved into advanced mathematics in order to find it, but thanks to our friend and his barrow I now have the method that I believe will successfully predict the next appearance, which as I have told you will be tonight at midnight." With this, he patted his notebook and tucked it away it in his jacket pocket.

After so many false leads and vain hopes, Titus, I had little confidence that Horace's method would bear fruit; but if I allowed even a very small probability of success, I was at once confronted by the question of what we should do then. I asked Horace for his thoughts upon this matter.

"Why, we shall capture the creature, dear Walter! There is no other way we may prove its existence to the world at large. We must capture it and transport it securely to London, where we shall be able to study it with the latest scientific equipment. It will be hailed as one of the greatest discoveries ever made!"

"But how? Even if such a thing were to materialise as you predict, it must be unnaturally strong if it can lift the wheelbarrow with ease when farm labourers cannot. It may have powers of which we know nothing."

Horace, somewhat triumphantly, showed in his bag a glimpse of a long iron chain, with a cuff at each end. "I have the answer," he said. "All of the research confirms that the Fae cannot bear the touch of iron and, if confined by it, cannot break free of its grasp. My friend the blacksmith has made me this manacle. It is very secure. While you distract the creature, I shall clap this cuff upon its wrist: the other end shall be already clasped about my own. It will be in our power completely from that moment."

I had doubts about the efficacy of this plan, but I decided to keep them to myself and, as it turned out, it was as well that I did for I was completely wrong about it: it worked like a charm! However, I am getting ahead of myself. Horace suggested that we install ourselves by the tree and rather than sit in silence whilst waiting, which might provoke suspicion in the object of our attentions, we should relax and talk naturally between ourselves. This we did, and I had in fact forgotten all about our mission by the time midnight arrived as we were having a very good discussion upon the history and meaning of the black shuck, or black dog, as a harbinger of evil in local folklore. It was with considerable surprise and fright, then, that I received the intimation that our prey was approaching from the watchful doctor. I followed his gaze and found myself not far away at all from a small figure that was pushing a wheelbarrow slowly up the hill. Our conversation faltered, and in the silence I could hear the creature puffing and gasping as it made progress towards us. As it drew level, it halted and looked us both up and down, and then grinned widely. It did not look human: it was short in comparison to the average man, it had a smaller cranium than a man, and a wider jaw in proportion to its head; its arms were long; its body thin and severely stooped at the shoulder. Its feet were bare and filthy, and it wore leather shorts and a stained leather apron over a dirty smock. "Good evening gents," it said, putting the barrow down and wiping sweat from its brow with the back of its hand. "I'm fair wore out, I don't mind tellin' you. I don't suppose either of you lively fellows would be a-willing to give me a hand with this here barrow? There's gold in it for you."

We were both astounded, of course. The experience had the quality of a dream about it, and that, I believe, was what saved me from simply running away as fast as my legs would carry me. Horace, recovering first, gave me a nudge and I remembered our plan. I stood up, very nervously, and took a step nearer. I heard Horace climbing to his feet behind me. "Heavy work, is it?" I asked, trying to sound casual. To be that close to a real fairy, after such a long and patient search, was, I can testify, both terrifying and exhilarating at the same time.

"It's a long way I've come, and a long way I have to go. It's not so much that it's heavy, but that I'm tired and in sore need of a little rest. If you'll take a turn, I'll pay you by the yard, so I will: one gold piece for every step. That's a fair wage."

"Where are you bound?" I asked.

"Nearer the way."

I could make no sense of this. "What's in the barrow?"

"Why, almost nothing at all! Take a look for yourself."

I edged nearer. The wheelbarrow was empty, so far as I could tell, bar a little chaff gathered in the corners.

"Alright, I'll have a go."

"Now there's a gentleman."

He stepped sideways away from the tines of the barrow and waved me forward. Horace crowded forward with me and soon I was in place, with Horace occupying the space between me and the fairy. I was studying the fairy closely; so much so that Horace was obliged to dig me in the ribs with his elbow to get me started. Realising that I was expected to continue playing along, I bent down and went to lift the handles, but found to my amazement, despite having heard the tales from Horace, that I could not raise the barrow even one sixteenth of an inch. As I strained away, there was a sudden flurry of arms and legs beside me and a shrill wail of dismay from the fairy, and I knew that Horace's plan had succeeded.

When I looked round, there was the fairy, sitting on the ground with tears pouring from its eyes and, like a dog with a sore paw, holding up its wrist, around which the iron cuff was securely fastened. The chain to which the cuff was attached looped down to the ground where it made one or two coils, and then continued up to another cuff around Horace's wrist. The fairy kicked its legs and wailed again, and then rolled around on the ground.

"Great Heavens!" I cried, "You've done it!"

This occasioned more rolling around and squirming and groaning. Horace coughed politely and then said to the fairy: "Please do stop all of that. We wish to talk to you."

At this, the creature sat up suddenly and gave Horace a sideways look in which cunning and hatred vied for dominance. "What do you want?" it said. "You didn't have to do *this*!" Here he shook his manacled wrist at us. "Wasn't I being nice with you? Wasn't I being straight?"

"We must oblige you to accompany us back to London."

"London, says you," the creature replied. "Well London's not for me. I have my barrow to wheel." It fell silent, and then, suddenly, it seemed jollier. "What say you we make a little bargain?" it said, smiling an unnaturally wide smile. "There's gold a-plenty, right under our feet. Let me go, and I'll get it for you, all of it. A king's ransom there is."

"We're not falling for your tricks, fairy," I said, but Horace had a light in his eyes that I didn't like to see, and he waved for me to be silent.

"Where exactly *is* this gold?" he asked, queerly.

"Why, right here!" The creature scratched at the ground where it sat, tracing the outline of a great stone slab that we had not realised was there. It brushed the soil and grass away with the flat of its hand. "Give us a hand here, will you? You don't think a poor old fellow like me can lift a great stone like this on his own, do you?"

After some hesitation, Horace edged cautiously forward and began to help with trying to lift the slab, and I followed him. Between the three of us it was just manageable, and with much straining and grunting we flipped it up and over on one side. It landed with a thud. Revealed was a crude stairway made of stone treads and earth, spiralling down into darkness the colour of pitch.

"There we are, you see!" The creature said triumphantly. "Now then, I'll fetch that gold for you. Just take this cuff off and I'll be down there and back inside five minutes."

"More likely you'll be gone Heaven knows where and we'll never see you again! No indeed, we shall not take off the cuff." Horace had a sly look to him. "We shall go with you."

"Let us take this… ah… *gentleman* with us, back to London. That will be fortune enough," I said, looking into the well with trepidation. "We have no need of this gold."

Horace would not be swayed and shook his head firmly. "Lead on, fairy," he commanded. "Take me to the gold."

So it was that we found ourselves descending the stair, with the creature in the lead, followed by Horace, to whom he was chained, and I close behind.

Down and down, around and around. The steps were uneven in places, and it quickly grew freezing cold. "How much farther?" Horace demanded after a long minute's descent.

"Not far," came the answer. We continued, step by step upon the stone treads, and the darkness was kept from devouring us whole only by our sputtering lamps. Down and down, we went, in increasingly stale air, surrounded only by the clatter of our own descent.

"How much farther?" Horace asked once again, much later.

"Not far."

After a further, unbearably long descent, Horace came to a stop. "How long, then? For God's sake, how long will it take to reach the bottom?"

"How long? Why, it's but a hundred years and a day. Not long."

"A hundred years and a day? But that's impossible!"

"It's no time at all."

I could feel the distance below us as one feels the pull of a great chasm. "Horace, this is madness! We must turn back!" I shouted.

I believe Horace could feel it too, but he addressed the situation with a composure I could only admire. "I fear you are right. We have come this far, but… it seems there is no end to this stair." He turned to the creature. "Where are you taking us? Is this your trick? Well, it has failed. We are going back. Come!" With that, he yanked upon the shackle and began to climb, but was brought to a sudden halt when he reached the length of the chain. The fairy had not moved.

"We made a bargain," the creature said out of the darkness. "Take you to the gold, was your demand, in return for my freedom. That I shall, and that I must, for a hundred years and a day or however long it takes. Come! Come with me! Come!" And with that, the creature recommenced its descent, dragging Horace behind. Horace tried to brace his feet against it, but could not obtain purchase upon the damp stone, and he slipped. For a moment he caught himself, but then the chain tugged at him again and he was pulled off balance. He let out a scream of terror. I tried to catch his wrist but missed it, succeeding only in knocking his lantern flying, which shattered and went out, and then he was gone into the dark. His terrified screams, receding below, were at length brutally cut off and superseded by the horrid bumping of his bulk and the rattle of the chain as he tumbled down and down and down for an interminable age. At last, long after I could bear it no more, there came a silence in which the darkness swallowed all.

Then I ran. Cowardly, I know. In mitigation, I can only say that in my horror I lost all sense of myself, of knowledge and logic; all I knew was that I must go up as fast as I could. I climbed and climbed, until my legs were aching and I could not lift my feet, and then my lantern died and I went on my knees and elbows and wormed my way up and up, never stopping for dread of what was below, step by painful step, until at last I breathed in fresh air and emerged from that abominable stair to lie upon clean, fresh grass, looking up at stars that had not moved since we had first arrived by that accursed tree, and then my senses left me.

I was found, lifeless, bloody and covered in dirt, by a hiker out for an early morning tramp, and brought to the doctor in the village. When I had recovered sufficiently to be able to speak, I told the doctor I must have had a bump on the head and could offer no explanation of my injuries, and so he could do no more than patch me up and send me home. Whilst I am sure that I was the subject of village gossip for a while as a result, which would not be the first time, it appears no-one had seen me with Horace and not a soul has asked me about his disappearance.

I have of course been back many times in the last week to the place where we encountered the creature on Stoney Down. I have never been able to find any trace of the stone slab or of the stairway, or the creature's wheelbarrow. The hiker saw nothing. The notebook is lost with Horace, and I would not know where to start to replicate his calculations. I do not think I shall find the way back.

Poor Horace has not turned up, and I am afraid the only conclusion can be that he is dead. Time and place do not mean the same to the Fae as they do to us, he said. The creature told us that it would retrieve the gold in less than five minutes, but once we were on the fairy stair it told us it was one hundred years and a day to the bottom. There and back would take five minutes in our world, two hundred years in theirs. On that basis Horace's remaining natural lifespan lived out on that fairy stair would equal less than the passing of one minute in ours, and that supposes he survived the fall and did not subsequently die of thirst or hunger or take his own life once he realised his fate. He has been gone for a week.

It is especially sad for me to realise, after much reflection, that Horace's vulnerability to the enchantment of the gold, which I believe led to his decision to follow the fairy to it rather than bring the creature to London and claim the fame and fortune he undoubtedly would have earned, and deserved, stemmed not from greed, as many would suppose, or from a spirit of scientific discovery, which he would have preferred us to believe, or even an enchantment, but from his wounded pride at having accepted the charity of his friends for so long. He was answering the urge to pay back what he owed. It makes me feel that I am to blame.

I am so sorry to burden you with this testimony, Titus. What now? Am I mad? Should I tell the police what I know? Should I say nothing? I shall do whatever you advise.

Your friend,
Walter

Chapter 41: *A Funny Thing*

I had been waiting about twenty minutes in the English Tea Room at Brown's Hotel in Mayfair when Mother floated in. I stood up as she approached, and a waiter, who had appeared from nowhere, pulled out her chair for her.

"Hello Mother."

She sat gracefully, not bothering with any pretence of a physical greeting, and dismissing the waiter with a wave of her hand. "Hello Nicholas," she said. There was something unusual in her voice. If I hadn't known her better, I would have said she was nervous – but that was plainly nonsense. The meeting was at her request, and on neutral ground. She held all the cards.

I hadn't made any arrangements for the repayment of her loan. I had spent quite a lot of the money one way or another, without much in the way of assets to show for it, so I was a long way short. Compensation from the council on the community centre deal was unlikely to be settled for a long time yet, if there was to be any at all. The only financial solution was to sell my flat, which I didn't wish to contemplate at all, so I had no choice but to play for time and hope I could win her round. I looked closely to see if I could detect any sign of softening in her demeanour, but of course she looked as tough as steel, as usual.

"I hesitate to ask," I said, re-taking my seat, "But would you like something?"

"Thank you, darling. I will have a chamomile tea."

This was unusual, and I thought immediately that something must be wrong: she so rarely ate or drank anything, this had to be a symptom of something serious like an illness, or a death. I ordered for her, while she rummaged in her handbag for some pill or other, and then we sat facing each other in silence. Again, this was unusual: normally Mother said what was on her mind before you could get a word in.

"How's the extension coming along?"

"Do you know, I have no idea. I expect it must be nearly finished by now. I haven't been out there for a while."

I couldn't bear it any longer. "If this is about the loan…"

"It isn't. We will be having words about that, Nicholas, rest assured, but that isn't why I'm here. No, it's something nice, for a change."

I hardly knew what to say. "Really?"

She lifted her chin, paused theatrically, and then enunciated carefully: "Henry Wychwood, Annabel's father, and I are an item."

"What?"

"We've been seeing each other for a while. It's not a secret, but of course, you wouldn't know because you keep away from me as much as possible, and if I didn't chase you down we'd never speak at all."

"Henry Wychwood?"

"Yes. Don't look so surprised. He's such a charming man, and so good looking. Anyway, the thing I wanted to tell you is, we're going to get married."

"What?"

"He asked me, and of course I said yes. It will seem a bit rushed to you, but when Henry suggested that we make it a double wedding with Clifton and Annabel I had to agree. Why wait, at my time of life? I did think that perhaps it wouldn't be fair to Annabel to steal her moment of glory, and we could always do a quickie at the registry office, but she was marvellous about it, thought it was an excellent idea, and Clifton was his usual generous self. There! What do you think? You can walk me down the aisle."

"Walk you down the aisle."

"We're going to announce it tomorrow. I thought you'd prefer to know in advance, even if it did mean sitting down with me for five minutes. I know you didn't want to. Well, aren't you going to say congratulations?"

I didn't know quite what I wanted to say at that moment. Congratulations was not on the list of phrases forming in my mind, but now that Mother had suggested it I grasped it with the gratitude of a drowning man thrown a life buoy. "Congratulations!" I mumbled, "Marvellous."

Mother was looking at me strangely. "I see this has come as something of a shock to you. I suppose it would. Nicholas, it has been five years. I didn't think I would ever want or find someone else after your father died, but life is a funny thing."

I concentrated upon my breathing, but everything was spinning and it didn't seem to help. A few things had become clear at least, deeply unpleasant as they were. Mother's appearances at Clifton's house instead of being where I had expected, which was frying herself on a sunbed in Spain and ogling the pool boy, were no longer a mystery: she had been staying at Wychwood Hall, sleeping with Henry Wychwood and sharing all of her family issues with him over breakfast muesli in the orangery, for God knows how long. The withdrawal of her funding for my business had no doubt been prompted by Henry, who had other ideas about how to use the money. Just as soon as he and Mother were married, my inheritance was going to be flushed down the Wychwood plughole along with Clifton's. It made me feel vomitously ill. It was all out of my control, and very much under the frighteningly firm control of Henry Wychwood, peer of the realm, and there was not a single thing I could do about it.

"It certainly is," I said. "A very funny thing. Very funny indeed."

Chapter 42: *Do Not Look Out Of The Window This Night*

Do Not Look Out Of The Window This Night

Do not look out of the window this night:
    Bar the shutters, and turn all the locks.
Leave cold the grate and extinguish the light,
    Do not answer if anyone knocks.
Stop up the keyholes with sealing wax,
    Turn the looking glass face to the wall;
Block off the mouse holes and caulk all the cracks,
    Wrap yourself in your cosiest shawl.
Wear that straw hat with the widest of brims,
    Say your prayers well, hum some comforting hymns;
Do not stray from your bed 'til the morning is near,
    Lock your heart, and consign me the key;
For if the fairies see you, my dear,
    They will steal you away from me.

By WP

Chapter 43: *The Journal of Davey Bone*

I did sleep for barely one hour, and yet a dream came to me in that slight interval that shall haunt me for as long as I shall live and beyond into the afterlife, I shouldn't wonder. In my dream I rose silently from my bed like a spirit leaving a cadaver and betook myself downstairs once again in darkness to see if the objects I had left upon the kitchen step were still there. The house was quiet, for once; so quiet indeed that it might have been empty of every soul save my own. When I opened the back door I did disturb there an especially large and ugly rat that was lurking upon the step and it gave me an evil leer, bared its long teeth, and, bristling, hissed at me as if I were not the pinnacle of God's creation, Man, with dominion over all creatures, nor one hundred times larger to boot. I had by the door my stout walking stick, and I took it up and was outside in a trice, aiming a blow that would end it there, but the creature leaped aside and ran for it, and so I gave chase. It was ponderous slow in its movements for a rat – I thought perhaps it must be old and diseased – and I kept up with it, which gave me much encouragement to pursue it farther, but in spite of my best efforts I was never able to make up any ground upon it. Into the bushes, it fled, and I followed, brandishing my stick and leaping through the undergrowth with the zest and zeal of a much younger man. On and on, and we were soon deep in the wood and I must jump over roots and fallen branches; and all the while it persisted in remaining just beyond the reach of my cudgel. In its sly efforts to escape it changed course several times, but with God-given agility far beyond my normal powers I remained fast and true at its heels and it led me onward and downward, into ever darker and more overgrown places. Soon I was following by sound as much as sight, but of a sudden it stopped and turned to look at me with piercing yellow eyes, and I was almost upon it, but it snarled and dove suddenly into a dark hole; and I made a great leap after it, aiming a tremendous blow at its disappearing hind quarters, but instead of falling to the ground as expected I found myself tumbling into darkness, and then I landed upon soft dirt, and, looking up, I found myself to be in the great throne room under the earth, this time in gloomy darkness. What I had previously taken for fine tapestries were no more than twisted roots, the great pillars were but boulders and the throne upon its dais a tree stump. Hideous, stinking creatures pressed towards me, baring their teeth, hissing and jeering and prodding with sharp sticks as they jostled me towards the throne. Seated upon it and dressed in a filthy green smock was a pale and malformed mockery of the human form with a wide, lopsided face, great pointed ears and long, yellow teeth in a slit of a mouth. Its yellow eyes, each at a different angle, narrowed at my approach and regarded me with pure malice.

"The bargain is broken," it spat. "The time has passed. The price must be paid. Fool and knave! You might have been a king among men and celebrated forever in the songs of my people, but you have chosen unwisely."

"You have asked too much of me," I said. The creatures around me cried out discontentedly and stamped their feet.

"You have asked too much of yourself. Enough, mortal! You have robbed me of my prize. The price is that ye shall forfeit a thing of equal value. May your bitter tears at the consequence of your bad faith never cease. Begone!"

I awoke, and it was yet early but there was no possibility of more sleep and so I dressed and went downstairs, and when I looked out upon the kitchen step I found the objects still there. Not long afterwards, my dear Anne came to me and asked whether I had seen Lilly Grace, who had been missed from her cot and not found in any of the beds upstairs. I replied that I had not, thinking first that this was some game of the children's, but cold fingers of dread clutched suddenly at my gut and I ran upstairs calling her name, going from room to room. She was not there. I hurried back downstairs, and my fervent haste transmitted itself to my wife and the other children, who began to call her name also and seek her out in her favourite places, but she could not be found. Soon the search extended out of the inn and into the yard and the garden beyond, and then out into the village, where I asked my neighbours for their help, and before long the whole village was out looking for her, and not a barrel, cellar or chimney was missed. Out in the woods we went then, spread out, calling her name, and then out onto Stoney Down under a pale sky, but there was no sign of her anywhere. All the while I had it in my mind that she had been taken by the fairies as punishment for my failure, and this strengthened my resolve threefold, for not only do I love my Lilly Grace more than I love myself and would not see any harm come to her at any price, but also in finding her I should prove that she had not been spirited away, and thus the entire construction of fairies and gold and burning down houses was no more than nonsense, and this would mean that her disappearance was not my fault.

When I broke from the search in the evening to see how the remainder of the Bone family was faring, I was weak with fear for Lilly Grace. I found Anne beyond tears: in her desperation she had turned to prayer and, on her knees

236

before Lilly Grace's empty cot, was reciting The Lord's Prayer over and over, her eyes closed tight. My children were huddled together in the kitchen, silent and weepy, except for young Davey who was out with the men, still looking. Hope had long passed, however, after such a time, and all involved knew that the search continued as a thing to do rather than there being any chance of success. I went back out to join the men nonetheless, and it was not until darkness had overtaken all that the search was halted. Young Davey came home just before me, exhausted, and fell asleep sitting in a chair. The other children were all sent upstairs, and all remained together, piled into their parents' own bed. Anne was in the girls' bedroom continuing her frantic prayer, and would not be comforted. My own exhaustion was several notches beyond any level I had ever known; but fearing the worst for Lilly Grace, distracted still by the search, and by the needs of my other family members, I could not sleep and it was not until the small hours that I finally knew what I must do.

Chapter 44: *Near The Bottom Of The Bottle*

I knocked on the door of Charlie's van. The day, which had now aged into twilight, had been glorious. If the weather held, as seemed likely, for another twenty-four hours, then Belle would have her perfect wedding day - as if that had ever been in doubt. There was a light on inside, so I knew he was there, but he didn't answer and after about a minute I started to worry. Charlie wasn't well: you could tell that just by looking at him. I knocked more loudly, and started wondering whether any of the windows would be large enough to provide access in case I needed to get to him. Then I called: "Charlie? Charlie?" And again, louder: "Charlie?"

It was something of a relief when at last I heard noises from inside and, finally the sound of the latch. The door swung open a few inches, and Charlie's face appeared. He looked awful. He said nothing; just looked at me dully. His eyes, rimmed with red, had a yellow glaze. I thought perhaps he had been dozing.

"Any chance of a cup of tea?" I asked brightly.

He grunted in an unwelcoming way, but turned around and shuffled back into the interior of the van, leaving the door open. I followed him in. It looked much more grubby and disorderly in there than it had before. Above the smell of old socks and musty paper there was a sharp odour coming from the sink, which was piled high with dirty crockery. There was an empty half-bottle of Bell's whisky on the table, and an empty tumbler beside it. He put the kettle on the stove and lit the gas. Then he shuffled back towards me. At close range his face was unpleasantly waxy and pale. The capillaries in his nose and cheeks looked blue, and he had shaved, but there were clumps of white stubble he had missed. I noticed that his hands were shaking.

"How are you, Charlie?"

"Never better," he said defiantly.

"Are you sure?"

"I said I'm alright, didn't I?"

"Alright. Shall we sit down?"

Charlie plonked himself down with a sigh behind the table. Despite the show he was making of not wanting me there, I couldn't help feeling that he was secretly pleased to see me. It was cold in the van. Keeping my jacket on, I sat opposite him and then, catching a sudden whiff of his breath, I had to turn away for clean air and I made a pantomime of having something in my eye. When I turned back he was regarding me with hostile impatience.

"I'm finished."

"What do you mean?"

"It's all a mess. Everything." And it all came flooding out: Clifton's ascent to putative lord of the manor, and my descent to the gutter; Mother cutting me off without a penny; her forthcoming marriage to Wychwood; Belle's inexplicable preference for Clifton.

Charlie scrutinised me carefully. "Lost the money, lost the girl. Dumped you, did she? Clearing the decks before the wedding?"

"Charlie, can't you be a bit kinder about it?"

"Perhaps your cousin isn't such an arse after all."

The barb caught me with my guard down, but I didn't complain because I deserved it. I laughed bitterly. "I've lived in his shadow all my life. Even my own mother favours him over me. I've never beaten him at anything, ever, and the worst thing is he doesn't even try. So perhaps you're right, Charlie. Clifton's not the arse. I'm the arse."

I could feel Charlie's eyes on me, but I regarded the threadbare beige cardigan he was wearing, which had what looked like heavy gravy stains down the front.

"It can't be that bad. There's always something."

"No. I'm done. There's nothing left." I shrugged.

Charlie sat in silence looking at me, and I couldn't meet his gaze. We stayed like that for a long moment.

"What's happened to the tea, by the way?" I said eventually. "I thought you put the kettle on."

Charlie turned and looked at the hob, where the flame had gone out under the kettle. "Out of gas," he said. "Fuck it!" He reached unsteadily under the table, fished about, and came up with a new bottle of Bell's whisky in his hand. He wheezed a couple of breaths and then said: "Let's have a proper drink."

"Why not?"

"If you look in that cupboard over there," he said, "You might find some clean glasses." I got up and opened the cupboard door he was pointing to. It was full of all kinds of kitchen junk. I looked back at Charlie and shook my head. He waved his hand. "At the back! You may have to rummage a bit."

Charlie broke the seal with a practised twist of his wrist and poured with a shaky hand into two mismatched tumblers. "A toast," he offered. "May you find the way."

"Cheers!" We clinked glasses and drank. Charlie drained his in one, and so I followed suit. He poured again as soon as I put the glass down.

"Death to the evil fairy!" I offered by way of a return, raising my glass.

Charlie put the bottle down heavily and just sat staring at me. "That is not a proper toast."

"That's what they say around here."

"Find something else please."

"Jesus! Alright." I thought for a moment. Words dropped into my head, although I couldn't say where they came from: "May your enemies be scattered as smoke blown away on the wind."

Charlie thought for a moment, and then raised his glass and clinked it against mine. "That I will drink to," he said.

Less than an hour later we were deep into the bottle. I had told Charlie far more than I had ever meant to about my life and my family, poor chap, but he kept asking more questions and refilling our glasses and I didn't have a chance to ask him anything much. Then he said: "Wychwood has no relations left alive, other than his sister and his daughter Annabel."

"He's an evil bastard," I said. "He's like a criminal mastermind. He's stolen everything I ever had."

"You're not listening. Pay attention, Nicholas. Once this double wedding has taken place, I wonder what would happen to the estate if by some terrible chance the Wychwood line and their spouses were wiped out? A tragic car crash, perhaps?"

"Wouldn't that depend on wills and clearing debts and stuff?"

"Let's say for the sake of argument that if there were any wills they couldn't be found."

"They all died in the car crash."

"Yes."

"Clifton?"

"Yes. All of them."

"Mother?"

"All of them."

"In the same car crash?"

241

"That's right."

"Christ!"

"It's hypothetical."

"What if they all died of food poisoning? Salmonella?"

"It doesn't really matter."

"Or…" I held up my finger, "In a nasty hunting accident."

"Unlikely, but it doesn't matter. The question is, if they all died, what would happen to the estate?"

"I don't know. I imagine it would go to surviving direct relatives who… survived." I paused, wheels turning in my head. "Which is me. Only."

"Exactly! In due course, you yourself would be the Master of Wychwood."

"So you're saying after the wedding I'm going to be to be fifth in line to inherit or something."

He snorted. "Bet they haven't thought of that."

"I bet they have. There'll be a will, or a trust or something."

"I don't think so." Charlie looked smug, as if he knew something.

"What makes you so sure?"

"Call it premonition."

"You mean intuition."

"I'm not drunk," Charlie said.

We were somewhere near the bottom of the bottle when I said: "The thing is, Charlie, nobody's ever really loved me."

"Don't worry. I love you."

"No, I'm serious. I mean, when I think about it there's really no-one. Father was always working. Mother… well, Mother is Mother. She's always treated me as someone to torment. I'm just a dog who gets kicked and beaten but

242

always comes creeping back on its belly for more. She never loved me. She never loved anyone but herself."

Charlie patted me on the back of the hand. "You're nothing like a dog," he said.

"I thought perhaps Hazel… but you know, I fucked that up. I don't know how it happened but I found myself treating her just the way Mother treats me. And after a while she ran away. I don't blame her. And Belle. I thought maybe Belle would fall in love with me. I really wanted her, Charlie, more than anything. That should have counted for something, right? She was it!" I took a sip from my glass and shrugged hopelessly. "But she's in love with Clifton. With that fat lump. Can you believe it?"

Charlie put his glass down and stood up. I looked up at him, and my eyes were brimming with tears of self-pity. Charlie looked down at me disdainfully. "Are you going to stop whining about it and do something about it?" he said. "You let these people piss all over you and you come here and complain about it as if you hadn't lain down in front of them and begged them to do it." He put on a whingy voice. "Clifton won't share. Belle doesn't love me. Mummy took my toys away. Wychwood robbed me."

"I don't deserve that, especially from you, you… self-pitying old git."

"Says the self-pitying young arse. Look in the mirror, sonny boy." He pointed to his own face. "Am I what you aspire to be?"

Charlie's red-rimmed eyes held mine with a dead stare. I shook my head, and found myself grinning through the tears. "No offence, Charlie."

Charlie bared his teeth in response. "Well then. Do something. Do what you have to do. They think they can treat you like that? Walk all over you?"

I put my hand to my forehead, rubbed it. "I don't know what to do."

"Yes you do."

I shook my head, suddenly feeling very drunk. "I'll be leaving now," I said. I stood up. "Thanks for the whisky, and… and good luck. Good luck with… with whatever it is you're up to, Charlie. I'm done." Charlie's expression didn't change. I turned away quickly and found my way out with a little more difficulty than usual, and then staggered up the lane in the direction of the church.

Chapter 45: *Miss Burtenshaw's Ogre*

In other circumstances the arrival of Miss Estella Burtenshaw at Wychwood Hall might have been the cause of considerable speculation on the part of those below stairs concerning the object of her visit since she was, after all, of marriageable age, of a good family, and by all reports possessed of a considerable array of charms, albeit not a large fortune or the prospect of such; but it so happened that the household was preoccupied with another, more urgent matter that had only recently arisen: a matter that prompted her chaise and four horses, which presented itself in the gloom of early evening a shade after the church clock had struck six, to be received discreetly and Estella and her lady's maid to be quickly spirited inside the Hall with a minimum of ceremony; and thus her advent, notable as it was, earned no more than a whisper in the ongoing considerations of the house, and thereby the parish, at that time.

The face of the stately edifice that was Wychwood Hall wore a sombre expression and was surrounded by stillness and silence that hung about the lawns and gardens like a ghostly cloak. In the welcome light of the entrance hall Estella bounded forward in joyous haste to greet her dearest friend, only to find that noble and normally energetic person surprisingly subdued and, indeed, upon the verge of tears. They fell into each other's arms. "Jane, whatever is the matter? Something is wrong, I know it is. You must tell me at once!"

"Oh, Estella! I wish I could offer you a more cheerful welcome. You must prepare yourself." Jane paused at this moment to suppress a rising sob.

"Where is Jonathan?" Estella asked, fearful of the worst, looking around her in vain. Jonathan was Jane's brother: a captain in the Royal Horse Artillery, presently returned from duty to convalesce following the overturning of a gun in which he had suffered serious injury.

Jane continued in a faint voice: "He is missing."

"Missing? What do you mean? I thought he was here!"

"He has not been seen by anyone since yesterday evening. Something terrible has happened to him, I know it has. It is not like him to just disappear: he is so very dependable."

Estella was momentarily overwhelmed, for, as the servants' whispers had correctly surmised, she had undeclared feelings for Jonathan that she had strong hopes were reciprocated, but her emotion was swiftly tempered by unselfish compassion for her friend and she found herself facing the unwelcome tidings with a calm resolve she had not known was within her. "Oh, my poor, dear Jane," she said. "You must not worry. I am sure that he shall soon be found, safe and sound."

A pearly tear escaped the corner of Jane's eye and slid down her cheek. "His leg is not yet healed. He could barely stand upon it yesterday, but he insisted upon going out. We only realised that he had not come home again at dinner. They searched for him until very late, and all day today, but they found… they found no trace of him anywhere."

"There, there. Do not cry so, Jane. He *shall* be found, you shall see."

Estella comforted her friend, who then begged her to see to her own needs after such a long journey, and took her upstairs and walked with her as far as her room, leaving her only so that each could make their toilette in preparation for the evening meal. Dinner was a sombre affair: no-one had much appetite for conversation or food alike, there was no more news of Jonathan, and afterwards each one at the table mumbled their excuses and retired early. When Estella arrived back in her chamber she was attended by Sally, her lady's maid.

"A desperate time, Madam. The servants are all beside themselves. Can nothing more be done?"

"I am told everything that can be done has already been done."

"But Captain Jonathan cannot just have vanished."

"Indeed no. There must be a rational explanation."

"And no sign of the hound either. Perhaps they are together, at least."

"Hound? What hound?"

"Oh! Well mister Norfolk said that the young master had gone off after one of the hounds: Hengist, I think he said its name was. It had got out of the yard when he opened the gate and ran off." Norfolk was the butler to Jonathan and Jane's father, Lord Wychwood, the master of Wychwood Hall.

"Did he indeed?! And what else did mister Norfolk say?"

"He said the young master was uncommonly fond of that dog, and when it went off towards the village with a great howl, like it was on a scent, and set the others baying and making a hullabaloo, the young master cursed himself for a fool and straight away limped off after it saying he would fetch it back himself."

When Sally had completed her duties and retired, Estella lay in bed, her head whirling with cruel apprehensions and new conjectures provoked by Sally's gossip; but she was so deeply fatigued after her long journey that she was very soon obliged to abandon her battle with those circling imps and spectres, and settled, with an unsatisfied sigh, into a deep sleep.

As the faint fingertip of an overcast dawn brushed the window panes of her bedroom, she awoke from her repose refreshed and resolute, and soon afterwards, dressed but without having broken her fast, was proceeding along the path to the kennels beside well-tended lawns, listening to a blackbird singing in the surrounding woods, with the far-away cawing from a rookery near the churchyard and the yelping and growling of the hounds at their morning feed providing tenor and bass accompaniment. A long, low building with a tiled roof and a large, walled yard, the kennels adjoined the huntsman's neat and well-kept cottage where Cobbett, who was the current resident, introduced her to some charming puppies, in whose playful company she would have happily remained all day were it not that she had other plans, and at the same time obliged her with answers to her questions; from which she learned that the young master was committed heart and soul to the hunt, and was a naturally excellent horseman, although he had been forbidden by the doctor to ride until his injury had healed completely; and that Hengist had never run away before and, like the young master, there was yet no sign of him. On being asked what he thought may have happened to the hound, the huntsman could only give a terse shake of his head and a shrug of his wiry shoulders.

After breakfast, finding her friend Jane cruelly indisposed due to a sleepless night, Estella embarked upon a walk to the village with Sally at her side.

"How I wish I had seen those pups, Madam. They sound a proper tonic."

"Indeed they are most delightful, and you shall accompany me next time. Mister Cobbett the huntsman is a dear man, but he is a little too firm with the hounds in my opinion, although not cruel. I understand also that he is unmarried…" At this, Sally blushed and Estella laughed aloud. "I see you have made enquiries already!"

The lane took them up a gentle hill, and when they mounted the crest the sun ventured to appear for the first time that day through a gap in the clouds, treating them to a most perfect view across the valley in which the nestling church, the village green, and the neatly ordered gardens and fields yielded to a surrounding downland landscape of grassy hillsides and woodland slopes. Here their viewing was interrupted as their attention was drawn by a trail of white smoke that was arrowing towards them between the hills at an impossible speed.

"Madam...?" Sally was quite taken aback.

"I believe we shall see it come by quite close to us! It is the new steam train from Brighton, Sally. Do you see the route it will take? It will follow the line of those trees, and then come by beneath us, where they have cut that channel through the hill. They say it is the fastest engine ever built!"

"It frightens me, Madam. It is like a monstrous dragon flying across the countryside. Oh, I beg you, do not say it is coming here!"

The steam locomotive indeed raced towards them, seeming to increase its furious velocity as it approached. From their vantage point they breathlessly observed it rampage through the cutting below, great billows of smoke and steam streaming behind it.

When the noise had abated, Estella said: "Do not be afraid, Sally. It is a great beast, indeed it is, but a friendly one I believe and we must become accustomed to it for they say none shall stop its progress now."

Soon afterwards they arrived at the outskirts of the village and Estella came to a halt at the first dwelling: a modest, flint-walled cottage upon the doorstep of which a small girl of perhaps six years of age, wearing a coarse smock that was too small for her and no shoes, was sitting, prodding idly at

249

the ground with a short stick, with a pair of white geese foraging nearby in the yard. The sun had retreated again, taking refuge behind a thick, grey curtain of cloud.

"The hound ran in this direction, or so Cobbett said. We must ask if anyone saw it."

"Leave it to me, Madam." Sally approached the girl in a friendly way, contriving somehow not to mind the geese, and soon had her talking freely despite some initial shyness on the girl's part, and in only a little time she brought her over to Estella. "This is the lady I was telling you about as what lost her dog," she said. "She is very sad about it. Will you help us?"

Estella bent down to bring herself level with the child. "Hello. Why, how pretty you are! What's your name?"

"Rose, Miss."

"Well, Rose, my dog has run away and I am looking for him. It would have been the day before yesterday when he came by. He has white socks and a brown back and a white tip to his tail, and he is very friendly. His name is Hengist. I am sure he would not have passed you by without stopping to say hello. Did you see him?"

"No, Miss."

"Have you heard anyone talking about him?"

Rose looked at her feet and kicked half-heartedly at something she had seen in the dirt. "No, Miss."

"And the young master from the Hall - you know who I mean? – did you see him come by looking for my dog?"

"No Miss."

"Thank you, Rose. You are well-named: pretty as your namesake, and when you are grown up you shall be a famous beauty, I have no doubt." Estella rose to her full height. "Come, Sally, let us try farther along the lane."

"Miss?"

"Yes, Rose?"

"My Nana lost her dog. It ran off, like yours did, and it never came back neither."

"Really? Your Nana? And when was this?"

The child's eyes filled with tears. "I don't know, Miss. I don't like to think of it."

Soon afterwards Estella and Sally were uncomfortably installed at the kitchen table in the tiny cottage of Rose's grandmother, Mrs Fielding. The cottage's interior was small and cramped; this situation being made worse by the prodigious number of objects crammed into the available space: baskets of dried flowers competed with clay jars, glass bottles, and sacks full of rags, whilst the furniture was laden with uncomfortable numbers of old cushions, bolsters and blankets in the process of being repaired. Mrs Fielding offered to put the kettle on the fire for a pot of nettle tea, but was dissuaded from this when both women politely declined; then, having established that Estella was a visitor to the Hall and in search of Captain Jonathan and the escaped hound, the venerable dame unhesitatingly took it upon herself to reassure her that she must not worry about the young master, as he had been called back to his regiment at short notice, which tidings she said she had from a neighbour whose son was in the army, so he should know. This being patently no more than a false and idle rumour that could only bring her mistress and her friends at the Hall more misery, Sally was about to let go a sharp response about raising vain hopes and making thoughtless tittle tattle when she felt a jab in her arm from Estella's elbow and instead held her tongue. It was only then that Mrs Fielding finally began to relate the tale the women had come to hear concerning her dog, a mongrel named Crumpet of incomparable looks, intelligence and dependability that had been her constant companion, she said, for more than ten years. The faithful Crumpet had suddenly disappeared about three weeks before, and no sign of her had been seen since by anyone in the neighbourhood. When Estella asked if she had any thoughts about what had happened, Mrs Fielding first weighed her up with a long, careful look and then sent Rose away upon an errand and shut the door firmly.

"Indeed I do have an idea, my dear Miss Burtenshaw, although you will think me a silly old woman for it, just as everyone else does," and here she sighed at having to carry the burden of such adverse opinion. "My poor, dear Crumpet, God rest her soul, is not the only dog to have gone missing in the last few months. I could name three or four, and then there's the cats as well. Now when I went looking for her, I had more than half an idea already who had taken her, and so that's where I went: Elias Mutton's house."

"Elias Mutton. Is he a local man? What made you think of him?"

"I have known him for sixty-seven years, and he never was much of a one for company, especially not after his wife and son died. Ill-tempered and mean, he is, to everyone - with no exceptions. Not much of a one for churchgoing, neither. But for all that, I have always known that he was never a bad 'un. Not deep down. And he never took no dogs belonging to someone else. But since last Michaelmas, Crumpet took to barking at Elias Mutton whenever she got the chance, and she had never done that before! After that, if I took her past his house, she wouldn't stop with her barking and whining until we were well down the lane, and if we came to pass him on the road she would give him a wide berth and keep her eyes on him, all the while bark, bark, bark, until he was long gone by, and there was nothing I could do to stop her, neither. He didn't like it, of course, but he never said anything; just gave me these nasty looks. So when Crumpet went missing, he was the first person I thought of, you see."

"You went to his house?"

"I went there alright. I wasn't afraid of him. Not then, I wasn't. The place was more run down than ever: holes in the roof, and weeds in the yard, and a terrible smell coming from it like something had died and was left laying where it fell. I knocked on the door, and when he came he just stood there in the doorway and didn't ask me in, just left me standing there. He looked terrible, and at first he wouldn't look me in the eye or say anything, even when I said I knew he had taken her. Then I said I was going to come back with help, and he just laughed and said I wouldn't remember, and even if I did no-one would listen to me. He was right about the second part, anyway, because they all think I am a fanciful, superstitious old woman. Then he did look at me, and that look was so cold and hateful that I wanted to run away there and then but I wouldn't give him the satisfaction. He started muttering under his breath, cursing and swearing I am sure, and so I gave him one of my looks and then I turned my back on him and I walked away. Walked with my head held high, I did, but I did chance a look back over my shoulder: Elias Mutton is seventy-three years old and bent over with the palsy, but when I saw him staring after me from the doorway he was standing as straight as a broom-handle."

The village green was unusually quiet, and those people that were out hurried about their business with their heads down as if they were expecting a storm, although there were none of the usual atmospheric signs of one coming. "What now, Madam?" Sally asked, pulling her shawl about her as they emerged from the front door of Mrs Fielding's cottage.

253

"I am minded that we should pay a visit to Mr Elias Mutton," Estella said, "But before we do so, I should like to take the opportunity to make a few more enquiries here in the village."

They asked a farmer's wife, but she had not seen or heard of any hound on the loose from the Hall, and when Estella asked her if she had seen Captain Jonathan she repeated the story they had heard from Mrs Fielding about him being recalled to his regiment, at which Sally could not restrain herself, and put the poor woman right about the situation in the strongest possible terms. After that, they could not get another word.

The innkeeper proved to be more talkative, and although he had no information about Hengist the hound, he did say that there was a lot of old nonsense being talked recently about dogs and cats going missing when probably they had just crawled away under a bush to die, as animals do when their time comes, as their instincts dictate. He said he had a strong feeling the young master would turn up safe and well, and wished Estella and Sally well. When asked about Elias Mutton he seemed surprised that Estella should be interested in him, shook his head and said it was a shame he had no friends and no one to help him in his old age, but that was what came of being ill-tempered and rude to one's neighbours for an entire lifetime; there was no talking to him, even now when Old Scratch was no doubt stoking up the flames to receive him shortly.

To reach Elias Mutton's house they had to walk through the village on the road and then take a narrow track that ran eastward through orchards and then grazing land. The track became narrower, the hedgerow on each side being overgrown, and before long it was little more than a barely-trodden path, overhung by trees and choked with weeds and bushes. Sally was all for turning back as soon as the going became difficult, but Estella was determined and led the way, which, it proved, was not at all as impassable as it seemed and for a while they made good progress; but the trees meeting overhead blocked out the light and in the gloom Sally lost courage with every step, and at last she halted and would go no farther.

"Come, now Sally. We must be nearly there. Indeed, I believe it is just around this next turn." Estella said.

"Sorry, Madam, but I cannot take another step in this awful place."

"We have come this far. We may as well see it through. Come now, Sally. Put your best foot forward."

"My feet are not my own, Madam. They will go in one direction only, which is backwards."

Estella took a few paces down the path and peered into the gloom. "I am sure it cannot be much farther. Sally, you stay here. I am going to walk on a little way to see if I can see Mr Mutton's cottage."

"Oh, Madam, please don't leave me alone!"

When Estella had walked twenty paces, she was surprised to find that Sally had followed her and was holding onto her coat-tails like a child. She took Sally's hand in hers and led on. Just around the turn, as Estella had predicted, they received their first view of Elias Mutton's cottage: situated in a close dell, small and roughly made, it was undoubtedly the most poorly-maintained and unwelcoming structure Estella had seen here or anywhere else on her travels. The walls were covered in creepers that had become as thick as tree-trunks before giving up the ghost, having torn great cracks in the walls with their exploring tendrils; the roof was full of jagged holes; the glass in the windows cracked and filthy, the window frames rotten. The yard was overgrown and littered with debris, the gate hung partly off its hinges, and great fir trees had grown up all about, ensuring that it remained permanently in shadow. There was no sign of any life, animal or vegetable, anywhere near it. It was a dispiriting sight, and enough to make Sally entirely lose her remaining powers of locomotion.

"This surely cannot be the place, Madam. No-one could live here."

"It must be. Strange… it does look uninhabited."

"I am so frightened. I would not go any nearer for all the tea in China. Can we go home now?"

"We have come this far. I am going to knock upon the door." Estella steeled herself and marched towards the gate, with some difficulty on account of the briars and weeds that impeded her way, but Sally would not release her hand and stumbled along beside her. At last they stood in the yard before the door of the cottage, which was firmly shut. Estella knocked loudly, and then took a step back and waited.

A minute passed and there was no reply. She knocked again, more loudly. "Perhaps he is not at home," she said. "Perhaps it is the wrong place." Sally could not muster any words in reply. Then there was the sound of footsteps from inside, and a bolt was drawn; whereupon Estella and Sally both found themselves edging away from the door. Sally's eyes were fixed upon the latch, which rattled and then lifted slowly, at which she let out a short squeal of fear; and then the door swung open inwards, creaking loudly, and standing in the doorway was a man who answered the description of Elias Mutton. All of his clothes were much too large for him: he was wearing a shirt with no collar that might once have been white, with a waistcoat over it; his trousers were baggy and his legs bowed, and on his feet he wore heavy boots. He might once have been tall, but age and toil and diet had worn him down and disease bowed him to the point that he was on the same eye level as Estella. His complexion was very pale, his skin thinly stretched and blotchy; indeed, he looked unwell and anaemic. He said nothing; just stood in the doorway and looked Estella and then Sally up and down, sizing them up, but not meeting their gaze.

"Mister Mutton?" Estella asked. "How do you do? I am Estella Burtenshaw." Mutton did not reply, so she continued: "I am looking for a dog. A foxhound. It ran off, you see. It came this way."

The old man grunted noncommittally. There was a very bad smell emanating from the doorway that reminded Estella of the odour she had encountered once when there was a dead rat found under the floorboards, only much stronger.

"I was wondering if you had seen it, perhaps?" she added.

Mutton shook his head slowly. "No," he said in a low, hoarse voice. His eyes darted back and forth without meeting theirs.

"And there was a young man that may have come this way looking for the dog: Captain Jonathan from the Hall. Did you see him?" The smell from inside came at her in waves.

There was more slow shaking of the head. "No." Mutton licked his lips

"I see." Estella paused, realising that she had little more to say but nonetheless sure that she had more business to pursue with Elias Mutton. She tried to find a way to continue the conversation, but was also fighting a strong urge to leave and so in the end could only come up with: "Well, Mister Mutton, I am sorry to have troubled you."

Mutton firmly closed the door in her face. Estella and Sally turned together and walked away from the house.

"I am so glad that Jonathan is safe and well," Estella said after a few paces. "I am not at all surprised his regiment called him back. They must rely upon him a great deal."

"Indeed," Sally replied, entirely recovered from her fears of only a few moments before. "And as for that silly hound, he is probably twenty miles away by now and still running." They continued out of the gate and took a path through the trees in a direction they had not previously been at a brisk pace.

"We must hurry. I am sure everyone will be wondering where we have been."

"Yes, Madam; I'm sure you are right." Sally looked around her, slowly registering her surroundings. "Madam, where *have* we been?"

"Where have we been? Don't be ridiculous!"

"Sorry Madam, but... where are we?"

"Where are we? Why, it's perfectly obvious where we are. Perfectly obvious... we're... we're..." Estella stopped walking and frowned. "We're lost."

"Please don't say that." Sally frowned. "I don't like it around here. I don't feel safe."

"I am afraid I don't know where we are, Sally. I don't recognise it at all."

"How did we get here?" Sally's voice trembled. She caught hold of Estella's arm and clung on to it tightly.

"That is a very good question! How did we get here? Where have we been?"

"I don't know." Sally's voice was barely a whisper.

"No, I don't know either. We were staying at the Hall, I remember that. That's where we are going: back to the Hall."

"The Hall. Of course! That's right."

"We went for a walk... is that it?"

"A walk… we went for a walk." Sally clapped her hands to her head. "The train! I remember the noise and clouds of smoke when it came past us: I was so frightened!"

"The train! That's it. We were looking for something! Jonathan! But no, he's been recalled by his regiment. No! He's still lost! We were looking for him, and…" The memories came crowding back into her head, dispelling the fog that had somehow crept in there. "We went to Elias Mutton's house."

"Madam, please. Let's go home, back to the Hall. I can't stand this a moment longer, any of it! I can't bear it!"

"There is something very wrong here, Sally. We must get to the bottom of it. I fear that Elias Mutton knows exactly what has happened to Jonathan and to Hengist. I know this sounds silly, but I think he did something to us, I don't know how, to make us go away and forget him." Estella frowned, and her eyes grew steely with resolve. "I want to look inside Mister Mutton's house."

"Oh Madam!" Sally was crying with fear.

"We shall retrace our steps to his house and watch until he goes out."

"No, Madam. I can't go back there. I can't go in there."

"I shall go in. We shall wait together, and then when he has gone I shall go in and I shall need you to stay hidden outside and keep watch in case he comes back."

It was only twenty minutes later that Estella, watching the house from behind a large holly bush with Sally still quailing at her side, witnessed Mutton leaving: he emerged from the door looking bent and aged, took a long and cautious look around him, and - on seeing no-one – straightened and loped off through the trees on a path only he knew at surprising speed. Estella waited for a moment to see if he would come back, and when he did not she took both of Sally's hands firmly in her own and looked her in the eye. "Sally, it is most important that you remain here and watch the house while I go inside. If Mister Mutton comes back you must warn me. Do you understand?"

"Madam, I beg of you: please do not go in there."

"Sally, please. You must warn me if he comes back."

"How, Madam?"

Estella thought for a moment. "You must scream very loudly and shout: 'Fire! Fire!' As loudly as you can, Sally. That will alert me and confuse him, which will give me a chance to slip out of the door."

Estella approached the house cautiously, it having occurred to her that there may be someone else at home, and her first action was to knock upon the door, softly at first, and then more loudly when there was no answer. At last, confident that there must be no-one inside, she tried the latch, but the door had been locked and wouldn't budge, and so then she walked carefully around the building, peering in through the grimy windows in vain, finding only internal shutters that were closed. The poor state of repair of the building came to her assistance in the end, as, when she came to the back door and tried it, the wooden door frame, which had rotted badly, gave way easily around the bolt and the door came open far enough, with a few tugs, for her to slip inside.

The door opened directly into the kitchen, which was dingy, ice-cold and damp; there were bare boards underfoot, the walls were decorated in grubby, flaking whitewash and cobwebs, and the stove, which occupied the fireplace, had not been used for some time. Little light came in through the kitchen window, which was not shuttered, but nonetheless crusted with grime; the larder, the door to which had been left open, was empty save for shards of broken pots and glass jars and some torn paper; and there was a small table, upon which there lay a selection of rusting, dirty utensils. Nothing had been cooked or consumed there for weeks, if not months.

Estella passed through the room taking care not to make noise or disturb anything. She reached the door that led into the living quarters and gently tried the latch. It lifted smoothly, but the door creaked when she pushed at it. She tried again, even more cautiously, and managed to swing it open silently by pushing only very slowly; her immediate care to establish that the room was unoccupied. This achieved, she turned her senses to exploring it. The smell was much stronger here: a pungent, animal smell of fur and rotting flesh. It was very dark, the shutters being closed, and it took a while for her eyes to accustom themselves, but once they had she perceived that the floor consisted of bare boards and was very dirty and heavily stained in places; the fireplace was cold and had not been cleaned; a rocking chair lay on its side by the hearth, the uppermost rocker splintered in twain; there was a cot in one corner with clothes and blankets heaped upon it, and a chest stood in another corner, the lid open and partially pulled from its hinges. Estella took a step forward into the room. At once she heard a long, low moan that chilled her blood and made her stop in her tracks: it was the exact, terrifying sound that she might have thought a lurking ghost would make, had she believed in such things. The sound stopped and she remained absolutely still, straining her hearing to pick up any further disturbances that might be associated with it. It was otherwise remarkably silent inside the cottage: not a clock ticked, not a board creaked. She could feel her heart pounding inside her chest like a hammer upon an anvil. Then the noise came again: a deep, slightly muffled moaning that did not originate from any particular part of the room insofaras she could tell but emanated from the very walls and floor. The urge to run was extraordinarily strong, but Estella concentrated upon breathing steadily and remained where she was. It must come from somewhere, she maintained to herself, and indeed as she listened she began to feel certain that the sound was emanating from the corner of the room occupied by the broken chest, where the stains upon the floor were particularly bad. She slipped quietly back into the kitchen and on a shelf found a stump of candle, which she lit with a match from her purse. Returning, she approached the corner cautiously, using the candle to peer ahead at the chest. The silence amplified every tiny noise she made as she moved. The floorboards around the chest were very deeply stained and scuffed. Another step and the stink of putrefaction rose up before her like an invisible wall. There came another long groan, this time from almost directly before her. She hesitated, reluctant to look into the chest for fear of what she might see, but at the same time determined to discover the source of the sound; then she leaned forward, holding the candle at full reach in a shaking hand so that she could view the contents. The light flickered, but at last the dark shadows resolved themselves and she saw: a pile of stinking brown bones lay there, rotting sinew and gristle still attached. At that very moment there came another long moan from the chest, louder this time, and it was accompanied by a muffled knocking sound. Estella felt light-headed and backed away towards the door, but her careless footsteps on the wooden floor provoked even louder knocking, and she feared that she might faint at any moment. How she found the resolve to remain inside the room she did not know, but instead of fleeing she halted, leaned upon the doorframe for support, and breathed deeply, reasoning with herself as she did so. She was in no doubt now, if she had

262

suffered any before, that she would be in mortal peril if Mutton were to return and discover her, for she was certain that Mutton must be behind the disappearances of the dogs, it being canine bones she had seen in the chest. However, far from adding to her terror, which was already beyond measure, this grim realisation made her spirits soar, for it suggested that the sounds she had been hearing, far from being the terrible moaning of supernatural creatures to be feared, might represent the groans of a victim in captivity. This hope spurred her on, and it was not long before she was back in front of the chest and looking closely at the floor around it. Then she began tugging at it, although it was very heavy; dragging it out of the corner and into the centre of the room. Beneath the chest she had exposed a trapdoor, of size about two feet squared, which she proceeded hurriedly to lift by means of a short, knotted rope, thinking all the while not of herself but of the victims she imagined groaning below; although her chief hope she dared not admit to herself for fear of disappointment. The trap door opened to a ladder descending into darkness!

From the depths, the rising stink of death and decay was overwhelming. Summoning all of her courage, she shouted down into the cellar below. "Hello? Do not be afraid! I am coming to free you." She climbed carefully down the ladder, and by the light of her small stub of candle found herself in a confined space that was nothing less than a charnel house. Bones littered the floor, dark bloodstains bespattered the walls, and the partially butchered remains of animals lay in disorder around the floor. She could barely breathe, but a very short search of the room led her to discover the object of her search: the figure of a man, bound with rope and with a sack over his head, who lay groaning upon the ground. She hurried over and, upon removing the sack, uncovered the pale and haggard face of none other than her dear Jonathan, blinking blindly in the – to him – bright light. He was wounded and fought weakly against her at first, but she spoke softly to him and reassured him that she was no dream phantom but indeed his Estella, come to rescue him, and he slowly understood and then wept tears of joy.

She freed him from his bonds and helped him to his feet: he was frail and in much pain, and must lean his weight upon her, and only very slowly were they able to make their way, one step at a time, to the ladder. He climbed ahead of her, rung upon rung, and at last they emerged into the cottage, where he lay trembling and exhausted upon the floor. "Up! Dear Jonathan, you must get up. He will come back, and he must not find us here," Estella urged, and he responded heroically with his last reserves of strength. Together, they stumbled through to the kitchen and made their way to the back door. The day, although overcast, seemed bright and joyous after their confinement and Jonathan uttered a cry of delight at it. It seemed to Estella that the daylight and sweet, fresh air replenished them both with strength and resolve, and she led him staggering to the trees where Sally, already terrified beyond the bounds of her wits, did not know what to make of his bloody and dishevelled state, and burst into more tears.

The journey back to the village was slow going, with Estella supporting Jonathan upon one side and Sally supporting him upon the other, and fraught with terror on the part of all three at the prospect that Elias Mutton might return and, finding his captive gone, come loping after them down the path at any moment, so when at last they reached the cluster of houses around the village green it was with great relief. They quickly attracted a small crowd; Jonathan was lain under a tree and attention given to his wounds. As he was gently tended to it became clear that his leg, which had been on the mend, was swollen and painful, and he was bruised and cut on his arms and face. That he had been beaten, mistreated and starved was not in doubt. As soon as could be arranged, the innkeeper's son was dispatched on horseback to the Hall with the joyous news that the young Captain had been found and was safe, and bearing requests from Estella for a carriage to take him home and for the doctor to be sent for. Estella explained to those assembled how she had found Jonathan a prisoner in Elias Mutton's house, and although it took some time for her meaning to be clearly understood and given credence by the many present who had known Elias Mutton all their lives, by the time she had finished the assembled folk were clamouring for action to bring Mutton swiftly to account.

The innkeeper held up his large hands for silence. "Justice must be served, indeed it must. And things look very black, very black indeed. But fair is fair and I for one will not condemn a man without allowing him his say before the judge."

"But he's a danger to every one of us: you heard what she said. We need to defend ourselves!"

"Aye, and he ate my poor Crumpet!" Mrs Fielding added firmly.

"We shall go to his house and find him, but I don't want no-one shooting him or setting fire to nothing. We'll take him and lock him up until the magistrate comes."

"And I say we will do what must be done."

"And any as takes the law into their own hands will have to account to me first and the magistrate after, is that clear?"

"Aye!" came the muted response from many throats.

"Then let us waste no further time!"

When the men had left, Estella and others helped Jonathan into the village inn, where a makeshift bed had been set up for him, and Estella sat at his side, mopped his brow and held his hand while he drifted in and out of wakefulness, muttering unintelligibly.

Sally brought some clean towels. "Madam, we are safe now, aren't we? Please say we are."

"Quite safe, Sally."

"I was so frightened. Dearest Madam, I am so sorry. I am afraid I was of no help to you at all."

"Quite the opposite! I really could not have done without you."

"It all seems such a blur. I feel so woolly headed. I remember meeting Elias Mutton. I had forgotten about him, but I remember now. And then we were lost in the woods. And then we came to ourselves and went back, and you saved Master Jonathan from that dreadful place. What happened to us, Madam?"

"I cannot explain it myself."

"It's when I think about it the woolly clouds form in my head."

"Dear Sally, try to get some rest. The carriage will be here soon enough."

After an hour or so the men returned with the news that they had not found Elias Mutton at home, but they had forced entry and witnessed the charnel carnage inside just as Estella had described. The party was surprisingly silent: even the innkeeper was cowed by what he had seen, and could only repeat "Ain't natural, it ain't. Ain't natural." He produced a bottle of brandy from behind the bar and made sure everyone that had been on the expedition had a good tot. The bravery demonstrated by Estella and Sally in rescuing Jonathan had been shown in a new light, and the two women were the subject of many a respectful toast and "God bless!"

The coach sent from the Hall arrived soon after, and with it Lord Wychwood himself to see his son alive after all and thank his son's valiant rescuers, and by his side was a tearful Jane, who would not be left behind in spite of her sleepless state. When he had bathed Jonathan's forehead himself several times and heard the story from Estella's own lips, and wrung her hand more than once from sheer gratitude, he could not contain himself longer but sprang to his feet. "By thunder, we shall hunt down this miserable wretch and feed him to the hounds or I am no knight of the Order! The huntsman is on his way, gentlemen, and then we shall see what we shall see!" Then he stood everyone in the inn two rounds of the best ale, which meant that by the time the hunting party had arrived the mood had lifted considerably.

After embracing Estella and offering her a long and rambling thank you, and extending the same courtesy to Sally with no less warmth, Jane displaced Estella from her brother's side and would not be moved thence until the doctor had arrived. That gentleman, after a thorough examination of the patient, pronounced him fit to be moved, whereupon Jane accompanied her dear brother into the carriage and went off to the Hall with the doctor, leaving Estella, who had hoped for that honour herself, and Sally, who had hoped to accompany her mistress, with no immediate prospect of transportation home.

The hunt rallied on the green outside the inn. Lord Wychwood and the huntsman, Cobbett, led the hounds and riders on a sortie to Mutton's house to pick up the trail. The pack was alert and purposeful and flowed down the country lane like dry autumn leaves bobbing down a swift stream. The villagers on foot were sent to search through the woods and flush the quarry out into the open. Estella and Sally watched them depart from outside the inn.

"What shall we do now, Madam?"

There had been several offers of shelter from the women of the village, who were conscious that Estella and her companion, being gentlefolk, may not feel comfortable with waiting at the inn; and Mrs Fielding, who could not have been more delighted with them now that they had so dramatically confirmed her suspicions beyond the doubts of her fellows, had invited them back to her house, and the innkeeper's wife had put her upstairs parlour at their disposal for as long as they needed it. Estella, however, had other ideas.

"Do you remember the hill we climbed on the way here, where we saw the engine? We should climb up there. We shall be able to see everything for miles."

"But... it's not safe, Madam. He is out there."

"It is the safest place of all. We shall be able to see danger long before it comes anywhere near us. It will be much safer than remaining indoors and waiting for him to steal in through an open window."

"Oh, how I wish we had gone back to the Hall!"

It was late afternoon and although it would not be dark for some hours yet the wind had picked up, driving the accumulating clouds in ominous shapes across the sky and bringing a premature and threatening gloom to the landscape. Estella and Sally stood upon the top of the hill above the railway cutting and surveyed the countryside around them; Sally looking anxiously about her in fear of an imminent attack, but Estella standing straight and tall and searching the land before her methodically. There was the hunt, on the far side of the village, still casting about in the woods near to Mutton's cottage; so distant that it resembled a swarm of black ants scavenging a garden lawn. Coming from the South West, and much nearer, was the line of men from the village. They had spread out line abreast, armed with cudgels and farm implements, and were advancing at a slow pace through the woods towards the more open orchards and fields near the village; their far-off cries slowly growing louder as they approached, beating trees and bushes to flush out the quarry. The rooks from the churchyard, disturbed from their treetop stronghold by the approaching tumult, circled on a rising current of warm air above, cawing warnings.

The faint call of a hunting horn drew her attention back to the hounds and riders, who were in motion now, spreading into a long line as they advanced quickly through the wood. The hounds pulled away, more agile in finding a path between the trees. "Sally, look: they have the scent! See how eager they are," Estella cried. Emerging from the wood, the hounds accelerated across a field and through a gap in the hedge, following a course that would take them around the village to the north. The riders came out of the trees next, the huntsman Cobbett way ahead of the field having been barely slowed in the wood thanks to famously fine horsemanship. Next came Lord Wychwood on his very large grey hunter, and behind him a motley assortment of horses and riders of all descriptions. Estella could hear the excited baying of the pack more clearly as it pursued the lead hound on the scent: before long it had a lead of a field and a half on the huntsman and was turning south west, skirting the village and following a line of trees that would bring it eventually to the road.

"Madam, they are coming this way!" Sally squealed.

"Sally, look! There he is! It must be him!"

A solitary figure had appeared from behind a clump of trees to the north of the hill on which Estella and Sally stood, and had loped off northwards on a trajectory that would bring it directly into the path of the approaching pack.

"It is him! They will catch him now for certain!" Sally cried. At that very moment the figure halted, paused, no doubt upon hearing the cries of the hounds, and then turned about and came away southwards, bearing directly towards the hill upon which the two women had mounted their vigil.

"Oh no! Whatever shall we do?"

Estella was watching the unfolding events calmly. "Do not fear. The hounds are nearly upon him even now." Indeed, the pack was closing down the approaching figure, which Estella now had no doubt was the murderous Elias Mutton. At last he turned at bay and met the pack leader head on. The hound seemed somehow smaller than Estella had expected now that it had caught up with Mutton, but she was surprised indeed when he lifted the animal clean off its feet with unnatural strength and twisted its neck with a turn of his wrist. The hound went suddenly limp in his grasp, and the remainder of the pack, which had surrounded him and was closing in, fell silent and began to back away. At that moment the huntsman galloped up and came to a halt, staring incredulously at the tableau before him. Moments later Lord Wychwood and the other riders began to arrive. Cobbett tried to rally the hounds with shrill cries, but he had lost all control of them. Mutton turned and, swatting at some of the hounds with the carcass of their brother, continued on his way southward. Whether anything was said to him could not be heard, but he showed no signs of responding. However, he had made little progress when the first of the men of the village rounded the hill ahead of him bearing staves and hooks and scythes. Mutton stopped in his tracks,

270

looking uncertainly back at the hunt and then forward at the villagers, whose numbers were multiplying as those behind caught up. In the drama of the moment, Estella was not at all surprised to hear the long, low rumble of distant thunder: the storm everyone had been expecting. A cry went up from the villagers, and Mutton seemed to make a decision. He turned in the direction of the hill and looked up at the crest purposefully. Estella drew herself up to her full height, expecting the worst.

With long strides, Mutton began to climb. Both women knew there was nothing to be done now but face the end - they were revealed! All hope lost, Estella stepped forward with an exclamation and placed herself between Mutton and her servant. "He shall not harm you, Sally!" she declared. Mutton halted and regarded the two women for what seemed an eternity. At that moment the wind dropped and a crack appeared in the clouds through which the sun poured its light. Estella could not know it, but from where Mutton stood, with the sun directly behind and her long shadow reaching almost to his feet, he beheld her outlined in golden light, her dark silhouette as terrifyingly strong and tall as the English knights of old; and indeed innocence was her armour, and virtue her shield. Mutton snarled and tucked the dead hound effortlessly under his arm, brandishing his fist defiantly, and seemed to grow even more in stature; his legs becoming thicker and longer, his shoulders broader, his arms more muscular. He roared a challenge to his pursuers, who had stopped and were staring in horror at their neighbour; and then Mutton turned away from the hill and loped off into the deep railway cutting that was his only remaining way of escape, the limp bundle under his arm hampering him not in the least. The huntsman blew his horn, summoning the hunt to give chase, but the distant rumbling had resolved itself not into a summer storm but into the clatter and whoosh of an oncoming train, and suddenly, spitting smoke and cinders, it filled the cutting with all the hulking menace of a raging dragon. In a long moment Mutton faced the approaching engine and seemed to grow greater still, changing before the horrified eyes of his pursuers into a monstrous creature with heavy shoulders and thick arms, answering the sound of the train with its own bellowing challenge from a great mouth lined with ragged, pointed teeth. Mutton seemed ready to take on the onrushing iron beast with his bare hands; but then the locomotive struck and there was nothing where he had been standing as the engine swept all before it. Mutton, or whatever he had become, had quite gone.

Estella drank from the Wychwood Cup at last, wedded to her Jonathan in a grand ceremony attended by the great and the good of the county, and Sally married her huntsman in a separate but no less well appreciated service, and each event was attended and enjoyed beyond measure by both women, and each couple settled into some semblance of happy married life. Estella and Sally remained close companions for the rest of their days. Hengist, the missing hound, turned up again at Wychwood of his own accord, having not been dined upon by Elias Mutton as feared but rather having found a bride of his own on a farm some miles away and sired a wriggling clutch of new pups, and was welcomed back by Jonathan and Estella like a long-lost son. Not long after the wedding, Estella learned from her new husband after much pressing that when they had found Elias Mutton's remains there had been nothing more than an unrecognisable bundle of skin, smashed bone, blood, jellified tissue, hair and teeth deposited by the track. The post-mortem had concluded that it was not only impossible to identify the remains as Elias Mutton, but impossible to tell dog parts from man. At this Estella refrained from observing, as she truthfully could have, that from her vantage point she had witnessed the dead hound thrown clear of Mutton's grasp by the collision with the engine, and that therefore the remains must be those of Elias Mutton and no other. She also neglected to say that if the remains did not appear to be entirely human, that was not a surprise to her, at least.

In time, when Jonathan could no longer ride because of the pain from his imperfectly healed injuries, Estella became Mistress of the Ashdown Bewick hunt. She maintained all of its traditions, carrying out her duties, ordinary and extraordinary, with utmost determination and diligence for more than twenty-five years.

Chapter 46: *It Isn't You*

Dear Nick

When you sent me that first story about the faun I knew it was one of your traps, and yet as you so cleverly judged I haven't been able to help myself. I've spent hours and hours poring over and researching all the articles and stories you've sent me as if they were some kind of puzzle. I think I wanted them to be. Stupidly, and even after everything you've put me through, I wanted to believe that you would go to the trouble of making something wonderful just for me, tailored to contain everything I love, everything that makes me happy. I was content for it all to come to nothing in the end if it just meant you had tried.

But it isn't coming to nothing, and in my heart I know it isn't you. You could never have done this. You just stole it, didn't you? Sending it to me one piece at a time, drawing me in slowly, and all the time giving the impression that it's you sharing your discoveries, creating a mystery for us to solve together, showing me that you love me, when really it's nothing to you, just a way of manipulating me.

I know it was Walter Peachey who collected all this together. Please don't bother lying about it. I know. Poor Walter Peachey. He really believed in fairies. He spent his whole life looking for them. He never found any actual evidence of their existence, only stories, but he never gave up, he always thought that the great discovery was only just round the next corner. In the end, they locked him up. They committed him because he tried to burn down the local manor house, Wychwood Hall. He would never say why, and they say he never lost his mania for it. They only released him when he was dying and too weak to carry out his threat.

These papers you've stumbled upon are Walter's. I believe somewhere in there is the explanation of what happened to him: why he went mad, and what it has to do with the fairies and with Wychwood Hall. I want you to send me all the papers you've got left, straight away. All of them: no more teasing. Sending them to me one by one won't make any difference to us. It's too late for us, Nick. It's over. You know it in your heart. But if I had them all, then... then I could solve it, Nick. I could find out. Please, Nick. Don't you want to know?

H

Chapter 47: *The Wedding*

The autumn solstice sun imbued a golden burnish to the scene of the bride, in her pearl-and-white wedding gown, riding a magnificent white horse slowly and gracefully across the meadow. She was flanked on each side by four young bridesmaids in blood-crimson shifts with matching floral garlands in their hair who were carrying wicker baskets, the contents of which they took turns to run scatter in her path, throwing handfuls of rose petals high into the windless air so that they would flutter prettily to the ground before and around her. The children from the village were following the procession, running and playing, their voices blending with the birdsong and the chatter of the crowd as it gathered outside the church. Ambling steadily under Belle's guidance, the white mare, its long mane and tail plaited artfully, took a direct route towards the gate, which was being opened by top-hatted ushers dressed in charcoal tailcoats and grey trousers, with wing collars and bright ties, and the bridesmaids streamed ahead as the party approached, scampering through the gate and preparing the way with more petals. The horse snorted as it arrived and clattered to a halt on the roadway, where the wedding traffic chaos had been temporarily halted, and an usher took the bridle. Belle's father, in a grey morning coat, reached up and helped his daughter down from her perch.

"Thank you, Daddy," she said with a gracious smile. The bridesmaids scurried to arrange her long train while the watching crowd pressed forward to get a closer look. The mare stamped her foot on the road, and Belle turned to her, pressing their heads briefly together and whispering something; then the usher led the horse away. As I was absently watching from my vantage point on the path up to the church, Henry turned suddenly and looked straight at me, as if he had somehow sensed my presence: a look of pure malice. I was unprepared and for a moment was a butterfly on a pin, but then someone stepped between us and we both turned away.

"My lords, ladies and gentlemen, kindly take your places in the church: the ceremony is about to begin." The voice belonged to another of the ushers. The crowd began to break up, a steady flow of people making their way at different speeds, in a variety of best suits and dresses, through the lich gate and up the path to the church door. Some of the gathering did not have an invitation to the church, and remained where they were, gawping at the bridal party. I looked for Charlie among their number, but there was no sign of him, so I left them to it and strolled, somewhat reluctantly, up the path myself.

I had hoped that I might avoid having to play any part in the ceremony, the whole thing being somewhat contrary to my own interests after all, but Mother had soon put paid to that and it had swiftly transpired that I would have the ignominious pleasure of giving her away, although thankfully no speech would be required from me at the reception. I hadn't been invited to the rehearsal, my role, according to Mother, being so straightforward that even an idiot could do it, and so when I had climbed the hill I found myself waiting awkwardly outside the church, wishing that I could be somewhere, anywhere else and dreading the day ahead.

It being a double wedding, the co-ordination of the walks down the aisle was a tricky business. Belle and her father would go first, while I waited outside for Mother to arrive as soon as they had gone. This required split-second precision, or the illusion of it at least: Mother would actually be on a circular flight path in Wychwood's vintage Jaguar until being given the signal for permission to land; a compromise on her part that she had described as silly nonsense, and to which she had agreed only when directly and firmly requested to do so by Henry. It also required my presence there at the church door waiting for her; an uncomfortable intersection with Belle and her father since I was now persona non grata with both. However, they were both preoccupied and when I got there I got away with saying a brief hello, which was barely acknowledged, and then retreating to a corner of the churchyard until they had gone through the doors.

I leaned against the churchyard wall and closed my eyes. It was the end of all things, this wedding. I puffed out some air and opened my eyes, and as I did my gaze fell upon a gravestone directly in front of me. It was granite: tall and rectangular, with a slight convex curve to the top edge. The face was worn, but very legible; and the legend read as follows:

Walter Peachey
1842-1909
The way beneath the wood they took,
From sight of man were hence enveiled;
Rain wept, wind howled, fire died, earth shook;
The beasts and birds the loss bewailed.

"Hello Walter, fancy meeting you here!" I said under my breath. "I'm between a rock and a hard place. Any suggestions?" But I already knew what Walter would say.

It seemed an age before Henry, Belle and bridesmaids set off through the church doors. Their journey to the altar began to the accompaniment of thunderous organ chords, and then the doors shut again and Mother arrived exactly as

278

scheduled. She had decided not to compete with Belle in the earlier donkey derby, or indeed for the meringue prize, and had opted for an tea-length dress in ivory lace that made her look like a refugee from the 1960's, which I suppose she was. There were no bridesmaids for her either: Mother had very few friends who were not single middle aged men. "Nicholas!" she called piercingly, quite unnecessarily since I was already on my way back to meet her at the church door. There were still a couple of ushers manning the doors, but for a horrible moment Mother and I were more or less alone. She was on ridiculously high heels, and only a little shorter than I was, but she looked up at me somewhat pathetically and said: "Be happy for me." I tried to smile, really I did.

The ushers opened the doors and then the organist began playing the Trumpet Voluntary, the congregation turned as one to look, and we began to advance slowly. Mother's hand gripping my forearm was more physical contact than we had had in a very long time.

Faces I mostly didn't recognise floated past in the pews; some curious, some enjoying the occasion, some whispering to each other as they cast knowing glances at us. Mother enjoyed the attention, her triumphant eyes flicking from one face in the crowd to another. Her grip tightened and she began walking more and more slowly, whilst I found myself wishing the tombs below the stone flags of the church floor would open up and swallow me, or better still swallow everyone, right down into the rotting bowels of Hell. Ahead of us, the wedding party stood in front of the altar: the priest, Belle and Clifton, with Henry at Belle's side and the best men, Clifton's a hulking, lump-faced rugby player I didn't know and Henry's a grey haired man I thought I recognised from the hunt, flanking them. The bridesmaids were gathered behind on both sides, leaving a space for Mother and I between Henry and his best man on the left.

Was that a hint of sneering triumph I could detect in Henry's face? Clifton was ruddy faced, trying hard to look happy, but sweating in his tight collar like a prize porker at the abattoir door. As for Belle, she wasn't looking at Mother and I at all, but had her eyes fixed on Clifton with what looked to be an adoring smile on her lips; a tableau that hurt like a knife thrust vigorously again and again right between my ribs. I willed her to look at me, to show me even the tiniest flicker of recognition of something still between us; not in hope that there was a way back, because there was none, I knew that, but in hope that the consequences of what had happened in the chapel might be hurting her, even if not as much as they were me. Closer and closer we came, and not once did she so much as flick a glance in my direction.

We lined up beside the others and I waited in utter dejection for my father-of-the-bride line to come around. I couldn't really see anyone other than the priest from where I was standing without looking ninety degrees right, which was fine by me. When I did risk a glance, all I could see was Mother glaring at the quite wonderful flower arrangements with which the church interior was bedecked: calla lilies, roses, dahlias, rudbekia, sunflowers, with berries, twigs and pine cones, and even an occasional pumpkin. Having come late to the party she had had no say, and as a consequence was finding fault with everything, or perhaps she was taking the autumnal theme personally. The burning autumnal reds and oranges took me back to the beech wood and that spellbinding first kiss with Belle, deepening my misery.

When at last, after Henry had given Belle away, I was asked to give Mother away, I managed to snap out of that sad woodland reverie, spoke up and played my part. It was almost as if someone else was saying the words. After that I was supposed to sit down, but when I turned to take my place in the reserved front pew I found that the bridesmaids and family members had poached my seat and were showing no desire to push up to make room for me. I considered making a fuss, but I knew it would only get me into more trouble and it provided a convenient excuse for me to slink away into the empty side chapel where I could still see something of the proceedings but no-one would be looking at me - or so I thought. When I had taken my seat I encountered Cissy giving me the blackest of black looks from the second pew to my right. She looked much older than I remembered, her eyes watery and tired, eyelids droopy with excessive mascara, and jowly cheeks over-rouged. Her large-print white and navy dress and matching hat placed her squarely with the frumpy brigade. I gave her a short nod of acknowledgement, and she responded by closing her eyes and turning her face away.

As the ceremony droned on, I found my eyes wandering idly around the church. They settled upon a white marble memorial stone set in the wall to my left; one of many plaques, but this one had tiny winged skulls in the corners and black lettering, which made me think how much Hazel would have liked it. It said:

TO THE MEMORY
OF
SIR JOHN STRUDWICK, BARONET
OF THE ORDER OF ST DUNSTAN KNIGHT MARSHAL,
HIS BELOVED WIFE AGNES, LADY STRUDWICK
AND ONLY SON GEORGE, AN INFANT,
WHO DYED IN THE GREAT FIRE
OF WYCHWOOD HALL 21st JUNE MDCLXXV

Et post haec mittam eis multos venatores et venabuntur
eos de omni monte et de omni
colle et de cavernis petrarum.

The moment when the priest asked if anyone knew cause
or just impediment why these persons should not be joined
together in Holy Matrimony brought a silent pause in
proceedings and a ridiculous, twitching smile to my lips that
I was helpless to control, but I sat in silence and the priest
moved on. It took an inordinate time to reach the kiss. We
stood up and sat down about a dozen times, and then they
spun things out even further with a holy communion. While
people were queueing for their morsel of Jesus a baby went
off like a car alarm at the back of the church and was walked
up and down for a bit, providing a diversion until its mother,
worn down by waves of disapproval both real and imaginary
from the congregation, took it outside. Then a toddler ran
down the aisle, making a bolt for the exit. He deserved to be
rewarded for his initiative, but he was chased down and
carried back to endure more, saying very articulately "But
why, Mummy? Why?", which encapsulated some of my own
thoughts with prodigious accuracy.

At the end of the ceremony a pair of the older bridesmaids
came forward with a huge silver wedding cup held between
them. It was filled with wine by an usher, which took several
bottles, and each bride and groom drank from it three times.
The Wychwood Cup, as it was known, was large enough for
everyone in the church to have a sip if they wanted. It was
passed around the family in a deeply unhygienic way, which
took an age. When it came to me, I passed it on without
partaking: no-one seemed to notice or indeed to mind; and
then it was passed to friends and distant relatives, until it
had done the rounds of the entire congregation.

When the last sip had been taken and the cup retrieved, the wedding party set off on its final triumphant procession from the altar towards the church door, bringing the church service mercifully to an end. The organist played the recessional: Mendelssohn's 'Bridal March' from A Midsummer Night's Dream. First came the four youngest bridesmaids, walking backwards and scattering yet more rose petals before them; next another, slightly older, carefully bearing the – now empty, the dregs having been drained foolishly, or perhaps heroically, by one of the ushers - wedding cup. Then came the newlyweds: Clifton and Belle first, Belle beaming radiantly at all and sundry and Clifton shuffling alongside looking like a landed codfish. Two bridesmaids followed, managing Belle's long train between them. Henry Wychwood, processing with Mother on his arm next in line, had the smug air of a wolf with a goat in one pocket and a ewe in the other. Mother was basking in whatever attention was left in Belle's wake, occasionally waving and blowing kisses to people she recognised. After them, the remaining bridesmaids, best men and ushers paired up and were joined by those emptying out from the pews. Progress was slow.

As the doors were thrown open the church bells joyfully hurled their clangour from the tower, only to be cut immediately and shockingly short, the dying cadence of the first peal interrupted by a single clang, and then nothing. The wedding party was already outside, with a press of family behind and others at the back still waiting to exit the pews, and I hadn't yet moved from my seat. There was a secondary rattling and clattering from the direction of the tower door. The organist continued to play, bent over the keyboard in rapt concentration as if nothing had happened, but I caught some swift movement behind me in the corner of my eye and turned to see the priest and a few of the officiators rush from the vestry. Others still in the church stopped shuffling and followed my gaze. Frozen in my seat, I could only watch as the tower door swung open with a bang before the priest could get to it and a half dozen ashen-faced bell-ringers hurriedly exited in a thin cloud of dust. One sat down in a pew quickly, fanning herself, and the others grouped around her. The priest did a silent count of them, and then the ringers and officials gathered into an urgent knot, communicating in low voices. Then the priest went over to the tower door, looked inside, and disappeared into the interior. Meanwhile two of the men advanced towards the frozen congregation, their faces in set expressions that were designed to hide their underlying anxiety.

"Ladies and gentlemen, please keep moving and exit the church," one of them announced over the continuing organ music. "No cause for any alarm. No need to rush. Take your time." In response to a clamour of questions, he added: "There's a slight technical problem in the bell tower. Nobody hurt. Nothing to worry about. Please keep moving. That's right."

We emerged to long shadows in the churchyard. People began to cluster in small groups in the remaining sunny patches, discussing what had happened in low tones and sending off inquisitors to find out more. Mother came to find me because she wanted me in the photographs; the only person who did, including me. She took a firm grip of my arm and began shepherding me to where the photographer trying, with little success, to conduct his business. "What on Earth is going on? Where have you been? This isn't anything to do with you, is it?" she demanded.

"Certainly not," I replied indignantly. "Why on Earth would you think it's got anything to do with me?"

Belle was furious and barking orders at anyone who came near her, and even Mother kept her distance. Henry had disappeared back into the church, no doubt taking charge in his brisk, military fashion. Eventually intelligence began to emerge, and was passed from cluster to cluster. "It was deliberate sabotage by vandals," a man declared with Sherlockian certainty to the group next to us. "Apparently they cut through the bell ropes so that when they were pulled the last strands would break. All the ropes came down. Someone could have been killed."

"Who would do such a terrible thing?" Mother demanded theatrically, looking at me suspiciously.

The man didn't answer: in his mind he had already solved the crime. "It's a miracle no-one was hurt," he replied. "The police will have to be called."

"But why? Why would anyone do that?"

He shrugged. "Their idea of a joke."

It was Charlie, of course. It had to be. Charlie, bolstering my resolve. Charlie, reminding me that I had a choice, that they couldn't have it all their own way. Charlie, silencing the fucking bells, bless him.

The photographer doggedly pursued his task of trying to shepherd both happy couples into position for pictures, a task worthy of Sysiphus. I stayed out of as many of the official photographs as I could: not much of a challenge, especially for someone so generally unpopular, but I couldn't avoid some of the group shots, and inevitably Mother wanted some tedious shots of us together. She, of course, made sure she was in as many of the pictures as possible.

When at last photographs had been taken to the satisfaction of all parties, calm had been restored, bell ringers had been visited and fussed over, all due greetings had been exchanged between family, friends and acquaintances, and all was ready, which had taken a period of not less than two hours, both pairs of bride and groom formed up and paraded out together through the church gate over a carpet of petals and under a rain of confetti, and climbed up into an old open topped carriage drawn by two beautifully groomed bay horses to cheers from the crowd. Then the carriage clopped away up the lane, on its way to Wychwood Hall.

Chapter 48: *The Journal of Davey Bone*

Thursday 24th June 1779

In the early morning hours of 23rd June Wychwood Hall was burned to the ground. When all is said and done, it was not at all as difficult as I had imagined and feared, and fortune was my ally in all things. I gathered up a black lantern, some flasks of oil and some rags, a bag of six-inch nails that I had in the barn and a heavy hammer, and after a walk in which I was persuaded on many occasions of the sound of footsteps or hooves upon the road but in the end met with none, I found myself at my destination. Girded with grim determination I circled quietly around the house, thanking providence for a westerly wind that would not take my scent to the kennels and start the hounds off baying and howling. The window of the library had been left slightly open by a careless servant, and what better place could there be than a library in which to start a fire? I prepared the rags with oil and slid up the lower sash. The lantern provided me with flame, and without even needing to enter I tossed burning rags left and right onto the bookcases, where the fire caught at once. I emptied the remaining oil onto the floor through the window, putting the flasks back in my bag, and made certain that the fire had taken well. Then I walked around the house, first nailing each door to its frame and then pinning each window shut with only a few blows. From a safe distance standing under the trees I watched, and for a long while it seemed that nothing more was happening and I feared lest the fire had not caught, but then there was a crash as the library windows shattered and thick smoke began pouring out. At that, I waited no longer, but made my way home through the fields to ensure that I should not be seen, and arrived under cover of a dark sky and new moon to find all asleep, even my dear wife Anne, who I found by the side of Lilly Grace's cot, curled up in a ball. I lay down beside her myself and was immediately asleep.

I did not know my way to the great faerie hall, but the briars parted to make a track, the branches of overhanging trees lifted from my way, and the moon lit the path like a great, argent lamp. The grass on Stoney Down shone silver and opened before me into a great arch, beneath which ornate, silver-wrought doors swung back at my approach. Inside the high entrance hall was empty, and I marched through it full of purpose to the royal chamber, where I found the faerie host assembled around the throne, upon which was seated the man in green, smiling in a way I did not much like.

"I did what you asked of me," I said, straining to keep my voice under control. "Wychwood Hall is razed to the ground."

"It is so, indeed. But our bargain was that you must complete the task by Midsummer's Eve. That, you did not. You have broken our agreement, and you must pay."

"Where is my daughter?" I demanded, facing him. "Give her back to me!"

The green king's eyes glittered. "Why should I let such a prize slip through my fingers? You have failed. She is mine by rights."

I began to walk slowly around the throne, and the assembled fairies followed me with their eyes.

"Give her back to me."

"I will not."

"You refuse? I have murdered a dozen or more poor souls in burning torment at your whim and now you refuse?"

"That I do. A bargain is a bargain."

"And that is your last word?"

"Begone, mortal, and never return. Be grateful that your loss is no greater."

"How could my loss be greater? I have lost my daughter and I have damned my immortal soul, such as it is, and I have been cheated of my fortune." I completed my journey around the throne. "I shall go." I took a step towards the doorway, and then stopped and turned back. "But ye shall not. Remain here, then, a hundred years, until these nails have rusted away." And I shewed the green king and his fairy kin the nails I had scattered on the floor as I had walked around them all. Thick they lay, in a completed circle of iron that the fairy kind could not pass and could not break. "The very same nails with which I hammered fast the windows and doors of Wychwood Hall and imprisoned and murdered all those poor souls inside. Now they shall serve to make another prison, for you!"

The screeching and howling that followed as the fairy horde realised their plight was terrible to the ear, but music that I much appreciated nonetheless. I bowed to the green king in mockery, and turned to leave.

"Hold!" he cried, high above the shrieking din, and I stopped and turned back, and the fairy folk fell silent in fear of their monarch. "Hold, mortal. Remove this iron cage and I shall reconsider."

"No indeed. Bring me my daughter and I shall reconsider," I replied.

"She is here. Why, can you not see her?" He held up a bundle of rags. "Break the circle and I shall bring her to you."

"Give her to me and I shall break the circle."

"It seems we have struck another bargain. Take care that you keep to this one. My vengeance is cruel."

"Pass her to me, then."

The green king bore the bundle of rags to the edge of the circle, and I leaned in and took it from him. It felt the right weight and size, and I lifted back a cloth to find her peacefully sleeping face. It was my darling Lilly Grace, returned to me after all, and the love I felt for her filled my eyes with tears.

"And now for your part of the bargain," the green king demanded. "Remove these terrible iron nails, break the circle."

"Indeed I shall," I said. "I shall… when I am ready. That may be in a few years' time, and it may not; but keep to my side of the bargain I shall, you may rest assured."

"But the way is open! After all these years, it is opened and we must leave. We must take the way beneath the wood. The moment will be lost! You cannot leave us confounded thus! Does your cruelty know no bounds? Wait! You shall have riches, and more. Anything!"

"I have all the riches I need, thank you kindly," I said, and with that I left the faerie hall bearing my daughter in my arms.

When I awoke I hurried downstairs and threw open the kitchen door, and there I found Lilly Grace sitting quietly upon the doorstep. I swept her into my arms and pressed her to my chest, but she barely responded and I knew at once that something was wrong. I bore her inside and up the stairs to Anne, who took her with a cry of joy and smothered her in kisses. My little girl put her arms around her mother's neck, but did not speak or make any other sign of emotion or recognition. After more cuddling Anne washed her clean, checking her at the same time for hitherto unseen injuries, of which there were none, and put her into her cot, with a thousand more kisses, where she fell asleep immediately.

"Something is wrong with her," I said to Anne urgently when we were in our own room. She demanded to know where I had found her, and could scarce believe that I found her sitting upon our own doorstep. She said that she thought Lilly Grace must be very tired and very frightened from whatever ordeal she had endured, and that it may take some time for her to come to herself, and from this I took great comfort, although there was much in my mind on the matter that I would not share with Anne, and never shall.

My little Lilly Grace is returned to me, but I am not so sure that the fairies have not played one last, wicked trick. I have tried many a time to find my way back to the faerie hall and complete my side of the bargain, to put things right, but I have never found the way. Why does she sit so lifeless at the kitchen table and why do her eyes avoid the gaze of her siblings and doting parents? She will not eat the food that we set before her, save that she is always hungry for the same thing, which she demands in a croaking voice that I do not recognise: "Bread and milk... bread and milk... bread and milk!"

Chapter 49: *The Reception*

I managed to dodge the horrendous task of standing in the line-up to greet the wedding guests by the simple ruse of slipping around the back. No-one missed me, or if they did they didn't come looking for me. I grabbed a glass of champagne and went on a tour of the set-up while it was still empty. The wedding marquee looked very different to the marquee for the hunt ball. It was grander, taller, and newer: Clifton's money at work already, no doubt. Pennants in the wedding colours of deep red and russet orange fluttered from the posts at the apex of the roof. Inside, Belle had tried hard to elevate the décor a long way above the standard set by the hunt ball: it was draped in the same autumnal colour scheme as the church and decked with flowers and harvest produce, with flower displays at regular intervals around the walls of the marquee and on each long table. There was a long high table on a dais, and I went over to find out if I had been put next to Mother, but fortunately I wasn't on the top table at all, which pricked my pride only a little. Then I heard a voice I recognised coming from the entrance.

"Hello Nick." It was Jenny-from-Oxford, who had evidently also skipped the line-up. Her tone was warm but with an undertone of uncertainty. I went over, giving her my best sunny smile, and gave her a peck on the cheek. She looked at me closely. "How are you? You disappeared into thin air at the ball."

"I had to go home. I wasn't feeling well," I lied.

She brightened up a bit. "I hope you're better now."

"Oh yes. Better than I've been in ages. How are you?"

"Well! I'm well! It's lovely to see you."

"Yes, you too!"

A voice interrupted us. "I'm sorry sir, madam, the marquee is not open yet. Could I please ask that you make your way to the ballroom for the reception?" It was one of Wychwood's staff; a balding man in his forties with bad teeth, indicating the direction with an open hand.

I turned back to Jenny. "We've been rumbled. We'd better go."

"Mister Carpenter, is it?" the servant asked. I nodded. "The reception line will be finished in a few minutes. Lord Wychwood asks that you wait for him in the library."

"Does he?" I said, showing off a bit for Jenny's sake. "I'm not sure I'm available at this precise moment for waiting in the library. I'm at a wedding reception, you see."

"If you would care to follow me?" He waved with an open hand, attempting to shoo me into the house.

"Not just now, thank you."

"Please, sir. He's very busy. It is his wedding day, after all."

This appeal to my better nature seemed rather impertinent. "I sure he is," I said. "Much too busy to come and find me himself, apparently." The man looked very uncomfortable.

"I think you'd better go," Jenny said.

I winked at her. "Alright," I said to the man, "But only because you asked me so nicely."

I took Jenny's arm. "Are you staying in the haunted house tonight with the horned devils?"

"Here? No, I'm in the Joiner's Arms in Snedley. What about you?"

"Good choice," I said. "Wish I'd thought of that one. Let's catch up later, eh? I'll find you."

I left Jenny to find her own way to the ballroom. The servant led me back into the house and through to the library, showed me in, and then left me there.

I wandered slowly up and down the rows of shelves full of leather-bound volumes, breathing in the dusty, dry fragrance of old paper and reflecting that the collection must be worth a lot of money if my experience of buying books for Hazel was anything to go by. Another asset that had just fallen into Clifton's lap. And then I turned a corner and found myself again in front of what could only be the Brodie Cabinet.

There is something about looking at biological specimens, which many of the items on display were, that connects straight to the stomach. Things in a jar that should not be in a jar; specimens whole and partial, imperfectly preserved; freaks of nature: such objects trigger in the mind a primitive warning to turn away, and yet the eye is drawn back to them in morbid fascination. Perhaps it is this cognitive dissonance that causes what begins as mere queasiness to amplify to the level at which vomiting becomes a real risk. I once had to run out of the museum at Guy's hospital due to just such a mounting feeling of nausea, and here in front of the cabinet I could detect the beginnings of it again.

At the same time, as I stood there looking at the contents of the cabinet, I could feel other connections forming in my head. There was something in the way the items on show were set out that was trying to tell me something, and I almost had it. Just a little longer, I knew, and it would come.

Wychwood entered with hurried strides and went over to his desk. "Nicholas, please come and sit down. Thanks for waiting." He sat down in his padded leather office chair and waited for me to take the seat opposite, drumming his fingers.

"Congratulations!" I said.

"Thank you." Henry sat back and looked at me appraisingly. "I know you have a… ah… difficult relationship with your mother," he said at last.

"I don't think that's any of your business."

"Ah, but it is. Anything that affects Margaret's happiness is a very direct concern of mine. I also appreciate that you and I haven't exactly seen eye to eye since we met. But I'd like to ask you to try to be happy for us."

"Well that sounds very reasonable. But I don't suppose whether I'm happy about it or not means anything to anyone. What you really mean is, don't make waves. Well, don't worry. I'm sure you'll be very happy together and, for the record, I have no plans to come between you."

"Good." The conversation was going the way he wanted, and he became more confident and brusque. "It would suit me, as no doubt it would suit you, for you and I to see as little of each other as possible. Your mother will be moving into Wychwood Hall, granted, but that will not entitle you to visit Wychwood whenever you feel like it. Do you understand?"

"So you're saying you want to control when and where I can see my own mother. Is that right?" I could feel the insistent presence of the cabinet behind me and I kept wanting to turn round and look at it.

"You've managed to upset my sister, my daughter, and my wife. That is not acceptable. So yes, in the circumstances, I feel making arrangements in advance will be necessary."

I laughed. "Good luck with getting Mother to comply with that. No, that's utterly ridiculous and I won't do it."

Wychwood snarled. "Do you think I don't know what you've been up to? About your plans to buy Wychwood? That's right, the agent told me all about you. About your family money. You ridiculous upstart! Wychwood is not for sale. It will never be for sale!"

"Not now that you've sold your daughter and seduced my mother."

The sudden fury disappeared, controlled and hidden behind a mask of cold hostility. "Very well. If you have any ideas about disrupting the proceedings today, then please forget them. I will not have my daughter's wedding day ruined. After today, to be crystal clear, I do not expect to see you again in this house or anywhere near it. You may see your mother anywhere else you like, whenever you like. If you disregard my wishes on this in any respect there will be unfortunate consequences. Do I make myself clear?"

"I'm not interested in your expectations or instructions," I said curtly. "But actually your wishes and mine do appear to coincide rather nicely: I very much hope that I shan't see you again after today. So you see there is really no need for empty threats." I walked to the door, and, as I did so, something changed and I knew what the meaning of the cabinet was. "Goodbye, Henry."

When I got through the door into the hallway I kept walking until I reached the ballroom and found myself a large glass of wine and a quiet corner. Fuck Henry! What he had to say meant nothing to me. Besides, there was little doubt in my mind that I would have the last laugh, once Henry realised exactly what he had let himself in for with Mother. I almost felt sorry for him. I raised my glass and silently made a toast to the happy couple.

A few enjoyable moments thinking of all the ways in which they were going to get on each other's nerves followed, but these were curtailed soon enough as my thoughts turned back to the Brodie Cabinet. A very different explanation of the objects in the cabinet had come to me in those last moments with Henry; one that made more sense to me, having seen what I had seen, than it being a mere cabinet of curiosities, and the more I thought about it, the more convinced I became by it. It was a collection of a quite different sort, taken for a very different purpose and under very different circumstances. It was a *trophy* cabinet.

"Clifton, many congratulations. I am so happy for you, really I am." There had been more photographs taken in the garden in which I had been made to participate by Mother, but my role had been minimal and as the shoot had moved away to another location I had found myself left behind, standing side by side with Clifton.

Clifton grunted non-committally, looking annoyed to have been caught on his own.

"What a beautiful ceremony," I added. "I didn't realise it'd be a Catholic service. Puts about half an hour on the running time, eh?"

He didn't meet my gaze. "Yes. Yes, I've been having instruction, actually. It was important for Belle. She's pretty serious about it."

"Mmm… I had no idea."

He eyeballed me with bloodshot orbs. "What's that supposed to mean?" he hissed. "Look, Nicko, it's my wedding day, alright? No trouble. Comprendo?"

I smiled. "Comprendo."

Clifton continued glaring at me. Then he nodded, shifted his gaze back to the ground, and said: "Alright. I'll take that." Then he looked over at where the photographer was herding the wedding party, took a deep breath, and blew it out again, gathering himself. "Yet more photographs await, I'm afraid," he said, waving me on. "Lead on, MacDuff."

"You go on. I'm going to sit out this round."

"Right-oh."

As Clifton walked off I said: "I hope you're very happy together. You and Wychwood Hall."

For a moment I thought he was going to ignore me, but he stopped and came back.

"You're not very nice, are you Nicko? I wish you weren't so bitter and twisted, for your own sake. Belle and I are married now, and I have every hope and expectation that we'll live happily ever after, alright? Everything else is entirely circumstantial. And that's an end to it."

I fought with myself over what I was going to say to that. Eventually, I just said: "I wish we'd been closer over the years. We could have been friends, don't you think?"

Clifton shook his head in disbelief, made a half-hearted gesture of throwing up his arms and looking to the skies, harrumphed, and then walked off. He was still shaking his head as I watched his receding back, and for a moment I found myself appreciating his point of view.

After that, I went off in search of somewhere to hide. I wandered round the gardens and walked all the way round the house, enjoying the remaining sunshine, and then, thinking that the food might be ready, made my way back to the marquee.

"Ah, there you are!" Mother had drunk more champagne than was good for her on an empty stomach, and was also high on all the attention she was receiving. It was too late to run for it, so I smiled the smile of the damned and obeyed her summons. The people she had been talking to, who I didn't know, made their excuses and left us to it. "They're calling me Lady Wychwood," Mother said, putting her hand on my shoulder to steady herself.

"That's what you are now. You'd better get used to it."

"Yes, I suppose I had." Mother scanned faces around us to see if there was anyone more interesting to talk to. "You could look a bit happier about it."

"You do look gorgeous," I said, trying to distract her. "I love that dress."

"Come and meet some of Henry's friends. You need to circulate."

"I'm working my way around."

"I want you to build some bridges, darling. Make some friends. I can help. You've upset quite a few people somehow or other. I know this must be difficult for you, but honestly, I couldn't be a lonely old widow for the rest of my life, could I? Can't you be nice to them?"

"Can't they be nice to me? I've just been hauled into the library by Henry and banned from ever visiting Wychwood again."

"I know. He's terribly cross."

"You knew?"

"Yes. I think the bells were the last straw."

"I told you, that wasn't me."

"I'm sure he'll get over it. In time."

"And you're okay with me being unwelcome in my own mother's home."

"Yes. For now. Until you've made up."

She really was in an unassailably good mood; a party balloon full of helium. I decided to try my luck. "Look, do you really have to call your loan in? I'll have to get a job as a barman or an estate agent or something and spend the rest of my life paying off my debts."

"I told you, I've made up my mind. What you do is up to you. Besides, Henry and I have plans."

"What plans?"

"Plans."

"Well he's wasted no time in spending all your money, has he?"

"Nicholas! There is nothing wrong with me speaking to my husband about financial matters and making plans. That's part and parcel of a marriage."

"You do realise that he's only married you for your money."

The balloon popped. "That is an awful thing to say." Mother's face flushed. "I want you to apologise immediately."

"I'm afraid I can't because it's true."

"I didn't tell you how Henry and I met, did I? I was visiting Clifton and Annabel, and I wanted to see the view from on top of the downs, so I went for a walk. I didn't think it was far. But somehow I got lost, and then I just couldn't seem to get anywhere, and I kept walking and walking for hours. I'm sure I must have just walked round and round in circles. Luckily for me Annabel had the sense to call her father and ask him to look for me. He sent out all his staff, but they couldn't find me and I was getting very tired and desperate, and then suddenly he turned up on a white horse, would you believe, like a knight in shining armour, and he got down and lifted me up into the saddle, and then he led the horse back here. It couldn't have been more romantic. I knew at once, and so did Henry."

"That doesn't sound like you at all. Did they put something in your gin?"

"I knew you'd scoff. Anyway, we hadn't met before, you see, so there was no question of it being about money. He didn't know anything about me."

"Yes he did. He knew everything about you. He probably engineered the whole thing. And I suppose Annabel isn't marrying Clifton for his money either?"

"You really can be horrid when you try. I do try not to let it get to me, but really… today of all days." She put her fingers to her forehead, a sure sign that one of her fake migraines was on the way.

"Margaret! Can I get you another drink?" I looked round, cross at being interrupted when I had Mother on the ropes. It was the Mayor. "Is everything alright?" he asked.

Mother looked up, miraculously better all of a sudden, and primped her hair. "Oh, absolutely fine, thank you. Do you know my son Nicholas?"

"I don't believe we've met."

We shook hands. "I know one of your colleagues," I said, "Councillor Howland Greenwood."

"Ah, Howland. Our Chair of Planning. He's been on the council for years and years, you know. Longest serving councillor. I don't think he'll ever retire."

"I believe I would like another glass, thank you," Mother interrupted, determined to spite me and regain her position as the centre of attention. She offered her arm to the Mayor. "Shall we?" The Mayor waved to me in good humoured resignation as she dragged him away.

"Hello Belle." She gave me a peck on the cheek and went to move on, but I had her by the arm. She stopped and looked theatrically at my offending hand, but there was no-one nearby to notice and I didn't let go. "I want you to know that I wish you every happiness, truly I do," I said in a low voice. "I will always wish it had been me you chose."

"Let go of my arm," Belle demanded with an implied threat that if I didn't she would make a scene. The last guests were exiting the ballroom on their way to the marquee, and in a few seconds we would be alone. I complied anyway, and she went to walk away, but then she came back looking flustered and was about to say something when I interrupted her.

"I just don't understand - why Clifton? He's a selfish, lying boor."

"No he isn't."

"I always thought the idea was to marry someone you love."

"Meaning you, I suppose. I've never said I was in love with you."

"But you are."

There was a moment of silence between us in which emotions rose and fell like ocean waves. "You sad, spoilt little pretty boy," she said at last. She took two steps towards me. "How dare you patronise me? You really think I'm in love with you? What have you ever done that amounts to anything? All you ever did is sponge from your parents. Property developer? They buy you a portfolio to manage, and what do you do? You bugger it all up and they have to bail you out. Oh, yes: everyone knows about that. Your mother's been pulling her hair out trying to cope with you since your father died. You can't stay in a relationship for more than five minutes because you're so self-centred you actually sulk if the conversation isn't about you! You're a crashing bore. Poor Hazel ran away from you because you were so awful to her. What on earth makes you think I could ever care about you?"

"Fucking me all those times maybe? I suppose that meant nothing to you."

"Nothing, that's right. A last fling, which I'm really starting to seriously regret."

That stung. "Why him?"

"It's none of your business, Nick."

I said it for her: "Daughter and country pile for sale, cash only, apply within?"

Belle hissed.

"Oh my God! That *is* it."

"No."

"I thought that kind of familial duty nonsense went out with the Victorians. But there we have it! It's Clifton's money to the rescue. This is your father's doing, isn't it."

"You have no idea, do you Nick? You live in your own little world."

"You don't love him."

"It's my fucking wedding day! Of course I love him. Can't you just leave me alone?" Her eyes were brimming with tears.

"Okay, you don't want to listen to me. I'm telling you for your own good. You don't love him. You love me."

"Nick, listen to me." She collected herself. "I was going to write you a letter, but I'll say it now. I'm sorry, but Clifton and I have discussed it and we've decided that… that after today we'd rather not see you again." Her face was suddenly composed, cold and hard. A solitary tear escaped the corner of her eye and ran down her cheek. "Don't come to St Dunstan's, and don't try to contact us. You won't be welcome. Please respect our wishes. Goodbye, Nick."

Henry's father of the bride speech was quite excellent. It was sincere, funny, fulsome in its praise of Clifton and sentimental about Belle. No-one in their right mind would have wanted to follow it, and I was just congratulating myself on not having to make a speech at all when an irresistible urge to stand up and say something came upon me, and suddenly, before I could consciously resist, I was on my feet and announcing myself. "My lords, ladies and gentlemen, my name is Nicholas Carpenter and, earlier today, I gave my mother away." There was a stunned silence. I felt stunned myself, since I had no idea what I was going to say, but it didn't seem to matter as it appeared all I had to do was keep breathing and the words came out of their own accord. "We've heard all about Clifton and Annabel, but as the substitute father of the other bride, and a proud son, I feel that I must say a few words to mark the occasion. This isn't planned, so please bear with me." Henry's face was thunder. Mother looked aghast. "After this morning's double wedding, the Carpenters and the Wychwood family are entwined about as much as any two families can be without social services being called." I paused to allow for laughter, but none was forthcoming. I looked around the room and other faces came into focus, tight lipped and hard eyed. I ploughed on: "Henry Wychwood is now my stepfather, Annabel my step-sister, and Clifton, my cousin, is also my brother-in-law." I turned to Henry. "Hello Daddy," I said. More silence. If eyebeams had any substance, Henry's would have sizzled twin holes through my skull.

"A double wedding involving only two families is pretty unusual in this day and age, but this one is also unusual for being a union between town and country. I admit that as an unashamed townie I arrived expecting pitchforks and a wicker man." I could feel the hostility growing. "Instead, I was inducted more warmly than I had a right to expect into the country way of life," here Belle refused to meet my gaze and Clifton's face had turned purple, "And I would like to thank Henry Wychwood and his family and assure them that their kindness will be returned, measure for measure."

I waved my arm around. "I'm still a townie at heart, but who could fail to be impressed by the magnificence of Wychwood Hall and its estate? This beautiful part of the country has an extraordinary history, and the more deeply I delve into it, the more fascinating things I uncover. There's something quite... unique about it, and Wychwood Hall is right at the centre." Here I looked directly at Henry. "It's a joy to me to know that as a result of the happy unions we are celebrating today the Carpenter family will have a significant role in ensuring that Wychwood will continue to serve as a monument long into the future."

"Concerning the bride, who, did I mention, is also my mother, I should state the obvious, which is that she is very beautiful, and never more so than today. For those of you who don't know her as I do, she is also an extraordinarily strong and determined woman who knows her own mind. She's always two steps ahead of everyone else, and three steps ahead of me, never loses an argument, has uncanny business sense, and knows everyone who is anyone."

"These terrifying qualities might have intimidated a lesser man, but in Henry she has found her knight in shining armour; a man who literally rescued her on a white charger, who has ambitions worthy of her strengths, and who intends to put all of her personal assets to work for the benefit of the Wychwood estate."

"I should therefore like to propose a toast to my mother and new stepfather, the other bride and groom. A perfect match, may they be happy together for as long as they live. Please stand and raise your glasses to Henry and Margaret, Lord and Lady Wychwood."

The first dance had begun in the marquee. I was standing at the back where the noise from the band was not too deafening, a safe distance from where the two newly married couples were giving it their best endeavours, when a husky voice beside me said: "Bad luck. You can't win them all, you know."

I turned and found Cissy facing me, a step away. "Hello. I don't know what you mean."

"Oh, I think I'm entitled to lay claim to a little insight."

"I suppose you are. Look, Cissy, I'm very sorry. I really never..."

"Such a good match, aren't they? Belle's so very much in love with him."

"And I thought she was marrying him for his money."

"Hides true nastiness behind such a *thin* façade of charm. Such a pity. Anyway, it's not true. Curious, really. I never thought for a moment she would go through with it, but you can never really tell what's going on under the surface of things, can you? It turns out he's the love of her life. She told me no one has ever measured up to him, and no-one ever will."

"Is that right?"

"Oh yes. No-one." She caught the eye of a man passing us on his way to the dance floor. "Gordon darling! I'm coming!" she called, and then turned back to me. "You never had a chance." She gave me a long, complex look from under those overloaded eyelashes. "Goodbye," she said. "I don't suppose I shall see you again." Then she blew me a tiny kiss that got lost in the air somewhere between us, and was gone.

The wedding was over and the yellow Morgan was standing in the pool of light that fell on the driveway by the steps. Behind it the fountain gushed jubilantly, lit from within. There were white ribbons tied to the car's wing mirrors, bumpers and door handles, and attached to the rear bumper a textbook tail of tin cans on a string. The guests had gathered on the steps by the portico, and were watching the servants preparing three dozen paper hot air balloons, powered by methylated spirit burners. The happy couples emerged through the doors of Wychwood House. Mother and Henry hadn't changed outfits, having decided against an immediate honeymoon, and also in favour of allowing the younger couple the last piece of wedding theatre to themselves, but Clifton and Belle were dressed in their going away ensembles: Clifton in a brown Prince of Wales check suit that, on his frame, had just a hint of circus clown about it, and Belle looking perfect as ever in a classic Chanel hounds tooth two piece. The servants began releasing the balloons, which rose slowly in the night sky and drifted off, a line of magical orbs radiating a warm orange. Then Mother and Belle each took their turn to waggle their bride's bouquet at the crowd and throw it over their shoulder into a screaming scuffle of young women. Goodbyes were said, and there were tearful hugs and hands shaken, and kisses bestowed. Clifton took Belle by the hand and led her to the Morgan under a shower of confetti. He helped her to climb in; a feat she achieved gracefully in spite of the odds. Then, climbing in himself with practised ease, he started up the engine and with a spin of the wheels in the gravel, drove off to cheers and much waving.

"Where are they going?" asked Jenny-from-Oxford, who was standing next to me as Clifton took the Morgan around the fountain for the third time waving furiously, and then, instead of heading off down the driveway towards the gates, took the turning towards the stables.

"Nowhere," I said. "They're staying the night here before their flight tomorrow. It's handy for Gatwick, and why would you stay in a hotel there when you could be here?"

"Oh. No, I meant where's the honeymoon."

"I believe they're booked on a flight to Mauritius tomorrow afternoon."

"What are you laughing about?"

"Oh, sorry. It was just the charade of waving goodbye and driving three times round the fountain and stuff, and then parking round the back. It suddenly struck me as ridiculously funny."

There was a slight chill in the air, but the sky was clear and filled with stars. Thirty-six glowing dots were still ascending, cruising very slowly eastward. The last act of the drama had been played out, and it was time to leave. Others were already saying their goodbyes and making their way across the driveway to waiting cars and taxis.

"Shall we share my cab?" Jenny asked, taking my arm.

"I have one ordered already," I said. "And besides, we're going in opposite directions."

She let go. "Alright then. Well, it was nice to see you again." I didn't say anything, because there was nothing I could say that would do it justice, any of it. She pecked me on the cheek and walked off towards the headlights of the waiting vehicles.

I sat down on the steps and watched the receding balloons until they were specks, feeling empty and exhausted. When I finally looked round the crowd had thinned out considerably. Jenny would be on her way by now, if not already in her hotel. There was nothing here for me any more. It was time to go. Time to head back to my hotel and get some sleep. I stood up and went in search of my cab.

Chapter 50: *Reynard*

"Where do you think you're going?"

The voice, which came from behind me, was thick with alcohol and aggression. I looked round. It was Clifton's best man. I couldn't remember his name, and his speech at the wedding had been equally unmemorable, but his face was memorable: it was like a bag full of stones picked randomly from a rockery. One of the ushers was with him, also a big rugby type.

"Got a taxi waiting, thanks." I acknowledged him with a short wave and walked off. The next thing I knew I felt his hands fall heavily on my shoulders. He was trying to turn me round. I spun and faced him.

"Clifton sends his regards," he said, and swung a haymaker at me. I leaned back, turning my head, and his knuckles grazed my cheek as they whistled past. In the same microseconds I debated what to do. Fight, pacify, or run. Pacify.

"We don't have to do this. Let's have a drink, eh? Let's have a drink and talk about it." He swung at me again with his left. This one caught me on the top of the head as I ducked, glancing off, the sensation more like a slap. "Ow!" I said. I took a couple of steps backwards.

"That's right. Back off, you cowardly piece of shit," the best man bellowed, apparently enraged by my desire for self-preservation. A blur of motion caught my eye off to my right and then suddenly I was off my feet as the usher barrelled into me in a flying tackle. The impact drove the air out of my lungs and we fell together in a disorderly heap on the grass. As soon as I had orientated myself I tried to get up, but he was lying across my legs. Before I could wriggle them free, I took a kick from a highly polished Oxford on my right shoulder; the best man wading in with all his strength. I knew it ought to hurt, but strangely it didn't. Before he could launch another I rolled free with surprising strength and scrambled to my feet.

"You know what's cowardly," I said. "There's two of you and one of me. And look at the size of you! You can beat me up, no question. So there's nothing to prove. You win, okay? I'll just go and get my taxi and you'll never see me again." I began backing away again, hands up and open.

The usher was back on his feet, bleeding from a scratch on his cheek that he must have taken in the tackle. Both stepped forward after me, the best man leading the way.

"Oh no. You're going nowhere." He swung a fist at me again, missed. Over his shoulder I could see figures approaching, although I couldn't make out who they were in the gloom.

"Hey!" I said. "Help! These guys are beating me up! Help!"

The best man laughed. "No-one's going to help you. You're on your own, Romeo." He ran at me and I ducked, expecting a punch, but instead he pushed me with both hands and I staggered backwards, losing my balance completely. I was about to tumble over when rough hands caught me and pushed me forward again. I looked round. There were people from the wedding there. More of the ushers, and the older bridesmaids too, making a circle around us, their faces flushed, their eyes bright with excitement.

"What the Hell is this?" I shouted at them. "What's the matter with you people? Help! Help, somebody! Help!"

Some of the people in the gang around me laughed. "Help!" one of the girls squealed mockingly. "Help!"

The best man and the usher came towards me, closing from both sides. I tried to dodge them, dancing around the edge of the circle, and managed to escape their manoeuvre but someone in the crowd hooked out a foot and tripped me up. I received a couple of anonymous kicks before I could get up again, only to be pushed over by the best man, who started trying to land kicks on me again himself.

It dawned on me as the blows landed that my strategy of appeasement wasn't working. Time to try something else: fight or run.

I got up. "Alright, that's enough!" I yelled right in the face of the best man. He stopped. I jabbed him in the chest with my finger. "That's e-fucking-nough from you, you fucking cock." I pushed him as hard as I could, and it knocked him two steps backwards. I turned my attention to the usher. "Do you want some?" I shouted.

The best man started laughing. "That's the spirit," he slurred. "Make a fight of it." There were mocking cries from the circle around us.

"Smack him!" It was a girl's voice from the crowd. I didn't think her encouragement was directed at me. The best man look round to see who it was, and I took advantage of the opportunity to throw a punch at him. I got him right in the eye socket. I barely felt the contact, and the punch felt like it had no power in it, but he gave a howl of pain and staggered away. I looked at the usher. He was frozen, not sure what to do. Suddenly I was winning. I went after the best man. "Now who's a coward?" I shouted. He stood his ground, holding his eye, but didn't come for me.

Then a voice I recognised began a slow chant from the edge of the circle. "Rey-nard... Rey-nard..." I found her immediately, even in the half light. It was Belle. Belle in her going-away outfit, looking at me with the same bloodthirsty expression I had seen when the hounds had rioted and killed that... whatever it was at the hunt. "Rey-nard... Rey-nard...". Others voices joined hers. I looked at the faces surrounding me. Clifton was there, next to Belle, and other people from the wedding that had also been at the Hunt Ball. "Rey-nard... Rey-nard..." The volume of sound grew as more people joined the circle. Cissy was there too, a snarl on her face as she chanted.

I turned back to Belle. "Belle, what are you doing? What is this?" She ignored me and continued, egging on the people around her. "Rey-nard... Rey-nard..."

The sound seemed to reinvigorate the best man. I could see strength flowing into him second by second as the chanting got louder and louder. He stood up straight and grinned at me, rolling his broad shoulders. He said something, but I couldn't hear it. Around me the circle was shrinking, the people shuffling forward. I was suddenly very frightened, not in the adrenaline fuelled way I had been when the best man and the usher had started the fight, but in a deep-down bone-chilling way that left me glued to the spot, knees weak, arms powerless. This was way beyond anything I had ever known.

The best man came at me suddenly and grabbed me with his huge hands. He threw me across the circle, and I rolled to a halt against the legs of the crowd. The chanting suddenly stopped. I rose to my knees, and as I looked up the crowd before me parted to reveal Lord Wychwood and my mother. Wychwood looked at me as if I were no more than a worm. I focused on Mother. There was a strange expression on her face, a crazed look as if some battle were being fought behind her eyes. Wychwood put his hand on her shoulder. "Go on," he said. Mother's eyes came into focus and her expression hardened. There was absolute silence. Then, to my horror, with slow determination she lifted her foot, pulled it back, and then kicked me suddenly, right in the chest. I felt the point of her heel dig right in between my ribs and I screamed and toppled over.

She stepped back and the circle re-joined around her. Their silence continued for a long moment, broken only by sobs of pain that I realised with a shock were coming from me, but then a new chant started. It began like a low growl, the volume and pitch gradually increasing, and as it did the feet around me began to stamp the grass and move, inch by inch, towards where I was lying. "Kill... kill... kill..."

The faces of the throng were distorted into grinning leers. Their feet pounded the grass. "Kill... kill... kill..." I realised that my hands were covered in blood; mine, I thought. My blood. I thought of that creature, torn to pieces by the hounds. Only one stratagem left.

I leapt to my feet and without hesitation ran straight at Mother. She was a formidable foe but she only weighed just over eight and a half stone and I sent her sprawling. I shouldered past others, broke through the circle and into the dark open space beyond, and I ran as fast as I could without looking back. There was a clamour behind me: the howls of bereft predators, indistinct, confused shouting, excited whooping, and above it all the shrill cries of the hunter bidding the hounds. They came after me, every one of them, as I knew they would, giving voice in the sheer joyous blood-lust of the chase. I ran on for the trees, heart pounding, lungs sucking, fear fuelling my speed, knowing that I would surely be caught and certain now that I would not survive it, but not willing to give up; not this step, or this, or this...

A tree, and then another. The woods were close now. Nowhere to hide, nowhere to lose them, not yet. Keep going. My chest felt ready to explode, my whole body was signalling imminent collapse, but somehow the legs kept going and the arms kept pumping. The cries behind me had spread out on each side. They were trying to outflank me. I ran straight, hoping that I could out-distance them all. Into the woods, between the tree-trunks. There were shadows in the trees to my right, starting to pull ahead and converge. Faster. Go faster. The spaces between the trees ahead became narrower, the route harder to negotiate at speed, the visibility reduced in the gloom. Branches whipped at my arms and face. Keep straight. The going was hard and it was slowing me down. I hoped it was having the same effect on my pursuers too. The ground, cleared and well-trodden near the house, became ever more treacherous. There were fallen boughs tangling my legs, bushes that clutched and scratched at me, invisible tree roots that sought to make me slip and stumble. Keep going. I could hear branches breaking behind me and the occasional curse. It was so dark now that I could barely see where I was going. A low branch smashed me in the face, almost knocking me over. I staggered, regained my balance, and ran on with my arms out ahead of me, crashing through thick brush. Keep running, no matter what. I ducked under another bough that swung in at me from nowhere, got buffeted sideways, and my legs got caught up in a fallen branch, which tripped me. The twigs and branches of a low bush caught my fall, digging into and scoring my face and hands. I tried to get up, but the branch was still tangled in my legs. I kicked and kicked, and my legs came free, so I scrambled to my feet and set off running again. A few more steps, and then there was suddenly no ground under my leading foot and I pitched forward head first. There was a sound like a cricket bat hitting the ball right on the sweet spot and a burst of bright stars, and I was sucked into darkness.

Chapter 51: *Please Pick Up*

"Nick, if you're there, please pick up. Nick? Oh, sodding bloody answering machine! Look, I've finally worked it all out. You're going to say I'm mad, but I have to tell you. I'm sorry I was so awful to you in my last letter about sending me this stuff. I'm really glad you didn't stop. Grateful. It's so funny, because you've been sending it to me thinking you were just tempting me back into talking to you with stolen lemon bon bons, when all the time there was something amazing hidden in it. It was Davey Bone's journal that helped me to put it all together in the end. I don't think anyone's ever seen that before, by the way. It looks like it's the original pages, but even if it's not real, it's still brilliant. But there are still gaps. There has to be more. Please send it, Nick. Send me the rest of it. Call me and I'll tell you everything!"

Chapter 52: *Tinder*

Mother's heel had gone right through my shirt and had dug out a deep triangle of flesh like a flap, about a centimetre wide, which had been bleeding profusely but had now just about stopped. Charlie peered at it dispassionately in the dim lighting of his van. "You need to clean that and get a dressing on it. Wait there."

As if I was going somewhere! I heard the sound of rummaging behind me and then he came back with an almost empty bottle of Bell's whisky, a tea-towel, and an old box of sticking plasters that from the packaging looked like it must have been at least twenty years old. The whisky stung like blazes as he poured it on my chest. Tears came to my eyes. I swore constantly. He dabbed it away from around the wound and used the biggest plaster he could find. "Do you want some on your face?" he offered, holding up the bottle and the tea-towel.

"I'll do it," I said and took the bottle and the cloth from him. I drank the whisky in three long swallows, coughed, and then put the empty bottle and the cloth down on the table. "That's my face done," I croaked, eyes watering anew. "Thanks."

"There's more whisky."

"Yes please."

He reached down to a cardboard box under the table and came up with another bottle of Bell's, which he opened expertly. I took the bottle from him and added three big gulps to the liquid already working in my stomach. Charlie took the bottle back and drank from it himself.

"They tried to kill me." I put my head in my hands, and regretted it immediately. There was a huge lump on my forehead and the rest of my face was sore and puffy. I sat back up. "Ow!" I said. My shoulder was throbbing and if I tried to move it, it was agony.

"You'll be alright. No permanent damage done."

"No permanent damage? They were trying to kill me." A thought ran through me like an electric shock. "They might still be looking for me!"

"You're safe here."

It felt safe. I took the bottle from Charlie, took another swig. "You saved me. Thank you, Charlie. Thank you. How did you find me? How did I get back here?"

"I've no idea."

"What?"

"You woke me up, banging on the door, and then when I opened up you came barging in, sat down where you are now, demanded I make you a cup of tea, and passed out with your head on the table."

"Sorry, Charlie. Oh, God! You must be wondering what the Hell's going on."

"No, no. There's no need to tell me again. You've already told me twice."

"Oh Christ!" I took another slug of Bell's. "Sorry. Charlie, I think I may be concussed."

Charlie said nothing. He took the bottle away from me.

"What am I going to do? If I show my face they're going to try to finish the job, aren't they? Oh my God, I hope they're not going to set the dogs on me!"

Charlie looked at me flatly. "Hounds," he said. "They're hounds."

"Set the hounds on me, then." I caught sight of the sleeves of my jacket, which were torn and filthy. It prompted me to inspect the rest of my attire. "They've ruined my best suit!"

"They might," Charlie said. "Set the hounds on you."

"Oh Christ!"

He sat down at the table opposite me. "Nicholas," he said, "You have to finish this."

"I don't know what you mean."

"Yes you do." From nowhere, Charlie produced a wooden box and set it on the table.

I looked at it. And then I looked at Charlie.

"I've been meaning to give this to you," he said. "Do you know what it is?"

I nodded.

"Take it," he said. "Open it."

I picked it up. It was weighty, made of solid elm. The carvings were worn, but of excellent quality. A knight fighting a fire-breathing dragon, in a dense forest of trees. I opened the lid. Inside, one compartment was blackened with use, and the other, where the flint, striker and tinder would be stored, was empty but for three ancient gold coins, which lay heavily in the bottom. I looked at Charlie. He was looking back at me, his face an impenetrable mask that was barely human.

Chapter 53: *A Tiny Genie*

Charlie, are you alright?" I whispered.

"A few moments, please."

"Okay. It's not far now. Just the other side of those trees."

It was long after three in the morning. He leaned against the trunk of a scots pine, breathing heavily. Charlie was not in good nick. His drinking had been getting bad recently anyway, and since we had opened that new bottle of scotch he hadn't stopped. His mobility was worsening by the minute. It had been a long walk from his van back to Wychwood; much longer than I had remembered, and progress had been infuriatingly slow.

Eventually he cleared his throat with a long rattle and spat a glistening string into the grass. "Something to stiffen the resolve?" he asked, fumbling in his coat pocket and proffering a three-quarters empty bottle.

"Ok." I took it and turned away so that he couldn't see me wiping the neck clean before I took a long slug from the bottle. It seared my throat and assaulted my stomach, and then sent a very welcome wave of relaxing warmth through my belly. I took another mouthful and handed it back.

Charlie wiped the neck unselfconsciously, if rather ineffectively, and took a practiced nip. Then he straightened up. "Which way is it?" he asked, shoving the bottle back into his pocket.

"Come on," I said.

He resumed his slow stagger across the grass, wheezing like a pug dog, and I walked beside him, keeping him pointed in the right direction. It took another four long minutes for us to reach the stable block, which we skirted until we came at last to the lawnmower shed. Unable to muster any words, Charlie signalled with pointed fingers that he would remain outside and keep watch. As expected, the shed door was not locked. It was dark inside, but I knew where I would find what we had come for.

Charlie seemed to have bucked up a fair amount when I came out. "I'll carry it," he offered. I gave him a look to let him know what I thought of that idea, and then together we set off across the lawn towards the house, on the last leg of the journey. Charlie put in a surprising turn of pace, and the closer we got the more his condition seemed to improve. By the time we reached the last few yards we were moving as silently and efficiently as assassins in comparison to our previous progress.

Many great old houses of England were designed - in their original state – to be defensible, hence their thick walls, tiny ground floor windows, and stout oak doors banded with iron. Sometimes they even had a moat. Wychwood in its early years may well have been of this ilk, but its various reconstructions over the years had increasingly only nodded to these design features rather than employed them in a practical way, attack by men armed with poleaxes and swords having become less likely as time passed. Instead, other more contemporary security measures had been introduced: window grilles, and mortice and Yale locks on the external doors; although this technology itself was somewhat aged and a long way from state-of-the-art methods such as burglar alarms and close-circuit TV.

This very same security that served so well to keep invaders out was ironically also admirably suited to the task of keeping people in. The windows on the ground floor were secured against escape by their decorative but very functional iron grilles. The external doors were all made of stout oak and had plainly been reclaimed from past incarnations of the property, being studded and bound with

320

iron. Their only weak point was their relatively new mortice locks.

After watching and listening for at least a minute, during which time there were no signs of any movement from inside, I left Charlie propped up against the wall by the library window while I walked carefully and silently around the house. It was the work of only five minutes to fill each lock with superglue and then break off a superglued pencil in each barrel.

That job done in accordance with our plan, I re-joined Charlie, who had moved to a position on the lawn in full view of the house, standing unsteadily and staring up at the windows. It didn't really matter now if we were seen, so I joined him and there we stood, side by side under the night sky. No one looked out, but the house loomed over us, squaring up intimidatingly as if it knew what was coming next. I sensed that it was trying to mobilise, to resist...

Charlie nudged me, breaking the spell. I counted the windows from the portico and selected the correct one, and then stepped forward so that I could peer in through it. The library was in darkness, as expected. I was ready to smash a pane, but when I reached between the iron bars of the grille and, fingertips against the woodwork, lifted, the sash moved. I slowly raised it a few inches. There was no sound from inside, no light switched on in alarm. The still silence of the deepest hour of the night wrapped me in its cocoon.

The petrol can came with a flexible hose, which made it perfect for the job, and so lifting it up to my eye level so that the hose would reach over the sill, I began. The fuel glugged and splashed, and the fumes invaded my nose and mouth and stung my eyes. It took much longer than I had thought, and by the end I was desperate for some clean air to breathe, but I emptied it all through the window into the library; every drop.

It was a wonderful relief to put the can down: I took a few steps backwards and gasped fresh night air into my lungs. Charlie patted me on the back. Then I took out a thick splint of twisted paper; old, dry paper from the only source I had been able to lay my hands on. It seemed fitting, and I was done with sending it to Hazel. I brought out a cheap plastic lighter from my pocket too. We moved back to the window and I held up the splint. It was the point of no return, and we both knew it. We traded glances.

It was too late now to do anything else, even if I had wanted to. I flicked the lighter into life, and the flame danced like a tiny genie in the still night air. I put the paper to it without any second thoughts, and it caught at the first try and flames licked along its exposed edges. Once it was burning well I poked the paper carefully between the bars and launched it through the open window.

There was a flash and an enormous woof, and the glass blew out. Charlie and I dived to the ground. I stayed down for a few moments, and when I stood up again the library was ablaze, bathed in amber light. Fragments of glass in the grass around me reflected the glow like dewdrops in the early morning sun. The explosion had spread fire everywhere: items of furniture and curtains were burning and orange ripples of flame were already scaling the bookshelves.

I helped Charlie up and we watched for a short while. There is a moment with any fire when you're not quite certain it's going to take, and then relief when it passes the point of no return, but there was little doubt in this case and we both relaxed at the same moment. I took it as tacit approval when he rested his hand on my shoulder, although given Charlie's state it was probably more a way of keeping himself upright. Soon the blaze was roaring and crackling, and had spread with ease to the adjoining rooms. We could actually hear the air being sucked in from outside through the broken windows to feed the conflagration. From where I was standing the heat was beginning to feel uncomfortable, but it was the smoke that more than anything that persuaded me it was time to slip away to a safe distance.

We watched in silence from under the cover of the trees that crowded to the edge of the formal garden as the fire rampaged through the building. The emergency services would take a long time to come, even if someone had called them immediately, and there was no possibility that those inside would be able to control the blaze. It was burning like a furnace in parts. The fire would leave only a shell: it was now inevitable.

"We should get out of here," I said to Charlie.

Charlie continued watching the conflagration as if hypnotised. I touched him on the arm. "Charlie?"

"You go. I'm going to stay here a bit longer. I'll walk home across the fields when I'm ready. Don't worry - no-one will see me."

"Are you sure you're well enough?"

"Never better."

"Don't be silly."

He ignored me, unable to take his eyes away.

"Alright. I'll come by your place later then," I said. Charlie didn't answer. I set off on my way back to St Dunstan's to pick up the car, skirting the wood. It was hard not to keep turning to look at the house, but somehow I managed it.

Chapter 54: *No Traces*

The bedside radio clock in my hotel room told me it was 8.59am when I woke. I was just in time for the news on the BBC, so I reached over to switch it on. The pain was incredible. I could barely move my arm. My shoulder felt swollen and tender. My face burned. My chest ached. My legs ached. Very slowly, I turned and extended my arm until I could reach the switch on the top of the radio.

The fire at Wychwood received a brief mention. Fire engines were still at work, but the blaze had done its work and the building was a ruin. There were at least a dozen fatalities and no survivors. They were calling it a wedding fire tragedy.

The sky was clear and the day was warming up nicely as, much later, patched up as well as I could manage, I arrived in Stoney Hill. I had to park the car several hundred yards up the road from the church and walk back down: I had forgotten that the church would be busy, it being Sunday, and indeed it seemed that every resident of Stoney Down and the nearby villages had turned out for the service. People had congregated in the churchyard and on the road outside, and as I walked past on my way to Charlie's van, they turned to look at me and whispered to each other. A woman who had a scarf covering her head and was wearing a brown dress that I supposed was her Sunday best under an incongruous Barbour waxed jacket hurried over to intercept me. "I'm so sorry," she said. "What a terrible, terrible thing. We're all in shock." She took a close look at my face. "Oh dear! What happened to you?"

"Tangle with a rosebush. The bush won."

"You'll want a Tetanus shot for that." She gave a tiny smile of sympathy, and moved back onto her main theme.

"Everyone is stunned. Such a tragedy. If there's anything I can do… anything we can do…"

"Thank you so much. I feel it must all be a terrible dream, if I'm honest."

"I know! It's very hard to believe." She waved an arm at the people congregated outside the church and I realised she was shaking with emotion. "You're welcome to come to the service, if it would help."

"I hope you don't mind, but right now I need…" I was going to say some time to myself, but she put her hands up to stop me.

"Oh, of course. I don't mean to intrude. Anything I can do, you just let me know." Then she backed away with pantomime deference. I had no idea who she was. After that the villagers left me alone, watching me surreptitiously out of the corners of their eyes as I passed and cut down by the side of the church.

The silver birches that screened Charlie's van were only a few hundred yards down the lane. Yellow leaves fallen from their drooping branches had spread across the fields and peppered the track. Curled oak and chestnut leaves, less apt to stick to the ground, had begun to collect along the fence line and in the corners of the fields. The cawing of rooks was the only birdsong. When I reached the trees I stopped abruptly and stood looking for long seconds in complete astonishment at where Charlie's van ought to be. It wasn't there, and neither was Charlie. In its place was a tall stack of logs covered with a dirty tarpaulin, which looked as if it truly belonged there and, what's more, as if it had been there for a very long time. There were no signs whatsoever of a mobile home, nor indeed that one had ever been there.

It was utterly impossible, of course. My first thought was that I must be mistaken about the location, and so I walked further down the lane in case I hadn't reached it yet. I went quite a long way, finding nothing, and then turned back, hoping as I approached the birches again to see the mobile home back in situ; willing to write off my first impression as a hallucination of some sort, brought on by concussion, stress and fatigue perhaps. But as soon as I came back within sight of where it should be, it was apparent that the van was simply not there.

My mind raced, scrabbling for a solution. Was this the right lane? Could I have taken a wrong turning that happened to look very similar? Orientation with the church tower confirmed that this could not be the explanation. Could the van have been moved overnight and the logs put in its place? Someone – possibly Charlie – had gone to a lot of trouble if that was the case: there really were no traces of anything having been moved. It would have taken a huge lorry and a crane at the very least to move it in the time available, and there were no tell-tale ruts or tracks in the verge, no broken branches, no items accidentally dropped and left behind, however small. Besides, the woodpile really looked as if it had been there forever.

Chapter 55: *Deadheading*

When I arrived outside Howland Greenwood's house in Anning Green there was an elderly man in the garden, deadheading roses in the pleasant sunshine. About my height, he was wearing an old tweed jacket and brown corduroy trousers. His hair was white and combed across a balding pate, and he had a small white moustache. I went over and leaned over the gate.

"Excuse me?"

He stopped what he was doing and walked slowly over.

"Hello," he said. "Can I help you?"

"I hope so. I'm looking for Howland Greenwood."

"Well you've found him. What can I do for you? Is it about the bin collections?"

"You're Howland Greenwood?"

"The last time I checked, yes."

"Councillor Howland Greenwood?"

"Yes."

I paused, my mind churning.

"Chair of Planning?"

"Yes. Is it a planning matter?"

"No. Well, yes."

"I see. Well, I have to admit that I'm not up to speed with what's going on at the moment. I've been in hospital, you see." He took his gardening gloves off. "I'm trying to keep it quiet, so don't go spreading that around, please. I'm not supposed to be back at work yet, but tell me what it is, and I'll do my best to help you."

"Nothing serious, I hope.

"I don't think they know what it was, to tell you the truth. It was a very nasty experience, anyway."

"You're alright now?"

"I've had every test known to man and it appears I'm fit as a fiddle."

"Well I'm glad to hear that."

"Not as glad as I am!"

We laughed. "When are you back to work?"

"Officially? Next week. Unofficially, I'm back already. I can't just sit around, you see. I have to be busy."

"I'll leave it until you're back officially," I said. "You take it easy."

"It's quite alright."

"No really."

I went to walk away, but then turned back. "This is going to sound a little strange, but I don't suppose you've ever had problems with someone impersonating you before? You know, pretending they're you?"

"No?" He looked concerned. "I can't see what they'd have to gain. Why do you ask?"

"Oh, don't worry. I must have got mixed up. I could have sworn I met a Councillor Howland Greenwood, but he didn't look anything like you. I probably just misheard the name or something."

"It can happen. Well, as long as he didn't promise you anything I can't deliver on, then no harm done, eh?"

"No harm done," I said. "Absolutely."

Chapter 56: *The Kindness of Strangers*

It was twilight when I got back to the spot where I had left Charlie watching the fire consuming Wychwood Hall. The woods and the gardens were deserted and still. The day had been just like the day before: autumn halted in its tracks. The remaining people in yellow high vis clambering over the rubble were packing up for the day and the fire tenders were leaving. The TV cameras had gone.

I waited. I waited stubbornly for something to happen, there under the trees. The engine sound of the last vehicle to leave faded into the distance, leaving only the faintest susurrus of dry leaves in a breeze that itself dropped to nothing. The air thickened. Branches overhead clung to an orange sky that dulled to ochre and a deepening blue as the very last minutes of daylight ebbed silently away. Shadows reached and tangled and merged. I waited, and just at the end, in the moments before the day expired and night took the land in its grip, at last I felt a familiar presence beside me.

"Hello Charlie," I said.

Charlie looked thirty years younger. He stood upright, and moved freely without any sign of pain. And he hadn't been drinking. "Hello Nicholas Carpenter," he said.

We stood together for a while, looking at the ruin of the house, and then Charlie said: "You have everything you desired now, Nicholas. Wychwood will be yours. Your family's wealth, all yours."

I shook my head. "I didn't do it for the money, Charlie."

"That was our bargain."

I held up my hand, and in it was what was left of *Folklore and Topography of Bewick,* the book I had bought for Hazel's birthday. "Do you know what this is? There's nothing left of

329

it now; nothing except for the cover. Walter Peachey made it. I've been sending it piece by piece to Hazel, all this ridiculous, melodramatic, romantic stuff, because I thought it might bring us back together, you see; because she loves it so much. But it hasn't. And then I used the rest of it last night to light the fire at Wychwood Hall. And now there's nothing left. It's all gone. Just the cover, see? Such a pretty cover, too." Charlie's face might have looked younger, but was at the same time ancient, inscrutable. "And it's me," I said, "Do you see? A pretty cover and nothing inside. All the ridiculous, melodramatic, romantic, pathetic stuff that makes people *people*, is gone. I tore it all out. There's nothing left, just an empty shell." I opened and shut the boards to illustrate my point. "You chose well. I've been greedy and stupid. And I might just have been greedy enough and stupid enough to do it for the money. You did a good job on me, Charlie, you and your friends. Building me up, letting me think I'd finally made it with your irresistible deal of a lifetime, and making me think Belle had fallen for me, then bringing me crashing down so that I'd blame Clifton, and Henry Wychwood, and Mother, and Belle. So that I'd hate them enough."

"I killed all those people. All the people in Wychwood Hall. Murdered them. And I might have done it for the money. I might have done it for revenge. I might have done it because I hated them." I looked Charlie right in the eye. "But I didn't."

There was a long silence. "Why then?"

"I did it for you, Charlie."

Lines of puzzlement formed on Charlie's face.

"I did it for you. Because you're so fucking wretched. Because you're so fucking desperate. Christ, you're in even worse shape than I am. You want to leave, you've wanted to leave for such a long time, you and your people. But Wychwood was standing between you and the way, and you couldn't do it alone."

Charlie shifted his gaze away. "Why you would wish to help me?"

There were lots of things that I could say to that. That I felt closer to Charlie than I ever had any of my insufferable family. That I didn't belong here now any more than he did. But after consideration I decided to let Walter Peachey speak for me. "We are each one of us alone," I quoted, "But for the kindness of strangers."

Slowly, Charlie smiled – a real smile, not the grimace I had come to know; a smile that was joyful and mischievous and triumphant. "You may have removed all of the pages from that book, but in doing so I believe you have yourself been replenished," he said, and bowed to me, an old-fashioned, deep bow. "Please," he said, "Allow me to introduce my band of scoundrels, villains, and imposters."

He turned back to the woods, and gradually a line of figures began to emerge from between the trees; fantastic shapes of fauns and satyrs, goblins and elves, dryads and nymphs in smoke, coalescing from the darkness between the trees into human forms that swirled and solidified and stepped out into the open. Conrad Goldblum and Shitty Mary were there with their small crowd of protesters, minus placards; Councillor Howland Greenwood; the developer Duncan Brockbank; and others I didn't recognise. Each of them bowed to me in turn, and I acknowledged each one in the same way.

Chapter 57: *Farewell, Arcadia*

"Hello Hazel."

"Nick. Are you okay? What's going on? There's all this stuff on the news. I thought you might be dead."

"I'm okay." I paused. "Hazel, I rang to say goodbye."

"Goodbye?"

"Yes. I'm going away. I shan't call you again."

"Oh." Hazel was silent for a moment. "Where are you going?"

"I wanted to say that I'm sorry it didn't work out between us. I wish I had been better. I wish I had treated you better."

"You should have treated me better."

"Yes! Yes, I should. It was me. I lost you. I wish I hadn't. But it's too late now." There was silence, but I could tell she was still listening. "You're the only person who would understand. But I can't tell you."

"Didn't you get my message? I've been waiting for you to call me. I have so much to tell you!."

"I just want you to know that I'm sorry."

"So that's it? You don't care? I know what connects all the stories now, Nick. I know what sent Walter Peachey mad. I thought perhaps we could meet and… and talk about it."

"I have to go."

There was a pause. "You're not going to do anything stupid, are you?"

"Goodbye, Hazel."

"Nick, will you talk sense? Where are you going?"

"The way beneath the wood. They're waiting for me. But there's no way back. There's no way back, you see. Not any more."

A long silence. Then, she breathed: "It's all real."

"Goodbye."

"Nick..! Nick..?"

"Do you hear it? Listen… it's right at the edge of your hearing… you can hear it if you listen hard. A flute! It's playing such a strange, haunting refrain; so faint and far away that you can't quite be sure, and yet… there! So joyous, but beneath it all so sad, so mournful. Do you hear it? We are leaving! We are going home! Farewell, it laments. Farewell Arcadia."

Epilogue

The Way Beneath The Wood

From the way beneath the wood
    One Spring came they, a joyous host;
About the shaded grove, they stood:
    The righteous dead and Holy Ghost.

"Rejoice! The innocent are free!"
    His herald cried, and trumpets rang;
And trembling, 'pon bended knee,
    In witness of this, mortal man.

Close at hand, the beasts of tether,
    Creatures wild of vale and tor,
Birds of every hue and feather
    Did the Son of God adore.

O silent wonder, silent praise
    Of creatures mighty, creatures meek!
The rapt devotion of their gaze
    As waited they for Christ to speak!

Said the King of Kings: "I died,
    That Adam's sin may be forgiven.
Hell is harrowed; cast aside,
    The Adamantine Gates lie riven."

"Hell's might's defeated, Death undone,
    And Satan bound for aye," quoth He,
"And justice reigns where there was none,
    For every righteous soul is free!"

"Henceforth the way to Sheol's flame
    Is shut to all but those that sin:
The innocent shall mercy claim,
    The good to Hea'en are welcomed in."

The blessèd dead, exulting, loud
    Hosannas cried upon the sward,
And psalming joyously avowed
    The triumph of their sovereign Lord.

From the shadows stepped a shadow:
    Satyr, goblin, nymph or faun,
Peri, brownie, Rob Goodfellow,
    Nixie, pixie, unicorn.

"The way is shut?" it spake, unbending,
    "The way is shut? Then how shall we,
Folk whose lives are never-ending,
    Folk of under hill and tree,"

"Folk of river, folk of flower
    With no immortal soul to name,
Folk of charm and folk of power,
    E'er return to whence we came?"

"By ancient leave do we repair
  On shifting seas of spectral light
To Faerie's eldritch otherwhere -
  By ancient leave! Such is our right!"

Silent was the congregation;
  Proud, the tiny fairy stood
Before the King of All Creation
  In dappled light under greenwood.

"O sprite," proclaimed the Paraclete,
  "A bitter price must yet be paid
In consequence of Hell's defeat:
  Now from this world thy light must fade."

"The way is shut forevermore,
  From shadow-lands to men's domains,
Yet passage back, through yonder door,
  By God Almighty's Hand remains."

"Return ye hence and live forever,
  Prosper ye, proliferate,
Or tarry Earthbound, doomed to wither:
  The right is thine, to choose thy fate."

Within a frame of branches flailing
  Swirled an otherworldly mist:
The portal's arras, thinly veiling
  Fleeting shapes by darkness kissed.

Long the fairy stood as stricken,
    Long the hush upon the glade;
Stealing shadows dark did thicken
    Round the creatures there arrayed.

Unto the author of its doom,
    Obeisance resting unavowed
Til then, to wailing from the gloom,
    At last the prideful fairy bowed.

"Clothed evermore in sorrow,
    Know we now our exile starts.
Gone we shall be come the morrow:
    Leaving here, we leave our hearts."

"Follow, boggart! Follow, selkie!
    Hag, hobgoblin, brave centaur,
Ghoul, ifrit, and howling banshee:
    Follow, through Hell's open door!"

"In elven ships of glass we ride
    Across Damnation's deadly sea.
Now part we 'pon the instant tide:
    I, Oberon, do so decree."

Then from the brooding faerie band
    There keened a cry of great despair:
"Lost is our green and pleasant land!
    Lost to us is Arcadia fair!"

"No more the dance in elven ring
    Beneath Midsummer's starry night;
No more shall hunter, stumbling, bring
    The startled dryad's headlong flight."

"No more shall fairy maid in glamour
    With a smile shy youth enchant;
No more shall dwarven smith with hammer
    Shaping gold dark spells incant."

"No more by pool shall naiad preen,
    Nor cave-bound troll's tooth gnaw on bone,
Nor stolen babes be brought in lien
    Before Titania's golden throne."

Tribes of Faerie, anguish-ridden,
    By their liege-lord's edict bound,
Lamenting paradise forbidden,
    To the doorway slowly wound.

Came the Sidhe, the noble bloodline:
    Sylvan folk of aspect fair;
Wild of magic, pale as moonshine;
    Lords and ladies of the air.

Came the darkling children crawling:
    Goblin kin of lesser birth;
Delving kobolds, gnomes a-brawling,
    Creatures hatched in under-earth.

Came the salamandra: curling,
　　Coiling dragons belching flame;
Smoke-borne jinn; imps, torches twirling,
　　Playing Jack O'Lantern's game.

Came the undines, borne in water;
　　Jenny Haniver and fellows:
Fair Sabrina, river-daughter;
　　Nereids, limnads, sea-deep merrows.

The way beneath the wood they took,
　　From sight of man were hence enveiled;
Rain wept, wind howled, fire died, earth shook;
　　The beasts and birds the loss bewailed.

Shadow-haunting shapes a-hiding
　　In defiance slipped away;
Under hedgerows stealing, sliding,
　　Creeping into slow decay.

No fairy in the dell remained.
　　The trumpets took up their refrain,
The dead processed as was ordained
　　To Heaven; and all was still again.

This land shall sorrow ever after,
　　Echoes of their time shall sound:
Snatches brief of elven laughter,
　　Half-heard song from underground.

　　By WP

THE END

Acknowledgements

Thank you to all the people who have helped and encouraged me, especially my wife Jacquie, whose unconditional support and belief in me sustained me through the long, difficult bits, my amazingly talented kids Tia and Jack, Dave Etherington, my chief beta reader and advisor, and my brilliant cover designer, Luke Griffin.

If you enjoyed this book then please leave a review on Amazon or your favourite website, and tell your friends. I wouldn't ask you if I thought I could leave it to the fairies to do my viral marketing, but they are fickle and forgetful, and frankly if I did the chances are it might never happen.

Printed in Great Britain
by Amazon

21123152R00202